Copper Beach

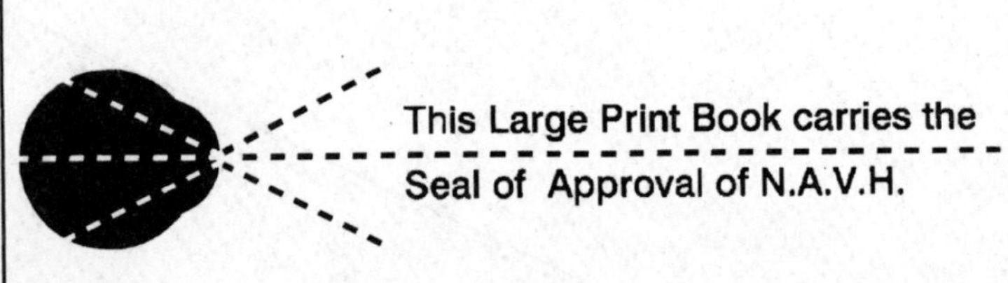
This Large Print Book carries the
Seal of Approval of N.A.V.H.

Copper Beach

Jayne Ann Krentz

THORNDIKE PRESS
A part of Gale, Cengage Learning

Detroit • New York • San Francisco • New Haven, Conn • Waterville, Maine • London

GALE
CENGAGE Learning®

A Dark Legacy Novel.
Thorndike Press, a part of Gale, Cengage Learning.

Thorndike Press® Large Print Basic.
The text of this Large Print edition is unabridged.
Other aspects of the book may vary from the original edition.
Set in 16 pt. Plantin.

LIBRARY OF CONGRESS CATALOGING-IN-PUBLICATION DATA

Krentz, Jayne Ann.
Copper beach / by Jayne Ann Krentz. — Large print ed.
p. cm. — (Thorndike Press large print basic)
"A Dark Legacy Novel."
ISBN-13: 978-1-4104-4516-2 (hardcover)
ISBN-10: 1-4104-4516-X (hardcover)
1. Psychics—Fiction. 2. Extortion—Fiction. 3. Large type books. I. Title.
PS3561.R44C66 2012
813'.54—dc23 2011044271

Published in 2012 by arrangement with G. P. Putnam's Sons, a member of Penguin Group (USA), Inc.

Printed in the United States of America
1 2 3 4 5 6 7 16 15 14 13 12

For Steve Castle, with love and thanks for the background on rare earths. Great brothers like you are even more rare. Sure glad we made it into the same family.

1

There was nothing like the drama of a deathbed scene to expose the skeletons in a family's closet. You never knew what would fall out when you opened the door, the nurse thought. Lifelong conflicts, absolution, regret, long-held grudges, enduring love or unrelenting hatred, whatever had been hidden for decades or generations was suddenly made visible at the end.

The night-shift staff was gathered at the nurses' station, drinking coffee, snacking on vending-machine munchies and speculating on the sexual orientation of the new orthopedic surgeon, when the dying man's son arrived. Emotions in the small group ranged from cynical to relieved.

They had all watched patients die without family at the bedside. It happened more often than most people realized. Everyone who did this kind of work understood that family dynamics were often convoluted and messy and sometimes downright evil. There were often very good reasons why relatives turned their backs on a family member who was dying. And there was no getting around the fact that the patient in 322 was seriously wasted not just from the cancer but from years of hard living and major addiction issues.

"Knox probably wasn't anyone's idea of a great father," the orderly said. "Still, it's about time someone from the family showed up."

The middle-aged nurse watched the visitor disappear through the darkened doorway of 322. Then she checked the computer file.

"He signed in as Knox's son," she reported. "But there are no relatives listed on the chart."

One of the orderlies popped a handful of potato chips into his mouth. "Guess it's safe to say it's not a close family."

Lander Knox knew what the crowd at the nurses' station was thinking. *The prodigal son shows up at last.* It amused him, but he had been careful not to let his reaction show. He understood that humor was not appropriate to the occasion.

He had learned long ago to fake the correct emotional responses for a wide variety of situations. His acting talent was worthy of an Oscar. He had gotten very good at pretending to be one of the sheep. He moved among the weak, emotional, easily duped creatures that surrounded him like the wolf he was.

He had considered taking a moment to charm the staff at the nurses' station. It would have been simple to give them a clever story about how he had been on the other side of the world in a war zone when he got word that his father was dying. He could have told them that he had spent three days without sleep trying to get back before the end. But it wasn't worth the effort. He was planning to stay only a few minutes, just long enough to take his revenge.

Shadows pooled inside room 322. The machines hummed and hissed and beeped like some high-tech Greek chorus heralding the inevitable. Quinn Knox's eyes were closed. He was hooked up to an IV line. His breathing was harsh, as if it took everything he had just to grab the next breath. He looked exhausted beyond bearing. The outline etched by the sheet revealed a painfully thin body. The cancer had been gnawing on him for a while now.

Lander went to the bed and gripped the rail. There was very little that could arouse strong emotion in him, but looking down at the father who had betrayed him, he felt something familiar and powerful stir deep inside. Rage.

"Surprise, I'm alive," he whispered. "But, then, I'll bet you've known all along that I didn't die in that boating accident. Hey, you're psychic, after all. But you sure hoped I was dead, didn't you? Well, I'm here. I won't stay long. Just stopped in to let you know that you lost and I won. Are you listening, you son of a bitch?"

Quinn's eyelids twitched. One withered hand moved slightly. Lander smiled. A euphoric satisfaction twisted and melded with the old fury.

"So you can hear me," he said. "That's good. Because I want you to go to your grave knowing that I know everything, how you lied to me, how you tried to cheat me out of my inheritance, *everything.* I'm on the trail of that lab notebook. I've traced it to the Pacific Northwest. Once I have that book, I'll be able to find that lost mine."

Quinn's eyelids fluttered and opened partway. Faded gray eyes, glazed with morphine and the oncoming chill of death, looked up at Lander.

"No," Quinn rasped.

"A couple of years ago I found the one

crystal that you kept as a souvenir. What's more, I've learned how to use it to commit the perfect murder. I've run a number of successful experiments so far. Very useful, that crystal. But now I'm going after the whole damn mine full of those stones, and there's nothing you can do to stop me."

"No, listen . . ."

"You're a dead man, or you will be very soon. They probably got a pool going out there at the nurses' station, betting on whether or not you'll make it through the night."

"Lab book is psi-coded." The breath rattled in Quinn's chest. "Try to break it and you'll destroy your senses. Maybe kill yourself."

"I heard the rumors about the code," Lander said. "But I haven't told you the best part yet. I've already located a code breaker in Seattle. She's a freelancer in the underground hot-books market. I'm going to use her to acquire the book for me and break the encryption. Sort of a two-for-one deal."

Quinn stared at him with an expression of gathering horror. Lander smiled, pleased.

"You don't fear death, but you're terrified that I'll get my hands on that lab notebook, aren't you?" he said. "And I will, old man, I will. I am so very close."

"No," Quinn wheezed. "You don't understand. The crystals are dangerous. You can't reopen the mine."

"The Phoenix Mine was my inheritance. You had no right to keep it from me. But I'm going to find it now. I've been working on my plan for months. Now everything is in place in Seattle. I almost wish you were going to live long enough to see me reopen that mine. Almost."

Quinn moved his head restlessly on the pillow. "You don't know what you're doing."

"You're wrong." Lander stepped back from the bed. "I know exactly what I'm doing. I'm going to claim what belongs to me."

"Please, listen . . ."

"Good-bye, you pathetic bastard." Lander started to turn away but paused, eyeing the IV lines. "You know, it's tempting to put a pillow over your face and finish you off right now. But I want you to have a little more time to think about how you failed to cheat me out of what's mine. I want you to suffer a little longer, *Dad.*"

Lander turned on his heel and walked swiftly out of the room. If he stayed for even another minute, he would give in to the rage and the urge to pull the plug on the old man.

Once out in the hall, he went quickly toward the elevators. He could feel the eyes of the medical staff boring into his back. *Screw them.* He was never going to see any of them again.

In room 322, Quinn's head cleared a little as he raised what was left of his old talent. The effort dumped a small jolt of adrenaline into his bloodstream, countering the effects of the drugs. After three fumbling attempts, he managed to press the call button.

The nurse appeared. Quinn dredged up the name out of his failing memory banks.

"Nathan," he rasped.

"Are you in pain, Mr. Knox?" Nathan came to stand beside the bed. "I can give you another injection."

"Forget the damn drugs. Help me make a phone call."

"All right. I can dial it for you, if you like."

"Number's in my wallet. It was with me when I got here."

"You aren't supposed to bring valuables with you to the hospital," Nathan said.

"Nothing valuable in my wallet except that phone number. Get it."

Nathan went to the closet, pawed through the meager assortment of personal belongings and produced the aged, well-worn wallet. He brought it back to the bed and opened it.

"Dial the number on that old card," Quinn said. "Elias Coppersmith. Hurry, man, I don't have a lot of time."

Nathan punched in the number. A man picked up. The voice had a faint, Western edge to it, the kind of voice you associated with cowboys and pilots. The classic Chuck Yeager twang, Nathan thought. The voice also had the ring of authority.

"Coppersmith."

"I'm calling from Oakmont Hospital," Nathan said. "A patient named Quinn Knox wants to speak with you, Mr. Coppersmith. He says it's urgent."

"Quinn? Put him on."

Nathan helped Quinn grip the phone and maneuver it to his ear. Quinn pulled on the last of his fading strength and his talent. He got one last rush of energy.

"Elias?" he croaked. "That you?"

"Damn, it's good to hear from you, Quinn. It's been at least twenty, twenty-five years. Didn't know you had my number."

"I kept track of you," Quinn said.

"Glad to hear it, but you should have stayed in touch. You sound awful. What the hell are you doing in the hospital?"

"Dying," Quinn rasped. "What the fuck do you think I'm doing? Shut up and listen, because I don't have a lot of time. I'm down to hours here, maybe minutes. I think someone may have found Ray Willis's notebook."

"Are you serious?"

"I just told you, I'm dying. Turns out people get real serious when shit like that happens."

"Quinn, where is that hospital?"

"Florida."

"I'll be on a company plane within the hour. Be there by morning."

"Forget it," Quinn rasped. "Not gonna last that long. Here's what I know. There's some rumors floating around in the hot-book market that the notebook has surfaced somewhere in your neck of the woods."

"Sedona?"

"Last I heard you bought yourself a whole damn island up there in the San Juans."

"Still got the island, but Willow and I just use it as a spring and summer getaway place. Moved the main headquarters of the company down here to Arizona years ago. There's one division left in Seattle, the R-and-D lab. My oldest son, Sam, is the only one who lives year-round on the island."

"You had another son and a little girl, too."

"Judson and Emma. All grown up now. Judson and Sam run their own private consulting firm. And Emma is . . . Emma. Lives in Portland, Oregon. Willow says she's still finding herself. I say it's time she got serious about life, but that's a whole other issue."

"So you're in Sedona." Quinn tried to smile. The smile turned into a painful, breathless, hacking cough. "You always had a thing for the desert."

"Tell me about the notebook, Quinn."

"Not much more to tell. But here's the thing you need to know. My son is going after it."

"I heard your son died a few years ago. Some kind of boating accident."

"Hate to say it, but it probably would have been better if that were true. But he's alive, Elias. He came to see me tonight. Says I deprived him of his inheritance. He's got my talent, Elias, but he's got a hell of a lot more of it than I ever had. And he's sick in the head. Evil sick. Be careful. That's all I can tell you. Gotta go now."

"Quinn, wait. For God's sake, man, don't hang up."

"You were the best friend I ever had, Elias. Always thought of you as a brother. All these years I tried to keep our secret, but I made the mistake of holding on to one of the crystals. Now Lander has it. I failed you."

"No, Quinn," Elias said. "Listen to me, you didn't fail me. You had my back forty years ago when Willis tried to kill both of us. And now you've given me the warning I need to handle this situation. I'll take it from here."

"Just like last time, huh?"

"Just like last time," Elias said.

"Good-bye, brother."

"Good-bye, my brother."

The phone fell from Quinn's hand. A strange calm settled on him. He had done what he could to protect the secret that he and Elias had vowed to keep forty years ago. It was up to Elias now.

In spite of the oncoming darkness, Quinn realized that he felt at peace for the first time in maybe his entire life. He could go now. He closed his eyes.

2

A crazy man and a gun was never a good combination. A crazy man with paranormal talent and a gun made for a very bad start to the day.

Abby Radwell watched the terrifying scene taking place in the library from the shadows of the doorway. The intruder holding the pistol on Hannah Vaughn and her housekeeper could not have been older than twenty-one or twenty-two. His eyes were fever-bright. His long hair was matted and disheveled. His jeans and ragged T-shirt looked as if they had not been washed in a very long time. He was becoming more agitated by the second.

The intruder's voice rose. "I'm not playing games, lady." He waved the pistol in an erratic pattern. "I know *The Key* is here in this room. You have to give it to me, and then she has to unlock it."

"You are welcome to take *The Key,*" Hannah said, somehow managing to maintain a calm, soothing tone. "But I can't unlock it for you. I don't know how to do that."

"She's supposed to unlock it," the intruder said.

"Who are you talking about?" Hannah asked. "Surely you don't mean my housekeeper. Mrs. Jensen doesn't know anything about unlocking encrypted books."

"Not the housekeeper," the intruder said. He used the back of his arm to wipe the sweat off his forehead. "The woman who is working for you here in this library. She knows how to unlock hot books."

"I don't understand," Hannah said. "Mrs. Jensen and I are the only people in this house. Please, take my copy of *The Key* and leave before this situation gets out of control."

Hannah was doing a magnificent job of lying, Abby thought. But the situation was already out of control.

Hannah Vaughn was eighty-two years old and confined to a wheelchair. She was helpless against the armed intruder. She was doing her best to defuse the mad tension in the room, but her tactics were not going to work. Mrs. Jensen was pale and shaken. She looked as if she was about to faint.

Abby's senses were wide open. Her intuition was screaming at her to rush back downstairs and out onto the street. The intruder was not yet aware of her presence. She could call nine-one-one once she was safely outside. But by the time the police arrived, it might be too late for Hannah and Mrs. Jensen.

Abby spoke quietly from the doorway. "I'll get *The Key* for you."

"What?" The intruder whirled around to face her, eyes widening in shock. "Who are you?"

"My name is Abby. I'm the one you're looking for, the woman who can unlock *The Key.*"

"Huh." The intruder blinked several times and shook his head as if to clear it. He was shivering, but he managed to steady himself somewhat. He gripped the gun with both hands, aiming it at her. "Are you sure you're the right woman?"

"Yes. What's your name?"

"Grady." The response was automatic.

"All right, Mr. Grady . . ."

"No, my name is Grady Hastings." Grady looked confused for a few seconds. He wiped his forehead again. "That's all you need to know. Get the book. Hurry. I don't feel too good."

"The book you want is encrypted?"

"Yes, yes." Excitement heightened the fever in Grady's eyes. "*The Key to the Latent Power of Stones.* They told me you could unlock it."

"It's in the crystals section, up on the balcony," Abby said.

"Get it. Hurry."

"All right." She walked into the room and headed toward the small spiral staircase that gave access to the balcony which wrapped around the library. "How did you know that it was in Mrs. Vaughn's collection?"

"The voices told me. Just like they told me that I needed you to break the code. I have to have that book, you see. It's vital to my research."

"You're doing research on crystals?" Abby asked.

"Yes, *yes.* And I'm so close to the answers, so *close.* I gotta have the book."

"Okay," Abby said.

Mrs. Jensen whimpered softly. Hannah had gone very quiet. She watched Abby with a sharp, knowing look. Her anxiety was a palpable force in the room.

"All right," Grady said. "That's good. Okay, then." He seemed to regain a measure of control. "But I'm coming with you. No tricks. You have to break the code. *The Key* is no good to me unless you unlock it.

That's what the voices in the crystal told me, you see."

"I understand," Abby said soothingly. She started up the spiral staircase.

Grady gave Hannah and Mrs. Jensen a quick, uncertain look and seemed satisfied that neither of them would cause him any trouble. He followed Abby up the staircase. Abby was aware of his heavy, labored breathing. It was as if he was exerting enormous energy just to hold the gun on her.

"You're ill," Abby said. "Maybe you should leave now and go to the emergency room."

"No. Can't leave without the book."

"What sort of crystal research are you doing?" she asked.

"Know anything about latent energy in rocks?"

"Not a lot, but it sounds interesting."

"So much power," Grady said. "Just waiting for us to figure out how to tap it. I'm almost there. Got to have that book."

Abby reached the top of the spiral steps and walked along the balcony to the section of shelving that contained Hannah's fine collection of volumes devoted to the paranormal properties of crystals. Many of the books were filled with the usual woo-woo and occult nonsense. Hannah said she collected those volumes for historical purposes. But a few of the titles contained the writings of researchers, ancient and modern, who had done serious work on the power of crystals, gemstones and amber.

The most valuable book in the Vaughn collection was Morgan's *The Key to the Latent Power of Stones.* Written in the eighteenth century, it was locked in a psi-code that added enormously to its value. In the world of antiquarian and collectible books that had a paranormal provenance, encrypted volumes were the rarest of the rare.

Abby stopped and ran her fingertips along the spines of the books on the shelf.

"Quit stalling," Grady said. The gun shook in his hand.

"Here it is." She pulled out the old leather-bound volume. The energy locked in the book whispered to her senses. "Morgan's *Key.*"

Grady eyed the worn leather cover warily. "Are you sure that's the right one?"

"Do you want to see the title page?"

"Yes. Show me."

Cradling the heavy book carefully in one hand, she opened the cover. Grady took a step closer and looked at the title page. He frowned.

"I can read it."

"Yes, you're lucky it was written in English. A lot of the old alchemists used Latin."

"No, I mean I can *read* it. *The Key to the Latent Power of Stones.*" Grady reached out and gingerly turned a page. "I can read this page, too. This isn't the right book. The voices in the crystal told me that the book I need is encrypted."

"Oh, right," Abby said. "You think that because you can read the text the book is not locked in a code. But that's exactly how psi-encryption works. It camouflages the real text in subtle ways, just enough to distort and conceal the true meaning. You could sit down and read this book cover to cover and think you were reading the original text. But in the end, it would be just so much gibberish."

"Break the code," Grady demanded. "Let me see if the text really does look different."

Abby braced herself for the inevitable shock and focused on the layers of energy that shivered around the old book. Few sensitives possessed the ability to lock a book or other written material in a psi-code; fewer still knew the oldest and most powerful techniques. Talents like her who could crack such codes were even more scarce.

The whole business was a dying art. Encrypting a book or a document required physical contact with the item that was to be encoded. In the modern world, people tended to store their secrets in digital form in cyberspace, a realm where old-fashioned psychic encryption did not work.

It figured that she had chosen a career path that was fated to go the way of buggy-whip manufacturing, Abby thought. But she hadn't been able to help herself. The old books filled with ancient paranormal secrets called to her senses. And those wrapped in psi-encryption were irresistible.

She found the pattern of the code. It was not the first time she had unsealed the old volume. She was the one who had acquired it for Hannah's collection in the first place. She had unlocked the book twice already, once to verify its authenticity and again to allow Hannah to make some notes. Hannah had requested that the book be relocked after she had read it, in order to maintain its value.

"Done," Abby said. "I broke the code."

"Are you finished already?" Grady eyed the book with a dubious expression. "I thought psi-encryption was tricky stuff."

"It is, but I'm good."

"I can still feel a lot of hot energy coming

off that book."

"Strong encryption energy leaves a residue, just like any other kind of energy," Abby said.

"So I can read the real text now?"

"Yes. Take a look."

She held the book out. Grady's hand closed around it. The physical contact was all she needed. She channeled the darkly oscillating currents of the encryption energy into Grady's aura.

The atmosphere was suddenly charged. Grady reacted as if he had touched a live electrical wire. His mouth opened on a silent, agonized scream. The gun dropped from his hand. His eyes rolled back in his head. He stiffened for a timeless moment. Then he shuddered violently. He tried to stagger back toward the spiral staircase, but he collapsed to the floor of the balcony. He twitched several times and went still.

There was a moment of stunned silence.

"Are you all right, Abby?" Hannah asked.

"No. Yes." Abby took a deep breath and silently repeated her old mantra, *Show no weakness.* She gripped the balcony railing and looked down at Hannah. "I'm fine. Just a little shaken up, that's all."

"You're sure, dear?" Hannah's face was etched with concern.

"Yes. Really. Breaking a code is one thing. Using the energy in it to do what I just did is . . . something else altogether."

"I knew you were strong," Hannah said. "But I hadn't realized that you were that powerful. What you just did was extremely dangerous. If that sort of energy got out of control . . ."

"I know, I know," Abby said. "I couldn't think of anything else to do." She glanced at the housekeeper, who was crumpled on the floor. "What happened to Mrs. Jensen?"

"She fainted. There was an awful lot of energy flying around in here a moment ago. Even a nonsensitive could feel it. What about that dreadful man? Is he alive?"

Dear heaven, had she actually killed someone? Horrified at the possibility, Abby went to her knees beside Grady. Gingerly, she probed for a pulse. Relief swept through her when she found one.

"Yes," she said. "He's unconscious, but he's definitely alive."

"I'll call nine-one-one now."

"Good idea." Abby drew a deep breath. She was already starting to feel the edgy adrenaline-overload buzz that accompanied the use of so much psychic energy. In a couple of hours she would be exhausted. She focused on the immediate problem. It was major. "How on earth am I going to explain what happened here?"

"There's nothing for you to explain, dear." Hannah rolled her chair to the desk and picked up her phone. "A mentally disturbed intruder broke into my home and demanded one of the rare books in my collection. He appeared to be on drugs, and whatever he took evidently caused him to collapse."

Abby thought about it. "All true, in a way."

"Well, it's not as if you can explain that you used psychic energy to take down an armed intruder, dear. Who would believe such a thing? The authorities would think that you were as crazy as that man who broke in here today."

"Yes," Abby said. A shuddery chill swept through her, bringing with it images from her old nightmares, the ones filled with an endless maze of pale-walled corridors, sterile rooms and locked doors and windows. She wasn't going to risk being called crazy, not ever again. "That is exactly what they would think."

"I have always found that when dealing with the authorities it's best to stick with the bare facts and not offer too much in the way of explanations."

Abby gripped the railing and saw the understanding in Hannah's eyes. "I came to the same conclusion myself a few years ago, Mrs. Vaughn. Those are definitely words to live by."

Hannah made the call and put down the phone. She glanced up at Abby.

"What is it, dear?" she said gently. "If you're concerned that word of what you did with that encryption energy might get out into the underground market, you needn't worry. I won't ever tell anyone what really happened here, and Mrs. Jensen passed out before she witnessed a thing. Your secret is safe with me."

"I know, Hannah. I trust you. Thank you. But there's something about this Grady Hastings guy that is bothering me."

"He is obviously mentally unbalanced, dear."

"I know. But that isn't what I meant. He was sweating so hard. He seemed on the edge of exhaustion. It was as if he was struggling against some unseen force."

"Perhaps he was, dear. We all have our inner demons. I suspect that Grady Hastings has more than most people."

The new nightmare started that same night.

She walked through the strange glowing fog. She did not know whom or what she was searching for, only that she desperately needed to find someone before it was too late. Time was running out. The sense of urgency was growing stronger, making it hard to breathe.

Grady Hastings materialized in the mist. He stared at her with haunted, pleading eyes and held out a hand.

"Help me," he said. "You have to help me. The voices in the crystal told me that you are the only one who can save me."

She awoke, pulse racing. Newton whined anxiously and pressed his furry weight against her leg. It took her a few seconds to orient herself. When she did, she was horrified to realize that she was no longer in bed. She was in the living room of her small condo, looking out the sliding glass doors that opened onto the balcony. The lights of the Seattle cityscape glittered in the night.

"Dear heaven, I've started sleepwalking, Newton." She sank to her knees beside the dog and hugged him close.

The first blackmail note was waiting for her when she checked her email the next morning.

I know what you did in the library. Silence

probably somewhat eccentric, but that hadn't bothered her. Eccentric collectors made up a good portion of her clientele. She had not, however, heard about the murdered fiancée. She'd taken time to run a quick background check on the Coppersmiths, but she had been in a hurry this morning. Maybe she should have done a little more research before coming to Legacy Island.

"Is that so?" she said politely, going for noncommittal.

"You know how it is when a woman dies under mysterious circumstances," Dixon said. "The cops always look at the guy she was sleeping with and the one who finds the body. In this case, that man just happened to be one and the same."

"Sam Coppersmith?"

"Yeah. But the sheriff cleared him. It was those damn bloggers with their conspiracy theories who tried to stir things up. It was the Coppersmith name that got their attention. When your family operates a big business like Coppersmith Inc., there's always folks who'll suspect the worst. No one here on the island believed a single damn word of what they wrote about Sam, though."

"I gather the Coppersmith family is respected here," Abby said. She kept her tone

will be maintained for a price. You will be contacted soon.

3

“You’ve probably heard the rumors about Sam Coppersmith.” The water-taxi pilot eased off the throttle, allowing the boat to cruise slowly into the small marina. “Don’t pay any attention to ’em.”

Abby pushed her sunglasses higher on her nose and took a closer look at the man at the helm. Half an hour ago, when he had picked her up at the dock in Anacortes, he had introduced himself as Dixon. He looked to be in his mid-sixties, but it was hard to be certain of his age because he had the rugged, weathered features of a man who had spent a lifetime on the water.

Dixon Charters was painted on the white hull of the boat. The name of the business was accompanied by a logo depicting an orca leaping out of the waves. Images of the magnificent black-and-white killer whales that prowled the cold waters of the Pacific Northwest in pods were ubiquitous through-

out the San Juans. Orcas graced sign bookstores, souvenir shops, real est fices and restaurants. They deco menus, greeting cards and calendars. ents bought cute, cuddly stuffed orcas their children.

Abby had grown up in the region. S understood the significance of orcas bo culturally and historically. And they wer certainly magnificent. There was nothing like the thrill of watching the sleek, powerful creatures launch their multi-ton bodies out of the depths and into the air and then plunge back beneath the surface. But in her opinion, most people tended to forget that orcas were anything but cute and cuddly. They were intelligent, powerful, top-of-the-food-chain predators. *Just ask a salmon,* she thought.

“I’m here on business,” she said coolly. “I can assure you that the very last thing I care about is Mr. Coppersmith’s personal life.”

“That’s good,” Dixon said. He nodded once, satisfied. “Because the gossip about him being the one who murdered his fiancée six months ago is pure bullshit. Pardon my language.”

Okay, didn’t see that coming. Abby’s pulse kicked up for a few beats. She had already figured out that Sam Coppersmith was

politely neutral.

"Well, sure," Dixon said. "But it's more than that. The Coppersmiths have been a part of the local community for damn near forty years. That's when Sam's parents' bought the old mansion out on the bluffs. Named it Copper Beach. There was hardly anyone else living on the island when they arrived. They pretty much founded the town. The first mayor and town council voted to name the town Copper Beach."

"If no one lived on Legacy Island before the Coppersmiths arrived, who built the mansion you just mentioned?"

"Man named Xavier McClain. He made a fortune in shipping and lumber back in the early nineteen-hundreds. Bought the island and built the big house. According to the legend, he was downright strange."

"Everyone has a different definition of strange," Abby said politely. *Trust me, I know whereof I speak,* she thought.

"The old stories say that McClain was really into the woo-woo stuff, you know?" Dixon aimed a forefinger at his temple and made a few circles. "He claimed he saw things other folks couldn't see. There are a lot of tall tales around here about how he got up to some real weird shit, I mean stuff, in the basement of the old house."

"What happened to Xavier McClain?" Abby asked.

"No one knows for sure. His body was found when it washed ashore in the cove below the big house. Most folks assume he fell from the bluff. Others say he jumped. A few think he was murdered. The kids like to tell you that his ghost still walks the bluff on foggy nights, but I don't hold with that nonsense. Anyhow, after McClain died, his descendants didn't want the house, let alone the island. Way too expensive. They sold out to Elias Coppersmith."

"Wait a minute. Are you telling me that the Coppersmith family *owns* Legacy Island, not just a house?"

"Well, they don't exactly own the town. They gave that property to the local residents. And folks around here own their own homes, of course, on account of Elias Coppersmith subdivided some of the land and sold it. But yeah, the family still owns most of the island. The only one who lives here year-round now is Sam, but the rest of the Coppersmiths are always coming or going. They've all got their own houses out there on the bluff now. Sam took the old house on account of no one else in the family wanted it. His mom never did like the place. Willow and Elias live down in Sedona; that's where the main headquarters of the company is located."

"Willow and Elias are Sam's parents?"

"Right. They'll be coming up here soon," Dixon said. "They always show up for the R-and-D lab's annual technical summit and staff family weekend. On the last night there's a real fine barbecue. The locals are invited. It's a big deal around here."

Abby examined the boats in the marina slips. The majority appeared to be hard-working craft of one kind or another. Several were rigged for serious fishing. The green plants and the curtains in the windows of others spelled live-aboards, people who lived full-time on their boats. Unlike the marinas on some of the other islands that catered to summer tourists, there were no luxury yachts.

One sleek, clean-lined boat caught her attention. The name on the hull was *Phoenix.* Dixon followed the direction of her gaze.

"That's Sam's boat." He said. "I'm surprised he didn't pick you up himself today. But he only leaves the island when he has to these days."

"Is Sam involved in the family business?"

"Sort of. He and his brother run their own consulting firm, real high-tech stuff, you know? But they do a lot of their consulting for the family business so I guess you could say they are involved."

She had learned a little about the family business in the course of her cursory online research this morning. The Coppersmith fortune had been built on the mining and research-and-development of so-called "rare earths," the elements and metals that provided the sophisticated materials and crystals so vital to modern technology. Rare earths with unfamiliar names, such as lanthanum and cerium, were used in everything from computers and cell phones to X-ray machines and self-cleaning ovens.

"Sam was always a bit of a loner, even when he was a kid," Dixon said. "But after he found his fiancée's body he really started keeping to himself in the old Copper Beach house. Lot of folks, including my wife, swear that losing the love of his life about broke his heart. They say his family is worried about him. They think he might be depressed or something, you know?"

Great, Abby thought. Thaddeus Webber had sent her all this way to hire a reclusive mad scientist with paranormal talents who was suffering from some form of depression due to the death of a fiancée he might or might not have killed. The long trip from Seattle today was looking more and more like a waste of time. She glanced at her watch, wondering if she should tell Dixon to turn the water taxi around and take her back to Anacortes, where she had left her car.

Dixon eased the boat against the dock. A gangly-looking boy in his teens trotted up to help with the lines. He gave Abby a curious once-over. She gave him a vague smile in return and turned to study the small cluster of weathered buildings that surrounded the marina. There were a few more structures along the short waterfront, but all in all there wasn't a lot to the town of Copper Beach. It barely qualified as a village. But that was typical of most of the remote communities scattered across the San Juans.

People moved to the islands for any number of reasons. Some sought privacy and a simpler, slower way of life. Others came looking for a serene environment that encouraged contemplation and meditation. The islands had been home to various cloistered orders, religious sects and assorted communes and marijuana entrepreneurs for years.

A lot of folks who chose to live in the San Juans arrived with one paramount objective in mind — to get off the grid altogether.

Their goal was to get lost and stay lost. It was not all that hard to do, because in the islands people minded their own business. Outsiders were stonewalled if they got too curious. Which only made Dixon's gossipy comments about Sam Coppersmith all the more intriguing, Abby thought. It was as if he felt some responsibility to defend Sam against the lurid rumors that had evidently circulated at the time of the woman's death.

Dixon and the teen finished tying up the boat. Abby stepped cautiously off the gently bobbing craft onto the planked dock and looked around, wondering if she was supposed to walk to her destination.

"Can I pay someone to drive me to Coppersmith's house?" she said to Dixon.

"You won't need a lift," Dixon said, angling his head. "Sam's here to get you."

A chill of awareness stirred the hairs on the back of her neck. Automatically, she raised her senses and turned to watch the man who was coming toward her along the dock. His dark hair was a little too long. A pair of black-framed sunglasses shielded his eyes, but the hard-edged planes and angles of his face told her a great deal about him.

It was the currents of raw power that burned in the atmosphere around Coppersmith that compelled her senses. She could literally feel the heat, both normal and paranormal, even from this distance. When he drew closer, she glimpsed a small spark of fire on his right hand. She took another look and concluded that the flash of light had been caused by sunlight glinting off the stone of his ring.

Her initial shiver morphed into a charged thrill. She could not decide if she was more excited than she had ever been in her life or merely scared out of her wits. It was a classic fight-or-flight response. There was obviously more than one kind of top-of-the-line predator living here in the San Juans.

She looked at Dixon. "I have one question for you, Mr. Dixon."

"Sure."

"Why are you and everyone else on the island so absolutely convinced that Sam Coppersmith did not murder that woman?"

"Simple," Dixon said. He winked. "Coppersmiths are all real smart, and Sam is probably the smartest of the bunch. If he had killed that woman, there would have been nothing at all to link her death to him. He sure as freaking hell wouldn't have left her body in his own lab. She would have flat-out disappeared. No problem making that happen here in the islands. Lot of deep water around these parts."

4

"Thaddeus Webber indicated that you had some experience with this sort of thing," Abby said.

"Obsessed collectors who send online blackmail threats to innocent antiquarian book dealers?" Sam Coppersmith leaned back against his desk and folded his arms. "Can't say that I have. But an extortionist is an extortionist. Shouldn't be all that hard to find the one who is bothering you."

"I'm glad you're so optimistic," Abby said. She drummed her fingers on the arm of her chair and glanced uneasily at her watch for the third or fourth time. "Personally, I'm getting a bad feeling about this meeting. I think there may have been some mistake. Thaddeus Webber must not have understood my problem."

"Webber wouldn't have sent you to me if he hadn't thought you needed me."

Sam had said very little during the short

drive from town. But she had known that his senses were slightly jacked for the whole trip because her own had been fizzing. They still were, for that matter. It was an unfamiliar sensation. She wondered if her intuition was trying to send her a warning. Or maybe she was simply sleep-deprived. Regardless, she was quite certain that Sam was assessing her, measuring her reactions, testing her in some way.

Her first view of the gray stone mansion that was the Copper Beach house had not been reassuring. The place was a true gothic monstrosity. It loomed, bleak and shadowed, in a small clearing on a bluff overlooking a cove and the dark waters of the San Juans. From the outside, the windows of the old house were obsidian mirrors.

She had concluded immediately that Sam and the house deserved each other. Both looked as if they belonged in another century, one in which it was considered normal for mysterious men to live in dark mansions that came equipped with attics and basements that held scary secrets.

Her sense of unease had deepened when she had gotten out of the SUV and walked to the front door with Sam. She had watched while he did something with his ring that unlocked the door.

"I've never seen a security system like that," she said. "Some kind of variation on a card-key security system?"

"Something like that." Sam opened the door. "My own invention."

She had anticipated another tingle of alarm, or at the very least uncertainty, when he ushered her into the shadowy front hall. But to her astonishment, the ambient energy whispering in the atmosphere had given her a small, exciting little rush. She knew that Sam noticed.

"I've got a lot of hot rocks down in the lab," he explained. "After a while, the energy infuses the atmosphere and gets embedded in the walls."

"That happens with hot books, too," she said.

"Not everyone is okay with the sensation. Gives some people the creeps, I'm told."

"Don't worry about my reaction, Mr. Coppersmith. I'm accustomed to being in the vicinity of paranormal energy."

"Yeah, I can see that." Something that might have been satisfaction had edged his mouth. "Call me Sam."

She had not offered her own first name. This was a business arrangement. The safest thing to do was to maintain at least minimal formality, at least until she figured out how to handle Sam Coppersmith.

He had removed his dark glasses at that point, revealing eyes that were a startling shade of gemstone green.

When he closed the door behind her, she had taken another look at his ring. It was made of some darkly gleaming metal and set with a small crystal. The stone was a deep, fiery red in color.

Sam had led her along a hallway and opened a door to reveal a flight of stone steps.

"Lab's in the basement," he had explained. "We can talk there."

She still could not believe that she had followed him downstairs into a windowless basement lab like some naive gothic heroine. Maybe she had been dealing with eccentric collectors for a little too long.

The cavernous, dimly lit chamber below the house was unlike any lab she had ever seen. It was crammed with display cases and drawers filled with crystals and stones and chunks of raw ore. If it were not for the low simmer of energy in the room, she could have been in the hall of gems and minerals of a world-class natural history museum.

But unlike the specimens in a museum, most of the stones around her were hot. The vibes in the atmosphere were unmistakable.

She was no expert in the field of para-rocks, but like most strong talents, she could sense energy that was infused in objects, especially when there was a lot of it in the vicinity.

In addition to the crystals and stones on display, there were a number of state-of-the art instruments on the workbench. There were also some devices made of iron, brass and glass that she was certain qualified as antiques. Several appeared to be from the seventeenth or eighteenth century, but a couple of the objects looked as if they had come from the laboratory of a Renaissance-era alchemist.

The low lighting in the room added to the weirdness factor. Unlike most modern labs, there were no overhead fluorescent fixtures. The stone chamber was lit only by the desk lamp and the faint paranormal glow of some of the charged rocks. Abby got the impression that Sam preferred the shadows.

She cleared her throat discreetly. "No offense, Mr. Coppersmith, but are you a real investigator?"

"Depends on how you define *real*."

"Do you have a private investigator's license?"

"No. But I do a lot of consulting work, if that makes you feel any better."

"What kind of consulting?"

"Technical consulting."

That did it, she thought. Thaddeus had sent her on a wild-goose chase. She did not have time to waste on mad scientists and gothic mansions. She gave Sam a cool smile and got to her feet.

"I'm afraid there's been some mistake," she said. "I need a real private investigator."

"You need someone like me. Webber wouldn't have sent you here otherwise."

"You're a technical consultant, for Pete's sake."

"Trust me when I tell you that technical consulting covers a lot of territory. You're here now; you may as well sit down and tell me about the blackmail threats."

She did not sit down. But she did not grab her shoulder bag and jacket and head for the door, either. As a compromise, she walked to stand in front of a glass display case and looked down at a chunk of what looked like blue quartz inside. With her senses still slightly heightened, she could perceive some of the energy locked deep inside the crystal. She wondered what the lab looked like to Sam. With his strong psychic sensitivity to para-rocks, the place probably glowed as brightly as if it was lit by sunshine.

She made her decision. Sam was right.

She did not know where else to turn. She had to trust Thaddeus Webber's judgment. He had been her friend and mentor for years.

"Here's the situation," she said. "I'm a freelancer in the underground hot-books market. Collectors in that market tend to be somewhat eccentric, especially those who possess some real talent."

Sam looked amused. "Are you saying those who collect paranormal books are crazy?"

She gave him what she hoped was a quelling look. "What I'm saying, Mr. Coppersmith, is that there are some collectors who are obsessed to the point of being quite dangerous. Others are just plain weird. And then there are those who actually believe in the occult. Witches, demons, sorcery, that sort of nonsense."

"Your clientele must be very interesting."

"For obvious reasons, I have to be careful. At the start of my career, Thaddeus Webber advised me to work only by referral. I have stuck to that advice. I do not accept commissions from collectors I don't know unless they are referred to me by someone I trust. And even then, I always check them out with Thaddeus. I go out of my way to keep a low profile. But word gets around in collectors' circles. The result is that once in a while a determined person manages to get my email address."

"That's how clients contact you?"

"Yes. I use a false name with that email address, of course."

"What name?"

"My clients know me as Newton. And that's all they know about me. When I do get a message from someone seeking my services who has not been properly referred, I never respond. That's usually the end of the matter. People who don't hear back from me tend to conclude either that I'm something of a myth or that I'm a complete fraud. But yesterday morning I received the first blackmail note. The second one came in last night. Both were sent to my Newton address."

"How hard would it be for someone to dig up that address?"

"Probably not hard at all if they hang out in the right chat rooms and hot-books sites. That's not what worries me. What freaked me out is that the blackmailer knows way too much about me. When I contacted Thaddeus to ask for advice, I got a one-line email back from him. He told me to contact you, and he gave me your email address."

"Let me see the notes."

"I printed them out for you." She turned away from the blue quartz and went back to her chair. Leaning down, she reached into the large shoulder bag, took out the manila envelope and handed it to Sam.

He opened the envelope and removed the two printouts inside. He studied the first one without comment. He read the second one aloud. *"In addition to knowing what you did in V's library, I also know about your past and why you attended the Summerlight Academy."*

Sam looked up from the page. "I assume V is Hannah Vaughn and that the incident referred to is the home invasion at her house that took place a couple of days ago?"

Startled, she watched his face very carefully. "You know about that?"

"Thaddeus Webber sent me an email, too."

In spite of everything, Abby found herself smiling. "To vouch for me? I gather you work by referral also."

Sam's mouth edged upward at one corner. "Whenever I can."

"In that case, you must have done some research on what happened in Mrs. Vaughn's library."

"According to what I found online, a mentally unstable man with a gun invaded Vaughn's home. He claimed to hear voices and may have been tanked up on drugs, which, in turn, caused him to collapse at the scene. He was taken into custody and is now sitting in a locked ward at a psychiatric hospital, undergoing observation to see if he is sane enough to stand trial. Statements were taken from the owner of the home, Mrs. Vaughn; her housekeeper, who fainted at some point; and an unnamed woman who was there at the time. That would be you?"

Abby took a deep breath and let it out slowly. "You seem to have all the facts, Mr. Coppersmith."

"Like you, I don't take every job that comes my way. And I do not have all of the facts, but I intend to get them." He slipped the printouts back into the envelope. "Any idea what the blackmailer wants from you?"

"Not yet."

"In that case, tell me what he has on you."

Abby began to pace the chamber, weaving through the maze of display cases while she composed her thoughts. She had known this was coming, she reminded herself. It had been highly unlikely that she would be able to hire Sam without giving him all the information he might need to find the extortionist.

"Everything in the police report concerning the Vaughn home invasion is true," she began.

"That makes me very interested to know what is not in the report."

"Right." She took a deep breath. "What's not in those reports is that I'm the one who caused the intruder to collapse that day."

Sam inclined his head once, as if she had confirmed a conclusion he had already reached.

"Thought so," he said.

"What?" She stopped and stared at him, slightly stunned.

"The convenient collapse of an armed intruder in the middle of a home invasion was a bit of a red flag," he said mildly. "You somehow used your talent to take down the intruder, didn't you?"

"Yes," she said quietly.

"You knew going in that you could do that."

"I knew that if I could manipulate him into touching one of the heavily encrypted books at the same time I was holding it, there was a good chance that I could channel some of the energy into his aura and temporarily destabilize his pattern, yes."

Sam looked intrigued. "So do you do that kind of thing on a regular basis?"

She glared at him, outraged and maybe

even scared now, although she was loath to acknowledge it. *Show no weakness.*

"Of course not," she said. She clasped her hands tightly behind her back and resumed pacing. "But for obvious reasons I do not want rumors of my ability to channel energy like that to start circulating in the collectors' market."

"You think it would hurt business?"

She whirled around to face him again. "Gossip like that could destroy me."

"How?"

"Look, Mr. Coppersmith, I work both sides of the book market, the normal side and the true paranormal side. My normal clients are mostly legitimate private collectors who are interested in the history of the study of the paranormal."

"Those would be your non-talent clients?"

"Yes. But to be honest, a small-time freelancer like me would starve if she catered only to that clientele. Talk about a niche market. The money is in the genuine hot-books world, which is, for the most part, an underground market. Deals conducted in that market have to be kept very low-profile. A lot of the most serious collectors prefer to remain anonymous. If they do invite me into their homes to appraise their collections, as Mrs. Vaughn did, they expect me to be extremely discreet. Generally speaking, the underground market pays well, but the clients tend to be a difficult bunch."

"Define *difficult,*" Sam said.

"The spectrum of difficult clients starts at eccentric and moves on through secretive, reclusive and paranoid, all the way to dangerous. But I try to leave that last category of client to my competitors. The true hot-books market is a pool that is very deep at one end. I stick to the shallows."

"Sounds like a smart business plan."

"There's less money at my end of the market, but it's definitely safer swimming. The point I'm trying to make, though, is that in my business, reputation is everything. Aside from the fact that I'm very good at what I do, my most important credentials are that I am considered one hundred percent trustworthy and that I am not perceived as a potential book thief. I regret to say that there are some freelancers in my business who are not above accepting a commission to acquire a particular hot book by any means possible."

"But if it got out that you can walk into someone's private library, zap the collector unconscious and walk out with any item you care to take, some would-be clients would be reluctant to hire you, is that it?"

"What do you think?"

"I think you're right," Sam said. "Power of any kind is always interesting, but people tend to react to it in one of two ways. Some folks are compelled and attracted or even obsessed by power. Others get very, very nervous."

"Exactly. I'm glad you understand what I'm facing here. When it comes to my underground clients, I walk a fine line. Like them, I try to keep a very low profile, and not only because I value my reputation. I do not want to become the subject of someone's research experiment or, worse yet, attract the sort of freaks who want to fire up a cult."

For the first time, surprise narrowed Sam's brilliant green eyes. "You've had trouble with one or both of those types?"

"When I was in my teens, and again in college, I attracted the attention of some people who wanted to study me. It was not a pleasant experience. And even though I try to vet every client carefully, once in a while one becomes obsessed with me because of my talent. Fortunately, no one has tried to get me to channel some ancient spirit, thank heavens, but my friend Gwen had some trouble in that department a while back. It was scary."

"Sounds like your talent-obsessed clients and the would-be cult founders have the potential to turn into stalkers."

"Yes." Abby paused. "I don't suppose you Coppersmiths have ever been bothered with problems like that."

"No, can't say that we have."

She gave a small sigh. "Must be nice to be part of a family that can insulate you from that sort of thing."

"Moving right along, whoever sent you the threatening notes mentioned something about keeping your old secrets as well as the new ones. What did he mean?"

"To tell you the truth, that was what made me contact Thaddeus." She cleared her throat. "When I was in my early teens and just coming into my talent, my family concluded that I had some major mental-health issues."

"I can see where that might happen if you grow up in a family that doesn't acknowledge the existence of the paranormal."

"In my case, there were some unfortunate incidents that confirmed their worst fears."

"Incidents?"

"Yes. As a result of those incidents, I was sent to a school for troubled teens. It was either that or a juvenile-detention facility.

My father made sure my legal file was sealed, but obviously the bastard who sent those blackmail notes is aware of at least some of my history."

"What kind of incidents?"

"Nothing serious, really." She unfolded her arms and waved one hand in a vague way. "I accidentally set a couple of fires, one of which partially destroyed a bookstore."

"No kidding?"

"But the owner was only mildly injured, I swear it," she said quickly. "And there was the time I did some damage to my family's house. Very minor damage, really. It was the water damage that occurred when the fire department put out what was a very tiny fire that was the biggest problem afterward. Well, that and the smoke damage."

Sam watched her with a fascinated expression. "You can do that? Set fires with your talent?"

She raised her chin. "I told you, the fires were accidents."

"Right. Any other incidents I should know about?"

"Nothing of significance. Look, this conversation is not going in a good direction. Let's get back on track. The problem here is that I've got a complicated past, and whoever is trying to blackmail me knows about it. He's threatening to spread gossip about me. That would be bad enough if the gossip was confined to the collectors' market, but I'm afraid that he'll go to the media."

"Why would the media care about your troubled childhood?"

She spread her hands apart. "My father is Dr. Brandon C. Radwell."

"A psychologist who specializes in family counseling. Wrote a book on marriage. Does some talk shows. I know. That much came up when I checked you out online."

"Clearly you haven't been paying attention to those talk shows."

"Guilty as charged," Sam said.

"My father has become one of those TV guest experts on families, child-rearing and marriage. His new book, *Families by Choice,* is being released this week. He is in serious talks with a television producer about a reality TV series. It would be similar to those shows that feature the dog experts who go into people's homes and deal with bad dogs, I think, except that he would go into people's homes and tell them how to fix their family problems."

"Okay, I see the picture here," Sam said. "If it gets out that the hot celebrity expert in family psychology has a daughter with a troubled past who thinks she has paranormal powers, it could kill book sales and the TV deal."

"And it would be all my fault. On top of that, the whole family would be horribly embarrassed. I'm the crazy daughter they would have preferred to keep stashed in the attic. That sort of thing isn't done much these days, though, so everyone, including me, goes out of their way to pretend that I'm normal. As far as the media is concerned, the Radwells are just one big happy family. Specifically, we are the perfect example of the modern blended family."

"You sound like you're quoting someone."

She wrinkled her nose. "Yeah. Dad."

"Your father and the rest of the family don't realize that you actually do have some true talent?"

"No, of course not. How do you prove a paranormal talent like mine to someone who isn't sensitive to that kind of energy?"

Amusement gleamed in Sam's eyes. "Setting fires wasn't proof?"

"That is not funny. My family concluded that I was not only delusional but seriously deranged. Hence my time in the Summerlight Academy, where I learned how to pass for normal. They like to think the intensive counseling and therapy were effective. I prefer to let them believe that. It works better for all of us."

"What do they think you do for a living?"

"As far as they're concerned, I'm a small-time online bookseller. I'm the official underachiever in the family, but that's better than having everyone think I'm still delusional." Abby glanced at her watch again. "I don't have any more time to waste, Mr. Coppersmith. Will you take the job?"

"Let's see what we've got here," Sam said. "You had a difficult childhood, you set a few fires, spent some time in a special school for troubled teens, and you currently live a double life that has a secret side involving the underground hot-books market. You have zapped at least one individual with your talent, and I'm betting there have been others."

Alarm flashed through her. "What makes you say that?"

Sam gave her a wicked smile. "Because you admitted you knew you could take down the intruder before you confronted him. That implies some prior experience, or at least a little practice."

She swallowed hard. "Okay, there may have been a couple of other similar incidents, but I can explain all of them, really.

One involved the owner of the bookstore that I accidentally burned down, and there was this creepy assistant professor in college who wanted to run experiments on me and tried to rape me when I refused. And a couple of years ago, a client became obsessed with me, but . . ."

Sam held up one hand, palm out. "No need to explain, Abby Radwell. You are my kind of client. I'll take the job."

5

Not just my kind of client, Sam thought. *My kind of woman.*

He watched from the dock until Dixon piloted the water taxi with Abby on board out of the harbor and out of sight beyond a cluster of small islets.

He was still feeling the rush when he climbed back into the SUV and started along the narrow winding road to the Copper Beach house. He flexed his hands and took a tighter grip on the steering wheel. Stirred by the energy that was still splashing through him, the Phoenix stone in his ring burned with a low, deep fire. He could not remember the last time he had responded to a woman this way. *Never,* he concluded.

Abby Radwell had hit his senses like sizzling, sparking, flashing heat lightning produced by some exotic, unknown crystal, one with incredible properties that he could not wait to investigate, that he was *compelled* to investigate. It was not curiosity or even just physical desire that energized him now, although desire was definitely a big factor in the mix. There was something else going on. Whatever it was, he had a hunch the prowling, hungry awareness was going to keep him awake tonight. Fine by him. It beat the hell out of the recurring dream that had plagued him for the past six months.

When he walked back into the big house, he discovered that a strange silence, a sense of emptiness, had settled on the old place. It was not the kind of silence that was associated with the lack of sound. The stone walls echoed, as they always did, with his footsteps. The thick oak floors creaked in places. The refrigerator hummed faintly in the kitchen.

But there was something different about the atmosphere now. It was as if an invisible hand had hit the paranormal mute button after Abby departed.

He went downstairs into the lab, cranked back in the chair and stacked his heels on the corner of the desk. He steepled his fingers and thought about his new client.

He summoned a mental image first, concentrating on what it was about her that had fascinated him. It was not any single aspect of her appearance, he decided. Warm copper and gold glowed in the depths of her auburn hair, which formed a vibrant cloud of curls around an animated, fascinating, intelligent but not classically beautiful face. Eyes the color of dark amber tilted slightly upward at the outer corners. There was a firmly etched nose and a soft, sensitive mouth to go with the eyes.

She was not tall, no more than five-foot-four at most, but what there was of her was curvy and feminine and healthy-looking in all the right places. She carried herself with the self-confidence of a woman who was accustomed to dealing with her own problems, a woman who was capable of handling a lot of talent. An aura of energy and power brightened the atmosphere around her.

After a while he took out his phone and hit a familiar code. His father picked up halfway through the first ring.

"Did she show up?" Elias demanded.

"She was here," Sam said. "Just left. She's on her way back to Seattle."

"Well? Were you right? Is she involved in this thing?"

"I think so, but I'm not sure how, yet."

"Webber sent her to you. He wouldn't have done that if there wasn't some connection to the lab notebook."

"I agree, but all I've got for certain at the moment is that an anonymous person has sent Abby two notes that qualify as blackmail threats. The sender is trying to coerce her cooperation. He wants her to do something for him, but he hasn't made any specific demands, just issued a few threats."

"What kind of threats?" Elias asked.

"Nothing physical, at least not yet. Abby has some stuff in her private life that she would prefer to keep secret for the sake of the family image. Also, she definitely does not want the news of what happened in Vaughn's library to become widespread gossip in the underground book market."

"So you were right? That intruder did not go down because of a drug overdose?"

"Abby broke the psi-code on one of the books in Vaughn's collection, and then she channeled the energy into the intruder's aura. The currents knocked the guy unconscious."

Elias whistled softly. "Takes a lot of power to channel energy that hot."

"It does."

"And the blackmailer *knows* she did that?"

"It's not clear if he knows that she took down the intruder. The blackmail notes are a little vague. But I think we can assume he is aware that Abby can unlock psi-codes.

My gut tells me that is what is important to him."

"Lander Knox," Elias said urgently. "Got to be him. He needs someone like Abby to acquire the lab book and break the code."

"I'd say there's a definite possibility that the guy who sent the notes is Lander Knox, but we're still in the theory-and-speculation stage. The rumors that the lab book has surfaced have been circulating for months now, according to Webber. There are a few other folks who would like to get their hands on that book."

"Helicon Stone." Elias's voice hardened. "Yeah, we have to assume that if that SOB Hank Barrett has gotten wind of the lab book, he'll be looking for it. Probably send his son out to do his dirty work."

Sam almost smiled. The feud between Elias and Hank Barrett, the owner of Coppersmith's biggest competitor, was legendary. No one knew the origins of the quarrel, but over time the hostility between the two men had helped fuel two empires.

There was a great fallacy taught in business schools. It held that successful multimillion-dollar companies were run by smart executives who based their decisions on hard data and logical marketing strategies.

The truth, Sam thought, was that, as with all the other endeavors that human beings engaged in, business was conducted by people who let emotions, egos and personal agendas rule the decision-making process. Sometimes it worked.

"I know how you feel about Hank Barrett, Dad," he said. "But blackmail isn't his style, and it's not Gideon's, either."

"Huh." Elias was silent for a beat. "Wonder why the blackmailer didn't just try to hire Abby Radwell outright?"

"She only works by referral, and she vets all potential clients through Thaddeus Webber."

"Must make for a small client list," Elias said.

"But a relatively safe list. You know as well as I do that there are some dangerous people in the underground market. Abby described it as a very deep pool. She told me that she prefers to swim in the shallows."

"Looks like somebody just tossed her into the deep end. Too bad Judson isn't available. You're on your own with this."

A week ago, Judson had taken what had looked like a routine consulting assignment for a regular client. He had sent one brief message indicating that the situation had become complicated and that he would not be in touch for a while. There had been no further word from him. That was not unusual with consulting jobs for this particular client, a no-name government agency that paid well for talent and discretion.

"Keep an eye on Radwell," Elias ordered. "We need to locate that lab book. For now, she's our best lead."

"Keeping an eye on Abby won't be a problem," Sam said. "She hired me to find the blackmailer."

"*Hired* you?" Sam was flabbergasted. "What the hell do you mean by that?"

"I thought you'd be pleased that I have a new consulting job. I know you and Mom have been worrying about me lately."

"Now, just one damn minute. Your job is to find that old lab book before Lander Knox does."

"Got to go, Dad. I'm on my way to Seattle. I'll update you later."

Sam ended the connection and went upstairs to pack an overnight bag. Anticipation crackled through him. He would be seeing Abby again soon.

6

Elias tossed the phone onto his desk and went down the glass-walled corridor that overlooked the patio, the pool and the great red rocks beyond.

He paused at the door of his wife's study. Willow was at her computer. He knew she was working on foundation business. It had been her idea to set up the Coppersmith Foundation twenty years ago. Although she staunchly denied having any psychic talent, her intuition combined with her financial expertise ensured that the foundation was managed brilliantly. No one in the Coppersmith Inc. accounting department could follow the money the way Willow could. As a result, no one got far trying to scam the foundation.

When he went through the doorway he felt the familiar sense of rightness that always thrilled him when he was in Willow's presence. He'd experienced that same thrill the first time they met. Nothing had changed over the decades.

He had fallen hard for Willow all those years ago, but he was pretty sure that he loved her more now than he had at the start, assuming such a thing was even possible. He had not had a dime to his name back in those days, just the land and mineral rights to a chunk of desert that everyone else thought was fit only for rattlesnakes and growing cactus. But Willow had believed in him. She had made a home for him in a secondhand trailer out there in the desert, never complaining about the lack of money, the blistering heat or the fact that the nearest mall was several hundred miles away. And Willow had kept his secrets. He counted himself the luckiest of men.

Life was very different now. It had taken several years and a lot of sweat before the mining venture proved successful. But in the end, the rare earths that his small company had pulled out of the ground had formed the foundation of the family empire.

He and Willow could afford anything they wanted these days. They enjoyed the money and lived well. But every time he looked at Willow, he knew an unshakable truth that warmed his soul. If he lost the company tomorrow and had to start over again, she would be by his side the whole way, even if it meant going back to that damned trailer.

"He called her Abby," Elias said.

Willow looked up from the computer. She took off her reading glasses with a slow, thoughtful motion and contemplated him with her knowing eyes.

"You're talking about the young woman in Seattle who freelances in the book market? The one Thaddeus Webber sent to Sam?"

"Abigail Radwell. Sam met with her today. Looks like someone is trying to blackmail her. I'm betting it's Lander Knox. Somehow he found out she can break psi-codes. He thinks he can force her to help him find the lab book."

"There are other people who are after that book," Willow said.

"Yeah, Sam reminded me of that, too. But Quinn warned me that his son was sick in the head. Evil sick. Blackmail is the kind of shit an evil man would try."

"Maybe. How does the situation stand now? Did this Abby Radwell agree to help Sam find that notebook?"

"Not exactly. As far as I can tell she hired him to find out who is blackmailing her."

Willow blinked. "She *hired* Sam?"

"That's what he told me."

"Hmm." Willow pushed back her chair and got to her feet. She went to stand at the window. "Well, I suppose that might work. Sam will persuade her that locating the book and getting it off the underground market is the best way to neutralize the blackmailer."

Elias joined her at the window. "That must be the plan. He said he was on his way to Seattle right now."

"He'll get the lab book, Elias." Willow reached out and took his hand. "It will be all right."

"For the past couple of decades, I've been telling myself that the lab book must have been buried in the explosion along with Willis. But deep down I always knew that it was out there somewhere. And now it's surfaced at last. If it falls into the wrong hands —"

"Stop blaming yourself for what happened at that old mine all those years ago. It was not your fault. You and Quinn Knox were nearly killed that day."

"I'm the one who found that vein of crystals. I'm the one who insisted we run those first tests to see what we had."

Willow tightened her grip on his hand. "What's done is done. You had no way of knowing how dangerous those rocks were."

Elias exhaled slowly. "I still don't. That's

one of the things that makes that lab book so damn dangerous."

"Sam knows that. He'll find the book. He's smart, and his talent will be an asset in this thing. You'll see."

Elias pulled her closer and wrapped his arm around her shoulders. Together they watched the fading sunlight splash across the red rocks. He knew they were both thinking about the past and the deadly explosion at the mine.

The repercussions of the paranormal energy that had been released that day had echoed down into the future, creating the greatest of all the Coppersmith family secrets, the one secret that he and Willow had never told Sam, Judson or Emma.

After a while, Willow turned her head to look at him with a speculative expression.

"He called her Abby?" she said.

"Yeah. After meeting her for all of maybe one hour. And now he's on his way to Seattle." Elias paused, trying to find a way to explain what he had heard in Sam's voice. "He sounded *energized*, Willow. As if he was looking forward to something."

Willow smiled. "In that case, regardless of how this turns out, I'm already grateful to Abby Radwell."

7

"Are you out of your mind, Abby?" Gwen Frazier leaned forward across the restaurant table and lowered her voice. "According to what I found online, Sam Coppersmith was implicated in the murder of his fiancée six months ago. You have no business hiring a man like that. He might be very, very dangerous."

"Relax, I'm employing him, I'm not sleeping with him. Big difference."

"That's supposed to reassure me?"

"Well, it certainly makes me feel better about the whole thing," Abby said.

They were in a booth in the bar section of the restaurant. It was seven-thirty. The after-work crowd that had drifted in earlier had come and gone. The place was now filling up with the locals from the nearby condos and apartment buildings. Several stylists from the hair salon on the corner, which closed at seven, were celebrating a birthday.

The low rumble of conversation and the music playing over the sound system provided a layer of privacy.

Gwen Frazier was the same age as Abby. Tall, dark-haired and hazel-eyed, she was an aura-reading talent who made her living as a psychic counselor. Her abilities allowed her to work with talents and non-talents alike. As she had explained to Abby, there was no real difference between the two groups of clients. Those with real psychical abilities of their own believed her when she explained that she worked by reading their auras. Those without talent wanted to believe that she could see their energy fields. It was a win-win situation for a woman in her line.

"This isn't a joke," Gwen said.

"I know. Sorry. It's been a very long day. The drive back from Anacortes took longer than usual. Accident on the interstate." Abby swallowed some of her wine and lowered the glass. "If it helps, I have been informed that there is no way Sam Coppersmith could have murdered his fiancée."

"Who told you that?"

"The water-taxi guy."

"He's an authority?"

"He certainly seemed to think so. Evidently, no one on that island thinks Sam did it."

"And what proof do they offer?" Gwen demanded.

"They seem to feel that if Sam had murdered someone, he would have done a better job of it."

"I beg your pardon. What's that supposed to mean?"

"He would have made the victim disappear." Abby waved one hand in a now-you-see-it-now-you-don't motion. "And he would have taken care to make sure that there was nothing left behind that pointed back to him."

"And you believed this water-taxi guy's theory?"

Abby looked at Gwen over the top of her glass. "Having met Sam Coppersmith, yes, I believe that theory."

"You do realize that there's a lot of money in the Coppersmith family," Gwen said ominously. "With money comes the kind of power it takes to make sure someone in the family does not go down for murder."

"Your cynical side is showing, Gwen."

"It's my best side. Is this Sam Coppersmith a real private investigator?"

"He described himself as a technical consultant."

"Oh, that's just wonderful," Gwen said.

"But I do think he's the best man for the job."

"Why, for heaven's sake?"

"Because this situation involves a very hot book, and I need an investigator who at least takes the paranormal seriously. Not a lot of those floating around, in case you haven't noticed. Besides, you know as well as I do that Thaddeus Webber would never have sent me to Coppersmith if he had believed there was a better option."

"Point taken." Gwen sat back. "Have you received any more email from the blackmailer?"

"No, thank goodness. But there's something else I want to talk to you about."

"What?"

"I've had a really weird dream two nights in a row. They both featured Grady Hastings."

Gwen frowned. "The crazy guy who staged that home invasion in your client's house?"

"Yes."

"Well, it's not surprising that you would have some bad dreams for a while. That was a very frightening situation."

"True, but what is freaking me out about the dreams is that I've started sleepwalking.

I've never done that in my life."

"There is nothing unstable about your talent," Gwen said, "if that's what's worrying you."

"You're the one who told me that a disturbance in the dreamstate can be an early indication of serious problems with the para-senses."

"It's true, but that kind of disturbance is visible in the aura. You're fine."

Abby framed the base of her glass in a triangle formed by her thumbs and forefingers. "Take a look. Please."

"Okay, okay."

Gwen heightened her talent. Abby felt energy shiver gently in the atmosphere. A few feet away, a middle-aged businessman who was slouched on a bar stool suddenly turned his head and looked around, as though searching for someone or something. Abby knew that he had felt the tingle of psi in the vicinity but probably did not know what it was that had lifted the hairs on the nape of his neck. Over in the corner, a redheaded stylist drinking a cosmopolitan glanced uneasily around the room before turning back to her colleagues.

Abby waited while Gwen did her thing. After a couple of minutes, the energy level in the atmosphere receded.

"I'm not picking up any bad vibes," Gwen said. "Just the indications of stress that I've mentioned before. There is some deepening in the intensity of ultralight coming from the hot end of the spectrum, but nothing alarming. I didn't see anything that I associate with instability of the para-senses. Also, for the record, I didn't see the kind of dreamlight that is associated with regular sleepwalking."

"Then what in the world is going on?"

"I've tried to explain to you that what happened to you in the Vaughn library was the equivalent of a category-five hurricane, as far as your para-senses are concerned. You channeled an enormous amount of volatile energy. For heaven's sake, you managed to render a man unconscious. There was bound to be some blowback, to say nothing of the fact that you could have been killed that day. You need to give yourself time to recover from the shock."

"I can't continue sleepwalking," Abby said. "What if I open the sliding glass doors and decide to take a walk off the balcony?"

"Calm down. You're not going to do that. Your para-senses would kick in fast if you tried to do anything that might put your life in danger."

"You have more faith in my senses than I do."

Gwen grew thoughtful. "In this dream, do you have any sense of where you're going or what you want to accomplish?"

"I see Grady Hastings. He's reaching out to me, begging me to help him. He tells me I'm the only one who can."

"Is that all?"

"Pretty much."

"Okay, I'm sticking to my theory that the fugue states you're experiencing are being triggered by stress you experienced the other day. But there is another possibility that you should not overlook."

"What?"

"Your intuition may be trying to tell you something important."

"Such as?"

"I don't know," Gwen said. "But you're too smart to ignore the implications. Try turning the dream into a lucid dream, and then take control of it."

"Easier said than done."

"Well, it's certainly easier for a strong talent than it would be for someone who doesn't have much psychic sensitivity," Gwen said. "Before you go to sleep tonight, set your psychic alarm clock to alert you when you start dreaming. Then take control of the dream."

"That will work?"

"Yes, if you do a good job of setting the alarm. The trick works on the same principle that makes it possible for you to tell yourself that you have to wake up at a certain time in order to catch an early plane. Lots of people, even people with very little talent, do that all the time."

Abby took a slow breath and reminded herself that this was Gwen's area of expertise. "Okay, I'll give it a shot."

Gwen aimed a finger at her. "You know what you really need?"

"Please don't say a new boyfriend."

"You need a vacation. You should come with me to Hawaii tomorrow. It's not too late. I'll bet we can find you a seat on my flight. There are always last-minute cancellations."

"Sure, at full fare. You know I can't afford that. Besides, leaving town now is out of the question. How can I enjoy a vacation if I know there's a blackmailer waiting for me when I get back?"

"I guess that would put a damper on things," Gwen conceded. "But you've hired Coppersmith to take care of the extortionist for you. Let him do his job while you relax on a beach."

"I don't think you can just hire an investigator and then go merrily off on vacation while he cleans things up for you."

"Why not? You're finished with the Vaughn job, and speaking as your friend and psychic counselor, I'm telling you that you need some time off to let your senses recover. Put the ticket to Hawaii on your charge card and tell your investigator to file reports of his progress by email."

"I don't like the idea of turning Sam Coppersmith loose, unsupervised, on what is essentially my very personal and private business."

Gwen smiled knowingly. "You like to be in control."

"Who doesn't? But trust me, if you ever meet Sam Coppersmith, you'll know why staying in charge is a very sensible idea."

"What's he like?"

"Think mad scientist with a basement lab."

"Doesn't sound like the typical profile of a private investigator."

Abby picked up her glass again. "There's nothing typical about Sam Coppersmith."

When they emerged from the restaurant, a light misty rain veiled the Belltown neighborhood. The wet pavement glowed with the reflected light of the streetlamps. Neon signs illuminated the windows of the innumerable restaurants, pubs and clubs that lined both sides of First Avenue.

Gwen shoved her hands deep into the pockets of her trench coat. "I'm thinking that maybe I should cancel Hawaii tomorrow. I don't like leaving you here alone to deal with Coppersmith and a blackmailer."

"You are not going to cancel. Your new client is paying you a huge fee and all expenses just to have you go there to do a reading. You can't turn your back on that kind of money."

"Screw the money. I'm worried about you, Abby."

"I'll be fine."

"Promise me that if you start to feel like you're in more trouble than you can handle you'll call Nick, first, because he'll be the closest. And right after you call him, you'll call me. I'll be on the next plane back to Seattle."

"I promise," Abby said.

Neither of them mentioned the possibility of her going to her family for help. It was not an option, and they both knew it. Gwen and Nick Sawyer constituted her real family, Abby thought. The bond among the three of them had been forged in the fires of their years together in the Summerlight

Academy. Nothing could sever it.

She was about to add more reassurance, but a flash of intense awareness stopped her cold in the middle of the sidewalk.

"Abby?" Gwen stopped, too, concerned. "Are you okay?"

"He's here," Abby said quietly.

"Who?" Gwen asked.

Abby watched a shadowy figure detach itself from a darkened doorway and walk forward into the light. The man wore a black leather jacket open over a dark crewneck pullover and dark trousers. The collar of the jacket was pulled up against the chill and the rain, shadowing his features.

He carried a black leather gym bag in one hand. With her senses on alert, she had no difficulty at all perceiving the faint heat in his eyes. A thrill of excitement fizzed through her veins.

Sam looked at her, eyes heating a little. "I've been waiting for you. You know the old saying."

"What old saying?" Abby asked.

"You can run, but you can't hide."

Abby looked at Gwen. "Meet Sam Coppersmith."

8

Sam heard the clicks of dog claws on a wooden floor before Abby got her door unlocked.

"That's Newton," Abby explained. "He isn't keen on strangers, especially strange men."

"I'll try to make a good impression," Sam said.

She turned the key and pushed the door open. A scruffy gray dog of uncertain ancestry lunged forward to greet Abby as if she had been gone for a year.

"Sorry I'm late, Newton." Abby leaned down to scratch the dog affectionately behind the ears. "We've got company."

Newton regarded Sam with an expression of grave misgivings.

"I'm with her," Sam said.

"Generally speaking, he doesn't bite," Abby said.

"You don't have to make that sound like a

character flaw," Sam said.

Newton was on the small side, but that was about all he had in common with the typical condo dog, which, in Sam's experience, tended to come in two versions: tiny, white and fluffy or chunky pug. Newton was a condo-sized version of a junkyard dog.

"Where did you get him?" Sam asked.

"The animal shelter." Abby gave Newton an affectionate smile. "It was love at first sight, wasn't it, Newton?"

Newton spared her a brief glance, acknowledging his name. Then he turned his attention back to Sam.

Sam set the leather duffel bag on the floor, crouched and extended his hand toward Newton. The dog tilted his head slightly to the side and pricked up his ears. He sniffed Sam's hand and then condescended to allow himself to be patted a few times.

"Congratulations," Abby said. She slipped out of her coat and turned to hang it on the red enamel coat tree. "Newton approves of you. He doesn't take to everyone."

Sam got to his feet. "I think it's more a case of tolerating me."

"Well, yes, but at least he doesn't look like he's going to go for your throat."

"He's a condo dog," Sam said. "The most he could go for is my ankle."

Abby glared. "Do not, under any circumstances, underestimate Newton. He picks up on vibes in the atmosphere. He knows when he's being insulted."

Sam looked at Newton. "Is that so?"

Newton gave a disdainful little snort and trotted off down the hall.

Sam looked at Abby. "Since your guard dog has decided to allow me over the threshold, is it okay if I take off my coat?"

Abby flushed. "Yes, of course. Sorry. I didn't mean to be rude, it's just that I wasn't expecting to see you again so soon."

"I got that impression."

He shrugged out of his jacket and handed it to her. When she took it from him, her fingers brushed against his, sending an intimate little thrill of awareness across his senses. He knew she felt the small flash because her brilliant eyes widened slightly in surprise. She gave him a startled look and then just as swiftly looked away.

She hung his jacket on the coat tree and led the way down the short hall to the living and dining area.

A few minutes ago, Gwen Frazier had discreetly vanished in a cab to her own apartment a couple of blocks away. Sam had felt the energy shiver in the atmosphere when Abby had introduced him to her friend. He was fairly certain that Gwen had used some talent to make a judgment call. She had evidently decided that Abby was safe with him, at least for now, because she had not tried to hang around.

Things were looking up, he decided. He had managed to get through two lines of defense tonight, the protective friend and the protective dog. He was on a roll.

"Your friend is also a talent, isn't she?" he asked.

"Yes. Gwen is a psychic counselor. She does aura readings in a shop in the market."

"Aura readings. Right."

Abby gave him a severe look. "I know what you're thinking."

"Do you?"

"You think Gwen is using her talent to con people. For the record, she doesn't do fortune-telling or palm-reading. And she certainly doesn't pretend to talk to the dead. She really can read auras. Her clients come to her for advice and guidance. She analyzes their energy fields and tells them what she sees and makes recommendations. She's a kind of therapist."

"Got it."

Abby sighed. "I'm probably overreacting here. It's just that so many people think Gwen is a fraud. Storefront psychics aren't exactly held in high esteem by psychologists and traditional counselors. Would you like some herbal tea? I'd offer coffee, but I don't drink it at night, at least not lately."

And that was all the information he was going to get on Gwen Frazier, he thought. "Tea will be fine. Thanks."

"I'll get the water started." She hesitated, as if she wasn't quite sure what to do with him. "Please, sit down."

He studied his options. The condo was small, but it was a corner unit with an open, flowing floor plan. The walls were a sunny Mediterranean gold with dark brown accents. The floors were hardwood. There were two area rugs decorated with modernistic designs in deep red, teal, green and yellow. Newton was lounging on the one near the window. He watched Sam with deep suspicion, but he showed no signs of going for the jugular or the ankle.

There was a comfortable-looking L-shaped sofa, a reading chair, some bookshelves, a lot of healthy-looking plants and a glass-topped coffee table. There was a book on the table. He took a closer look. *Families by Choice: A Guide to Creating the Modern Blended Family* by Dr. Brandon C. Radwell.

"That's my father's new book," Abby said.

He picked up *Families by Choice* and turned it over. The back-cover photo showed a smiling Brandon C. Radwell holding hands with an elegant-looking woman who had to be his wife. Behind the beaming couple stood Abby, a man about her age, and two very attractive women who appeared to be nineteen or twenty.

"This is your family?" Sam asked, holding up the book to show the photo.

"That's the Radwells, the perfect modern blended family," Abby said. She turned away and became very busy with the teakettle. "That's my stepbrother, Dawson, and my half sisters standing with me behind Dad and Diana."

"Your half sisters look like twins."

"They are. They're in college." Abby set the kettle on a burner. "I was twelve when they were born. Dawson was thirteen."

He put the book down on the coffee table and finished his examination of the room. One corner had been turned into a home office outfitted with a desk, a computer and some storage cabinets.

The tiny balcony and wraparound floor-to-ceiling windows took full advantage of the cityscape view. The lights of the Space Needle glittered in the night.

The whole place glowed with a cozy, inviting warmth that suggested a very personal touch. A lot of time and attention had been lavished on the little condo to transform it from a living space into a home.

"Nice," he said.

Abby smiled, the first genuine smile he had gotten from her. She was suddenly radiant. Deep satisfaction and delight lit her eyes. "It's my first home. I've been renting forever. But I finally managed to save enough for a down payment. Moved in three months ago. Did the decorating myself. My friends helped me with the painting and built-ins."

There was more than just pride of ownership in her voice. "It's my first home" said a lot. The little condo was very important to Abby. Something else she had said struck him, too. Her friends had helped her paint and decorate. There was no mention of any assistance from her stepbrother and half sisters.

He walked to the granite counter that divided the living area from the kitchen and angled himself onto one of the bar stools.

Abby took a canister down out of the cupboard. "I assume you came to see me tonight because you've made some progress on the investigation?"

"Nope. I've got zip."

For a heartbeat or two she did not move or even blink. Her stillness was absolute. She recovered quickly and frowned.

"Then what in the world are you doing here?" she asked.

He folded his arms on the counter. "My job. I told you I don't have any startling revelations, but I do have a few questions."

"You could have called."

"I prefer to get my answers face-to-face." He smiled. "Less chance of a misunderstanding that way."

"Fine, whatever." She removed the lid of the canister and started spooning loose tea into a pot. "Ask your questions."

"You said you don't know what the blackmailer wants."

"I told you, he hasn't made any specific demands."

"Do you have any theories?"

"I assume he's after some very hot, probably encrypted, book. He wants me to get it for him."

"But you don't know which book?"

"Not yet." She put the lid back on the canister. "At any given time, there are always a few extremely rare volumes with a paranormal provenance floating around in the underground."

"Did Thaddeus Webber give you any clue?"

"No." She opened another cupboard and took down two mugs. "Our communication on the subject thus far has been via email. Thaddeus lives alone in the foothills of the Cascades. He's very reclusive. Quite paranoid. He doesn't have a phone. Says they're too easy to tap. When he insisted that I contact you immediately, I emailed him a couple of questions, but the only response I got was 'Talk to Sam Coppersmith. He'll know what to do.' "

"I think he's right. I have a better idea of what may be going down than you do."

She gave him a wry smile. "I've come to the same conclusion. Talk to me, Sam."

"I'm pretty sure that Thaddeus Webber sent you to me because he thinks your blackmailer is after an old lab notebook that my father spent years trying to find."

"For the record, whoever he is, he's not *my* blackmailer, but go on."

"Eventually, Dad concluded that both the notebook and the man who had recorded the results of his experiments in it had been buried in an explosion in an old mine called the Phoenix. But now there is reason to believe that the notebook has surfaced in the collectors' market. We know of at least one very dangerous man who is after it."

Abby raised her brows. "I assume that you are not referring to yourself?"

For a second, he didn't comprehend. Then it hit him that she had just let him know that she considered him dangerous.

"No need to insult me," he said, going for offended. "I'm on your side in this thing, remember?"

"Actually, it's starting to sound like you've got your own agenda, but I'm good with that. Everyone has an agenda, right?"

He did not dignify that with a response. "What I'm trying to explain here is that it's reasonable to assume that Webber sent you to me because he thinks that you're in danger from someone who is after that notebook. He understands that I'm the best-qualified person around to look after you until we find that damned book and get it off the market."

"Okay, I get that, but remember that you're supposed to be working for me."

"Trust me, I am not going to let you out of my sight until we find the notebook and the person who is trying to blackmail you."

"I'm not sure that translates into working for me."

"You will have my full attention until this is over," he assured her gravely.

For a long moment, she studied him with deeply shadowed, unreadable eyes. The shriek of the teakettle's whistle broke the tense silence. She turned away to pour the hot water into the pot.

"All right," she said. "I guess that's the best deal I'm going to get. You find my blackmailer and make him go away. In exchange, I will find the lab notebook for you."

Irritation sparked through him. "This isn't a business arrangement."

"Yes." She set the kettle down. "That is exactly what it is. Never mind. I take it you think this lab book is locked in a psi-code?"

"According to the rumors, yes. We don't know when it was locked or who did the encryption."

"This man you mentioned, the one who kept the records of his experiments in the notebook, you say he died in a mine explosion?"

"Yes."

"When?"

"About forty years ago. His name was Ray Willis. He and my father and another man named Quinn Knox were mining engineers who all had some intuitive sensitivity for the latent energy in rocks and crystals and ores. In addition, they had the vision to see that the future of technology was going to be dependent on the so-called rare earths. They formed a partnership and went into the exploration business. They hit pay dirt, literally, when they picked up the mineral rights to an old abandoned mine out in the Nevada desert. Whoever sank the shaft originally was probably looking for gold. There wasn't any there. But Dad and his partners were after twenty-first-century gold."

"The rare earths."

"Right. They were all convinced that the Phoenix was the modern equivalent of a gold mine."

"Did they find the minerals and elements they were looking for in the Phoenix Mine?"

"Yes, but they found something a lot more interesting and, according to Dad, a lot more dangerous. They discovered geodes filled with quartzlike crystals unlike anything they had seen before. There was no data on them in the research literature. But they eventually turned up a few old references to similar crystals in some ancient books on alchemy."

Abby made a face and poured the tea into the mugs. "Alchemy. That figures. The old alchemists were always coming up with secret formulas and running experiments with para-crystals and amber and other stones in an effort to enhance their powers."

"Dad, Willis and Knox could sense the energy locked in the rocks, but they had no idea how to access it, let alone figure out how to use it. They set up a small on-site lab and started conducting experiments."

Abby set one of the mugs on the counter in front of him. At least she was no longer looking skeptical. Instead, she appeared to be reluctantly fascinated.

"They found out that the crystals had paranormal properties?" she asked.

"Yes. But they soon realized that they were playing with fire." He was suddenly very conscious of his ring. "Maybe literally. All they could tell in the field lab was that the energy in the stones was volatile and unpredictable, and that it was paranormal in nature. Dad and Knox wanted to stop the experiments until they could get some of the specimens to a properly equipped facility. But Ray Willis was obsessed with the stones. He was convinced they had enormous value, and he decided that he didn't want to share the potential profits."

Abby picked up her own mug. "There was a falling-out among the partners?"

"You could say that. Ray Willis tried to murder Knox and my father. Dad never told us exactly what happened in the mine shaft that day, but in the end there was an explosion. Knox and my father escaped through an air shaft. Willis didn't make it out."

"What happened?"

"Afterward, Dad and Knox made a pact. They decided that for the foreseeable future, the crystals should stay in the ground. Those rocks were just too dangerous. There was no telling what would happen if they fell into the wrong hands. They agreed to keep the location of the mine a secret, and they tried to destroy all traces of its existence."

"The foreseeable future has turned into forty years?"

"Yes, but Dad still hasn't changed his mind about the Phoenix. He does not want it found, not yet at any rate. He says if the time comes to reopen that mine, Coppersmith Inc. will handle the job."

"Meanwhile, your father is committed to keeping the secret."

"His old partner, Quinn Knox, kept the secret, too. But he died a couple of weeks ago. Before he passed on, however, he warned us that his son, Lander Knox, who is evidently a full-blown bad guy with a lot of talent, is on the trail of the lab book."

"You say your father and Knox searched

for the book after the explosion?"

"Not just the notebook. Several of the crystals that Ray Willis was using in his experiments went missing, too. Dad and Knox couldn't find the book or the stones. Eventually, they gave up and told themselves everything had been buried with Willis in the explosion. But over the years there have been occasional whispers that indicated that the book and at least some of the crystals survived. In the beginning, Dad chased down every lead. Now my brother, Judson, and I do it. But until now, nothing has ever come of any of the rumors."

"What happened to your father's partnership with Knox?"

"They worked together for a while. Found a new mine, one that produced copper. They sold out to a big mining company and split the profits. That was the end of their partnership. My father spent his share of the money on exploration and development of another rare-earths mine that became the foundation of Coppersmith Inc."

"What happened to Quinn Knox?"

"He and Dad lost contact over the years. Knox evidently had a problem with gambling and a few other addictions. But Dad heard from him for the first time in decades when Knox called from his hospital bed to warn him about Lander Knox. Apparently, Lander found one of the crystals that Quinn had kept and learned about the existence of the Phoenix Mine. He has concluded that he was deprived of his rightful inheritance, and he's determined to find it. To do that, he needs the lab book."

"You really think this Lander Knox is the person who is trying to blackmail me?"

"I think there's a very high probability that he's the blackmailer, yes. But we have to assume that there may be others who will do whatever it takes to get that book."

"Wow, a lost mine and a missing lab book." Abby looked genuinely amused. "You know, if it weren't for the blackmail part, this would actually be one of my cooler gigs."

"I'm glad you can see the positive side of this situation."

He studied the tea she had placed in front of him. Normally, he never drank tea, herbal or otherwise. But this tea was a mysterious golden green. He picked up the cup and swallowed cautiously. The brew tasted oddly soothing. He could feel the warmth flooding through him, and it felt good. It occurred to him that he had been cold for a while now. Strange that he had not been aware of it until tonight.

They drank the tea together in silence. Eventually, he put down the cup.

"By now you've probably heard the rumors about me," he said.

9

She didn't pretend that she didn't know what he was talking about.

"Well, sure," she said. "Even my friend Gwen has heard them."

"I didn't kill Cassidy Lawrence."

"I know."

That was not the response he had expected.

"How do you know that?" he asked.

Abby shrugged. "Gwen would never have left us alone together if she thought you were capable of that kind of thing."

He frowned. "She's that good?"

"She's that good."

"Huh."

So much for the fantasy of Abby throwing herself into his arms and swearing a vow of unqualified trust. *Take what you can get, Coppersmith.*

"There's one other thing I'd like to clarify," he said.

"Yes?"

"For some reason, a lot of folks seem to believe that Cassidy and I were engaged."

"Not true?"

"No," he said. "We saw a lot of each other for a while, and people made some assumptions. We had an affair, but she was not my fiancée."

"I see."

Abby's phone chimed into the sudden, acute silence. She flinched, clearly startled, and picked up the device. She glanced at the screen, smiled and took the call.

"Talk about a psychic intercept," she said. She walked out from behind the kitchen counter, heading toward the small desk. "We were just chatting about you, Gwen. . . . Yes, that's what I told him. You can take off for Hawaii without having to worry about me."

Abby stopped in front of her desk and began to flip through a small stack of mail.

"Yes," she said. "I promise I'll call Nick if I think I need backup. But I'll be fine. . . . Yes. . . . Good night. Safe trip. I know it's a job, but try to have some fun in Hawaii, okay? . . . Yes, I promise I'll call with updates."

She closed the phone and set it down. "Good news. Gwen just gave you a clean bill of aura health."

"I appreciate that," Sam said.

Abby tossed the last of the mail aside and reached for the small package that sat on the desk. "I don't remember doing any online shopping recently."

A visible shiver went through her when her fingers closed around the parcel. She gave a sharp, audible gasp. Energy sparked in the atmosphere.

"Oh, my," she breathed.

Newton jumped to his feet, ears sharpened. He whined softly.

Sam was already moving, crossing the room to where Abby stood, gazing raptly at the package that she held in both hands.

"What's wrong?" he asked.

"Nothing is wrong." She had recovered from the initial shock. Anticipation sparkled in her eyes. "I think someone sent me a very special gift, a book, judging by the energy. An old one."

He could sense the subtle shiver of energy around the package now. "Whatever is in there is hot."

"Yes, indeed," she said. She began to unwrap the package with great care. "Very hot."

The hairs lifted on the nape of his neck.

"Who sent it?" he asked.

"I don't know yet. There's no return address. Maybe there will be a note inside. I have a hunch that it's a thank-you gift from one of my clients."

"Your clients have your home address?"

"No, of course not. Too many crazies in my line. All of my business correspondence goes to an anonymous private post office box and is then forwarded here."

She got the outer wrapping off, revealing an ornately carved wooden box.

"Those are alchemical designs," Sam said.

"They certainly are."

Abby opened the hinged lid of the box. There was a small leather-bound book inside. She used both hands to take it out. She smiled.

"What?" Sam asked warily.

"It's encrypted with a delicate little psi-code." Abby opened the cover with great care and studied the title page. Pleasure and a little heat illuminated her eyes.

Sam looked over her shoulder and studied the Latin. "What does it say?"

"The title translates to *A Treatise on the Herbs and Flowers Most Useful in the Art of Mixing Perfumes.* It's a guide to perfume making, written by someone who obviously had a psychic talent for the craft. According to the title page, it contains some of Cleopatra's own personal recipes. Isn't it lovely?"

"Abby," Sam said, "it wasn't mailed to you."

"Yes, I know. I told you, my mail goes through a private post office."

"That's not what I meant," he said evenly. "It wasn't mailed anywhere. There's no postage on it. That package must have been hand-delivered."

Abby looked up at last. Her eyes narrowed faintly. He realized he finally had her attention.

"Well, I do have a few friends," she said tentatively. "I suppose one of them could have dropped it off."

"Is there a note?"

"I didn't notice one." She looked at the wooden box. There was a small white envelope inside. "Wait, there it is."

She put the book down and opened the envelope. She pulled out the small card inside and read the handwritten message: *"Please accept this small gift as an expression of my admiration for your unique talents. I wish to commission your services with a view to acquiring a rare item that is rumored to be coming onto the market. Price is no object. There will be a generous bonus if you are successful. Regardless of your decision, the herbal is yours to keep."*

"Someone is trying to bribe you to take him on as a client," Sam said. "And he knows where you live."

"Oh, crap," Abby said.

10

Icy energy electrified the atmosphere. Abby knew that Sam was jacked. So was she, but in a different way. It made her uneasy to realize that a potential client had found her home address, but she could not bring herself to believe that the little herbal represented a truly dangerous threat.

"I take precautions," Abby said, "but everyone knows that these days you can find anyone if you look hard enough. I would point out, for instance, that you found my address tonight. I don't recall giving it to you this afternoon."

"I had your license plate," Sam said.

"I beg your pardon? I left my car in Anacortes when I went to see you." Then it struck her. "Oh, for heaven's sake, it was Dixon, wasn't it? He made a note of my license plate when he fetched me at the marina. You used it to trace me."

"My family takes precautions, too," Sam

said. "How many of your clients have gone to the trouble to track you down like this?"

"It's never been much of a problem, to be honest. Everyone knows my reputation. There's no point approaching me unless you have been referred by someone I trust. Even if someone got as far as the front door of this building, none of the doormen would let him in unless I gave my approval."

"Mail and packages are delivered to the lobby. How did these get up here today?"

"I was supposed to be out of town for the next few days. I had a job down in Portland that I rescheduled after the blackmail threats arrived. The day doorman, Ralph, always brings up my mail and waters my plants when I'm gone. I forgot to tell him that my plans had changed."

Sam picked up the note and read it silently. "This isn't the same guy who is sending you the threatening notes."

"No, I'm sure it isn't. Whoever sent me this herbal is trying to impress me. This is a very generous gift. I could probably sell it for several thousand dollars, enough to cover my mortgage payments for a while and pay off my new furniture."

"*Are* you impressed?" Sam asked softly.

She drew one finger across the elegantly hand-tooled leather cover. Hushed power locked in stasis stirred her senses.

"Oh, my, yes," she whispered. "No one has ever given me anything like this in my whole life. The book is valuable in and of itself as an antiquarian text, but the psi-encryption makes it worth much, much more to the collectors in my market. Who knows what secrets may be hidden inside."

Sam's jaw hardened. "In other words, the person who sent it to you is wooing you."

She smiled. "You could say that. Giving me this book is the equivalent of giving another woman a very nice set of diamond earrings."

She could see that Sam did not like hearing that. She wondered why it bothered him so much. She had merely been trying to illustrate a point.

"It's not personal," she said quickly. "I mean, it's not like he wants to have an affair with me or anything. He just wants me to know that he can afford my services and that he'll pay well for them." She touched the herbal again. "This gift also tells me that he respects my talent."

"Don't get any ideas about dumping me and taking him on as a client," Sam warned. "You and I have a deal."

She sighed. "Yep, I'm committed."

"You don't have to act like it's a tragedy.

That blackmailer is still out there, remember."

"Believe me, I haven't forgotten."

"Can I have a look at that herbal?" Sam asked.

"Sure." She handed it to him with some reluctance. The energy of the book was mildly intoxicating. Like an exotic perfume, she thought.

Sam opened the book with due care. "I can feel a little heat, but nothing that would warn me that it's encrypted."

"Whoever locked that book was very skilled with the old techniques. You probably wouldn't notice anything at all unless you actually tried to concoct some of the recipes. Then you would find out, probably the hard way, that the perfumes you created were all off in some fashion."

Sam looked up. "The hard way?"

"The results might vary, from foul-smelling concoctions to some that are downright poisonous. It would depend on just how serious the person who set the code was about protecting her secrets."

"You think a woman locked this book?"

"Yes," Abby said. She smiled. "Every psi-code is unique. It's like a fingerprint in that it reveals a lot about the individual who set the encryption. You'll have to take my word for it when I tell you that you do not want to re-create any of those recipes unless the code is broken first."

"I believe you." Sam put the book down on the desk. "What are you going to do with the herbal? Keep it?"

"No, I really can't do that. The person who sent it was very gracious and very generous about insisting it was a gift, but I could never accept such a valuable item for services that haven't been rendered."

"How will you return it?" Sam asked. "You don't know the sender."

"I'm sure that won't be a problem. I'll give the book to Thaddeus Webber. He'll find a way to return it to whoever sent it. Thaddeus has connections throughout the hot-book market. Unlike me, he works the deep end."

"Do you think that the person who sent you the herbal is a deep-end collector?"

"Yes." She placed the herbal carefully back into the box. "I do."

"Think he knows you'll arrange to return the book if you don't accept him as a client?"

"Certainly." She smiled. "I told you, I have a reputation in this business."

"In other words, he didn't take much of a risk when he gave you the herbal."

"No. But it was a very elegant gesture, regardless."

Sam watched her close the lid of the box. "You know, I had no idea until now how delicate business negotiations are in your world."

"I thought I made it clear. In my line, reputation is everything. All my transactions involve an element of trust."

"Well, that attitude explains why you aren't yet ready to hold hands and jump off the edge of a cliff with me," he said, without inflection.

She blanked for a couple of beats. Then she chuckled. The chuckles turned into laughter, and she was suddenly laughing harder than she had in some time.

"That's hilarious." She wiped the corners of her eyes. "You are a very unusual man, Sam Coppersmith."

"You want to know the sad part? I wasn't trying to make a joke. I need your trust to do my job, Abby."

She sobered and blinked a few times to clear her eyes. "Oh. Sorry. I didn't realize. Never mind. As you just pointed out, we have a deal, and I do trust you to honor your part of the bargain. I give you my word I'll honor my end. I'll do my best to find that lab book. Speaking of my little problem, just how do you plan to go about finding the blackmailer?"

Sam looked as if he wanted to pursue the topic of trust, but he must have concluded that the conversation was not going to be useful. He turned away and went to stand at the window, looking out into the night. Newton joined him.

"A chat with Thaddeus Webber would be a good place to start," Sam said. "But I'd like to do it in person, not via email. Unlike you, he isn't so easy to find. Think you can get him to agree to talk to me?"

"Yes, I'm sure I can. I want to see him, myself, in order to give him the herbal. I'll email him tonight and set up a meeting. He's quite security-conscious, though, so he'll want to choose the time and place."

"Fine by me, so long as he makes it soon, preferably tomorrow."

"I doubt that will be a problem. Thaddeus is the one who sent me to you in the first place, after all. He'll be as helpful as he can."

"Good."

She waited a beat. Sam did not say anything else. He and Newton continued to contemplate the night.

She cleared her throat. "So do you plan on returning to Copper Beach tonight? It's a long trip."

"What?" Sam sounded distracted, as if she had interrupted his train of thought. He turned around. "No, I'm not going back tonight. I thought I made it clear I'll be sticking close to you until this is finished. Got a spare blanket for your sofa?"

Blindsided. She stared at him, speechless. A tiny tingle of panic iced her spine. *Should have seen this coming.*

"I really don't think it's necessary for you to spend the night here," she said quickly. "It's not like there is an immediate threat to my safety."

"Sure there is."

"I don't see it."

"Let's review," Sam said. "You are suddenly very hot, in more ways than one. Every time I turn around, someone else is either trying to bribe you or trying to blackmail you into working for him."

"Just two people," she said. "Three, counting you."

"That's two too many. Sooner or later, someone may decide to take more direct action. This place is not exactly a fortress."

"I've got Newton," she said. But she was grasping at straws, and she knew it.

"I'm sure Newton is a fine animal, but he's not exactly a pit bull or a rottweiler. Tonight, I sleep here."

She thought about the black leather duffel he had left in the entry hall. "I'm guessing that whatever is inside that bag you brought, it's not your gym stuff."

"Overnight kit, a change of clothes and some of the equipment I use in my consulting work. I never leave home without it."

"You came prepared."

"We're in this together, Abby."

"Right." She took a deep breath. "Actually, there are three of us involved in this thing. You, me and Newton. And right now Newton has priority. It's time for his late-night walk."

"Please don't tell me that you make a habit of going out onto the street alone at this hour every night?"

"No need for that," Abby said. "The main reason I chose this particular condo building is because it has a lovely dog garden on the roof."

Newton bounded toward the front door, claws skidding on the floor.

"He knows the word *walk,*" Abby explained.

"Maybe you're right," Sam said. "Maybe he is a little bit psychic."

"All dogs have a psychic vibe," Abby said. "But Newton has more talent than most. I knew that the instant I saw him in the animal shelter."

Some time later, she closed her bedroom door, turned off the lights and pulled back the covers. The curtains were open, allowing the nighttime glow of the city to spill into the room.

Newton jumped up onto the foot of the bed and settled down.

"Feels weird knowing he's out there in the other room, doesn't it?" Abby whispered.

Newton regarded her alertly, his proud, intelligent head silhouetted against the city lights.

She pulled the down quilt up to her chin and contemplated the shadows on the ceiling. She should have been more uneasy about the situation, she thought. She was not accustomed to having a man spend the night. Her dates were never invited to stay until morning. Even with Kane, she had not taken that step. Maybe that had been a sign that the relationship was doomed, she thought. A woman should long for that kind of domestic intimacy with the man she was thinking of marrying. But she had never felt the need to have Kane stay. And in the post-Kane era, she had been living something of a cloistered life. There had been no other relationship that had even come close to being serious.

Her new home was her refuge, her fortress, her private, personal space. It was the first place that had ever truly belonged to her. She had filled it with things that had meaning to her. She had decorated it with the colors and fabrics and furnishings that she loved. And tonight a man she had known for less than a day was sleeping on her new sofa. She was still making payments on that sofa.

"I probably won't sleep well tonight," she said to Newton. "But what if I have that damn dream and go sleepwalking out into the front room? It would be so embarrassing."

Newton put his head down on his paws.

Abby looked out into the night and thought about the lucid-dreaming advice that Gwen had given her. *Set your psychic alarm clock to alert you when you start dreaming. Then take control of the dream.*

11

"Help me." Grady Hastings was barely visible in the swirling mist. He reached out a pleading hand. "Please help me."

Abby looked at him through the eerie light that illuminated the dreamscape and knew that she was dreaming. The strange fog that ebbed and flowed around Grady was different tonight. It burned with an inner radiance that she had not noticed in the previous dreams. She could move through it, get closer to Grady.

She was dreaming, but she was aware that she was dreaming. Her psychic alarm clock had gone off right on time. She could take control.

"Tell me what you want from me," she said, speaking in the silent language of dreams.

The mist thickened around Grady. It was getting harder and harder to see him, but she sensed his desperation and despair.

"Help me," he said. "You're the only one who can."

She tried to grasp his hand. . . .

And came fully awake in a rush of energy, her senses sparking and flashing like dark fireworks in the night. The primordial instincts of childhood kicked in. She tried to hold herself utterly still, not daring to move, but she could not stop the shivering that racked her body.

Heart pounding, she opened her eyes, searching the shadows. No one leaped out of the closet. No monster crouched at the foot of her bed. Newton was not there, either. That was not right, because she could feel his warm weight pressed against her leg.

In the next heartbeat she realized that she was on her feet beside the bed. At least her psychic alarm had awakened her before she had actually started to walk out of the bedroom.

There was something very wrong with the shadows in the room. They seethed and shifted. It took her a few seconds to figure out that the pulsing, roiling ultralight was coming from the small, hot storm brewing on her dresser.

"Oh, crap," she whispered to Newton.

"It's the herbal. I accidentally ignited it in my sleep."

Newton growled softly.

She rushed to the dresser. Hot currents from the herbal were seeping out of the wooden box. She realized that she had inadvertently tapped some of the encryption energy in the old book when she tried to take control of the dream.

She looked at the box with a sense of dread. Currents of hot psi from the darkest end of the spectrum twisted and wreathed around it. Any minute now she would start to smell charring wood. And then the smoke alarms would go off. If the condo building's fire-detection systems were activated, the fire department would be called automatically. Even if no real damage was done, her neighbors and the condo board of directors would want to know what happened.

Disaster loomed.

She opened the box very carefully. Energy flared higher. Gingerly, she put her hand on the leather cover of the herbal. Shocks of paranormal electricity crackled through her. She ignored them and channeled her talent, dampening the currents. She could only hope that Sam was a really sound sleeper.

The last of the hot energy had almost winked out when the bedroom door opened abruptly. She looked over her shoulder and saw Sam's shadowy frame silhouetted against the city lights that illuminated the living room. Icy energy chilled the atmosphere. The room was suddenly very cold.

"What's going on?" Sam asked. His eyes burned. The strange crystal in his ring glowed with an inner fire.

Newton spared him a brief glance, ears sharpened, and then returned his full attention to Abby and the hot book.

Abby winced and stifled a groan. So much for the faint hope that Sam would sleep through the disturbance.

"Nothing is wrong," she said. Her voice sounded half an octave too high, even to her own ears. The book was almost dark now. She got the lid back on the box and turned to face Sam. "I had a bad dream and got up to walk off the energy. You know how it is with nightmares."

"Yes," he said. His tone was as cold as the energy that enveloped him. "I know how it is with nightmares. I also know that you're lying through your teeth. Why are you trying to hide the herbal?"

"Excuse me," she said. Her voice was firmer now. It would have been easier to pull off stern and deeply offended if she had not been standing there in a plain, unadorned cotton sleep shirt that fell to her knees. "In case it has escaped your notice, you are in my bedroom and I did not invite you in here."

He ignored her and glided toward the dresser. When he moved into the light slanting through the windows, she saw that he was barefoot but still partially dressed in his trousers and a black T-shirt that molded to his sleek, strong shoulders. She felt very vulnerable, not to mention seriously underdressed. She was aware of another sensation as well, an excitement that was decidedly sensual in origin. *Just the fallout from all the energy that you were using a minute ago,* she assured herself.

A heavy dose of adrenaline and psi often had a stirring effect on all the senses, although she could not recall feeling sexually aroused when she had gone into the zone on previous occasions. Usually, she just felt jittery and agitated afterward.

It was Sam's fault, she decided. All that powerful masculine energy emanating from him was messing with the natural wavelengths of her own aura. It was annoying. It was also unaccountably exciting.

Sam came to a halt and looked at the open box. She was intensely aware of him and the heat coming off him. He was so close now. It took an enormous amount of willpower not to touch him.

"You did something to the book, didn't you?" Sam said. "I can sense some of the residue of the energy. You're still jacked, too. What the hell were you doing?"

She abandoned the attempt to kick him out of the bedroom. The man was very focused.

"The book was a little hot, yes," she admitted. She cleared her throat. "But it has gone cold now, as you can tell."

Sam glanced at her, his eyes still burning a little with psi. His ring continued to heat with a fiery light.

"What triggered the energy in the book?" he asked.

"You know how it is with old objects that are infused with a lot of encryption energy," she said smoothly. "It doesn't take much to kick up a little heat."

"This thing didn't switch on all by itself. You got it hot, didn't you?"

"That's not exactly what happened."

"What the hell were you doing? Running an experiment? Trying to break the code? You should know better than that. You're the expert on para-books. Tests on objects known to be infused with unknown energy should be done under carefully controlled conditions, and never at night."

He was right, she thought ruefully. As a rule, paranormal energy was usually more powerful after dark. It could also be a lot more unpredictable at night, something to do with the absence of normal daylight energy waves. But the fact that Sam was quoting one of the laws of para-physics to her while she was engaged in putting out a fire was infuriating. She was so not in the mood for this.

"You are correct, I'm the expert here," she said, in her coldest voice. "You have absolutely no right to lecture me on the care and handling of old books."

"So you figured you were qualified to conduct a night experiment on a highly encrypted book?"

"I was not running an experiment." She angled her chin. "For your information, I did not deliberately trigger the energy in that thing. I was sound asleep. I woke up and saw that it was giving off some psi-light, so I got up and shut it down."

"If you expect me to believe that book ignited all on its own, you can forget it. Tell me what the hell is going on here."

"It's complicated . . ."

Sam clamped his hand across her mouth. Furious, she glared at him. But he was not looking at her. He was watching the bedroom doorway.

The room was suddenly much, much colder. *Sam's energy,* Abby thought. He was running very hot, but the bedroom was deathly cold. Something sparked at the corner of her eye. Sam's ring.

She realized Newton had gone very still, very alert. He, too, was gazing fixedly at the doorway, looking down the short hall and into the living room.

Sam put his mouth very close to her ear. "Keep Newton quiet."

She nodded once to show that she understood.

He took his hand off her mouth and gripped her shoulder. He squeezed gently, silently warning her to stay put. She nodded again to show she had got the message. When he took his hand off her shoulder, she was once again aware of the icy chill in the atmosphere.

She crouched beside Newton, wrapped one arm around him and put her hand over his muzzle. Newton shivered, not with fear, she thought. The energy crackling through him was the tension of the hunter.

Sam crossed the room and disappeared through the shadowed doorway.

12

It was the faint clink of metal out on the concrete balcony that had alerted him. Even a very small amount of impact noise traveled in steel-and-concrete buildings.

Sam waited in the kitchen, watching the balcony from the shadows of the refrigerator. He gripped his most recent invention in his hand. It resembled a cell phone, but the crystal-powered device had a very different purpose. He was pretty sure that the theory behind the design was solid, but he had not yet had a chance to conduct any real-world experiments. Tonight promised to provide the opportunity for a field trial.

His intuition had been riding him hard all day. It had spiked into the hot zone after dark. He had the sense that things were moving fast, and that Abby was in danger. He had not even tried to sleep tonight. He had spent the night mentally and psychically standing guard.

Out on the balcony, a dark shadow appeared. It dropped easily down from the floor above. For a second or two, the newcomer dangled on the rope he had used for the descent. Then he stepped nimbly onto the railing and down to the floor of the balcony. It was clear he had done this kind of thing before. An expert.

He left the rope dangling and moved swiftly to the sliding glass doors. A small tool of some kind appeared in his gloved hand. A moment later, the sliding glass door slid silently open.

Chilled night air and faint currents of psi whispered into the room when the intruder entered. A talent of some kind, Sam concluded, and definitely a professional. It was a good bet that he had gained access to the building via the parking garage, always the weak point in the security system of any condo tower. Once inside, he would have had access to every floor and the roof.

The intruder moved across the room, going directly to Abby's desk with the certainty of a man who knew his way around the condo. That raised some intriguing questions, Sam thought.

The guy had a second-story man's sense of style. He had definitely nailed the cat-burglar look. He was dressed from head to toe in tight black clothing. A black stocking cap concealed his hair and all of his features except his eyes.

At the desk, he stopped, flicked on a small penlight and began to sort through the mail.

Sam walked out of the kitchen and around the end of the dining counter.

"No need for that," he said. "Abby went through her mail earlier this evening."

"What the . . . ?" The intruder swung around, spearing the shadows with the penlight. "Who are you?"

"A friend of Abby's."

"No, you're not. Abby doesn't have any boyfriends. Who are you, and what are you doing in her place?"

"I was just going to ask you the same question."

"Like hell."

The intruder sprinted for the open slider. Sam was already moving. He managed to seize the man's shoulder and succeeded in touching the crystal device to his arm. He sent energy into the fake cell phone. There was a small flash of paranormal lightning. The intruder grunted and started to crumple. He struggled to straighten and resume his flight to the balcony, but he fell slowly to his knees, arms wrapped around his midsection.

Sam yanked off the stocking cap, revealing platinum-blond hair cut in a short, crisp, vaguely military style.

"What the h-hell d-did you do to me?" the intruder got out, teeth chattering.

There was a sharp, excited yip. Newton charged into the room. He went straight to the intruder and started licking his face.

"Hell of a guard dog, all right," Sam said.

Abby appeared. She had taken the time to pull on a robe. She had a large object clutched in her hands.

"Sam." Her voice was tight and anxious. "Are you all right?"

"Yes," he said. "Get the lights."

She flipped a wall switch, illuminating the heavy lamp she carried. Her eyes widened, first in shock and then in outrage, when she saw the man shivering in the middle of her living room.

"Nick?" She put the lamp down on the coffee table. "What in the world are you doing here?"

Nick gave her a disgusted look and continued to shudder. "Your taste in boyfriends is going downhill, Abby. This one just tried to kill me."

Abby glanced at Sam, frowning. "Whatever you're doing to him, you can stop, at least until I decide whether or not to call the cops."

"He'll be all right in a few minutes," Sam said. "Probably." He pocketed the crystal device. "I just temporarily shocked his senses. You know this guy?"

"Nick Sawyer," she said. She regarded Nick with seething irritation. "And yes, I know him. You could say we're colleagues of a sort. We both work the book market, but Nick isn't quite as selective as I am when it comes to clients. I was, however, under the impression, until tonight, that he was my friend."

Nick muttered something unintelligible. Newton bounced around him, waiting for the new game to begin.

"Give him a minute," Sam said.

Nick managed to get to his feet. He was still shaky. He was about the same age as Abby, a lean, athletically built man with the sort of clean, chiseled features that could have ensured him a successful career in modeling. His silver-white hair and artificially tanned face served to enhance the vivid blue of his eyes.

He shot a hooded look at Sam, did a quick assessment of the situation and evidently concluded that his best option lay in an appeal to Abby.

"Sorry about this, sweetie," he said. "I

thought you were out of town."

"That's supposed to excuse what you just did?" Abby waved a hand toward the open slider. "You just broke into my home. You'd better start talking, and fast, or I'm going to call the police, I swear it."

Nick exhaled heavily and leaned over to scratch Newton behind the ears. "Take it easy, sweetie. I can explain everything. You know you're not going to call the cops."

"Before you say another word," Abby warned, "if you call me sweetie one more time, I will use that lamp on your head."

"It's a little complicated, sweet — uh, Abby."

"I think we can uncomplicate this thing real fast," Sam said. "Tell us why you broke in here tonight."

Nick scowled. "Who is this guy, Abby? I can't believe he's a new boyfriend. Definitely not your type."

"Talk," Sam said. "Fast."

Nick shot him an irritated look. "I didn't break in, I let myself in."

"That wasn't a key you used to open the slider," Sam said.

"Abby and I are old friends." Nick turned back to Abby and flashed a smile that was as brilliant as his hair. "Isn't that right?"

"We both know that I never gave you a

key to my home," Abby said. "Gwen has a spare, but you don't. Why are you here?"

"Believe it or not, just looking out for you. There's a real hot book floating around. Some kind of lab notebook dealing with crystal experiments. It's supposed to be about forty years old, and rumor has it that it's encrypted. If that's the case, there's a good chance that some of the people who are after it will be trying to hire you."

"Don't give me that blather about looking out for me," Abby snapped. "You're trying to locate that book yourself, aren't you? You came here hoping that you would find a lead."

"So you are working that job." Nick jerked a thumb at Sam. "He's a new client, isn't he? What's going on here? You never let clients into your home."

"You know, I really don't have to answer your questions," Abby said. "You are supposed to be explaining why you are here in my living room."

Nick shrugged. "Like I said, just looking out for your best interests."

"I got that much," Abby said, bristling with impatience. "Tell me the rest of it."

"Okay, okay, calm down. I don't know a whole lot more than what I just told you. I don't have a client yet, but the word on the street is that the book is worth a fortune to more than one person. Figured if I got to it first I could hold an auction. This could be the big one for me."

"Where did you hear the rumors of the book?" Sam asked.

"Like I'm going to tell you that," Nick muttered.

Sam took the aura-suppression device out of his pocket.

Nick looked bored. "The rumors cropped up in the usual places online. Tell him, Abby."

Abby folded her arms. "There are chat rooms where collectors and dealers exchange gossip and leads. I haven't had a chance to check out the usual suspects lately, because I've been preoccupied with my own problems. Guess I'd better visit some of the online sites."

"What have you heard about the collectors who are after the encrypted book?" Sam asked.

"Damn it, who is this guy, Abby?" Nick demanded.

"The name is Sam Coppersmith," Sam said.

He was still trying to get past the comment about not looking like Abby's type. It occurred to him that no one would think it odd if a cat burglar fell from a tenth-floor balcony while engaged in an act of breaking and entering. Stuff happened. Abby, however, would probably not approve of that disposal plan. She clearly had a history with Nick Sawyer. So did Newton.

"Coppersmith." Nick frowned. "Name rings a faint bell. How did you find Abby?"

"She found me," Sam said.

"You're a talent of some kind." Nick gave him an accusing look and then turned back to Abby. "You never trust strangers."

"Sam was referred to me by Thaddeus," Abby said. "Or maybe it would be more correct to say that I was referred to Sam. Either way, Thaddeus vouched for him."

"Okay, so Webber approved him. That still doesn't explain what he's doing here in your apartment at two o'clock in the morning. You never let your dates stay over."

Abby flushed. "I thought I made it clear, Sam is not a date. My arrangement with him is strictly business."

"You never let clients do sleepovers, either. What the hell is going on here, Abby? Why did Webber send you to him?"

"If you must know, Thaddeus thinks I may be in some danger because of that book you're looking for," Abby said.

"Damn it, I *knew* this had something to

do with that lab book. You should have come to me."

"I've been a little busy," Abby said. "Someone is blackmailing me."

"Shit," Nick growled. "Who?"

"That's where I come in," Sam said. "I'm going to find the bastard."

Nick frowned. "But you're after that old lab book, aren't you?"

"That, too," Sam said. "But the two projects go together."

Nick looked at Abby. "Sounds like you've fallen into the deep end."

"Yes," Abby says. "It appears that is the case."

"There are some real sharks out there. Are you sure you trust this guy to take care of you?"

"Yes," Abby said.

Sam told himself that he should take heart from that simple response.

"What is the bastard using as the extortion threat?" Nick said. "You've always been squeaky-clean. You don't even get parking tickets."

"He knows about my time at the Summerlight Academy and why I was sent there, and he knows who my father is. You know what would happen if my past suddenly became an issue in the media. It could ruin

Dad's chance at the reality series."

"Screw it," Nick said. "Let your father take care of himself. You don't owe him or anyone else in that family a damn thing. They don't deserve your loyalty. Hell, even if they knew that you were trying to protect them, they wouldn't appreciate your efforts."

"It's not just about protecting them," Abby said. "We're not entirely certain yet, but it looks like the blackmailer may know exactly how I took down Grady Hastings in Mrs. Vaughn's library. If he knows what I can do with encryption energy and decides to fire up rumors about me in the chat rooms, he could destroy my business."

"Okay, that would not be good," Nick said. "But according to the rumors, this lab book is attracting some dangerous collectors. I don't want to see you get hurt."

"She won't," Sam said. "That's why I'm here."

"I'll be okay, Nick," Abby said. "I think you'd better leave. It's late."

"All right, I'm going." Nick gave Sam one last glare and then turned back to Abby. "But promise me you'll call me if you need backup."

"I will," she said. "By the way, please use the stairs on your way out. I don't want any of my neighbors to wake up and see you climbing past their balconies from this floor. I've got my reputation to consider."

"Yeah, right." Nick coughed. "I, uh, left some of my stuff out on the balcony."

"Get it," Sam said. "And then go."

Nick pretended not to hear the order, but he went out onto the balcony and collected the rock-climbing equipment. When he came back inside, Sam followed him down the short hall and into the small foyer. Newton accompanied them.

Nick opened the door. The outer hall was empty. He gave Newton one last pat and then straightened to give Sam a hard, cold look. He lowered his voice.

"If anything happens to Abby, I'll be holding you responsible," he said.

"Understood," Sam said. "Believe me, if I thought she would be safer far away from this situation, I would have arranged that. But running wouldn't do her any good. Problems like this tend to follow a person. And even if you escape for a while, they're lying in wait when you return."

Nick thought about that for a few seconds. Then he nodded. "You're right. Guess that makes you her bodyguard."

"That's pretty much what it comes down to," Sam said.

"That gadget you used on me is sort of impressive. Can I assume that you've had some practical experience in the bodyguard business?"

"I've done some occasional consulting work for a private firm that gets most of its business from a government agency."

Nick widened his eyes. "You've got experience as a *consultant?* Gosh, darn, that sure makes me feel a whole lot better. Which government agency are we talking about? The post office?"

"Close enough. Time to leave, Sawyer."

Nick looked down at Newton. "At least you've got Newton to help you."

"Right."

Nick narrowed his eyes. "Don't underestimate the dog. Or Abby."

"I won't."

Nick went out into the elevator lobby and vanished into the emergency stairwell.

Sam closed the door, threw the dead bolt and looked down at Newton. "Just you and me, pal."

Newton looked hopefully at the leash hanging on the coat tree.

"Forget it," Sam said. "It's two o'clock in the morning."

He went back into the living room. Abby was in the process of closing the sliding glass door. The chilly breeze stirred the wild curls of her hair and caused the hem of her robe to flutter around her ankles. She had very nice ankles, Sam thought. Dainty, feminine, sexy.

Abby got the door locked and turned around to face him.

"So do you date a lot of cat burglars?" he asked, before he could stop himself.

Abby made a face. "That is not amusing. But just to be clear, Nick and I never dated."

"Why not? Seems like you two have a lot in common, what with being in the same business and all."

Why was he pushing her like this? he wondered. They had more important things to talk about, such as the lab book. But he knew the answer. He had been feeling increasingly territorial all afternoon and evening. Watching Sawyer come through the balcony door and then act as if he had every right to do so because of his personal relationship with Abby had triggered some very primal responses.

"Nick is a friend," Abby said quietly. "He and Gwen and I go back a long way together. The three of us are like family. For the record, Nick is gay."

"Huh." Okay, now he felt like a certified ass. That's what the old primal-response thing did to a man, he thought. It made him stupid.

Abby watched him with her mysterious eyes. Energy continued to swirl gently in the atmosphere around her. He realized that he was still running a little hot. An edgy hunger stirred things deep inside him.

"That gadget that you used to stun Nick," she said after a while. "Is that your own invention?"

"Works on crystal energy. But it can only be triggered by psychic currents."

"In other words, only someone with talent can use it?"

"Yes. I think of it as a bug zapper." He rubbed the back of his neck, trying to suppress the restlessness. "This isn't a good time to talk about technology. We both need sleep."

Newton appeared from the hallway. He looked plaintively at Abby.

"He wants to go out," Abby said.

"He went out earlier. I can't believe you're in the habit of taking him out at two in the morning every night."

"Of course not," Abby said. "But we don't usually have so much excitement going on in the living room at this hour. Now he's wide awake, and so am I. We could both use a stroll to work off some of the adrenaline. I'll take him up to the garden."

"In your nightgown and robe?" It dawned on Sam that he sounded like a scandalized husband.

Abby was amused. "Calm down. I'll put on a coat and a pair of shoes. No one will know that I'm in my nightgown."

Sam thought about saying something along the lines of "It's the principle of the thing" but decided that it would only make him look like a Neanderthal.

Abby went down the hall and opened a closet door. Newton trotted enthusiastically in her wake.

"Hang on," Sam said, resigned. "You're not going up there alone."

They took the elevator to the rooftop terrace, went through a set of glass doors and out into the crisp summer night. Low-level lamps marked the winding path through the elaborately planted rooftop garden. Abby and Newton went ahead, to the gate of the section that had been set aside for dogs.

Sam pulled up the collar of his jacket. At least it wasn't raining, he thought. Abby was bundled up in a long trench coat. She had on a pair of shoes that his sister, Emma, would have called slides, but they looked a lot like slippers to him.

He watched her stoop down to unclip

Newton's leash. As soon as he was free, Newton hurried through the gate and began to investigate a row of bushes, selecting just the right spot. *Choices, choices,* Sam thought. It seemed like there were always choices to be made in life. And once a man had made his decision, he was committed.

He moved to stand beside Abby, savoring her scent and her unique vibes. She did not try to put any distance between them.

"Sorry I zapped your friend tonight," he said.

"Nick had it coming. He had no business sneaking into my home tonight to go through my mail. As long as there was no permanent harm done."

"He'll be fine. At least I think he will."

"I beg your pardon?"

"Relax. According to my design calculations, there won't be any permanent damage."

She looked up at him, her eyes pools of mystery in the darkness. "Have you ever used that gadget on anyone else?"

"No. Haven't had the opportunity. But I've had some experience with a prototype."

"Great. Wonderful. I'm so relieved to hear that."

He exhaled slowly. "Nick asked me if I was qualified to act as a bodyguard."

"You're not my bodyguard," she said quickly. "You're my hired investigator."

"Comes down to the same thing. And you have a right to know my qualifications."

"As a bodyguard or as an investigator?"

"Both. I told Nick that I've done some consulting for a private contractor that does some work for a government agency."

She smiled. "The post office?"

"You know, you and your friend have a warped sense of humor."

"Nick already made that joke?"

"Yeah."

"Sorry. Couldn't resist. Go on."

"I'm trying to explain that I do have some experience in this kind of work. Thought it would make you feel better."

"You don't need to tell me your credentials," she said. "Although I admit I'm curious. But the bottom line is that I know you can handle my situation. I wouldn't have let you spend the night under my roof if I thought otherwise."

"What makes you so sure I'm qualified for the job?"

"My intuition, of course. Hey, I'm psychic, remember? You give off all the right vibes."

He turned to face her. "What kind of vibes would those be?"

"I knew the moment I met you that you're

the kind of man who does what he says he's going to do. No excuses. In some ways, you're as hard as any of those rocks in your collection, but you can be counted on to complete the job or go down trying, and it would take a lot to bring you down. You've committed yourself to protecting me while we hunt for the blackmailer and the lab book. You would not have made that commitment unless you thought you could carry it out. I realize you have your own agenda, but that doesn't mean you won't honor your commitments."

"You've known me for less than twenty-four hours. How can you be so damn sure of me?"

"I don't know," she admitted. "Just something about your energy. But I'm not basing my conclusions entirely on my own intuition. Thaddeus Webber thinks you're the right man for the job. But more to the point, Gwen and Newton approve of you. And Nick, for all his faults, is a pretty good judge of character, too. He has to be, because he deals with some very shady clients. He wouldn't have left without a struggle tonight if he thought you couldn't be trusted to do your job."

"In other words, you trust me because your friends and your dog signed off on me."

"They're my family, Sam. I've got another, picture-perfect family, but it's not the same thing. Gwen, Nick and Newton are my real family. Do you understand?"

"Yes." He reached out and framed her face between his hands. "But there's something you need to understand. The lab book is important, but you are my number-one priority in this thing. I give you my word on that."

Her eyes burned with a little heat. "That's good to know."

"Is there any other man who might climb through your window tonight?" he asked. "Some other guy who might feel he has a claim on you?"

"No," she said. She rose slowly on her toes, as if she was making her decision on the way up. The energy around her got a little hotter. "No one else. Not tonight. Anyone I should know about who might feel she has a claim on you?"

"No," he said.

"That's all right, then."

She put her arms around his neck and kissed him lightly, carefully, as if she was conducting a delicate experiment, the outcome of which was designed to satisfy her curiosity but not to oblige her to make a commitment.

Fire roared through him. He lifted his head.

"Don't know about you," he rasped, "but as far as I'm concerned, we are not running a field test or a lab experiment here."

Her eyes widened. "What do you mean?"

"I'll show you."

He crushed her close and kissed her hard and deep, making it clear that he wasn't running a test. This was the real deal, and he wanted to make sure she knew it.

She was clearly startled, and for a terrible moment he thought she would retreat. But she gave an urgent little gasp and tightened her arms around his neck. Her mouth softened invitingly under his.

Heat lightning snapped and flashed in the atmosphere. He was suddenly more aroused than he had ever been in his life. It was as if the energy of his aura was resonating with hers in a way that made every sensation more intense, more volatile, more vital.

He was trying to decide how to get her out of the coat and down onto one of the loungers when she planted both hands against his chest and pushed herself a little distance away. She was breathless.

"Newton," she managed.

He looked down. Newton was sitting at their feet, his head tipped to one side with an expectant air. He had the leash between his teeth.

"Your dog has lousy timing," Sam said. "But he's got a point. It's too cold out here for this kind of thing."

Abby giggled. Her laughter sparkled in the night. Sam grabbed her hand and made for the glass doors. Newton, leash still in his teeth, dashed after them, excited and enthusiastic.

"He thinks we're playing a game," Abby said. She punched the elevator button.

The elevator door opened. Sam pulled her inside. Newton trotted in with them.

Sam hit the button for the tenth floor and pinned Abby to the wall.

"No games," he vowed.

She struggled a bit. He held her still and kissed her fiercely.

When the elevator doors opened, he was forced to release her. She clamped a hand over her mouth and looked at him with laughter-filled eyes.

"What's so funny?" he asked.

In response, she pointed up at the ceiling of the elevator. He saw the security camera and realized why she had resisted a moment ago. He laughed and yanked her back into his arms, making sure that he was kissing her as the elevator doors closed, making sure that the last image recorded on the security camera was that of Abby in his arms.

Staking his claim.

13

She was hot and cold and shivering so hard she could not even get the key into the lock. What was wrong with her? It was as if she was in the grip of a raging fever, but she did not feel ill. Just the opposite. She was wildly exhilarated. She was flying.

The key fell to the floor.

"This is embarrassing," she said.

Sam scooped up the key, opened the door and propelled her inside. She was vaguely aware of Newton's nails clicking on the floor behind them. He disappeared down the hall to the living room. Sam got the door closed, peeled off his leather jacket and immediately went to work unfastening Abby's coat.

Part of her was shocked by the force of her response. It was as if the physical contact had awakened something deep inside her that had been dormant all these years, as if she had been *waiting* for this encounter.

Sam wrenched off her coat, hurled it in the general direction of the coatrack and closed his hands deliberately, powerfully, around her shoulders. Yet for all the strength that she sensed in him, both physical and paranormal, there was an exquisite tenderness in his touch that was incredibly seductive. *As if he was handling fine, delicate crystal,* she thought.

She slipped her hands up under his black T-shirt and flattened her palms on his chest. The feel of sleek, hard muscles beneath his warm skin excited her senses. She could see the heat in his eyes. He tangled his fingers in her hair and kissed her throat. For the first time in her life, she understood what it meant to be thrilled.

"Yes, yes, *yes,*" she whispered.

He pulled back just long enough to tug off his T-shirt. With her fingertips, she traced the outline of an elegant bird with wings of fire that covered his left shoulder.

"It's a phoenix, isn't it?" she said.

"Yes."

"You know, I would never have pegged you as the type to get a tattoo."

"I was nineteen," he said.

He cradled her jaw in one hand and used his thumb to tease open her mouth, tasting her, drawing her deeper into the embrace.

The world spun around her. It took her a few heartbeats to realize that Sam had picked her up in his arms. He angled her carefully and carried her down the hall, through the dimly lit living room and into the darkened bedroom.

He tumbled her down onto the bed and sprawled heavily on top of her, anchoring her with his weight. His mouth moved over her as if he craved her.

She could feel the damp warmth gathering between her legs. He had done little more than kiss her, but her body was already preparing for him. The sheer urgency of her need should have made her hesitate, pull back. And somewhere a faint alarm was sounding, warning her that what she was doing held all manner of unknown risks.

But she was in no mood to pay attention to the weak protests that emanated from the part of her mind that was still trying to think rationally.

Sam dragged his mouth across hers one last time and then wrenched himself free. He rolled off her and sat up on the edge of the bed.

"Give me a second here," he said. His voice was low and husky, and his breathing was rough. He stripped off his pants and fumbled briefly in a pocket. "Damn. My hand is shaking so hard it will be a wonder if I can get this thing on."

She exulted in the knowledge that she was the reason he was having problems with the logistics of the situation. A sense of her own feminine power arced through her. Tonight she was a goddess.

Sam managed to sheath himself in the condom. He came back down on top of her, crushing her into the bed. In the darkness, his eyes were ablaze with a desire that crossed the spectrum from normal to paranormal. On his right hand, his ring glowed with a muted coppery radiance.

Her own senses were spiking wildly now. She was unbelievably sensitive to the slightest touch. She flinched when he pushed her nightgown up to her waist and pulled it off over her head. And then his mouth was on her breast, and she would have screamed with the intense pleasure of it all if she had been able to catch her breath.

"You are on fire," he said. The words were filled with wonder and awe.

"So are you." She stroked the contoured muscles of his back. His skin was streaked with sweat. "You're burning up."

"Never felt better in my life."

A sliver of uncertainty pricked the lush fog of sensation at last. She clutched his taut upper arms.

"I'm not sure this is normal," she said.

"So what? Neither of us is exactly normal."

He was right, she thought. She pushed the concern to the back of her mind and abandoned herself to the exhilarating resonance of the energy in the bedroom.

He cupped her hot core and stroked her. Fire and ice sleeted through her. She twisted beneath his touch, straining into the embrace, trying to pull him into her.

He kissed the curve of her shoulder. "I can't wait any longer. I need you now."

"Yes," she said. "Now."

He moved, making a place for himself between her thighs. She gasped when she felt him pushing slowly, heavily, into her. Once again she thought she heard a whisper of warning. *This isn't normal.* Something more was happening here, something she did not fully comprehend. Whatever it was, the meaning was still encrypted.

But he was inside her now, filling her completely, and it seemed to her that their auras were resonating together in some unimaginable way. Then she could not think about anything else except the overpowering need that was building inside her.

Sam began to move. She raised her knees

to let him sink deeper. Until tonight, she would not have believed that she was capable of experiencing such intense sensations.

In the next heartbeat, her release cascaded through her in waves of energy that defied easy descriptions of both pleasure and pain. *Not normal,* she thought again. *But incredible.*

She cried out and sank her nails into Sam's back. He went rigid, and then his climax broke free, surging through him in heavy waves. His fierce growl of triumph and satisfaction echoed in the shadows.

In that senses-shattering moment, she could have sworn that the flaring ultralight currents of their overheated auras had established a harmonic link, a breathtakingly intimate resonance.

She had just time enough to think, *Such a thing isn't possible.*

And then they were collapsing together into the damp sheets, and she could not think coherently at all.

14

She awoke to the intoxicating fragrance of freshly brewed coffee.

Sam.

She opened her eyes to the early light of a Seattle summer morning and bolted upright on a tide of adrenaline. *Sam had spent the night in her bed.*

She knew he had not gone back to the sofa, because she had a distinct recollection of him returning from the bathroom after the heated lovemaking. Mentally, she corrected herself: *the heated sex.* No love involved on either side. They barely knew each other.

It came down to a one-night stand. She never did one-night stands. Too risky.

Newton was nowhere to be seen. A shiver of alarm shot through her. He was always there to greet her first thing in the morning.

As if on cue, she heard Newton in the hall. He trotted into the bedroom, put his front paws up on the bed and licked her hand.

"Well, good morning to you, too," she said.

She rubbed his ears. Newton gave her another perfunctory lick on the hand and bounced off, tail high. He disappeared back down the hall, as if he had more important things to do.

She forced herself to focus on the chain of events during the night. When Sam had returned to the bed, he had pulled her close and fallen into a profound sleep. She had expected to spend the short time left until dawn lying awake, worrying about the weird, unsettling sensations she had experienced and the possible ramifications of what had happened.

But the exhaustion that had come over her had been beyond any normal postcoital languor. *Probably because there had been as much paranormal as normal energy involved,* she thought. She had never before engaged in sex with all of her senses wide open. Until last night, she would not have believed such an encounter was even possible.

Her phone chimed, snapping her out of her reverie. She scooped it up off the nightstand and glanced at the screen. The familiar caller ID calmed her. Ralph, the day doorman.

"Good morning, Ralph," she said. She glanced at the clock again. "Early-morning package delivery?"

"There is a gentleman here to see you." Ralph spoke very quietly into the phone. "A Mr. Strickland."

"Dawson? Are you sure?"

"Says he's your brother, but you never mentioned a brother."

"Dawson is my stepbrother," she said. She spoke automatically while she tried to think. "What does he want?"

Sam came to stand in the doorway of the bedroom. Newton was at his heels. Sam had obviously showered and shaved. His dark hair was still damp. He wore a charcoal-gray pullover and a pair of black trousers. He had a cup of coffee in his hand and a little heat in his eyes. She was suddenly very conscious of her wild hair and the faded nightgown.

"Mr. Strickland says he wants to talk to you," Ralph said, his voice still barely above a whisper. "But if you'd rather not see him, I'll be happy to tell him that you're not at home. After all, you were scheduled to be out of town this week, anyway."

She smiled a little at Ralph's protective

tones. He knew she had spent the night with a man and that said male was still under her roof. The door staff knew everything that went on in the building. He was trying to shield her from any possible awkwardness that might result if her stepbrother walked in on the situation. *As if Dawson has ever shown any interest in my social life,* she thought. So long as she kept a low profile and did not embarrass the clan, Dawson and the rest of the perfect blended family pretty much ignored her.

"I appreciate that, Ralph, but it's okay," she said. "Tell Dawson that I'm just heading into the shower. I need about thirty minutes to get dressed. If he wants to wait that long, you can send him up then."

"Let me see if he'll wait," Ralph said.

There was some mumbled conversation on the other end of the connection. Ralph came back on the phone.

"Mr. Strickland says he'll go down the block to Starbucks and get a latte," Ralph said. "He'll be back in half an hour."

"Thanks, Ralph." She ended the connection and tossed the phone down onto the nightstand. She looked at Sam. "Dawson will be coming up here in thirty minutes."

Sam walked to the bed and set the coffee on the nightstand. "Who is Dawson? Or should I ask?"

"Technically speaking, he's my stepbrother. He's the son of my father's current wife by her first marriage."

"The man standing next to you in the back-cover photo of your father's new book."

"Right."

"I get the feeling you're not close."

"No kidding," she said. She grabbed her robe off the foot of the bed. "Which is, as Gwen has pointed out, a real shame, because Dawson is the heir to a fortune on his mother's side. His Strickland ancestors made a ton of money in the lumber industry and later did some very shrewd investing in commercial real estate here in Seattle."

"Dawson is connected to those Stricklands?"

"Yep, those Stricklands. His grandmother, Orinda Strickland, controls the family money now. Dawson and his mother, Diana, are the only heirs." She pulled on the robe and picked up the mug. "Thanks for the caffeine."

He gave her a slow, sexy, intimate smile that raised the hairs on the back of her neck in an exciting way.

"Any time," he said.

She flushed and looked toward the

dresser, searching for a distraction. The old herbal was gone. Suspicion slashed through her. She whirled around.

"Where's the book?" she asked.

"In my duffel bag. Figured it would be safer there."

"What, exactly, do you mean by 'safer'?"

"By 'safer,' I meant a little more secure than it was lying on top of your dresser." Sam's voice hardened. So did his eyes. "I'm not planning to steal the damn thing, if that's what you're thinking."

She reddened. "I didn't mean to imply that you would do that."

"Sure you did. It was the first thing that popped into your mind when you noticed that the book was missing."

"Sorry," she mumbled. "That was rude." She sipped some coffee.

"Do you always wake up this suspicious after a date?"

Shocked, she choked on the coffee and sputtered for a few embarrassing seconds. Eventually, she managed to compose herself.

"That wasn't a date," she managed weakly. "Not exactly." She fumbled to a halt.

"Let's see, there was tea and conversation, a kiss in a garden, and there was sex. Really great sex, I might add. I admit that the late-night prowler in your living room, the burning herbal and taking the dog out for a walk at two in the morning were a little unusual, but aside from that, I'd say we met most of the requirements for a date."

"Or a one-night stand," she said.

"Or that," he agreed, a little too readily.

She was feeling cornered, and she knew she sounded surly. She did not dare look in a mirror. Her face was probably scarlet. She drew herself up and squared her shoulders.

"Excuse me. I need to get into the shower and get dressed," she said.

She fled toward the bathroom.

"Coward," Sam said behind her. He sounded amused.

She closed the door very firmly.

15

Sam did a quick survey of the freezer, cupboards and refrigerator. The refrigerator was mostly empty, but he located half a loaf of bread and some eggs. He unearthed a package of frozen soy sausages in the freezer and scored a jar of peanut butter in a cupboard.

Newton sat alertly in the middle of the kitchen, watching each step of the breakfast preparation process with rapt attention. Sam tossed him half a slice of toast slathered with peanut butter. Newton snagged it neatly out of the air and wolfed it down.

Abby finally emerged from the bedroom. Sam punched the button on the microwave to nuke the pale gray sausages. He glanced at the clock.

"We've still got a few minutes before your brother arrives," he said.

"My stepbrother," she corrected. She walked into the kitchen and picked up the coffeepot. “And I’m glad we’ve got some time, because I think I need another cup of coffee before I deal with him. I can’t imagine why he wants to see me. Something bad must have happened. Maybe someone fell ill or is in the hospital. But I would have expected a phone call if that was the case.”

He watched her carry the mug around to the other side of the counter and perch on one of the stools. She was wearing a pair of snug-fitting brown trousers and an amber sweater that was about the same color as her hair. Her eyes were shadowed with anxiety.

The microwave pinged. He opened the door and took out the fake sausages.

“You’re sure you don’t have any idea of why your stepbrother is here today?” he asked.

“Nope.” She watched him place the sausages on the two plates that held the fried eggs and slices of toast smeared with peanut butter. “That looks good. I think I’m hungry.”

He set the plates on the counter and walked around the corner to sit down beside Abby. He eyed the soy sausages and reminded himself to keep an open mind. “I take it you’re a vegetarian?”

“Not entirely.” She took a bite out of a

slice of the toast. “I eat fish.”

He picked up a fork. “When was the last time you saw Dawson?”

“A couple of months ago. He’s got a house on Queen Anne. We ran into each other by chance in a restaurant here in Belltown. I was with Gwen and Nick. Dawson was having dinner with his fiancée. We said hello. Introductions were made, and that was about it.”

“You meant it when you said that you aren’t close, didn’t you?”

She shrugged. “We have nothing in common, certainly not a bloodline. I was twelve and he was thirteen when I went to live with my father and his new family. That happened because my mother died. Dad didn’t have much choice except to take me in. Dawson and I both developed immediate resentment issues. I didn’t like his mother, Diana, trying to parent me. Dawson didn’t like my father trying to parent him. Things got even more complicated when the twins were born later that year.”

“Okay, I think I’m seeing the dynamics here.”

“And then there was the inheritance issue. Dawson’s grandmother did not approve of her daughter marrying my father. She insisted on a prenuptial agreement and made it clear that when it came to the Strickland money, I was not considered family. Not that I gave a damn about the financial aspects of the situation. I was just a kid, but by then I already understood that money follows blood. I didn't have a problem with that fact of life. The little lecture that Orinda Dawson gave me when I turned thirteen was entirely unnecessary, however."

Sam winced. "She gave you the talk about inheritance issues when you were just a kid?"

"The financial stuff wasn't a big deal. Like I said, I already understood how that worked. But Dawson's grandmother is one scary lady. She certainly scared the daylights out of me, at any rate. But in hindsight, I think it's only fair to say that she was horrified by me. Actually, everyone was."

"Because of your talent?"

"I was just coming into it when I moved in. But within the year, it was obvious that I was going to be a little different. Orinda did not want anyone to think that the family bloodline was tainted by weirdness."

"She didn't understand what was going on with you?"

"No, and neither did the others. I made them all very nervous. I saw a series of counselors and shrinks, and made the fatal mistake of trying to convince each of them that I really did sense paranormal energy in some books. And then there were the incidents I mentioned."

"The fire-setting stuff?"

"You wouldn't believe how that kind of thing upsets folks. Eventually, the decision was made to send me to the Summerlight Academy. That's where I learned to pass for normal. Mostly."

The doorbell chimed. Newton growled softly and glared down the length of the front hall.

Abby sighed and set down her cup. "That will be Dawson."

She slipped off the stool and went down the hall. Newton followed, hovering near her in a protective manner. Maybe Abby was right, Sam thought, maybe the dog was a little bit psychic.

A moment later, he heard the front door open. Polite greetings were exchanged, not the relaxed, familiar sort that friends and colleagues employed, and not the more intimate kind typical of family members. The relationship between Abby and Dawson fell into another category altogether, he decided, one that was not easy to identify.

Abby reappeared. Newton was still at her heels.

"Sam, this is Dawson Strickland. Dawson, Sam Coppersmith."

Dawson looked exactly as he did on the back cover of *Families by Choice.* Medium height, brown-haired and endowed with what, in another era, would have been labeled patrician features. He had the toned-and-tanned look that spelled expensive athletic clubs and a lot of time on ski slopes, golf courses and private yachts. His shirt and trousers bore all the hallmarks of hand-tailoring. His watch had cost as much as a European sports car. He carried an Italian leather briefcase in one well-groomed hand.

But it was the anxious, edgy energy that shivered invisibly in the atmosphere that interested Sam. Dawson was nervous. It was clear he was not looking forward to the conversation ahead.

Sam came up off the stool and offered his hand. "Strickland."

"Coppersmith." Dawson shook hands briskly, frowning a little in polite concentration. "Name sounds familiar. Any relation to Coppersmith Inc.?"

"Some."

"A pleasure to meet you." Dawson bestowed a dazzling smile on Abby. "I didn't know you were seeing anyone."

"Of course you didn't." She gave him a polite smile. "Why would you? It's been a couple of months since we last met. How's the engagement going? Have you set a date for the wedding?"

"Next month." Dawson affected an air of surprise. "Didn't you get an invitation?"

"No."

"Must have been an oversight. Carla is handling that end of things. I'll make sure you get one."

"Don't worry about it," Abby said. "I think I'm going to be out of town on that date, anyway."

Dawson frowned. "How would you know that if you don't know the date?"

"Just a wild guess. Would you like some coffee?"

"Sure, thanks. Had a latte down the street, but I could use some more caffeine." Dawson set down the briefcase and took the stool that Abby had just vacated. "So how long have you two been seeing each other?"

"Not long," Abby said, before Sam could answer. She put the coffee in front of Dawson. "What is so important that you had to track me down at this hour of the morning?"

Dawson stopped smiling.

"Sorry about the timing," he said. "I came

in person because I don't like to have these kinds of business discussions over the phone."

"You're starting to scare me," Abby said.

But she looked irritated and maybe a little apprehensive, Sam thought, not frightened.

"Relax." Dawson flashed a closer's smile. "I want to hire you."

Abby stiffened. "What are you talking about? You don't collect books of any kind, let alone the type I handle."

"Let me explain," Dawson said. He grew serious again. "I'm in the middle of some very high-level negotiations with a potential investor. This guy is hugely important to me and to my firm. Needless to say, I've got some competition. Evidently, the man has a thing for old books."

"Oh, crap," Abby said very softly.

She looked at Sam. He knew what she was thinking, because he was thinking the same thing. *There are no coincidences.*

Oblivious, Dawson pressed on, very intent now. "It has been made clear to me that I can improve the odds of bringing this very heavy hitter on board if I can produce a certain book that is rumored to be coming up for sale in the paranormal books market. That's your market, Abby."

Icy fingers brushed the back of Sam's

neck. He was suddenly jacked, all senses on alert. He knew that Abby was running a little hot as well.

"What old book would that be?" she asked, without any inflection.

"Not what I'd call a real antiquarian book," Dawson said. "It's only about forty years old. Hang on, I'll get the details." He got off the stool and hoisted the briefcase onto the counter. Opening the case, he took out a sheet of paper. "Let's see. It's a laboratory-style notebook containing the handwritten record of experiments that were conducted on various specimens of ore and crystals taken out of a mine in the Southwest. Exact location of the mine is unknown. Whoever kept the notebook evidently believed that the crystals possessed paranormal powers." Dawson grimaced. "In other words, he was some kind of nut job."

Abby raised her eyes to the ceiling. "Why me?"

Dawson put the paper back into the briefcase. "Because you're the only expert on rare books dealing with the occult that I know."

Anger flashed across Abby's face. "I do not deal in the occult. I've explained that."

"Paranormal, the woo-woo thing, whatever," Dawson said quickly. "You're not just the only paranormal–rare-books expert I know, you're the only rare-books dealer I know. Naturally, I came to you."

"Sounds like the man you're negotiating with is aware that you have a connection in the paranormal-books market," Sam said.

"Sure," Dawson said. "Probably why I was invited to the negotiating table. In my world, you use whatever edge you've got."

"So you decided to use me?" Abby asked.

Dawson had the grace to redden. "Sorry. That didn't come out right. I'm not trying to take advantage of you, Abby. I'll pay you for your time. In fact, I'll give you a very hefty bonus if you can turn up that lab book before my competitors get hold of it."

"Any idea how many other people are looking for the book?" Sam asked.

"No," Dawson said. "But I have to assume that at least a couple of the other players who want the account have hired their own experts. What do you say, Abby? There's a lot of money at stake, and a big chunk of it can be yours if you find that book for me. I'm on a deadline, by the way. I need to get it as soon as possible."

Abby shook her head. "I'm sorry. I realize the account is important to you, but you don't know much about my world. Some books are dangerous. Some collectors are ruthless. Your investor may be one of the bad guys."

"The bad guys in my world are focused on the money. They operate Ponzi schemes. They don't set up elaborate scenarios just to acquire old lab books."

"The fact that your investor knows enough about you to figure out that you're connected to me is not a good sign," she said. "That means he knows he can't approach me directly, because he can't get a referral."

"He needs a referral to get you to broker a deal for an old book?" Dawson asked, incredulous.

"Yes," Abby said. "That's how I work."

"That's crazy."

Abby said nothing. She just looked at him. But there was suddenly energy in the atmosphere. Sam heard a low growl and looked over the counter. Newton was on his feet now, very still, very focused. His whole attention was fixed on Dawson.

Dawson flushed. "I didn't mean anything personal. Just an expression. Come on, Abby, it's just an old lab notebook. I know it's valuable to this particular collector, but we're not talking illicit drugs or the arms trade here. People don't kill each other over forty-year-old notebooks."

"Actually, they do from time to time,"

Abby said. "Which is why I try to stay out of that end of the market."

Dawson's face was a study in outraged disbelief. "You expect me to believe that this book is that valuable?"

"I don't know," she said. "But I do know that it is associated with the paranormal, and collectors in that market are often eccentric and unpredictable."

"Abby, this is supposed to be your specialty. You find weird books for weird people who believe in the paranormal, right?"

She smiled faintly. "Something like that. It's nice to know you have so much respect for my professional expertise."

Dawson grimaced. "Come on, I know you're holding a grudge because of the past. And let's face it, you did have some serious issues when you were in your teens. Remember the time you came home with that old book you picked up at a yard sale? That night you set fire to it in the bathtub."

Abby's shoulders were rigid. "That was sort of an accident. But no one believed me."

"Because you scared the hell out of everyone and set off the alarm," Dawson shot back. "We ended up with a house full of firefighters and a lot of water on the floor. Mom was furious. You embarrassed her in front of the neighbors. That was when Grandmother said you should be put into an institution."

"I'm well aware of your grandmother's opinion of me," Abby said.

"It's not like that was the only scary incident. You exhibited some very bizarre behavior when you were in your teens. Mom had every reason to worry about the twins."

"No, she didn't. I would never have hurt anyone."

"What about the time you disappeared for nearly two whole days? Mom and your father were frantic. The police wouldn't look for you, because they said you were probably just a runaway. Then we got that call from the cops saying you'd been found at the scene of a fire that had started in a bookstore. The dealer was injured and had to be taken to the hospital. The only reason you didn't end up in juvenile detention was because your father got you a good lawyer who got the charges dropped."

"Got news for you, Dawson," Abby said. "The Summerlight Academy was only about half a step up from jail. The doors and windows were locked. There were forced therapy sessions. There were counselors who wanted to test me and my friends, over and over again."

"What was the family supposed to do? They couldn't risk keeping you at home. The shrinks told us that you really believed you had paranormal powers."

Abby's smile was edgy and cold. "I do believe that. Which is why I'm in a position to warn you that the lab notebook is dangerous."

"It's just a damn book." Dawson's voice hardened. "I need to find it. I'm not fooling around here."

"I realize that the account is worth a lot to your firm, but there are other gazillionaires out there," Abby said. Her voice softened. "Let this one go. Find another."

"Damn it, this is business. I'm not asking for a favor. I told you, I'll make it worth your while."

"Thanks, but I can't take the job."

"This is about the past, isn't it?" Dawson's face reddened with anger and frustration. "About the fact that your father married my mother for her money and found out too late that my grandmother had it locked up in a trust."

"Believe it or not, this is not about the past."

"It is all about the past and the money. Don't you get that? Grandmother saw through your father right away, but Mom wouldn't listen."

Newton had stopped growling. More than ever, he resembled a scaled-down version of a junkyard dog. He looked remarkably dangerous. There was a little wolf in every dog, Sam thought. People who forgot that sometimes had nasty encounters with teeth.

"It's all right," Abby said to Newton. She stooped and touched him lightly with her hand. "It's okay."

Newton did not take his focus off Dawson.

"Whatever happened in the past isn't important here," Abby said. "Everyone has moved on, including me. We're the perfect blended family now, remember?"

"Bullshit."

Her mouth curved slightly. "True. But family is family."

"This isn't funny," Dawson said tightly. "You've had it in for me from the start because Grandmother made sure you and your father would never get a dime of her money."

"I don't suppose it will do any good to tell you that I never cared about the money," Abby said.

"If there's one thing I've learned, it's always about the money," Dawson said. Bitterness edged his mouth. "And right now you're letting the past get in the way of both of us making a hell of a lot of it. Want some brotherly advice? Grow up and get over it."

"I repeat, this isn't about the past." Abby locked her arms beneath her breasts. "It's about you getting involved in something you know nothing about."

"I realize I don't know anything about rare books," Dawson said, exasperated. "That's why I'm here. What I know is that I need this investor and you're the only one who can get him for me." He closed one hand into a fist. "Name your price, damn it."

"No," Abby said.

Dawson's jaw twitched. "You know, don't you?"

"Know what?" Abby said.

"You know that my firm is in trouble."

She frowned. "No, I wasn't aware of that."

"I took a real hit a couple of months ago when a major project, a sure thing, went south. It was a Ponzi scheme, and I fell for it. My clients don't know about the losses yet. I can juggle the numbers for a few months while I recover. But the only way I can dig myself out of this hole is with new capital. I have to close the deal with this investor. If I don't, I'll go under."

"Oh, damn," Abby whispered, shocked.

"Lawsuits will be the least of it. You think

some of your clients are dangerous? I've got a couple who will go to the Feds. I could wind up in prison."

"I'm sorry," Abby said. Her tone was surprisingly gentle. "But you can recover. You're good at investing."

"Abby, I'm standing on the brink of bankruptcy and maybe looking at jail time. I need to land this account."

"I'm sorry," Abby repeated. "I'm sorry, but I can't help you."

"Why not?"

Sam picked up his coffee. "For one thing, she's already got another client for that lab book."

Dawson swung around, jaw working. "You?"

"Me," Sam said.

Dawson pulled himself together immediately. "I'll buy the book from you. Just name your price."

"I don't have the book yet," Sam said. "If and when I do get it, I won't be selling it."

Dawson turned back to Abby. "This is your idea of revenge, isn't it?"

"No," she said. "I swear it's not."

"I hope you enjoy it." Dawson slammed the briefcase shut, picked it up and went down the hall.

The door closed behind him.

"Excuse me," Abby said.

She rushed out of the kitchen and disappeared into the bedroom. Newton hurried after her.

Sam got up and followed the pair, not sure what he should say or do. It was clear that Abby was accustomed to handling her problems all by herself or with the help of her close-knit circle of friends. But he happened to be the one who was here today.

He walked into the bedroom. Abby was sitting on the edge of the bed, clutching a tissue. She was not crying. She had one hand on Newton, who had his front paws propped on the bed beside her.

"Please go away," she said, a little too politely. "I'll be fine."

Sam went to the bed. He pulled her to her feet and into his arms.

"We're a team now," he said. "That means you're stuck with me."

She pressed her face into his shoulder and sobbed.

16

After a while she realized that the humiliating bout of visible weakness was finally over. She stopped crying. The temptation to stay where she was, wrapped warm and tight in Sam's arms, was almost overwhelming. It took everything she had to push herself away from him.

"This is so embarrassing," she said. She stepped back and managed a shaky, rueful smile. "Sorry about the drama. Sorry about your shirt, too."

He glanced down at the damp spot. "It'll dry."

"I'm okay now. Just lost it there for a while." She grabbed another tissue and blew her nose. "I haven't been sleeping well lately, and now there's the blackmail thing and that stupid lab notebook and Dawson facing bankruptcy and . . . and last night."

"I thought last night went well," he said neutrally. "It certainly did for me."

"I didn't mean that. Not exactly." Utterly mortified now, she tossed the tissue into the little wastebasket and rushed past him toward the bathroom. "Never mind. Give me a few minutes to wash my face."

"Sure," he said.

She fled into the bathroom, closed the door and turned on the cold water. She winced when she saw her tear-swollen face in the mirror. She was not one of those women who cried in an attractive way. But, then, it wasn't as if she'd had a lot of experience. She rarely cried these days, and when she did, she made certain that she was always alone.

It was the stress. She'd been under a lot of it lately. She had to get a grip.

She leaned over the sink and splashed the cold water on her face for a couple of minutes, then turned off the faucet and grabbed a towel. When her face was dry, she took another critical look at the wan features of the woman in the mirror. *Show no weakness.* She reached for a lipstick and a compact.

A short time later, feeling back in control, she went into the front room. Sam was standing at the window, looking out over the rain-dampened city. He turned around when he sensed her approach.

"You can't stay here," he said. "Not now."

She stopped in the middle of the room. "What?"

"There are too many people after that book, and a lot of them have decided you can get it for them. I'm going to take you to a different location, one that is more secure. You'll be safe there, while I look for the blackmailer."

"What on earth are you talking about? I can't just disappear."

He smiled. "Sure you can. You'll see."

"What are you proposing to do with me? Stash me in a hotel room under a different name?"

"No. I'm going to take you to the Copper Beach house. I've got good security there. In addition, strangers stand out like sore thumbs on the island. It's hard to get ashore without being noticed."

"Whoa, whoa, whoa." Horrified, she held up both hands, palms out, and waved him to silence. "Thanks but no thanks. I appreciate the thought, but that is not going to work."

"Why not?"

She lowered her hands. "You said it yourself a few minutes ago. We're a team. We're going to have to work this thing together. You don't stand much of a chance of finding that lab book, let alone breaking the code, without my help. And I need you to track down the blackmailer. Let's face it. Finding out that my stepbrother is under a lot of pressure to come up with that book really put the icing on the cake, didn't it? I'm in this thing up to my neck now, and there's nothing either of us can do about it except see it through."

He looked at her for a long time.

"Do you always get to the bottom line this fast?" he asked finally.

"Believe me, if there were viable options, I'd be running for the exit by now. You need me, Sam Coppersmith. And I need you."

He raised his brows. "Like I said, we're stuck together."

She smiled. "Well, we do have Newton."

Sam looked at Newton. "Good point."

Bored, Newton trotted into the kitchen and began to slurp water out of his bowl.

Abby walked across the room to stand directly in front of Sam. "But I can't think of anyone else I would rather be stuck with in this situation."

"You're sure about that?"

"Absolutely certain," she said.

"Okay," he said. He stroked her cheek with the back of the finger on which he wore the fire-red crystal. "I agree we're in this together. But I'm not changing my plans. We're going to Copper Beach."

"Why?"

"We need a secure base of operations. Copper Beach is built like a fortress. Most of your work is done online, right?"

"Well, yes."

"Looks like a lot of my work will be done that way, too."

"You're going to try to find Dawson's major investor, aren't you?"

"It's a solid lead. Worth pursuing."

"I can't just walk away from my life here in Seattle. Among other things, I need to put in an appearance at my father's book-launch event. That's on Friday night. He's giving a talk and signing *Families by Choice.* There will be media. Dad has made it clear that it's very important that the whole family show up."

"You're not going into exile. You're just going to Copper Beach. We can get back here for the book-signing event."

She looked around, searching for other excuses not to leave her new home.

"All of my stuff is here," she whispered. Okay, that sounded excessively juvenile. She squared her shoulders. "But you're right. No reason I can't leave for a while. Like going on vacation, right?"

He smiled. "That's one way to look at it."

"Newton will enjoy the country. He loves to visit Thaddeus because he can run around in the woods." She turned toward the bedroom. "I'll go pack."

She was in the process of folding her nightgown, the lacy new one that she had bought on impulse and had been saving for some special occasion that had never seemed to come, when she heard the chimes that told her she had new email.

She put the nightgown into the small suitcase and picked up her phone. She recognized the code instantly. For no good reason, a chill of apprehension iced her senses.

"Thaddeus," she said softly.

She opened the email and read the brief, cryptic note. She hurried out into the living room. "We need to see Thaddeus right away. He says he wants to talk to both of us in person. Something about an auction for the lab book."

Sam tossed his two soy sausages to Newton and dumped the dishes in the sink.

"Let's go," he said.

17

"Did he give you any details about the auction?" Sam asked.

He was at the wheel of his SUV, driving into the foothills of the Cascades along a narrow, winding road. The terrain was turning steeper and more heavily wooded. Abby was strapped into the passenger seat, her attention focused on the view through the windshield. Newton was in the backseat.

Abby had been unusually quiet since she had locked up her condo and stowed her suitcase and her dog in his vehicle. He had sensed how hard it was for her to accept that her home was no longer safe. He wanted to tell her that she could trust him to take care of her, but he knew that would not make up for the temporary loss of the one place that was hers, the small, cozy space where she was in complete control. He understood about control issues. Hell, he had them, too. Who didn't?

"No, but obviously rumors are circulating that the lab book will soon be up for auction," Abby said. "That's good news and bad news."

"What's the good news?"

"I know how to track that kind of chatter. I don't usually do business with the dealers who work the deep end, but thanks to Thaddeus and Nick, I know who they are and I know how to contact them. I'll try for a preemptive bid for the lab book. Failing that, I can guarantee that my client will top any other offer." She gave him a quick, searching look. "That's right, isn't it?"

"Yes. I want that lab book." He tightened his hands around the wheel. "Price is no object. What about the bad news?"

"Once the announcement of the auction is made, one or more of the high rollers who want the book will be able to drive the price sky-high."

"Not a problem."

"That's nice to know. What has me worried is that we are now officially in the deep end of the market. Like I told Dawson, some of the collectors are dangerous. If one of them decides he won't be able to buy the book, he may go after it some other way."

"He'll try to steal it?"

"To do that, he would have two likely options. The book is most vulnerable during a transaction. So he can try to identify the current owner or the dealer who is brokering the sale. That won't be easy. If that doesn't work, he'll get a second shot at acquiring the volume if he can ID the new owner."

"Me."

"Your problem is that you are not exactly a low-profile collector in my world. Dawson, for instance, now knows that you are trying to acquire the book. If he tells his investor . . ."

"I see where you're going with this. But once I have the book, I'll make sure it's secure. The word will go out that it is permanently off the market. Even if some people know that my family has it, there won't be many collectors who will take the risk of trying to steal it from Coppersmith Inc. We've got some serious security and an even more serious interest in making sure that notebook stays locked up. We'll take good care of it."

"Okay," she said. But she did not look satisfied.

"What's wrong?" he asked.

She hesitated. "I'm not sure. I've got a bad feeling about Thaddeus's last email."

"We'll be at his place soon."

"Take the next left."

"There's no road sign."

"Thaddeus likes it that way."

He slowed and turned left onto an even narrower strip of badly cracked pavement. The trees loomed close on either side. "Mind if I ask you a personal question?"

"Depends on the question."

"I'm pretty sure I know what happened when you accidentally started the fire in the bathtub. You tried to unlock a book, and the energy got out of control."

"I had no idea what I was doing, let alone that it might start a fire."

"Paranormal fire is unpredictable. Get it burning hot enough and it will affect the energy in neighboring bands on the spectrum, all the way to the normal." Sam whistled softly. "Must have been a lot of energy released when you broke that code."

"Uh-huh."

"What about the time you disappeared for a couple of days and nearly got arrested for trying to burn down a bookshop?"

"That was a little more complicated," Abby said slowly. "I thought the owner of the bookshop was just a nice old man who recognized my talent and wanted to help me learn how to handle it. I realized later that he wanted to use me to unlock an old volume that he had in his collection."

"Did you?"

"No. And to this day, I'm not sure why. When I picked up the book, I got the overwhelming sensation that whatever was inside was dangerous, or at least it would be in his hands. I just knew that I did not want him to be able to read that book."

"What was it about?"

"Hypnotic poisons. So I lied and told the bookshop owner that I couldn't break the code. He went a little crazy. He locked me inside his rare-book vault and told me that he wouldn't let me out until I agreed to break the encryption."

"The son of a bitch imprisoned you?"

"I was terrified. I held out for as long as I could. I had some fantasy that someone, my dad or the police, would realize what had happened and rescue me. But eventually it dawned on me that no one knew where I was and that I was on my own."

"You told the bastard that you would break the psi-code."

"Yes. When he opened the door I told him I had done what he wanted. I handed the book to him. When he touched it, I channeled some of the energy into his aura. I was acting entirely on intuition. I had no idea what would happen. He screamed and collapsed. The next thing I knew, the book was on fire."

"A shop full of old volumes and manuscripts. Talk about a firetrap."

"I had no idea how to put out the flames. I pulled the fire alarm and managed to drag the owner out of the vault. That's where the firefighters and the cops found me. When the dealer recovered, he claimed that I had attempted to burn down his shop."

"And you ended up in the Summerlight Academy for troubled youth. What happened to the dealer who forced you to decode the book?"

"He died of a heart attack a few months later." Abby held up one hand. "I had nothing to do with it. I was locked up at the Summerlight Academy."

He flexed one hand on the wheel, aware of the cold tension simmering in him. "Wish I could have taken care of him for you."

Abby looked disconcerted. "That's very . . . sweet of you."

He smiled. "Sweet?"

"I didn't mean to offend you. It's just that no one has ever offered to do anything like that for me before. I'm touched, truly I am. So, uh, have you done anything like that before?"

"Most of the time I prefer to use less

permanent methods."

"In other words, you have done that sort of thing before."

"Maybe."

"When you work for that private contractor you mentioned? The one who does some business with the post office?"

"To be clear, the post office is not the client," he said. "It's a different agency."

"When was the last time you worked for the contractor?"

"About three months ago." He paused. "But I was on an assignment the night Cassidy was murdered."

"Ah," she said softly. "No wonder you had a hard time establishing an alibi."

He did not respond to that. It was enough that she believed him, he thought.

"Take that gravel road to the right," she said.

He slowed the SUV and turned into a rutted lane that wound through the trees and dead-ended in a small clearing. A high steel security fence protected a run-down house and a yard filled with large stone pots. As far as he could tell, the only things growing in the planters were weeds.

He brought the vehicle to a halt and studied the scene. "You're sure this is the right place?"

"I told you, Thaddeus is a bit eccentric." Abby unfastened her seat belt and opened the door.

"Doesn't look like he's much of a gardener."

"The pots and the weeds are all that remain of an experimental garden he planted years ago. He was trying to grow some exotic herbs that he found for sale online. Supposedly, the herbs had psychical properties. But they didn't do well in this climate."

Sam got out of the car. "How do we announce ourselves?"

"There's an intercom at the gate." Abby started forward. "I'll let Thaddeus know we're here. He'll disarm the security system and let us in." She opened the rear door of the SUV. "Come on, Newton. We're going to visit Thaddeus."

Newton bounded down, but he did not look like his usual enthusiastic self. Instead, he flattened his ears and moved close to Abby.

"Maybe he's not a country dog at heart, after all," Sam said.

"I don't understand it," Abby said. "Usually he loves to come up here."

Small shards of ice touched the back of Sam's neck. He jacked his senses a little and looked around, trying to decide what it was about the scene that was bothering him.

"Wait," he said, making it an order.

Abby stopped and looked back at him. "What is it?"

"Looks like the gate is unlocked."

"That's impossible. Thaddeus always keeps the gate locked." She took a closer look. "Good grief, you're right. It's not like Thaddeus to get sloppy with his security system. He's totally paranoid, and he's got reason to be. He deals with some very dangerous collectors."

Sam went back to the SUV, opened the cargo-bay door and unzipped his duffel bag. He took out the small pistol, shut the door and went back to the gate.

"That's a gun," Abby said. She sounded oddly shocked.

"Good observation."

"But I thought you used that crystal gadget for self-defense."

"Sometimes a gun works better. It gets people's attention faster."

He gave the gate a cautious shove. It swung open easily enough. He walked into the yard. Abby followed quickly. Newton trailed behind. He whined softly.

"Something is wrong," Abby said.

"Yes," Sam said. "But I think the trouble

has already come and gone."

"You can tell things like that?"

"I've got pretty good intuition when it comes to this kind of stuff." He glanced at Newton. "So does your dog."

"Maybe Thaddeus fell ill or took a fall," Abby said anxiously. "If he managed to call an ambulance or a neighbor, that would explain why he unlocked the security system."

"Maybe." But he knew before he went up the three concrete steps that whatever he found inside the little house was going to be bad.

The front door was ajar. He pushed it wider.

Abby eyed the open door. "This isn't good."

"No," Sam said. "It isn't."

Sam took another look at Newton. The dog's ears were flat, and his tail was down. He stayed close to Abby, but he did not have the go-for-the-throat vibe he'd had earlier, when Abby had confronted Dawson.

Sam moved across the threshold. An all-too-familiar miasma iced his senses. He knew that Abby felt it, too. But, then, most people, psychic or otherwise, could sense death when it was close by.

"Dear heaven," she whispered. "Not Thaddeus, please."

Sam went along the small front hall. The house felt empty and filled with the silence of the dead. There was no other sensation like it. He heard Abby and Newton behind him.

The place looked like the home of a hoarder, but as far as he could tell, the only things Thaddeus Webber had ever hoarded were books. There were thousands of them on the floor-to-ceiling shelves. Hundreds more were stacked on the floor.

"It's hot in here," he observed. "Psi-hot."

"Most of the books in this house have a paranormal provenance," Abby said. "Get enough hot books together, and you can feel it. If you think it's warm up here, you should see the vault."

"Where is it?"

"Downstairs in the basement. That's where Thaddeus keeps his most valuable books."

Sam turned the corner at the end of a row of shelving and stopped at the sight of the crumpled form sprawled on the floor.

"Thaddeus," Abby said.

She said the name with grim resignation. She had known this was coming, Sam thought.

She slipped past him and hurried to the

end of the aisle to crouch beside the body. Newton hung back, whining a little.

Abby touched the dead man's throat. Sam knew there would be no pulse. He was sure that Abby knew that, too.

She drew her fingertips away and looked up at him. There was a forlorn sadness in her eyes that he knew he would not soon forget. He walked to the body and hunkered down beside it.

"I'm sorry," he said quietly.

"There's no blood," Abby said. "I don't see any wounds. Perhaps he died of a heart attack or a stroke. He was eighty-six, after all."

"The authorities will conclude that the death was due to natural causes, but you know as well as I do that is probably not what happened here."

"He was just an old man who loved his books," she said.

An old man who loved his books so much that he was willing to do business with some very dangerous people, Sam thought. But he did not say it.

He turned Webber faceup. The body was surprisingly heavy. *They always are,* he reflected. There was a reason the term *dead weight* had been coined a long time ago.

Scraggly gray hair and a wildly overgrown,

unkempt beard framed sunken cheeks and a bulbous nose. Webber was dressed in a tattered robe and ancient pajamas.

"He heard an intruder during the night," Sam said. "Came out of the bedroom to see what was going on."

"Someone got past his security system." Abby rose and looked around. "It would have taken a lot of digging to find this place. He did all of his business anonymously over the Internet."

"As you pointed out, if you want to find someone badly enough, it's usually possible. Even the most sophisticated computer security systems are vulnerable."

"I know," Abby said. "Thaddeus shelled out for a high-end system, but it's not like he was a large corporation or the military."

"Which, as we all know, get hacked, too. The thing that narrows our list of suspects in this situation is the cause of death."

"What do you mean?"

"I've seen this kind of thing before, Abby. This was death by paranormal means. Not many people could kill this way. It almost always involves physical contact."

"Are you certain?"

He got to his feet. "This is the kind of crime I investigate for that private contractor I told you about. No, I can't be absolutely certain yet, but death by paranormal means is my working theory until proven otherwise. A heart attack would be way too much of a coincidence."

Abby took a deep, shuddering breath. "Maybe someone used one of his encrypted books to do this, someone with my kind of talent."

"It's a possibility, but I doubt it."

"Why?"

"For one thing, there just are not a lot of folks who can do what you do. For another, being able to short-circuit someone's aura long enough to knock him unconscious is one thing. The ability to actually stop a man's heart with psychic energy is something else. It would take a whole different level of talent."

"Maybe not." Abby rubbed her arms as if she was cold. "If the victim was old and frail and was having heart problems, a severe shock to the senses might be all it would take."

"There is that. Let's take a look at that vault you mentioned."

"All right."

She led the way to the small kitchen, Newton hanging at her heels, and opened what looked like a closet door. Sam saw a flight of stone steps that went down into darkness. Abby flipped a light switch, revealing a concrete chamber piled high with cartons, crates and shelves of books.

"I don't see a vault or a safe," Sam said.

"That's because Thaddeus took care to make it as invisible as possible. The door to the vault is in the floor."

She went down the steps ahead of him, wove a path through the crowded space and stopped at what looked like a nondescript section of the concrete floor. She shoved aside a heavy book cart and revealed a small computerized lock set into the floor. She crouched, entered a code and stepped back.

"Webber gave you the code?"

"I think I'm the only one he ever trusted," Abby said.

A large square section of the floor rose on invisible hinges. A heavy wave of psi poured out of the lower basement, jangling Sam's senses. At the top of the basement steps, Newton whined again.

"I see what you mean about the heat in the vault," Sam said. "It would take at least some degree of talent just to push through that high-energy atmosphere."

"Thaddeus kept all of his most valuable items down there." Abby descended a few steps and flipped another switch. She looked around. "I don't think the killer got this far.

Nothing appears to be disturbed."

"Whoever killed Webber was not interested in anything except the lab book."

"Which Thaddeus did not have." Abby turned off the lights and climbed back up the steps. "The bastard killed him for no reason."

"Not necessarily. The killer may have been after information."

Abby entered another code into the vault lock. She watched the section of floor glide back into place with an expression of pain mingled with anger. "Such as?"

Sam took a few seconds to put himself into the mind of the killer. "If it were me, I would have come here to get the identities of the most likely auction dealers."

Abby gave him an odd look.

"What?" he said.

"Nothing. It's just that for a moment there you sounded like you actually knew what the killer was thinking."

He said nothing.

Abby blinked and collected herself quickly. "Right. That's certainly a reasonable assumption. Thaddeus knows all the players. If there is an auction about to go down, he would have known the dealers most likely to handle it."

"The question, then, is whether or not

Webber gave up the information before he died."

"He would have had no reason to risk his neck to save his competitors. In the deep end, it's every man for himself. Yes, if he felt threatened, he would have given the killer a few names and contacts. I'm sure the monster got what he wanted, and then he went ahead and murdered poor Thaddeus anyway."

"Let's go."

She turned quickly and went up the steps to the main floor of the house. Sam followed her. Newton was waiting for them. He seemed relieved to have them aboveground again. Sam closed the basement door.

Abby surveyed the crowded shelves. "It won't be long before everyone in the rare-book community knows that a cache of extremely valuable books has been left unguarded. But only a very small number of people know the location of this house."

"The killer found Webber," Sam pointed out. "That means others can find this place, too."

"What are we going to do about Thaddeus? We can't just leave him there."

"Yes," Sam said. "We can, and we will. As soon as we get to an anonymous phone, we'll call nine-one-one and tell the authorities that we're concerned neighbors who are worried about Webber because no one has seen him outside his house for a time."

She frowned. "Why does the call have to be anonymous?"

"At this stage, I don't want anyone to know that we found the body. We need to leave. Now." He started toward the front door and stopped.

"What is it?" Abby asked.

He looked back toward the body. "What was Webber doing in that aisle when he died?"

"He was probably trying to flee the killer. He staggered that far and collapsed."

"Yes, but that row of shelving dead-ends at the wall," Sam said. "This was his home. He knew every inch of it. He must have realized that if he fled in this direction, he would be trapped."

"He was dying. He would have been terrified. At the very least, terribly disoriented. I doubt that he was thinking clearly."

"I'm not so sure of that." Sam slipped the pistol beneath his jacket and went slowly back down the aisle. He stopped a short distance from the body and studied the spines of the dusty, leather-bound volumes on the shelves. "I assume he had a logical way of organizing his books?"

"Of course." Abby came to stand at the far end of the aisle. "Thaddeus devised a very elaborate system years ago. It was based on alchemical symbols and numbers. Each section is labeled. See that little placard on the end of each shelf?"

He glanced at the nearest bit of yellowed cardboard. There was a handwritten notation on it. The combination of old symbols and numbers looked like some ancient, incomprehensible alchemical formula.

"Can you tell what kind of books he kept in this section?" he asked.

Abby came down the aisle and examined the faded handwriting on the cardboard for a few seconds. "This is a history section. Reference books that were written about alchemy by late-nineteenth-century scholars. These would all be secondary sources, as far as serious collectors are concerned. Some are interesting, but none are unusually rare or inherently valuable."

"None of them are hot?"

"No. Most of them are available from other antiquarian book dealers or large academic libraries."

Sam studied a small gap on one of the shelves. "One of the books is gone."

"He probably sold it recently."

"No, look at the way the dust on the shelf

is smeared. That was done by a hand groping for the book and pulling it away from the others. Whoever grabbed that volume was in a big hurry."

He went down beside the body again and took another look at the scene from the lower vantage point. A slim leather-bound volume lay just out of sight in the shadows beneath the last row of shelving. He retrieved the book, opened it and read the title aloud.

"*A Brief History of the Ancient Art of Alchemy,* by L. Paynter." He looked up at Abby.

"Paynter was a Victorian-era scholar," she said. "One of the first historians of science."

"I know."

"By that time, alchemy had long since fallen into disrepute. It was the province of crackpots and eccentrics. Anyone who considered himself a serious scientist or researcher was into chemistry and physics by then. But Paynter was of the opinion that if Isaac Newton had been intrigued by alchemy, there had to be something to it."

"Paynter was right." Sam handed the book to her. She paged through it quickly, pausing midway through the little tome.

"There's a page missing," she said. "It was ripped out, not cut out. The damage was done recently. You can tell because the crinkles and jagged edges haven't been pressed into place the way they would be if this book had been sitting unopened on the shelf for a few years."

"I knew I was missing something," Sam said.

The sense that an ominous darkness was closing in on them was getting stronger. *Spending time with a dead body will do that,* he reminded himself. *This is important. Take your time and think. You need to find whatever it is that you aren't seeing clearly.* He patted down Webber's pajamas and bathrobe. It was unpleasant work, but this was not the first time he had performed such a chore. When his palm passed over the pocket of the robe, he felt a small bulge. Probably a tissue or a handkerchief. There was a faint crackling sound. He reached into the pocket and drew out the crumpled page.

"That's it." Excitement quickened in Abby's voice. "That's the missing page. He tore it out of Paynter's history in the last moments of his life and stuffed it into his pocket."

"He knew we were on our way, that we would probably be the ones who found him. He did his best to leave us a message."

Carefully, he smoothed the old page and

studied the illustration. The cold sleet of psi that had been stirring his senses all morning transmuted into an ice storm.

"What?" Abby asked.

"This message isn't for you. It's for me. He knew that I would be with you when you got here." He shoved the page into the inside pocket of his jacket. "Let's move."

"I don't understand. What does that drawing mean to you?"

"I'll tell you when we're in the car."

Mercifully, Abby did not question the decision. She followed him quickly out the front door. Newton dashed ahead, more than enthusiastic about the prospect of leaving the grim scene.

He got Abby and Newton into the SUV, climbed behind the wheel and drove swiftly back toward the main road. The icy-cold feeling on the nape of his neck was getting more intense.

"What's the rush?" Abby asked, fastening her seat belt.

"Damned if I know." He took one hand off the wheel long enough to rub the back of his neck. "Just a feeling."

"What is it about the page that Thaddeus tore out of the book that has you so worried?"

Sam reached inside his jacket. He pulled

out the torn page and handed it to her. "Take a look."

She took the page and examined it closely. "It's an artist's rendering of an alchemist's laboratory. Competently done, but it certainly isn't Dürer's *Melencolia.* So?"

"Look at the setting."

"It's different from most pictures of an alchemist at work, because the setting is clearly Victorian," Abby mused. "Scenes of this type are usually set against medieval or Renaissance landscapes. This has got more of a *Frankenstein* vibe. The mad-scientist thing. But there is the usual mish-mash of allegorical images from Egyptian and Greek mythology." She looked up from the picture. "What makes this illustration different?"

"That picture is not an artist's generic vision of an alchemist's lab. Take a closer look at the fire on the hearth."

Abby glanced down. She stiffened. "The flames are formed by the stylized wings of a phoenix. Oh, geez, Sam. The bird looks an awful lot like that tattoo on your shoulder."

"Where do you think I got the idea for the tat?"

"You've seen a copy of this book?"

"Not that particular text but some related writings. I told you that when Dad and his partners found the crystals, they did a lot of research into the scientific literature. They were trying to track down references to previous discoveries of similar crystals. They didn't find much that was useful, just some old alchemy texts. But they did come across a few notes made by the guy in the picture. Dad gave them to me."

Abby read the title under the drawing. *"Scene from Dr. Marcus Dalton's laboratory."*

"Dalton conducted some experiments on crystals that he called the Phoenix stones. Very little of his work survived, unfortunately. He sensed the latent power in the stones, but he never figured out how to access it. He theorized, however, that in the hands of someone who could tap the energy of the crystals, the stones could be used, among other things, as weapons."

"Like that crystal bug zapper you used on poor Nick?"

He let the *poor Nick* comment pass. "Yes, but on a much larger scale. The most I can do with my little zapper is temporarily paralyze certain currents in an individual's aura. It's probably similar to what you do when you channel the energy in an encrypted book into someone's aura. And I need physical contact to achieve the results. Dalton believed the crystals had the potential to create much greater destruction, and from a distance. But he also theorized that the crystals could be engineered to create a source of power."

"Which, presumably, is why your father doesn't want to destroy all the records of the experiments and why he doesn't want to obliterate all traces of the Phoenix Mine."

Sam smiled. "Good guess. The world is going to need new sources of power in the future. Engineered correctly, those crystals might be an answer."

"What happened to Dalton?"

"He was killed in an explosion that occurred when one of his experiments went out of control. All of the crystals he was working on at the time disappeared, and most of his notes were lost."

"Just like the explosion in the Phoenix," Abby said.

"Yes. I told you, those crystals are dangerous and highly volatile."

Abby thought for a moment. "So Thaddeus was trying to warn you that someone is after the lab book. But we already knew that."

"I don't think that's what Webber intended as the takeaway from his last message."

"What, then?"

"I think he was trying to tell me that someone has one of the Phoenix stones and has figured out how to turn it into a weapon. That's what the killer used to murder him."

"Oh, my God," Abby whispered. "Lander Knox."

"Maybe. I knew that Thaddeus Webber was murdered by paranormal means. Now I know the nature of the weapon. We need to find that lab book, Abby."

She took out her phone. "I'll see if any of the deep-end dealers have responded to my offer of a preemptive bid."

He drove very fast along the graveled lane and pulled out onto the main road, accelerating hard. He saw a car parked sideways, blocking both lanes, when he came out of the first turn. A man was slumped over the steering wheel.

The psi-chill that had been riding him hard for the last hour flashed into full-blown awareness of impending disaster.

"Hang on," he said.

Abby looked up from her phone and saw the car. "There's been an accident."

"I don't think so."

He hit the brakes, slamming to a stop. He heard dog claws scrabbling wildly on the rear seat.

He snapped the SUV into reverse and shot back around the turn.

The maneuver got them out of sight of

the blocking car, but he knew that they had only a couple of minutes, at most. There was bound to be a second vehicle coming up from behind. A classic pincer move.

He braked again. "Out. Into the woods. Go."

Abby did not ask questions. She freed herself from the seat belt, opened the door and leaped to the ground, still clutching her phone. Sam followed. By the time he got out, Abby had freed Newton from the backseat.

"Head for the rocks," Sam ordered.

They ran up the hillside into the cover of the trees, aiming for the jumble of boulders that formed a natural fortress.

"What is going on?" Abby asked, panting alongside him.

"Not sure, but I think that whoever murdered Webber left some thugs to watch the house."

"But why?"

"Someone wants you, Abby. Someone wants you very, very badly."

18

He pulled Abby down behind the cover of the massive rocks.

"Keep Newton quiet," he said. "I don't want him giving away our position. Whatever you do, stay down."

She nodded and tugged Newton down beside her. She put her hand on his muzzle. The dog seemed to comprehend that this was not a game.

"What's happening?" Abby whispered.

He did a fast assessment of the available evidence.

"I think this was supposed to be a simple carjacking followed by a kidnapping. In a minute or so, they'll realize that it's gone bad. Won't take them long to figure out which way we went. From this location, I will be able to spot them before they find us."

"And then what?"

He took the pistol out from under his

jacket and settled onto his belly to peer through the narrow crack between two rocks. "Then I use this. With luck, they won't expect me to be armed. As far as most people are concerned, I'm just a guy who spends way too much time in a lab, studying rocks."

"Sounds like an excellent career path to me." Abby tightened her hold on Newton. The dog wriggled a little in her arms, trying to get free.

There was a fierce, all-too-familiar tension about Newton that Sam recognized. They were both experiencing the icy energy that accompanied danger, he thought, a unique kind of rush. He switched his attention back to the view of the road.

Down on the pavement, a man loped around the corner and into plain sight. It was the guy who had been slumped over the steering wheel of the blocking car. A second man got out of the chase car and joined his companion. Together they both looked at the open doors of the SUV, and then they turned to gaze up into the trees. One of them pointed at the pile of granite boulders.

"They just figured out that we're up here," Sam said.

"Not like we had much of a choice when

it came to hiding places," Abby whispered.

Down below, both men took out guns and started up the hillside They separated, working their way toward the boulders, trying to use the trees for cover. But it was clear that they were not accustomed to moving through heavily wooded terrain. One of them skidded on a pile of needles and stones and nearly went down. Dead branches crackled under their feet.

City thugs, Sam decided. Guys like this were used to dealing drugs in back alleys, conducting smash-and-grab robberies and carjackings, crimes more suited to an urban environment.

They were out of their element today, and working under a major strategic disadvantage, whether they knew it or not. They were advancing uphill on an opponent who had the high ground, a fortified high ground at that. And they didn't know yet that the opposition was armed.

Sam settled into the zone. *I can work with this.*

The second man stumbled again and fell to one knee. "Shit."

In the deep silence of the woods, the curse was clearly audible.

Sam squeezed off a warning shot. A

branch exploded above the second man's head.

"Shit," the second man yelped again. He lunged for the cover of the tree trunk. "He's got a gun."

The first man scrambled for cover. "Yeah, I can see that." He raised his voice. "You up there, the guy with the gun, listen, man. We're armed, too. But this doesn't have to get messy. We don't care about you. We want the woman. Send her out and everyone walks away from this now."

Sam let the silence echo. City thugs were no good when it came to the waiting game. They tended to be a jittery, impatient lot. They lacked the discipline for this kind of hunting.

"Hey, we're not going to hurt the woman if that's what you're worrying about," the second man shouted. "It's okay, man. We're just going to take her with us for a little while. We were hired to pick her up, that's all. There's this guy who wants her to do a job for him. When it's over, she goes home, safe and sound. Nobody gets hurt."

There was another long silence. The first man couldn't take it. He leaned around the tree and fired blindly. Most of the bullets plowed harmlessly into the ground. A couple zinged off one of the larger boulders.

When the silence became intolerable again, the second man called to his friend.

"Maybe he's out of ammunition," he said, sounding hopeful.

"Like hell," the first man responded. "He's going to wait up there and pick us off if we try to get to those rocks. Shit, this isn't going to work."

"I've had it," the second man said. "We didn't get paid enough for this. Let's get out of here."

"You up there in the rocks," the first man shouted. "You win. We're leaving. Don't shoot."

Sam let the silence lengthen once more.

Cautiously, both men edged away from the sheltering trees and half crawled, half stumbled back down the hillside toward the road. Sam fired two more shots by way of encouragement.

Newton exploded out of Abby's clutches. He charged around the tumbled boulders and raced down the hillside.

"Newton," Abby yelped, stricken. "No. Come back here."

"I knew that condo dog was going to be a problem," Sam said.

"Shit," the second man yelled. "There's a dog."

The first man had reached the chase car.

He jumped in behind the wheel and fired up the engine. The second man tried to open the passenger-side door, but Newton's jaws closed around his trouser leg. The guy yelled. He managed to kick free and get the door closed.

The chase car did a three-point turn and roared off, disappearing around a bend.

Sam got to his feet and went cautiously down the hill.

Abby followed quickly. "Newton, *Newton,* come here. Are you all right?"

Newton trotted back toward her, giving her a doggy grin. She went down on her knees and hugged him close.

"Good dog," she said. "Brave dog. You're the best dog in the entire world."

Newton licked her furiously.

"Always figured he'd go for the ankle, not the throat," Sam said. "Let's get moving." He urged her toward the SUV. "I want to make a stop before we head back to the island."

"Where?"

"The Black Box lab."

"Don't forget, we have to make that nine-one-one call to report Thaddeus's body," Abby said.

"We'll stop at a gas station on the way back to Seattle," Sam promised.

19

She felt the hot currents of energy swirling inside the lab as soon as she walked through the automatic doors with Sam. The interior of the Black Box facility, officially known as the Coppersmith Research and Development Laboratory, gleamed and sparkled with a lot of stainless steel and thick green-tinted glass. Instruments and high-tech equipment, including lasers that were clearly state-of-the-art and beyond, were arrayed on the workbenches. Computer screens glowed on every desk. Technicians in white coats hovered over chunks of raw ore and specimens of crystals and rocks.

There was a lot of heat in the room, Abby thought, and it wasn't all coming from the specimens. She was fairly certain that most, if not all, of the researchers and technicians were talents of one kind or another.

One of the techs looked up when Sam escorted Abby into the windowless room.

He yanked his safety goggles away from his eyes and got to his feet.

"Mr. Coppersmith," he said. "Sorry, sir, didn't see you come in. It's been a while since you dropped by."

Several other members of the staff noticed Sam and greeted him with a mixture of surprise and friendly respect. They looked at Abby with veiled speculation.

"I know I haven't been around as often as usual in the past few months," Sam said to the technician. "But I've been keeping tabs on things from my private lab. Abby, this is David Estrada. David, Abby Radwell."

David nodded at Abby. "Nice to meet you, Miss Radwell."

"Abby, please," she said. "A pleasure to meet you, too." She looked around. "I've never seen anything like this place."

"Not a lot of labs like this one around," David said. He did not bother to conceal his pride. "Rumor has it that our competition, Helicon Stone, operates a decent version of their own Black Box, but I doubt if they've got anything we don't have."

"If you ever find out that the Helicon lab does have something we don't have, let me know," Sam said. "We'll get it for you."

David laughed. "That's what I like about working here. I get every toy I want."

"How are things going?" Sam asked.

"Humming along," David said. "I'm working on a very interesting piece of amber today. Definitely charged. Would you like to see it?"

"I would, but I don't have the time. We're on the way to the library. I just stopped by to say hello. Where's Dr. Frye?"

"I think you'll find him in the library," David said. He smiled, as if at some secret joke. "With Miss O'Connell."

There were a few scattered snickers around the room.

Sam took Abby's arm. "I'll catch up with him there. See you all at the tech summit next week."

"Wouldn't miss it for the world," David said. "My kids can't wait to go kayaking again. They're still talking about the experience last summer."

Sam guided Abby back through the automatic steel doors and down a hall. She studied the stone- and steel- and glass-clad walls, floor and ceiling.

Sam guessed her thoughts. "Stone, steel and glass are the three materials that do the best job of stopping psi-radiation and ultralight."

"Stone and steel I understand. But glass?"

"Glass is still something of a mystery, and

it has a history of being unpredictable when it comes to paranormal energy, because it possesses the properties of both a solid and a crystal. But here in the Box we use a special type of glass that we designed ourselves. It doesn't always block psi or ultralight, but it does disrupt the oscillating pattern of the currents in many of the specimens. That works just as well as a solid barrier, in most cases."

He stopped in front of another set of steel doors and entered a code into the security system. The doors made almost no sound when they slid open, which, Abby decided, was why the two people at the far end of the room did not realize that they were no longer alone. The pair stood very close, their body language signaling an intimate relationship.

Abby looked around with a sense of spiraling excitement, her senses dancing to the beat of the hot energy in the room. Unlike the crystal-based heat in the lab, this was her kind of psi.

The Coppersmith Inc. technical library resembled the rare books and manuscripts room of a large academic library. The atmosphere was hushed and Old World. Leather-bound volumes graced the shelves. Some were quite ancient. Many of the hottest books were housed in glass cases. There were no windows, and the artificial lighting was kept to a minimum. Green glass shades covered the lamps on the reading tables. The difference was that many of the books in this library were hot.

Sam coughed discreetly. "Dr. Frye, Jenny. Sorry to interrupt."

The two people at the other end of the room jumped apart and turned quickly. The woman was clearly mortified. She appeared to be in her early forties and endowed with the scholarly, academic look that went with the library. Her silvering hair was cut in a sleek bob. She wore a navy blue skirted business suit and gold-framed glasses.

"Mr. Coppersmith," she said, flustered. "I'm so sorry. I didn't realize you were here."

"It's okay, Jenny," Sam said, moving forward with Abby. "Just stopped in to check on a few things and do a little research."

The man next to Jenny smiled. "Mr. Coppersmith. Good to see you again here at the lab. It's been a while."

"Been busy," Sam said. He sped through the introductions. "Dr. Gerald Frye, Jenny O'Connell, I'd like you to meet Abby Radwell."

Gerald Frye was obviously close to Jenny's age, but perhaps a couple of years younger, Abby thought. Thirty-nine or forty, although it was hard to be sure. It looked as if he had not bothered to run a brush through his shaggy mane of dark, graying hair that morning. His mustache and beard needed a trim. He wore heavily framed glasses and an unbuttoned lab coat that was liberally spotted with what appeared to be old coffee stains.

There was a polite round of *Happy to meet you.*

"Abby is an expert in hot books," Sam said.

"Is that so?" Jenny smiled warmly. "Always a pleasure to meet a colleague. There aren't that many of us who specialize in rare hot books. Do you work in one of the other Coppersmith labs?"

Here it comes, Abby thought. She braced herself for the inevitable reaction.

"No, I don't work in one of the other labs," she said. She gave Jenny her brightest professional smile. "I'm a freelancer."

Jenny blinked. Comprehension dawned in her expression along with ill-concealed disapproval.

"I see," Jenny said. "You work in the private market?"

"Right," Abby said.

Private market was polite code in the hot-books world for the paranormal underground market, and they both knew it. Professional librarians and academics who valued their scholarly reputations did not dabble in the underground market, or at least did not admit to dabbling in it. They had their own reputations to consider, and, besides, it was dangerous.

"Right now, Abby is working for me," Sam said.

Jenny's smile was stiff, but she kept her demeanor coolly polite. "I see," she said again.

Gerald Frye looked at Sam with a troubled expression. "I don't understand. Is Miss Radwell trying to find a specific book for you?"

"Yes, she is," Sam said. "It's one I want for the family collection, not the company library. It disappeared several years ago, but it's rumored to be coming up for auction. Abby has that covered. The reason we're here today is because I want to do some research."

"Yes, of course," Frye said. "In that case, I'll leave you to it. I need to get back to the lab." He bobbed his head at Abby. "A pleasure, Miss Radwell."

"Dr. Frye," Abby murmured.

Frye disappeared through the steel doors. Jenny gave Sam her own version of a professional smile.

"How can I help you, Mr. Coppersmith?"

"I'm looking for anything and everything you've got written by or about Marcus Dalton."

Jenny frowned slightly. "The nineteenth-century researcher who became obsessed with alchemy?"

"That's the one," Sam said.

"I'm afraid we don't have much. He was never considered a serious scientist. There is very little written about him in the literature, and as I recall, most of his own writings were destroyed in a fire or an explosion. Can't remember the details."

"Let me see what you've got, Jenny," Sam said.

"Certainly, sir."

It did not take long to exhaust the library's holdings on the subject of Marcus Dalton. An hour after Jenny produced a short stack of books, all secondary sources, Abby and Sam left the lab and walked across the parking lot to the SUV.

"Well, that was a waste of time," Sam said. "I had a feeling it would be, but I had to be sure."

"Jenny O'Connell was right," Abby said. "Marcus Dalton was not taken seriously in his own lifetime or by any of the historians of nineteenth-century science. Too bad so much of his own work was lost in that explosion."

Newton was waiting right where they had left him, his nose pressed to the partially open window in the rear seat of the SUV. Abby knew that he had probably been sitting there, his whole attention riveted on the entrance of the Coppersmith Inc. lab, ever since she and Sam had disappeared inside. He greeted them with his usual enthusiasm.

Sam got behind the wheel and drove out of the parking lot. "Not that it's any of our business, but did you get the impression that there was something personal going on between Frye and Jenny?"

Abby smiled. "Yep. We interrupted an office romance."

Sam looked thoughtful. "I hope it works for both of them. Jenny has been alone since her husband died a few years ago."

"What about Dr. Frye?"

"As far as I know, he's never been married." Sam took the interstate on-ramp, heading north toward Anacortes. "I saw Jenny's expression when you explained that you were a freelancer in the private market. Do you get that a lot?"

"Only if I deal with people like her, who work the academic and scholarly end of the market."

"How often does that happen?"

She smiled. "Not often. It's almost impossible for any of them to get a proper referral. Thaddeus held a major grudge against the academic world in general, because it disdained his insistence that the paranormal should be taken seriously. As a result, he almost never referred anyone from that world to me. On the rare occasion when I do agree to take on a client from any of the established institutions in academia, we rarely reach an agreement on my fees."

Sam grinned. "They can't afford you?"

"I always jack up my fees when someone from academia comes calling. Petty, I know, but we all have to have our standards."

"Guess I should be feeling lucky that you agreed to take me on as a client."

"Got news for you, Sam Coppersmith. Like it or not, you're from my world."

"I'm okay with that."

20

The urge to confide the full scope of the disaster to her special friend was almost overwhelming, but Orinda Strickland had resisted, at least until today. Some things simply could not be spoken of outside the family. Not that she didn't trust Lander Knox. He was a very discreet young man. He was the only one who really understood her. She looked forward to these luncheons so much. Nevertheless, one had one's pride. The loss of the family fortune and the possibility that Dawson might be facing bankruptcy, perhaps even prison, was simply too devastating to reveal. That sort of thing had to be kept secret.

"You look lovely today," Lander said. He held her chair for her.

She managed a light, gracious chuckle and sat down at the table. "You always say that. But thank you, anyway."

"I say it because it's true." Lander sat

down across from her. "You radiate qualities that are increasingly rare in the modern world. Grace, style, dignity. And wonder of wonders, you can carry on an intelligent conversation. Do you realize how few women of any age can do that these days? That's why I savor our luncheons together so much."

It was shortly after noon, unfashionably early for lunch, but the advantage was that the downtown restaurant was only lightly crowded. That meant there was less of a chance that she would run into an acquaintance, Orinda thought. She would have preferred to lunch at her club on Lake Washington. The Stricklands had been members for several generations. But she knew that there would be raised eyebrows and a good deal of curiosity if she were to show up with a handsome, distinguished man who was young enough to be her grandson.

There was absolutely no reason for her to feel awkward about her relationship with Lander, of course. He was a friend, nothing more. They were intellectual companions with a wide range of mutual interests who, sadly, happened to be decades apart in age.

They had met quite by accident at the opera during intermission. Both of them had attended alone that evening. It had been obvious from the start that Lander was well-bred and well educated. He did not say much about his background, but it soon became clear that he was descended from an old, established East Coast family. The faint hint of a Boston accent was so charming.

The conversation that had followed had been the most stimulating one she had enjoyed in years. Her husband, George, had never enjoyed the opera or the symphony or high art. His greatest pleasure had been a string of yachts, each one larger than the last. She had never liked being out on the water. Their marriage had been conducted along parallel lines that had suited both of them. Losing him ten years ago had been a shock, but she had not truly mourned.

In spite of the sick dread that was eating her up inside, Orinda managed a smile. But the phone conversation with Dawson had left her thoroughly unnerved. The realization that Abby was the key to the family's financial salvation had come as a terrible blow. She had been forced to take an anti-anxiety tablet to calm herself.

Dawson and Diana were right, Abby viewed the situation as a golden opportunity to take her revenge against the family. Dawson had reported that she wanted more than a simple cash payment for her services. She would no doubt demand to be named as a full-fledged beneficiary of the family trust. It was unthinkable. The woman was not a Strickland. There was no blood connection whatsoever. And she was mentally unbalanced.

As incomprehensible as it seemed, Orinda was starting to believe that Abby actually wanted to see the family lose everything. *The ungrateful bitch. After all I've done for her. Brandon Radwell could never have afforded the tuition and fees at that special school on his own.*

"I see your son-in-law is having a signing event for his new book on Friday night," Lander said.

"Yes." Orinda shook out her napkin. "It's the start of his book tour. He'll be gone for almost a month. I understand the publisher has scheduled a number of appearances."

"Have you read *Families by Choice?*"

"I glanced through it." Orinda sniffed. "I'm afraid it's the usual psychobabble that passes for deep insight and wise advice these days. But my daughter tells me that there's a very good chance it will sell quite well, and may even lead to a TV show."

Lander's smile held both sympathy and condescending amusement. "It's all about marketing and packaging, isn't it?"

"I'm afraid so. My son-in-law is very good at both."

Orinda opened her menu and reminded herself to be careful what she said about Brandon. Not that Lander wasn't aware of her feelings on the subject. He never pried into personal matters, but over the past few months it had become very easy to talk to him about so many things.

Their luncheons were supposed to be reserved for conversations about opera, literary works and other cultural matters. But all too often she found herself confiding certain matters that really should be kept in the family.

She gave thanks yet again that Lander could be trusted to be discreet. In spite of the difference in their ages, they were similar in so many ways. He had a charming, poetical way of describing their relationship. *We are old souls who have found each other.*

21

Sam gazed into the glowing computer with the brooding air of an alchemist pondering his fires.

"There was no indication that anything was stolen from Webber's home," he said. "The county officials have concluded that he died of natural causes."

"Well, we knew that would be the official cause of death," Abby said.

She sank down into the corner of the massive leather couch and curled her legs mermaid-style. Newton bounded up and settled down beside her. She rubbed behind his ears, taking comfort from the physical contact with him.

The toxic mix of adrenaline and nerves following the discovery of Thaddeus's body and the kidnapping attempt was starting to dissipate, leaving exhaustion in its wake. But she had a feeling that a restful sleep was going to be harder to come by than usual tonight.

"The local media mention that Webber appears to have been a hoarder who collected old books related to the occult, magic and the paranormal," Sam said.

"That is absolutely wrong," Abby said. "Webber had no interest in the occult or magic. But I don't suppose it will matter. So many people don't understand the distinction between the paranormal and the supernatural. Regardless, those reports will be enough to fire up the rumor mill in collectors' circles. My competition will be looking very hard for Thaddeus's house."

Sam got up from the computer. "The police will have locked up the place."

"I'm sure they did," she said. "For all the good that will do. I think it's safe to say the authorities have no idea of the value of some of those books. They'll assume that Thaddeus was just another eccentric hoarder."

"Did he have any family?"

"Not that I know of," Abby said.

Sam crossed the room to where a bottle of white wine was chilling in a bucket of ice. A bottle of whiskey and two glasses sat nearby. "Did he make any contingency arrangements for his collection in the event that something happened to him? Is there a will?"

"I have no idea. He always dreamed of founding a library of paranormal literature for serious researchers, but he never had the money to start such an ambitious project, and no academic institution would accept his collection."

"If he made a will, it will be on file somewhere. I'll have someone in Coppersmith's legal department check into it." Sam took out his phone and keyed a number. "If we can locate a will and the lawyer who drew it up, we might be able to take action to protect Webber's books, or at least those in the vault, before it's too late."

He spoke briefly to whoever answered the phone, giving instructions with a relaxed authority.

"Thanks, Bill," he concluded. "Let me know when you've got something."

Sam ended the call and reached for the wine bottle. When he realized that Abby was watching him, he raised his brows. "What?"

"Must be nice to be able to pick up a phone and have a lawyer snap to attention like that for you," she said.

"There are benefits to having access to the resources of a privately held company." Sam poured wine into one of the glasses. "But guys like Bill don't come cheap, and they don't exactly snap to attention, sadly."

He splashed some whiskey into the second glass and carried both across the room to where Abby sat.

"Thank you for trying to protect Thaddeus's collection," she said. She swallowed some of the wine and lowered the glass. "It meant everything to him."

"We might be able to protect his books, at least for now, but if there is an heir and if he or she doesn't appreciate the value of the collection, the books will probably go straight into the used-book market," Sam said.

"Or a yard sale."

Sam drank some whiskey and sank down onto the couch next to Newton. Absently, he scratched Newton's ears.

Abby smiled proudly. "Newton was a real hero today, wasn't he?"

"You're not supposed to anthropomorphize," Sam said. "Dogs don't think in terms of bravery and cowardice. He recognized a threat, and he followed his instincts."

"He was trying to protect me."

"You're his pack buddy. Like I said, he was just going on instinct."

Abby took another sip of wine. "You were protecting me, too. You're human. Am I allowed to call you brave and daring and heroic?"

"Nope." He drank some more whiskey. "I was just doing my job."

"Heroes always say stuff like that, you know."

"In this case, it's the simple truth. You hired me to find a blackmailer. Now it looks like I'm dealing with a blackmailer who is getting desperate enough to commit murder and attempted kidnapping."

"And you hired me to find that lab book. Which reminds me." She reached into her tote, took out her phone and checked her email. "There are a few new messages. Let me see if any of them are from those dealers I contacted earlier."

She ran through the new mail. There was a note from her father, reminding her of the signing event, and a message from her stepmother, demanding that she get in touch immediately. Ignoring the first two emails, she opened the third. In spite of her exhaustion, she experienced another flash of adrenaline.

"Here we go," she said, trying to keep her professional cool. "The auction is scheduled for next week. No preemptive bids are allowed, but it has been noted that my client will try to top any bid. We are guaranteed the opportunity to do so."

Sam sat forward, eyes heating. Energy

whispered in the atmosphere. Newton stirred and raised his head, ears sharpened.

Sam looked at the phone. "Which dealer is running the auction?"

"He calls himself Milton," Abby said. "But that's just his online alias. I don't know anything more about him, aside from the fact that he is one of the dealers who works with the most dangerous collectors and the most dangerous books. I've never done business with him, but he says he knows my reputation and trusts that my client is solid."

"I'll call one of the people in the IT department." Sam reached for his own phone. "See if he can trace Milton."

"I doubt that you'll be able to find him. Dealers like Milton don't survive this long unless they are very careful."

"Thaddeus Webber was careful," Sam pointed out. "Someone found him."

22

Imprisoned in the shadows, he watched her walk down the hall to the door of the lab. He called out her name, but in dreams there is no sound. He tried to move, desperate to stop her before she opened the door and disappeared inside the room where death awaited.

He managed to take one step and then another, but the darkness bound him as securely as a prison cell. He knew he would not get to her in time.

At the end of the hall, she stopped and looked back at him, her hand on the door-knob.

He said her name one more time, but she did not respond.

Cassidy.

She opened the door and entered the lab. The killer was waiting for her. . . .

Sam came awake as he always did after the

dream, breathing hard and drenched in sweat. He wrenched the covers aside and sat up on the edge of the bed. He forced himself to take a few deep breaths.

After a while he got up, yanked off his damp T-shirt, pulled on a pair of pants and opened the bedroom door. For a moment, he stood in the shadowed hall and studied the door across the way. Abby was inside that room. She had not invited him to join her. He had not pushed. His intuition warned him that she not only needed sleep, she needed time to come to terms with whatever had happened between them last night.

One night of hot, psi-infused sex did not a relationship make, he thought. Well, it had for him, but he could tell that Abby was having trouble with the concept. It was probably hard to focus on your personal life when you were worried about people with guns trying to kidnap you. A woman had to set priorities. So did a man, and keeping Abby safe was his one and only priority now.

He started down the dimly lit hall toward the stairs but paused when he heard the click of dog nails on the other side of Abby's bedroom door. Newton was awake and alert inside the room.

"It's okay," Sam said, keeping his voice to

a whisper. "Go back to sleep."

He went downstairs to the kitchen, turned on a light and took the whiskey out of the cupboard. He poured a medicinal shot and drank it, leaning against the granite counter. The heat of the liquor burned away the last fragments of the dream.

When the glass was empty, he thought about going back to bed, but that would be futile. He would not sleep again tonight. He never did after the dream. He would be awake until morning, so he might as well do something productive.

He turned off the light, left the kitchen and went down to the basement. He walked along the hall, the same hall that appeared in the damn dream. The ghostly images of Cassidy walking this path to her doom were not from his memories. He had not been in the house that night. But he had imagined how it must have happened so many times that his reconstructed version of events had become as detailed and as graphic as a photograph.

He opened the door and went into the chamber. The energy in the room stirred all of his senses. The lab was drenched in darkness, but the specimens in the glass cases were all hot. They burned most strongly at night.

He jacked up his talent and walked through the dazzling rainbow of paranormal light. The hues ranged across the spectrum, from icy ultrablack to hot ultrareds and on into the silvery ultrawhite energy that the old alchemists had called the Hermetic Stream, *the water that did not wet the hands.*

The raw-amber pieces were especially powerful to his heightened senses. He stopped in front of a glass case and studied the copper-and-gold radiation given off by the specimen inside. The same color as Abby's hair, he realized. He smiled a little and reached out to open the case.

Soft footsteps and the click of dog nails sounded in the hall. He turned away from the case and saw Abby and Newton silhouetted in the doorway. Abby had a flashlight in her hand. The beam speared into the lab, illuminating one of the glass cases.

Newton trotted into the room and immediately began to investigate the space, his nose to the floor.

Sam looked at Abby. She had put on her robe and slippers. Her hair was a wild storm of curls around her face. His slightly jacked senses got hotter.

"Didn't mean to wake you up," he said.

She moved slowly into the room. "Are you all right?"

"I'm fine." He went to the desk and flipped the switch on the lamp.

"Not much in the way of lighting," she said. She switched off the flashlight. "I think of labs as being sterile, brightly lit places, like the Coppersmith Black Box."

"They often turn off the lights in the Box. Paranormal energy is more vivid to the senses in darkness."

"Yes."

She walked slowly toward him, gazing into the cases that she passed. He felt energy shimmer in the atmosphere and knew that she had heightened her talent. He would know her aura anywhere and in any light, he thought.

"What do you see when you look at these stones?" she asked.

He looked at her, not the gems and crystals that surrounded them. She dazzled his senses more than any of the rare stones in the room.

"Fireworks, rainbows and a thousand shades of lightning," he said.

"I can sense that they're hot. Anyone with a scrap of talent could figure that out." She stopped a short distance away. "But I don't see fireworks, rainbows and lightning."

"That's because you're not looking at what I'm looking at."

"What are you looking at?"

"You."

She took a step closer, and then another, until she was only a foot away. She raised her hand and brushed her fingertips across the phoenix tattoo that covered his shoulder.

"Why couldn't you sleep?" she asked.

"A dream woke me."

"A bad one," she said. It was not a question.

"A recurring one."

"Was it about the woman you were dating? The one who was killed here in this room?"

"Cassidy Lawrence. Good guess."

"Not a guess," Abby said. "Intuition. What really happened that night?"

"Damned if I know." He exhaled slowly. "I was on an assignment with that private contractor I told you about. I finished the job early and got the feeling that I needed to get back here to the Copper Beach house as soon as possible. I arrived sometime after midnight. Knew something was wrong immediately."

"Bad energy?"

"There was definitely some of that, but the really big clue was that the alarm system had been turned off."

"By Cassidy?"

"I don't know. I never gave her the code. Maybe she had some good hacking skills. But my theory is that it was the killer who deactivated the system. I entered the house. Nothing appeared to be disturbed, but I could feel the psychic residue that murder always leaves. Same thing I sensed today at Webber's house. Death leaves a calling card. I found Cassidy's body in here. There was no obvious sign of violence. The authorities and everyone else concluded that she had taken an overdose of some exotic club drugs."

"Suicide?"

"No. I'm sure of it. Trust me, Cassidy was not the type."

"But you never found the killer."

"No."

"What do you think happened that night?" Abby asked.

"I've gone over and over all possible scenarios, and I keep coming back to the only one that works. It was a setup right from the beginning."

"What do you mean?"

"Cassidy must have helped engineer the whole thing. I don't want to believe it, because it makes me look so damned stupid, but there's no other explanation that fits. Serves me right for breaking the rules."

"What rules?"

"Never date the employees."

"Where did you meet her?"

"At a gem-and-mineral show in Arizona. I hit most of the big events each year, because you never know what might show up. Once in a while, there's a hot stone. At that show, one of the dealers had a very interesting chunk of psi-infused quartz. It was obvious that he didn't realize what he had. In fact, the only other person in the vicinity who clearly recognized the nature of the quartz was the spectacular-looking woman standing next to me."

"Cassidy."

"Right. One thing led to another. She was smart, gorgeous and talented. And she was as obsessed with hot rocks as I am. She wanted a job with Coppersmith. I introduced her to the director of the Black Box. Frye hired her immediately. Talent like hers is hard to come by."

"But the two of you continued to date," Abby said.

"I started bringing her here on weekends. But she wasn't supposed to be on the island the night she died."

"Why was she here? Did you ever figure it out?"

"The only logical explanation is that she

came here with her partner to steal the Phoenix stones."

"I don't understand," Abby said. "Why would she think they were here in your lab? You said that those stones disappeared in the explosion at the mine."

"That's only half true. The stones that Ray Willis had removed for analysis and experimentation vanished. But my father escaped from that mine with a small number of geodes containing hot crystals. The stone in my ring is from one of them."

Abby studied his ring, fascinated. "That's one of the Phoenix crystals?"

"Yes. Dad split one of the geodes and removed three of the smallest crystals. He had them made into rings and gave one to my sister, Emma; one to my brother, Judson; and one to me. But so far they've served mostly as reminders of our obligation to protect the stones. We can run a little psi through them, but none of us has been able to figure out how to tap the full power of the latent energy in the crystals. And we're not sure it would be smart to do so."

"But you can sense that energy?"

He glanced at the ring. "Yes. The three crystals are all different. Even though they came out of the same geode, they are not the same in color, and they appear to have different properties. Emma, Judson and I each responded differently to them. Each of us chose the one that compelled us the most. This was the stone that somehow resonated with me."

"Where are the rest of the Phoenix crystals?"

"They're in a vault here in the basement. But that's one of the problems with the scenario that I've been working on. I never told Cassidy about the stones. Never showed her the vault. As far as I knew, she had no knowledge of the Phoenix Mine or the rocks that Dad hauled out of it."

"Yet somehow she came to know your family secrets." Abby concentrated for a moment. "You said she was a talent with an affinity for stones that was similar to your own."

"Right."

Abby looked around the chamber. "She spent time in this lab with you. Maybe she could sense them."

"I doubt it. They don't actually give off a lot of energy unless you know how to tap into the heat. No one ever notices the one in my ring. It's the same with the crystals Emma and Judson wear. Besides, the stones in the vault are shielded behind an inch of steel. But maybe her accomplice knew something she didn't know."

"You're sure she had an accomplice?" Abby asked.

"It's the only answer. He's the one who killed her."

"Why would he do that?"

"That's one of the many things I don't know," he said. "The only thing I am sure of is that whoever was here that night, he or she did not get the vault open. The stones are still inside."

"Could be her accomplice wasn't all that good with locks," Abby said.

"Even a first-rate locksmith with some serious talent wouldn't be able to open the vault. It's got a one-of-a-kind crystal mechanism. Designed it myself." He held up his hand to show her the stone in his ring. "It can only be opened with one of the rings, and whoever did it would have to be able to push a little energy through the stone."

"What about explosives?" Abby asked.

"Sure, you could blow the safe, but it would be an extremely dangerous operation, due to the unpredictable nature of the stones inside. Whoever was here that night knew better than to try that approach."

"So Cassidy's partner got this far that night, realized he couldn't get into the safe and decided to cut his losses," Abby said.

"He started with his accomplice, Cassidy, the one person who could implicate him."

"I think that's how it went down. I also think it's time you had a look at what this situation is all about." He walked toward the far end of the room.

Abby trailed after him. "You're going to show me the lock?"

"I'm going to open the vault and show you the stones. You're in this as deep as I am. You have a right to see what my family has been protecting for the past forty years."

He went to the far end of the room and pushed the concealed lever in the wall. A panel of fake stone slid open to reveal the steel door of the vault.

"That safe looks much newer than the rest of the house," Abby said.

"It is. For years Dad used a top-of-the-line security system designed by the head of our Black Box lab, Paul Lofgren. He was an old friend of my father's. Lofgren died a few years ago. After I moved into this house, I wanted something more secure. I designed a new one. It was made to order by a firm in Seattle. I played around with various crystal devices until I came up with the obsidian lock and the Phoenix keys."

Abby gave that some more thought. "Did anyone outside the family know that you changed the lock?"

"No. It was another Coppersmith family secret. You're thinking that whoever arranged the burglary that night expected to find the old lock in place, aren't you?"

"It might explain why things ended the way they did."

"That's my conclusion as well."

He held his ring to the chunk of obsidian that was set into the wall and pushed a little energy through the crystal. The black stone glowed with dark light. The thick steel door swung open slowly. Faint currents of ghostly energy wafted out into the lab. Newton growled.

"I see what you mean," Abby said. She moved closer to get a better look. "Whatever is inside doesn't feel particularly hot. The vibes are definitely strange, however."

Sam hit the switch that turned on the interior light. He watched her face when she saw the small pile of dull, gray rocks inside the vault. She looked disappointed. He smiled.

"Not very exciting, are they?" he asked.

"Nope. If I couldn't sense a little of the energy, I wouldn't give them another glance."

"Each one is a geode. The hot crystals are inside. Dad split one of them, removed the three crystals for the rings and then decided he didn't want to risk cutting into any of the other geodes. Too many unknowns."

"Which one did he open?"

"This one." He picked up half of the split geode and removed it from the vault. "Good old-fashioned rock on the outside, but take a look at what's inside."

He turned the cut geode to reveal the senses-dazzling interior.

Abby gazed in astonished wonder at the breathtaking array of multicolored crystals that filled the heart of the stone.

"Oh, my," she breathed. "This is nature's version of a Fabergé egg, except that the decoration is on the inside."

"We think it may be more like nature's version of a powerful furnace," he said. "The problem is that we don't know how to safely access the full force of the energy in even one of these geodes. We haven't got the technology needed to control this kind of paranormal power."

"You're able to control the crystal in your ring in order to open the lock on the vault?"

"Sure, I can run a little psi through it, do a few parlor tricks." He put the geode, cut side down, back inside the vault. "But I have no idea what would happen if I could channel the full power locked in it."

Abby watched him close the vault door.

"What do you see in your dream?" she asked.

He reset the vault lock. "I see Cassidy walking along the hall to this room. I know she is going to open the door and come face-to-face with her killer. I try to call out to her, to warn her, but I can't move, and she can't hear me."

"Tough dream," Abby said.

"I've had better."

"I know it won't help, but I can tell you that I've got something similar going on," she said.

He looked at her. "Bad dreams?"

"Worse than that. I've started sleepwalking. Gwen says I shouldn't worry about it. She says it's probably just temporary stress caused by the incident in the Vaughn library. But she also said that it might be my intuition trying to tell me that I'm overlooking something important."

"What do you see in your dream?"

"Nothing that looks like any kind of clue, that's for sure. I see Grady Hastings, the crazy guy who broke in with the gun that day. He reaches out to me. Begs me to help him. I want to, but I don't know how."

Sam pulled her into his arms and wrapped her close and tight.

"Maybe there's a lesson here," he said.

"What would that lesson be?"

He dropped a kiss into her hair, and then he moved his mouth to her ear.

"Maybe neither of us should be sleeping alone," he said.

She slipped her arms around his neck. "Do you think that sleeping together would stop the dreams?"

"Worked for me last night." He kissed her throat. "What about you?"

"Well, I had the dream before we went to bed together. That's what woke me up. But afterward, I went out like a light. I don't remember any dreams."

He nuzzled her throat. "What do you say we rerun the experiment again tonight and see if we get the same positive results?"

She smiled. "Is that the way you science guys talk when you want to get a lady into bed?"

"Depends. Is it working? If not, I'll try another approach."

"Don't bother." She brushed her mouth against his. "It's working."

The lovemaking was compelling and intense, just as it had been the first time, but there was something different about it tonight, Abby thought. Last night she had experienced what felt like a metaphysical as well as a physical intimacy at the height of her release. The short-lived sense of connection had been unlike anything she had ever experienced, but she had told herself it was a result of the paranormal energy involved. They had both been running a little hot last night.

The same alarming, enthralling sensation of psychical and physical intimacy swept through her again tonight. But this time when she shivered in Sam's arms and wrapped herself around him while he powered through a shuddering climax, she knew that the connection was not temporary. Something much more permanent was going on with their resonating auras.

Her last coherent thought before she tumbled down into sleep was that even if she did not see Sam again for the rest of her life, the link between them would endure to the end.

She did not know whether to be thrilled or terrified.

23

Grady Hastings was enveloped in dream fog. He reached out to her. "Help me. You're the only one who can save me."

"Please, you must tell me what you want," she said.

"Help me."

She tried to grasp his hand, but she could not get close enough. She tried to walk toward him through the swirling fog of energy, but some unseen force stopped her. . . .

"Abby, wake up," Sam said. His voice was quiet but freighted with the weight of a command. "Can you hear me? You're dreaming."

Somewhere, a dog whined anxiously.

She came awake on the usual rush of energy, dismayed to find herself on her feet, almost halfway to the door. Sam was standing directly in front of her. He had both hands clamped around her shoulders. Newton pressed against her leg.

"Crap," she said. "I did it again. My own fault this time. I forgot to set my alarm."

"What alarm?"

"Gwen said I should set a psychic alarm so that I would go into the lucid dream state if I had the Grady Hastings dream again. She said that strong talents are especially good at manipulating lucid dreams, they just have to focus. She told me that if I took control of the dream I might be able to find out what my intuition is trying to tell me."

"So much for my theory that sex before sleep would ensure that you didn't dream," Sam said.

"Guess it's back to the drawing board."

"Let's not be too hasty here. We don't want to abandon the experiment just because we had one failure."

She looked at him. "I thought that doing the same thing over and over again and expecting a different outcome was the definition of insanity."

"Ah, but sex is never exactly the same." He pulled her into his arms. "Each time is different. I suggest that we keep rerunning the experiment until we get the right results."

She leaned into him. "The dream was

stronger tonight, Sam."

He held her close against him. "Was there anything different about it?"

"No. But I have come to a conclusion."

"What?"

"I don't think there's any deep, hidden meaning in my dream. I think the message my intuition is trying to send me is very simple and straightforward."

"What is it?"

"We need to talk to Grady Hastings."

24

Abby awoke with a start, aware that she was alone in the bed. Funny how fast you could become accustomed to sleeping with someone, she thought. She had slept alone all her life and had concluded that she liked it that way. Two nights with Sam had changed a lot of things.

A cold, wet nose pushed against her hand. She opened her eyes and found herself face-to-face with Newton. He was standing beside the bed, gazing at her with a fixed expression.

"Okay, okay, I'm awake. I thought I told you to forget that psychic-command thing."

She pushed back the covers, sat up and rubbed Newton briskly. He chuffed a little, licked her hand and then, evidently satisfied that he had performed his duty, turned and trotted out the open door. She could tell that he was headed downstairs to the kitchen. The sounds and smells of breakfast wafted up from the floor below.

Sleeping with Sam definitely had a few perks, she thought. He was fixing breakfast for the second morning in a row. She could not recall the last time anyone had prepared breakfast for her. Tomorrow morning she would have to return the favor.

The summer dawn had arrived with rain, all in all, looking more like a midwinter dawn. Through the window she could see the steel-colored waters of the sea, but the neighboring islets and islands were lost in the mist.

She took a teal-colored cowl-neck pullover and a pair of gray trousers out of her suitcase and headed for the adjoining bathroom. She had not packed for an extended stay. On the next trip into Seattle, she would have to stop by her condo to check her mail and pick up some more clothes and necessities.

She grabbed her phone and checked her email. There was a new note from Nordstrom, announcing the advent of a summer sale, and a nice message from her very good friends at Zappos, telling her that new styles were available from one of her favorite brands of shoes. There were no new emails about the missing lab book or the upcoming auction.

Phone in hand, she went out into the hall. The aroma of freshly brewed coffee and a hint of cinnamon warmed the atmosphere. When she arrived in the kitchen, she found Sam at the stove, spatula in hand. His hair was still damp from the shower. The very interesting dark shadow of a beard that she had noticed in the wee small hours of the night was gone. He was dressed in dark pants and a black pullover.

Newton was sitting on the floor, ears perked, watching Sam's every move. He spared a moment to greet Abby again, and then returned to supervising the breakfast preparations.

Sam looked at Abby, eyes heating a little. "Good morning."

"Good morning," she said. "Did Newton get breakfast?"

She felt awkward, not exactly shy but not really comfortable with the intimacy of their relationship. This was unfamiliar territory, she reflected, more easily navigated at night than in the daylight. But if Sam had any problems with the rapidly evolving status of their relationship, he gave no indication of it. He was acting as if everything from the psi-infused sex to eating breakfast together was all quite normal.

"I fed Newton some of that fancy kibble

you brought along," Sam said. "I think that he would rather have a slice of the French toast that we're going to eat."

"I told you, he's a very smart dog. And it's okay if he has a slice of French toast. Is the coffee ready yet?"

"Help yourself. Mugs are in there." Sam angled his head to indicate the cupboard.

"Thanks."

She opened the door of the cupboard and took down a mug. "Can I pour you another cup?"

"Yes, thanks." He scrutinized her closely. "Any more dreams?"

"None that involved Grady Hastings, thank goodness." She picked up the pot. "You?"

"None that involved Cassidy. I told you, we just need to perfect the experiment."

"Mmm." She poured the coffee, trying to think of what to say next.

"You're not real good with the morning-after conversation, are you?" Sam said. "Yesterday I made allowances because your brother arrived."

"Stepbrother," she corrected automatically.

"But this morning we've got time to talk."

She sipped some coffee. "I thought men didn't like the morning-after conversation."

He flashed her a wickedly sexy grin. "Depends on what actually happened the night before."

She flushed. "In our case, there always seems to be a lot going on the night before. There was me almost setting fire to a red-hot book in my bedroom. A midnight intruder. Bad dreams. A vault full of weird paranormal rocks with unknown powers. To say nothing of the stress of some of our pre-coital activities, such as finding a body and escaping a carjacking and kidnapping."

"Our relationship sure as hell hasn't proceeded along a normal path. I'll give you that."

"Exactly," she said. "Maybe that's why I'm not sure how to have a morning-after conversation with you. Or maybe I simply haven't had a lot of experience in that department. I've had a few relationships, including one or two that I thought might have the potential to go the distance. But they've never lasted long, and I somehow know that going in, so I try not to get overly committed. For some reason, not spending the entire night with someone has always been my way of drawing the line."

"As long as you don't have to face him at breakfast, you can tell yourself it was just a date, not a relationship, is that it?" Sam asked.

"Something like that, yes. According to the counselors at the Summerlight Academy, I have serious trust issues. My father the shrink says I have commitment issues. The combination makes for a one-two punch when it comes to relationships."

Sam shoveled large stacks of French toast onto two plates. "Well, the counselors and your father sure got the diagnosis wrong, didn't they?"

She sputtered on a sip of coffee. *"What?"*

He put the frying pan down on the stone counter. "You don't have trust issues. You're just real careful about whom you trust. And you don't have commitment issues. You've made plenty of commitments, and you've stuck to them."

"What on earth are you talking about?"

"Years ago, you formed solid friendships with Gwen Frazier and Nick Sawyer. You've maintained those friendships for years. You trust both Gwen and Nick. You made friends with Thaddeus Webber, a reclusive, highly eccentric old man who trusted almost no one. But he entrusted you with his secrets, and you kept those secrets. You dutifully appear in book cover photographs to help your father uphold the image of the modern family by choice, even though it wasn't *your* family of choice. And last but by no means least, you are one hundred percent committed to your dog."

She looked at Newton. "One hundred and ten percent."

"See?" Sam set one slice of toast aside to cool. "You can and do make commitments. Ergo, the shrinks at the Summerlight Academy and your father have never fully comprehended you or your issues. But you already know that."

She blinked. "Ergo?"

"It's a technical term." Sam carried the plates to the table. "Thus ends the lecture for this morning. Let's eat."

She went to the table, sat down and studied the French toast. Each slice was thick and puffy and golden brown.

"This is the most beautiful French toast I have ever seen," she said.

"You are obviously hungry."

"Yes, I am. Starving, actually."

One thing about her association with Sam, she thought. She was getting plenty of exercise and burning a lot of calories.

She spread a large pat of butter on the French toast and poured some of the syrup over the top. Working carefully, she forked up a slice of the toast. She munched and swallowed. And immediately went back for another bite. And another.

They ate in a surprisingly companionable silence for a while, no conversation required.

Eventually, Abby put down her fork and picked up her coffee mug. "What about you?" she asked.

Sam paused the fork halfway to his mouth and gave her a look of polite inquiry. "Me?"

"You obviously know how to make commitments. You're certainly committed to keeping the secret of the Phoenix stones."

"So?" He ate the bite of French toast.

"What happened with Cassidy? You said yourself that the two of you were very involved, to the point where many people assumed that you were either engaged or about to be engaged."

Sam lounged back in his chair and stretched his legs out under the table. "The answer is that I did consider marriage for a time. Everything about the relationship with Cassidy seemed perfect, maybe a little too perfect. But something was missing. I kept waiting for the click, you know?"

"The click?"

"The sense that this is the one. I never got it with Cassidy. All I can tell you is that while I was away on that last job with the private contractor, I came to the conclusion that it was time to end things with her."

"Instead, you came home to find her body in the lab." Sudden comprehension flashed through Abby. "That's when you made your real commitment to her. You committed yourself to finding her killer."

"She wouldn't have died if she hadn't been dating me," Sam said. "It was our relationship that put her in harm's way. I've known that since the night she was murdered."

"But if she seduced you and set you up for the theft of the stones . . ."

"Doesn't matter. I'm the one who asked her out on that first date at the gem-and-mineral show. I'm the one who introduced her to Frye. And I'm the one who continued to date her, even after she was hired."

"I understand."

Sam watched her for a long moment.

"Yes," he said. "I can see that you do. You're the only one who does. I'll get some more coffee."

He went to the counter and picked up the pot. He used his free hand to toss a slice of cooled French toast in Newton's general direction. Newton made an agile leap and snatched the toast out of midair.

Abby's phone chimed. She picked it up and glanced at the unfamiliar number.

"I can't imagine who this could be," she said.

She stabbed the connect key.

"Yes?" she said.

"Abigail? Is that you?"

Orinda Strickland spoke in the same clipped, cold, supercilious manner that had frightened the thirteen-year-old Abby. Orinda was no less daunting now that she was in her eighties, but there was a faint rasp that betrayed her age and something else. It took Abby a few seconds to find the right word. *Panic.* It was Orinda who was terrified today, and trying desperately to conceal it.

Abby took a deep breath and silently repeated her mantra. *Show no weakness.*

"Mrs. Strickland. What a surprise. I didn't know you had this number."

"I got it from Dawson."

"I see. Did someone die?"

"That is not amusing."

"It wasn't meant to be. I just can't imagine any other reason why you would want to get in touch with me."

"Nonsense," Orinda snapped. "You're family. Why wouldn't I want to keep in touch?"

"I knew it." Abigail slumped against the back of her chair and contemplated the woods outside the window. Newton came to sit beside her. She put a hand on his head. "This is about Dawson and that investor he's trying to land."

"Dawson told me that he talked to you about finding some old book that he needs to close the deal. He said you refused to help him."

"It's not that simple, Mrs. Strickland."

"Dawson said you won't get the book for him because you still have issues about the past."

"Well, sure, who doesn't? But I repeat, it's not that simple."

"Abigail, you were a very troubled girl. We did what we felt was best for you and the family. You're an adult now. I would have hoped that by this time you would have realized that we had no choice but to send you to that special school. You needed treatment."

"Uh-huh."

"Do you have any idea of how much it cost to send you to the Summer Hill Academy?"

"Summerlight."

"What?" Orinda asked.

"The name of the school was the Summerlight Academy."

"Well, you can't expect me to remember

the name of the school after all these years."

"Gee, that's funny," Abby said. "I've never been able to forget it. And no, in answer to your question, I don't know how much it cost you to dump me there."

"We spent thousands on tuition, room and board and counseling. You should be grateful for all that we did for you."

"Oh, I am," Abby said politely. "Very grateful."

She was aware of Sam watching her. He lounged against the counter, sipping coffee and listening to every word. Newton rested his head on her leg, offering silent comfort.

"The least you can do for the family is find that book for Dawson," Orinda said. "He tells me it is absolutely critical to closing the deal with the investor."

"Yes, he mentioned that. But you're going to have to trust me when I tell you that the book is dangerous."

"Nonsense. It's just a book, not even a very old one at that. We're not talking a medieval manuscript here. Evidently, the investor is obsessed with finding this particular book, however, and has made it clear that it is the price of doing business."

"A lot of people are searching for that same book, and at least one person has already been murdered because of it," Abby said.

"I don't believe that for a second. No one commits murder because of a forty-year-old book. You're making up stories, just like you did when you were a girl. This is about the money, isn't it?"

"No."

"Of course it is," Orinda said. "You have always resented Dawson's inheritance and the trust funds I established for the twins, even though I have explained that you have no right to that money because you have no biological connection to the Strickland line."

"I remember that talk. I told you then, and I'm telling you now, I'm not interested in the Strickland money."

"It's always about the money," Orinda shot back. Anger and conviction rang in her voice. "I would think that after all we've done for you, you would be willing to do this one small favor in return. If your sense of family obligation is so lacking, however, you have my word that you will be compensated for your efforts."

Maybe it was the rare show of emotion or simply the rising panic in Orinda's voice. Whatever the source, it triggered Abby's intuition. She straightened in the chair and braced her elbows on the table.

"This is as close to groveling as I have ever known you to come, Mrs. Strickland."

"I'm not groveling, you ungrateful woman. I'm trying to make you understand that you have a responsibility to help your brother in this crisis."

"Stepbrother," Abby said automatically. "No bloodline connection, remember?"

"That is beside the point. We are a family. Dawson says he could be looking at prison."

"Look, I understand that he's facing bankruptcy, but unless he was the one who was running the Ponzi scheme, I doubt that the Feds will charge him with a crime."

"Don't you understand?" Orinda said. "Whoever lured Dawson into that scheme made sure that when it fell apart, Dawson would take the fall."

"Okay, okay, calm down. Sounds like this all comes down to money. If Dawson is forced to pay off some clients, he can borrow the money from the Strickland trust. Surely he can get a loan from you."

There was a short, jarring silence.

"That is not an option," Orinda said in a flat voice. "The trust is almost entirely depleted."

"What?"

"I had Dawson invest almost the full

amount into that damned Ponzi scheme."

"Oh, for pity's sake. I'm no expert on financial management, but didn't anyone ever give you the talk on diversification of assets? And what about the if-it-looks-too-good-to-be-true-it-probably-is-too-good-to-be-true speech?"

"Don't you dare lecture me, Abigail." Orinda's voice was electrified with anger and tension. "What's done is done. It's not Dawson's fault that the money is gone. Dawson was the victim of a scam. But as a result, the entire family is facing financial ruin. You have got to find that book, Abigail. It's the least you can do after all the trouble you caused us."

The phone went dead in Abby's hand. She looked at Sam.

"In case you didn't figure it out, that was Dawson's grandmother, Orinda Strickland."

"The one who made sure you knew that you were not going to inherit a dime of her money?" Sam asked.

"Yep. Evidently, there is no longer a dime left to be inherited. It seems that she put virtually all of the Strickland money into the Ponzi scheme."

Sam whistled softly and shook his head. He did not say anything.

"I expect the next call will be from Dawson's mother."

"Your stepmother."

"Yes." Abby drummed her fingers on the table. "Although I suppose it's possible they'll get Dad to contact me. It's not like he was going to inherit anything, because he did sign that prenup, but as long as the marriage lasts, he gets to enjoy the many benefits of the Strickland money. If he knows the faucet has been turned off and that the twins' inheritance is at stake, he'll pay attention."

"You think he'll be worried about your half sisters' trust fund?"

"Jessica and Laura are Dad's do-over kids," Abby explained. "Part of the image of the modern family of choice. They're attending a very expensive private college. He won't want to see their tuition cut off."

"This situation," Sam said, "is getting complicated for you."

"Yes, it certainly is." She rose. "I'm going to take a walk. I need some fresh air to clear my head."

Newton sprang to his feet at the word *walk.*

"I'll come with you," Sam said.

Abby turned in the doorway. "I thought you said I'd be safe here on the island."

"You're safe." Sam put his empty mug on

the counter. "I just want to go with you. Do you mind?"

"Suit yourself."

"So gracious," he said, not quite under his breath. "And after all I've done for you."

For the first time in her life, she knew what it meant to see red. She was so outraged, she could scarcely speak.

"Don't you dare try to guilt-trip me," she fumed. "I've just spent the past few minutes talking to a world-class expert."

Sam grinned. "Couldn't resist."

She tried to stay mad, but she just did not have the energy for it. She burst into laughter instead.

"Your sense of humor leaves a lot to be desired," she said.

The misty rain had cleared. The day was starting to warm slowly, but the air was still cool and damp. Abby bundled up in a jacket. Sam put on a windbreaker. Once outside, Newton dashed about madly, bobbing in and out of the trees, glorying in his newfound off-leash freedom.

"I think he hears the call of the wild," Abby said.

"For a condo dog, he certainly has adapted to the country life in a hurry."

Abby looked at the three other houses just barely visible through the woods. "So this is the Coppersmith family compound."

"One of them. There's another one down in Sedona."

Abby gestured toward the houses. "Who lives in those places?"

"My folks built that one for themselves." He pointed to a modern-looking house that overlooked the water. "My mother never did like the old house. Judson and Emma use the other two when they're on the island. We're a close family, but we like our privacy. Also, my parents have long-range visions of a large, extended family with plenty of grandkids."

"But none of you have married."

"Not yet. Mom is starting to push. I think that's why she and Dad got so excited about my relationship with Cassidy. They were so sure she was the one. They're convinced that I'm pining away here on the island, nursing a broken heart."

"I know you aren't brokenhearted, but do you think it's possible that when you were unable to solve the murder you may have become somewhat obsessed with your sense of failure?" Abby asked gently.

"Sure." Sam smiled, a slow, cold smile. "But everything has changed now. I'm on the trail, thanks to you."

They walked across the clearing and came

to a halt at the top of the rocky bluff above the cove.

"Why did your mother name this cove Copper Beach?" Abby asked.

Sam's mouth kicked up at the corner. "One of these days you'll see for yourself."

Not far offshore, a pod of orcas sliced through the waters. The massive black-and-white creatures rose out of the waves in graceful, acrobatic leaps, only to disappear back into the depths.

"That's one of the resident pods," Sam said. "The researchers have them all identified, named and logged. No two orcas have exactly the same markings. Each pod even has its own dialect of the whale language."

"They're stunning when you see them up close like this," Abby said. "They look like they're dancing."

"They're hunting. Takes a lot of food to keep an eight-ton animal going. Looks like they've found a school of salmon. They'll work it as a team, driving the fish up against one of the underwater cliffs here on Legacy. Once the salmon are trapped, the orcas will pull out the knives and forks, otherwise known as very large teeth."

"Nature in the raw. Literally. I prefer my salmon cooked."

"Got news for you, the local fishermen

often use the same technique to catch the salmon you eat. Hunting tactics don't vary all that much from one species to another."

Sam's phone rang. He pulled it out of his jacket and checked the screen. Then he took the call. "Sorry, Dad. Nothing much to report. I told you I'd call as soon as I had something for you."

There was a short pause.

"That's not necessary, Dad," Sam said evenly. "You and Mom already have plans to come up here next week for the tech summit. No need to arrive early."

Another pause.

"I see," Sam said. He sounded resigned. He ended the call and looked at Abby. "That was my father."

"Bad news?" she asked, concerned.

"Depends on your point of view. He and Mom are on their way here to the island. They're due to arrive this afternoon."

25

The Copper Beach diner was nearly empty when Abby arrived. By the time the young waitress brought the coffee to the booth, the place was half full, and more of the locals were ambling in every minute.

"You're good for business," the waitress said in low tones. "Between you and me, the boss is thrilled. Problem is, the only things people are ordering are coffee and doughnuts."

The server looked to be about nineteen. She was cheerful, friendly and unabashedly curious. Her blond hair was secured in a tight ponytail. Her uniform consisted of a pair of jeans and a T-shirt. She was not wearing a name tag. In a town the size of Copper Beach, there was probably no need for one, Abby reflected. She had heard some of the other customers greet the waitress as Brenda.

"Don't knock the coffee and doughnuts,"

Abby said, in an equally soft voice. "High-profit items."

"Sure, for the boss. But people who only order coffee and doughnuts don't leave much in the way of a tip."

"Yes, I know. I've done this kind of work. Sorry about that. Maybe I should put up a sign that says minimum order of a hamburger required if you're here to see the stranger in town. And there will be an extra charge for viewing the dog out front."

Brenda snickered. Abby glanced around the crowded restaurant. Several pairs of eyes quickly slid away. The buzz of artificial conversation got louder. Most of it revolved around fishing and the state of the weather.

"I realize you don't get a lot of tourists here on the island," she said to Brenda, "but are they such a rare species that everyone in town turns out to view a specimen?"

Brenda giggled and leaned closer, on the pretext of collecting the menu. "It's true, we aren't exactly a destination stop in the San Juans. We're not Friday Harbor, that's for sure. Most folks don't even know that Legacy exists, and that's the way people around here like it. The biggest event here all year is coming up next week, that's the annual Coppersmith technical summit. The employees of the R-and-D lab and their families fill up the lodge and the bed-and-breakfast places. There is always a big barbecue on the last night. The whole town is invited."

"What makes me so interesting?"

Brenda winked. "The fact that you're staying out at Sam Coppersmith's place, of course."

"He doesn't have a lot of guests, I take it."

"Are you kidding?" Brenda straightened and did an eye roll. "He hasn't brought a lady friend here since his fiancée was murdered."

"The way I heard it, they were not engaged."

"Well, they weren't. She got killed before they could make it official. But everyone on the island knew that Sam was going to marry her. Losing her like that just about broke his heart."

"I see."

"There was a lot of nasty talk after he found the body. Online, they were calling him Blackbeard. They said any smart woman should be scared to death of him."

"Bluebeard," Abby said.

"Huh?"

"Bluebeard was the name of the seventeenth-century nobleman who was in the habit of murdering his wives, not Blackbeard."

"Oh, yeah. Whatever. Anyhow, the fact that he brought you here is a very big deal. Means his broken heart is mending."

Abby watched Sam walk down the street toward the diner. He had just come out of the post office, but he wasn't carrying any mail. He nodded at the people he passed. They greeted him in a comfortable, relaxed manner.

Newton, secured to a post by his leash, spotted Sam approaching and got to his feet to greet him.

"No one from around here believed for a single minute that Sam had anything to do with that poor woman's murder, you know," Brenda whispered earnestly.

Abby watched Sam pause to scratch Newton behind the ears. "I understand. They believed he was innocent because they knew him and knew the family. They couldn't imagine him committing murder."

"Well, sure, everyone knows the Coppersmiths. They own most of the island. But that's not the reason we all figured Sam didn't kill his fiancée."

"What was the reason?" Abby asked politely. She braced for the answer she knew was coming.

"Simple," Brenda said, with an air of triumph. "Like my dad says, if one of the Coppersmith men decided to murder someone, you can bet there wouldn't be anything left behind to tie him to the scene. Either it would look like an accident or else the body would just disappear. Not that hard to make that happen around here." Brenda nodded in the direction of the small bay. "Lotta deep water out there."

"I've heard that theory," Abby said.

"Yeah, well, obviously you don't think he killed that poor woman. You wouldn't be here if you did, right? Oops, gotta go." Brenda grimaced. "The boss is giving me one of his get-back-to-work looks."

She whisked herself off in the direction of the coffee machine.

Sam opened the door and walked into the diner. Every head in the room swiveled in his direction. There were several rounds of cheerful greetings. Sam responded to the friendly gauntlet with the easy familiarity of someone who knows everyone in the room.

He made his way to the booth where Abby sat alone with her coffee, and lowered himself down onto the vinyl seat on the other side of the table.

Brenda materialized instantly, a thick mug and a pot of coffee in her hands.

"Morning, Sam," she said, her cheeks pink with excitement. "Coffee?"

"Yes, thanks, Brenda. How's your grandmother? Heard she was having some problems."

"She went to see that specialist in Seattle, like your mom suggested. They ran some tests, and he put her on some new meds. They seem to be working. Her blood pressure is under control again."

"Good. Glad to hear it."

Brenda poured the coffee and gave him a dazzling smile. "Can I get you anything else?"

"No, coffee is fine for now. We're waiting for my folks. Dixon is bringing them over from Anacortes. Should be here in a few minutes."

"It'll be nice to see them again," Brenda said.

She went back behind the counter and started to pour coffee.

The background noise of conversation that had faded for a bit returned in full force. Sam raised his mug to swallow some coffee. He stopped when he saw that Abby was looking at him.

"Something wrong?" he asked.

"No," Abby said.

"Okay." Sam shrugged and took a sip.

Abby glared. "Don't be dense. Do you realize that everyone in this diner, probably everyone in town, assumes that we're involved in a relationship?"

Sam struggled with that question for a few seconds and then gave up. "We *are* involved in a relationship."

"Maybe, but it's complicated." She tipped her head slightly, to indicate the crowded restaurant. "Your neighbors here don't understand the nuances. They think we're in a more personal relationship."

"Yeah." Sam drank some more and lowered the mug. He smiled. "That, too."

She leaned forward. "I'm concerned that there will be some widespread misunderstanding here, Coppersmith. This is your home, not mine. What about the gossip?"

"What about it? This is a small town and a small island. Gossip is the lifeblood of the community."

"You're not taking this seriously, are you?"

"What do you want me to do? Stand up and announce that we're sleeping together but that we're not involved in a personal relationship?"

She sat back and drummed her fingers on the table. "Don't say I didn't warn you."

"Relax. You don't care what anyone around here thinks. Once this situation is finished, you'll never see any of these people again, right?"

She did another staccato drumroll and narrowed her eyes. "Right."

"Good. Glad we got that sorted out."

She gave him a steely smile. "Like my dad says in his book on modern marriage, communication is the key to a good relationship."

"Absolutely. Here comes Dixon's water taxi." Sam put down his mug, got to his feet and pulled some money out of his wallet. He dropped the bills on the table. "Time for you to meet the parents."

Abby slipped out from the booth and collected her tote. She walked side by side with Sam, past the curious stares and polite farewells.

Brenda waved a casual good-bye. Abby wiggled her fingers in response. Outside, on the sidewalk, Newton greeted her in his customary over-the-top style. She freed him from the post and wrapped the end of his leash around her wrist.

They walked along Bay Street and watched the water taxi ease into the dock. There were only two passengers on board. The resemblance between Sam and the broad-shouldered, silver-haired man was unmistakable. Same fiercely etched features, same fiercely determined eyes, Abby thought. It was not all that hard to imagine Elias Coppersmith surviving a murder attempt and escaping an underground explosion with a cache of dangerous paranormal crystals. Not so hard to envision a man like this going on to found an empire like Coppersmith Inc., either.

A trim, attractive woman with discreetly tinted blond hair stood beside Elias Coppersmith. Her hands were thrust deep into the pockets of her jacket.

Abby looked at Sam. "Are both of your parents strong talents?"

"Dad definitely has some serious sensitivity for the latent energy in crystals. But he isn't nearly as strong as Judson and Emma and me. He can't run a little psi through any of the stones the way we can, for example."

"What about your mother?"

"I'd say Mom has above-average intuition, but what mother doesn't? And she runs the Coppersmith Foundation like a forensic accountant. But I don't think her ability could be described as psychic. She's just very, very good when it comes to following the money."

"So where did you and your brother and sister get your talent for crystals?"

"Dad says it must have come from farther back on the family tree. Coppersmiths have been involved in mining of one kind or another for generations."

"Sounds like you don't buy that explanation."

"Let's just say that Judson and Emma and I have our own theory. We worked it out a few years ago, but we never told Mom or Dad, because we didn't want to upset them."

"Good grief. Surely you don't think you aren't your father's offspring. You've got your father's eyes, his bone structure . . ."

Sam grinned. "Not that kind of theory. But forty years ago, when that explosion occurred in the Phoenix, there was a hell of a lot of paranormal radiation released. We know that Dad and Knox must have caught a lot of it."

"Oh, my gosh." Abby felt her mouth fall open. She got it closed with an effort. "Are you telling me that you believe that the fallout from the explosion caused some kind of genetic mutation that manifested in you and your brother and sister?"

"Genetics are extremely complicated, even when you're dealing with the normal kind. We don't know much at all about the paranormal aspects."

"True."

"Promise me you won't say anything to Mom or Dad about the theory. Emma says they wouldn't handle it well."

"Okay," Abby said.

Sam went along the dock and grabbed the line that Dixon tossed to him. Then he caught the second one. He secured the water taxi with a few efficient, expert moves, straightened and took his mother's hand. Willow Coppersmith stepped lightly onto the dock. She gave Sam a quick maternal kiss, and then she turned to Abby with a warm smile.

"You must be Abby," she said.

Abby smiled. "Yes."

She started to put out her hand, but Elias bounded out of the bobbing water taxi, interrupting the polite greeting. He gave her a head-to-toe survey. Then he grinned, cold satisfaction glittering in his eyes.

"You got her." He clapped Sam on the shoulder. "Nice work, son. If she's half as good as Webber thought she was, we're going to get that damn book at last."

Abby gave him her best professional smile, the one she reserved for the most eccentric clients. "Nice to meet you, too, Mr. Coppersmith."

26

"You'll have to forgive my husband," Willow Coppersmith said. "Well, actually, you don't have to forgive him for acting as if you're just a useful employee that he can manipulate for his own purposes. But there is an explanation for his rudeness."

"I understand," Abby said.

They were sitting in the living room of the house that Sam's parents had built for themselves. It was not only much newer, it was a lot cozier and warmer than the old house. The modern, two-story windows provided a spectacular view of the water and far more natural light than those in the old stone house.

"To be honest, I thought Elias had abandoned the search for that old notebook," Willow said. "Maybe it would be more accurate to say that I hoped he had given up on it. But after he got the call from his old partner, Quinn Knox, he became obsessed with finding it all over again."

"I did get that impression, yes."

"If he does locate it, I know that he won't rest until he finds the crystals that went missing at the same time. He'll never believe that they were buried in the explosion, not now, after this business of the notebook surfacing."

"It's okay, Mrs. Coppersmith," Abby said, sticking with her polished, professional tone.

"Willow, please."

"Willow. The thing is, I'm accustomed to working for obsessed, difficult and eccentric clients. All part of the job, as far as I'm concerned."

"Ouch." Willow grimaced. "We're not just talking about Elias here, are we? You think Sam is a lot like his father in some ways."

"Well . . ."

Willow sighed. "I prefer to use words like *stubborn* and *determined* rather than *obsessed* and *difficult* to describe them, but you're right. They are good men, but I swear, once they set themselves an objective, it is almost impossible to make them rethink the whole idea."

"Not to worry, Mrs. Coppersmith," Abby said. "I've worked with even stranger clients, believe me. Collectors of the paranormal are always somewhat outside the mainstream."

Willow narrowed her eyes. "So are those who deal in the paranormal."

Abby kept her smile in place. "Takes one to know one."

Willow gave her an assessing look. "You're trying to convince me that your relationship with my son is strictly business, aren't you?"

"A business arrangement is the basis of our association. Sam and I made a deal, you see. He's trying to keep me from being kidnapped by some other collector who is after the notebook. In exchange, I'm trying to find the notebook for him. So far, he has upheld his end of the bargain. I'm still working on my half."

"If your relationship with my son is strictly business, I'm surprised you're staying in the old house. That's his personal residence."

"He had to stash me somewhere," Abby pointed out. "There weren't a lot of options. Someone did try to kidnap me, you know."

"Yes, I heard about what happened after you found Webber's body. That must have been a terrifying experience."

Abby pursed her lips. "I wouldn't say it ranked quite that high on my personal fear-and-panic meter. I reserve that category of terrifying for my step-grandmother. But the carjack incident definitely met the criteria for extremely alarming. Sam handled it brilliantly, though. Like I said, he is holding up his end of the deal."

Willow considered her with a thoughtful expression. "You are a very unusual woman, Abby."

"Just trying to do my job."

"Did Sam tell you that he's had some experience investigating paranormal crimes?"

"I think he said something about having done some work for the post office."

Willow's eyes widened. "The post office?"

"Never mind." Abby smiled. "Inside joke. Yes, he mentioned his consulting work."

"He told you about those jobs?"

"Not a lot," Abby admitted. "Between you and me, I think he was trying to reassure me that he does know what he's doing. Giving me his résumé, as it were."

Willow regarded her with a long, considering look. "Neither Sam nor Judson are in the habit of telling people about the nature of their consulting work. In fact, I would be willing to bet that Sam has never mentioned it to any of the other women he has been involved with in the past."

"To be clear, Sam and I are not exactly involved, at least not seriously involved. Not in the way you mean."

Willow brushed that aside. "I suppose you've heard about what happened to the last woman he dated."

"Hard not to know about it, under the circumstances. I got the first lecture on the subject from Dixon. Got another from a friend of mine who Googled Sam. Got the story from Sam. And last but not least, today I received yet another lecture on the subject from the waitress at the diner in town."

Willow's lips thinned. "I hate to hear that everyone is still talking about it."

"I understand."

"You don't seem concerned about the old rumors."

"Nope. Thaddeus Webber would never have sent me to Sam if he thought there was any danger involved. And my friend Gwen vouched for Sam."

"Who's Gwen?"

"She's a psychic counselor. Reads auras."

"Good grief. You decided to trust my son because your friend claimed to be able to see his aura?"

"Gwen is a genuine talent, and she is very, very good," Abby said coolly. "But I can see that even though you're married to a man who has a considerable amount of talent himself, and you've got two sons and a daughter with exceptional abilities, you don't really want to buy into the whole paranormal thing any more than is absolutely necessary."

Willow grimaced. "I've always realized that my husband and Sam and Emma and Judson all have unusual sensitivities. But I prefer to think of their gifts as being more in the nature of very powerful intuition."

Abby smiled. "You're okay with the concept of intuition?"

"Yes, of course." Willow moved a hand slightly. "I'm sure that most people have experienced a flash of intuition at one time or another in their lives. Unfortunately, they don't always listen to their inner voice."

Abby smiled. "That's true."

Willow's brows came together in a severe expression. "But that doesn't mean there is any need to resort to the concept of paranormal forces in order to explain my husband's and my sons' and daughter's abilities."

"Okay," Abby said.

"I don't want to debate the existence of the paranormal with you," Willow said quietly. "I want to make sure you understand my son. Cassidy's murder affected him very deeply. He did not realize that she was a complete fraud and had set him up until it was too late. He was heartbroken after he found the body."

"Well . . ."

"Now I'm afraid he no longer trusts his own judgment or his heart. In the past few months, I have become increasingly concerned about him. He has retreated into himself and that old house of his more and more. He only leaves the island these days when he absolutely has to go into the Black Box lab or when he takes one of those dreadful jobs for that private contractor. I think he uses the work to distract himself. He is not engaged with life, if you know what I mean."

"Hmm."

"What?" Willow asked, her tone sharpening.

"I agree with you that Sam has more or less imprisoned himself in the Copper Beach house. But it's not because his heart is broken or because he's afraid to love."

"No?" Willow watched her closely. "What, then?"

"You have to see the situation from his point of view. As far as Sam is concerned, Cassidy was a victim."

"She was a thief." Willow gripped the arm of her chair very tightly. "She seduced Sam so that she could steal the Phoenix crystals."

"He doesn't see it that way. He's the one who started the relationship and then continued it, breaking some unwritten rule about dating employees in the process. He blames himself for not getting a handle on the situation sooner. His heart isn't broken. But he's a man of honor, and he's got an over-the-top, steel-clad sense of responsibility. Plus he's just plain mad."

"He is not mad," Willow snapped. "Don't you dare say that."

"Sorry, I meant angry mad, not crazy mad. Poor choice of words. The thing is, it's intolerable to him that such a crime was committed in his home. He's been brooding over Cassidy's murder because he hasn't been able to bring the killer to justice."

"Good lord." Willow took a long moment to absorb that information. "You may be right. None of us looked at it from that angle. We were all so certain that Cassidy broke his heart with her betrayal."

"Don't worry, I'm sure it would take a lot more than that to break Sam's heart. Frankly, I'm not certain it's even possible."

"And here I was just starting to think that you knew Sam better than his own family does," Willow said. "You have a few things to learn about him as well, Abby."

27

Elias materialized in the doorway. "Well? any more leads on that Milton character?"

Newton, napping beside Abby's chair, stirred, raised his head, and focused on Elias.

"Maybe." Abby pushed herself away from the glowing computer screen and got to her feet. "But if you keep interrupting me every five minutes, it will take me forever to follow up on them."

Elias beetled his brows. "I thought I made it clear, we don't have a lot of time. You need to find Milton before he holds that auction. I don't want to take the risk of losing that damn lab book."

"I'm doing my best, Mr. Coppersmith. But in the meantime, I've assured Milton that we will top any bid, and he has agreed to give us that option."

"If Lander Knox gets to him first, there won't *be* an auction. He'll murder the dealer the way he did Webber and take the notebook."

"I realize that we're in a time crunch here. Which is why I would prefer to work without someone looking over my shoulder. But since you have interrupted me, I'm going to the kitchen to get some coffee."

She walked toward Elias. Newton sprang to his feet and padded after her. Faced with the oncoming woman and dog, Elias reluctantly fell back into the hall. Abby slipped past him, Newton at her heels, and headed for the kitchen. Elias stalked after them.

"What did you mean by 'maybe'?" he demanded.

"I meant maybe, as in maybe I have a couple of leads." Abby walked into the kitchen. "You need to understand that I don't usually work with dealers like Milton. I know how to contact him, thanks to Thaddeus and my friend Nick, but I don't know anything else about him."

"Thaddeus is gone, but what about this Nick you mentioned? Does he deal with Milton?"

"Yes, but I can't ask him for more information."

"Why not?"

"Because currently he's my competition. He's after the lab book, too. Knowing Nick, by now he'll have lined up a client."

"Knox."

"It's possible, but I think it's unlikely," Abby said.

"Why?"

"The clients in the deep end are more dangerous than the ones I usually work with, but Nick is not stupid. He takes precautions. Lander Knox is an unknown in the underground market. He's not a regular collector. Nick wouldn't want to take him on as a client, especially if he's got options."

"Hah. Options like Hank Barrett or his son."

"The owners of Helicon Stone?" Abby picked up the coffeepot. "That's a much more likely possibility. Can I pour you a cup?"

"Yeah, sure."

"You're so very welcome," she murmured, going for excruciatingly gracious.

Elias was oblivious to the sarcasm. He started to pace the kitchen. "Maybe I've been too focused on Lander Knox. No question that he's after the lab book. But if Hank Barrett has heard the rumors, he or his son will be trying to find it as well. They might be a bigger problem than Knox, if for no other reason than that they have the money to pay top dollar."

Abby handed him a full mug as he stomped past her. "There are other problems with auctions like this. I think that Milton is reliable, but we have to allow for the possibility that the book he is going to auction off is a forgery."

Elias's face worked in outrage. "Are you telling me that someone might try to pass off a fake?"

"A shocking notion, isn't it?" Abby smiled wryly. "I regret to tell you that forgeries are actually quite common in the rare-book business."

"If someone thinks he can scam me, he'd better start running now."

"Mmm."

"What?" Elias stopped to glare at her. "You don't think I know how to deal with con men and scammers?"

"I'm sure you would be a very dangerous man to cross, Mr. Coppersmith," she said politely.

Elias finally appeared to notice that he was missing something in the conversation.

"Are you laughing at me?" he said with a growl.

"Wouldn't dream of it. As I told your wife, I accept the fact that tolerating difficult, eccentric, obsessive clients is a necessary aspect of my work, but I should warn you that I have some limits."

For a couple seconds, Elias looked bewildered. Then comprehension lit his fierce eyes. "Are you calling me difficult, eccentric and obsessive?"

Sam appeared in the doorway. "Take it easy, Dad. You get used to her after a while." He looked at Abby. "Bill, the lawyer, tracked down the name and address of the psychiatric hospital where Grady Hastings is undergoing observation. We have to go into Seattle tonight for your father's book-launch event. We'll stay the night at your place and interview Hastings first thing in the morning."

"Sounds like a plan," Abby said.

"Any coffee left?"

"Yep," Abby said. She picked up the pot.

Elias rounded on Sam. "She thinks we're both wackos."

"I never said anything of the kind." Abby frowned. "If I thought you were both out-and-out crazies, I would not have taken you on as clients. And I definitely would not have hired Sam to protect me."

"What's the difference between Sam and me and a couple of crazies?" Elias roared.

Abby nearly choked on her laughter. She looked at Sam and knew that he was having a hard time biting back a grin. She cleared her throat.

"An interesting question," she said. She turned around to pour the coffee. "Let's just say I know it when I see it."

"Are you sure you got the right Abigail Radwell?" Elias asked Sam.

"Oh, yeah," Sam said, with deep feeling. "No way there could be two of them, trust me."

The wicked, intimate certainty in his words thrilled Abby's senses. The pot in her hand trembled ever so slightly when she poured the coffee.

"I don't get it," Elias grumbled. "If you think Sam and I are such difficult clients, why did you agree to work for us?"

"You and your son certainly top my personal list of demanding clients," Abby said. She put the pot back on the burner and turned around to face the men. "Furthermore, I am convinced that either one of you would cheerfully commit murder if you felt the circumstances warranted it."

"What circumstances?" Elias thundered.

"If you thought it was necessary to protect someone in your family, for example," Abby said.

"Hell, yes," Elias said.

"Sure," Sam said. "So what?"

"I like that in a man," Abby said.

28

". . . to summarize, the modern so-called blended family, the family by choice, is nothing new." Dr. Brandon C. Radwell surveyed his audience from the lectern. "There have always been families consisting of children and adults who are related not necessarily by blood but by a complex web of social connections. The major difference today is that while old-fashioned blended families came into existence out of necessity, today's blended families are formed by deliberate choices of the individuals involved."

"The *adult* individuals involved," Abby whispered to Sam. "The kids rarely have any say in the matter. It's Mom and Dad who decide to get divorced and start over with another spouse."

"Take it easy," Sam said. He patted her knee.

A couple of heads turned to glare at Abby.

Someone shushed her.

Abby glanced at her watch. *Not much longer,* she thought, relieved.

The small auditorium was full. She and Sam were seated in the last row. From her position, she could see her stepmother, Diana; the twins, Jessica and Laura; and Dawson in the front row. The room was packed with her father's adoring fans. Each one clutched a copy of *Families by Choice.* A video crew was busy filming the scene.

Her father might be a serial monogamist, Abby thought, but he did have a way with a crowd. No wonder his publisher was delighted to send him out on tour. The man could sell books. With his good looks, charisma and a knack for the thirty-second sound bite, he was the ideal talk-show guest.

A burst of applause went up from the audience. Abby clapped dutifully and leaned closer to Sam.

"Told you he was good," she said.

"You were right," Sam said. "The man's a natural for television."

At the front of the room, Brandon bestowed a beatific smile on his audience. "Before I sign those books you all bought at the door, I want to introduce you to my own family by choice. My lovely wife, Diana; my son Dawson; my oldest daughter, Abby; and my two younger daughters, Jessica and Laura. I'd like them to come up here now, so that I can tell them in front of this audience how proud I am of each of them and how grateful I am to have the support of such a warm and loving family."

"This is the worst part," Abby confided to Sam. She got to her feet. "But it doesn't last long. See you in a few minutes."

"I'll be waiting," Sam said.

It was just a casual remark, but for some reason Abby suddenly felt a little more cheerful. She pasted on her best professional smile. Under cover of another round of applause, she went down the aisle. By the time she reached the front of the room, the others had already joined her father on the stage. She climbed the three steps and took up a position next to Jessica and Laura. Dawson studiously ignored her.

Jessica leaned closer to Abby. "Mom said you probably wouldn't show. But I knew you would."

"Not like I had anything better to do tonight," Abby whispered back.

Laura and Jessica giggled. Abby smiled. She hadn't spent much time with the twins. She had been packed off to the Summerlight Academy shortly after they were born. The difference in their ages and the long separation had put a lot of distance into the relationship. Nevertheless, Abby was fond of the pair. For their part, Laura and Jessica treated her like an aunt rather than a sister, but the arrangement worked for all three of them. Abby suspected that the twins secretly admired her because she held the role of the proverbial black sheep of the family.

At the lectern, Brandon clasped Diana's hand and raised it upward so that their wedding rings glinted in the light. He smiled again, an icon of Perfect Father and Ideal Husband. Abby and the others smiled dutifully and did their best to look like a happy family.

"This is what the modern family by choice looks like, my friends," Brandon said. "It functions the way family is supposed to function. Sure, there are the occasional conflicts and arguments. Building a family by choice can be hard work. But anything in life that is worthwhile requires hard work. The Radwells have done it, and so can you."

Another round of applause swept through the room. Abby and the others kept their smiles fixed in place.

Under cover of the applause, Laura edged closer to Abby.

"Mom and Grandma and Dawson are really pissed at you," Laura warned.

"I know," Abby said out of the side of her mouth. "But Dad made it clear that this was one of those command-performance gigs."

Jessica wrinkled her nose. "Not sure what's going on, but we think Dawson screwed up big-time. I heard Grandma telling Mom that he's trying to close a really important deal. She said that you could help him, but you won't on account of you're jealous because you didn't inherit any of her money. Is that true?"

"No," Abby said. "Not true."

"Hah." Jessica looked satisfied. "I knew there was more to it." She immediately switched subjects. "Who's the hot new boyfriend?"

"Boyfriend?" Abby repeated blankly.

"The guy you came here with tonight," Jessica hissed in a low voice. "The one at the back of the room in the leather jacket. Looks a lot more interesting than Kane Thurston."

Abby followed her gaze and saw Sam. He stood with his arms folded, one shoulder propped against the wall, watching her.

"Oh, him." Abby pulled herself together. "His name is Sam Coppersmith, and he is definitely a lot more interesting than Kane."

"Uh-oh," Jessica said.

Abby looked at her. "Uh-oh what?"

"We heard Dawson talking to Mom about someone named Coppersmith. He said the Coppersmiths have tons of money. They even have a private island in the San Juans."

Abby was saved from having to respond, because the moderator had moved to the lectern and was announcing that the author would now sign his book and that refreshments were available.

Abby stepped off the stage, followed by Laura, Jessica, Dawson, Diana and Brandon. They ended up in a small cluster.

Brandon looked pleased. He glanced at Diana. "I think that went very well, don't you?"

Diana smiled, but there was a strained expression in her eyes. "They loved you, dear."

The event coordinator, a small, spare, middle-aged woman with glasses and neon-red hair, materialized at Brandon's elbow. She was as focused as an air traffic controller. "I'll escort you to the table, Dr. Radwell."

"In a moment, Lucy," Brandon said. "Family comes first. I want to have a chat with my eldest daughter before I sign books." He winked. "It's a father thing."

Out of the corner of her eye, Abby saw

Dawson grimace. Jessica and Laura rolled their eyes.

Lucy did not look happy about that, but she rallied. "In that case, I'll direct people to the refreshment table until you're ready."

"Good idea." Brandon gave Abby his patented paternal smile. "How about introducing me to the new man in your life, honey?"

A wave of anxiety swept through Abby. On the rare occasions when Brandon chose to play the concerned father, things rarely turned out well.

"Sam is a client," she said quickly. "There's nothing personal between us."

Brandon chuckled just loud enough so that people standing nearby could hear him. "You can't fool your dad. A father always knows when another man is interested in his little girl. I could tell from the way he walked into the room with you that there is definitely a very personal aspect to your relationship." He looked around, frowning a little. "Where did he go?"

Sam materialized out of the crowd directly behind Brandon.

"I'm right here, sir," Sam said. "Sam Coppersmith."

Brandon turned easily, radiating his charismatic smile, and extended his hand.

"Brandon Radwell. A pleasure to meet you. I have a few minutes before I start signing. Why don't we find a quiet place for a quick chat?"

"Sure," Sam said. He looked at Abby. "Don't wander off."

"We don't have a lot of time," Abby said through her teeth. "Dad needs to sign books."

"This won't take long," Brandon said.

The two men walked through the crowd to a quiet corner of the room. Abby watched, deeply uneasy. When she turned back, she realized that Dawson had vanished.

"Done," Laura said, relief evident in her voice. "Jessica and I get to leave now, right, Mom? You said we only had to stay for the perfect family scene."

"Yes, you can go," Diana said. She looked at Abby. "I want to talk to you."

"I'm afraid I'm a little busy this evening," Abby said. "I've got plans."

"After all I've done for you," Diana said, her voice low and hard, "and after all I put up with over the years, the least you can do is give me a few minutes of your precious time."

Abby sighed. "I knew I shouldn't have come here tonight."

29

Brandon switched off the engaging smile and slipped into concerned-father mode with effortless ease. The serious expression was just right, Sam thought. It consisted of a slightly furrowed brow, faintly narrowed eyes and a dash of paternal concern.

"My daughter tells me that you're one of her clients," Brandon said.

"Our relationship is complicated," Sam said.

One of Brandon's brows edged upward. "Aren't they all?"

"Good point."

Sam watched Abby and Diana disappear into a hallway. From where he stood, he could see that the corridor was lined with twin rows of offices. One of the doors was ajar. Abby and Diana went into the room. The lights came on. The door closed. *Not good,* Sam thought. But Abby had been dealing with her stepmother for a long time now. She could handle whatever was going down inside the office.

"How did the two of you meet?" Brandon asked.

"Through one of Abby's business connections," Sam said.

"She is in a rather unusual line of work."

"Antiquarian books that are associated with the paranormal. Yes, I know."

Brandon cleared his throat. "You collect those kinds of books?"

"I've got a few."

"I see. Has she told you that she doesn't just deal in books about magic, she actually believes in the occult?"

Annoyed, Sam jerked his gaze away from the closed office door. "Abby doesn't believe in the occult. Where the hell did you get that idea?"

"I don't know what my daughter has told you, but you need to know that she holds some weird theories."

"She believes in the existence of paranormal energy, not the occult."

"There's a difference?" Brandon asked drily.

"The occult is all about witchcraft, demons and magic," Sam said, impatient now. "Paranormal energy, on the other hand, is just that, energy. There's no magic, black or white, involved. Although there are a lot of fake psychics, mediums and dream analysts out there making a good living off the gullible."

Brandon's frown turned into a scowl. "Don't tell me you're into this paranormal crap, too?"

"I'm surprised to hear you say that, Dr. Radwell. You're in the psychobabble business. Surely you are aware that shared interests form the best basis for an enduring relationship."

Brandon's expression sharpened. "You read my book on marriage?"

"No. Just took a flying leap in the dark."

"Stop with the bullshit, Coppersmith. We both know why you're dating my daughter."

"We do?"

"You found out she's connected to the Strickland family, didn't you? You're not the first man to try to marry her for her inheritance. But there isn't one. The old bitch, better known as Orinda Strickland, controls the family money. Take it from me, she has gone to great legal lengths to make sure that Abby won't receive a dime. It all goes to my wife, and Dawson and the twins."

"I heard she cut you out, too."

Brandon snorted in disgust. "Prenup. And I was dumb enough to sign the papers.

Thought that after the old bitch died, Diana would change her mind and tear up the agreement."

"But?"

"But at the rate she's going, Orinda may outlive me, and I've had it with the waiting game. Time to move on." Brandon glanced across the room. "Lucy is signaling. Got to go sign some books. Just remember what I told you. Abby has no blood connection to the old bitch. In fact, Orinda is downright embarrassed that Abby is considered a member of the family. That translates into no inheritance."

"You think I'm after the Strickland money?"

"That sure as hell was the agenda of that bastard Kane Thurston."

"Who is Kane Thurston?"

"The last man Abby dated seriously," Brandon said.

"I'll be damned. You're a complete con and a hypocrite, Radwell, not to mention a lousy father, but in your own stumbling, fumbling way, you're trying to protect Abby from me, aren't you? Guess I've got to give you some credit for paternal instincts."

Brandon's jaw sagged. Shock blanked his eyes for a few seconds, but he managed to pull himself together.

"Abby is an adult," he said, between gritted teeth. "I can't tell her what to do, but I'm going to warn her about you. Don't think I won't."

He walked swiftly away through the crowd. By the time he sat down to sign books, he had his warm, father-knows-best smile firmly back in place.

30

"This is about Dawson and the deal he's trying to close, isn't it?" Abby said. "I've already explained to him that I can't help him."

"Keep your voice down." Diana glanced at the closed door of the office. "This is your father's breakout launch. I won't allow you to ruin it."

Abby measured the distance to the door. "I don't think this is a good idea."

The office was cramped and utilitarian. Metal file cabinets lined one wall. The window looked out over the street.

Diana folded her arms. "I'll come straight to the point. My mother says that she will redo the Strickland trust to include you if you agree to get that book for Dawson."

"Wow. She really is panic-stricken."

"That's putting it mildly. What's more, she's not the only one."

"The financial situation is that bad?"

"Yes," Diana said. "It's that bad."

"What about Dad's new book? If it sells well, that should help the family finances. And if the reality TV show comes through, that will be even better."

"The book and the TV project would both have to do phenomenally well to make up for what Dawson lost. Even if, by some fluke, the book does become a bestseller and the reality series takes off, the income will be Brandon's, not mine. That prenup my mother forced me to sign protects him, the same way it does me. He won't have to give me a dime."

"Oh, man. No wonder you and Orinda are having fits. Does Dad know what's going on?"

"No," Diana said, her jaw very tight. "I don't want him to find out. Do you understand? He married me for my money and my connections. I've known that for years. If he discovers that I'm on the verge of losing both, he'll be gone in a heartbeat."

"That is his pattern," Abby agreed. "His first wife dropped out of college to finance his Ph. D. He dumped her the day after he graduated. His second wife was one of his research assistants. That was my mother. He borrowed a lot of her work, which he published as his own. He divorced her to marry one of his wealthy patients. That would be you."

Diana reddened with fury. "Shut up. I know his history better than anyone, including you. That's why I know he's planning to leave me as soon as the TV show is a sure thing. In fact, I'm almost positive he's having an affair with the woman who is producing the pilot."

Abby said nothing. She looked down at her hands.

Diana made a soft, disgusted sound. "You were aware of that?"

"No, but I'm not surprised." Abby raised her eyes. "If you knew about his problem with monogamy, why did you stay married to him all these years?"

Diana's eyes glittered with barely subdued fury and frustration. "You haven't got a clue, do you? I divorced my first husband because he was an abusive man. My mother warned me not to marry him, but I didn't listen. But after Dawson was born, I realized I had to get out in order to protect him and myself. I married your father because I thought he truly cared for me and because I believed that he would be a good male role model for my son. Then the twins came along. Things were okay for a few years, but eventually I realized Brandon was having affairs on the side. I made myself tolerate his infidelity."

"For the sake of Dawson and the twins?" Abby said, surprised. "You didn't want to put them through a divorce? That was very self-sacrificing of you, Diana. I admit, I would never have guessed . . ."

"Don't be ridiculous. I didn't stay with your father because of Dawson and the twins. They could have handled a divorce. Half their classmates all through school were children of divorced parents."

"Right." Abby checked her watch again. "Okay, I get the picture. You're finally ready to divorce Dad, but suddenly you're trapped. You can't leave him, because you don't have the Strickland money to fall back on. And you think he's getting ready to leave you before his own ship comes in."

"Now do you see how important it is for Dawson to recover from the financial losses? I swear that if you help him get that book for his investor, I'll make sure that you receive a fair share of my mother's money."

"Always assuming Dawson can recover it for her."

"He will," Diana vowed.

"The thing is, I don't want your mother's money," Abby said quietly.

"Because you think you've landed on your

feet with Sam Coppersmith? Don't fool yourself, Abby. It won't last." Diana went to the door and wrenched it open. She paused in the opening and looked back over her shoulder. "Money doesn't just follow blood. When it comes to marriage, it usually follows other money. There are occasional exceptions, but they rarely end well. Witness my marriage to your father."

Abby looked at her. "There's just one thing here I don't understand. If you wanted to leave Dad and you didn't feel compelled to stick with the marriage because of Dawson and the twins, why in heaven's name didn't you file for divorce a long time ago?"

Bitterness edged Diana's mouth. "In a word? Mother."

"Why was she a factor? She never approved of Dad, anyway. I would have thought she would have been delighted to see you split."

"Oh, yes," Diana said. "She would have been thrilled. You want the truth? I didn't leave Brandon years ago when I should have because I didn't want to give her the satisfaction of proving that she was right. Again."

Diana went out into the hall. Abby listened to the fading echo of high heels on the tile floor.

Sam materialized in the doorway. "Everything okay in here?"

"Sure," Abby said. "Just a little family chat. But I learned something tonight."

"What's that?"

"Even for a Strickland, it's not always about the money."

"Funny you should mention that. I just had a talk with your father and came to the conclusion that it's not always about the money for him, either."

"What do you mean?"

"He wanted to make sure that I knew you weren't going to inherit a dime from the Strickland trust. He was trying to protect you from being married for your non-existent money."

"Oh." Startled, Abby took a moment to process that. "Huh."

"Can we leave now?"

"Yes," Abby said. "We can leave. In fact, I can't wait to get out of here."

31

Sam got behind the wheel, but he did not immediately fire up the engine. He contemplated the warmly lit windows of the auditorium across the street. There was still a large crowd inside.

"Tell me about Kane Thurston," he said.

Startled, Abby gave him a quick, searching look. "There's not much to tell." She buckled her seat belt. "He wasn't the first man I've dated who thought I was in line for a share of the Strickland money. People make that mistake all the time."

"Because everyone makes a show of pretending that you're all just one big happy family?"

"The power of branding."

"Who told Kane that you weren't fated to inherit the Strickland family fortune?"

"I did," Abby said. "As soon as I realized what he was after. Felt like an idiot for a while, because I can usually spot the con artists right away. But to give Kane his due, he is a very, very good con artist. He didn't fool Gwen and Nick, though. They saw right through him the first time they met him and warned me."

"You didn't doubt their verdict?"

"No, although I went into denial for a while before I admitted to myself that they were right. In the end, I knew I had to trust Nick and Gwen. And once I started looking at Kane with clear eyes, I realized they were right. Sorry you got the lecture from Dad. I've tried to make it clear to everyone in the family that you are just a client, but they all seem to be assuming the worst-case scenario."

"The worst-case scenario being that I might actually want to marry you?"

She winced. "I didn't mean it quite like that. Sorry. It's been a difficult evening."

"I assume your stepmother wanted to talk to you about Dawson's financial problems?"

"What else? She's desperate to recover the family fortune, in part because she wants to end the marriage to Dad. She figures my father already has one foot out the door, which is a logical assumption. If the book and the TV series do take off, he'll probably move on."

"He did say something about that. I think

he's given up on plan A."

"Which was?"

"Hoping that Orinda Strickland would kick the bucket first. He seems to think that if she wasn't in the picture, he would be able to convince Diana to tear up the prenup."

"Maybe once upon a time he could have done that. Dad has occasionally been known to use his knowledge of psychology to manipulate others. Got a hell of a track record in that department. But it's too late now. Diana definitely wants out. The only reason she's hesitating is because she does not want to end up broke."

"Why did she stay with him this long?" Sam asked.

"Didn't want to give her mother the satisfaction of being able to say I-told-you-so." Abby shook her head. "Can you believe it? Spend nearly two decades with a man because you don't want to admit your mother was right about him?"

Sam cranked the engine. "Families."

"A constant source of entertainment."

"They keep life interesting. You really think your dad hung around this long because of the Strickland money?"

"Sure. Even though he's not an heir, it has certainly made life very comfortable for him and provided him with a lot of social connections." Abby paused. "And to think that he doesn't yet know that it's gone. I wonder when they'll give him the bad news?"

"Good question."

Sam reversed the SUV out of the slot and drove onto the street, heading downtown. The lights of the city's office buildings, hotels and apartment towers glittered like watery jewels through the rain-splashed windshield.

"Just one more question about Kane Thurston," he said.

"What?"

"Was he ever there for breakfast?"

"Nope. Although I did meet him for brunch at a restaurant a few times. Does that count?"

"No," he said. "Brunch in a restaurant doesn't count."

Abby's phone chimed. She reached into her purse, grabbed the device and glanced at the caller ID.

"It's Nick," she said. Her tone was suddenly a few degrees brighter. She took the call. "Hey, Nick."

Sam heard the easy familiarity and affection in her voice and felt a tug of simple, primal jealousy. Knowing Nick was gay did nothing to assuage the response. Abby was closely bonded with her friends. She'd had years to forge the connections among herself and Nick and Gwen. He, on the other hand, was a newcomer in her life, and as far as she was concerned, their relationship was not easy to define. The passion was high-energy, but he knew she did not fully trust the intimacy that it generated. It was all happening too fast for her.

She needed time to recognize and accept the bond between them, he thought. But meanwhile, he did not have to like the fact that he was playing second fiddle to a cat burglar and a psychic who read auras for a living, to say nothing of the dog.

"Are you sure?" Abby's tone altered abruptly. Alarm edged her voice. She leaned forward in the seat, phone clamped to her ear. "Nick, wait, don't hang up. What do you mean? Tell me what's going on. . . . Okay, okay, I've got it. Code red. . . . Yes, he's with me. . . . Yes. Ten minutes. I promise."

She ended the connection and sat very still, phone clenched in one hand. She had been tense all evening, but what she was radiating now was off the charts.

"What's wrong?" Sam asked.

"There's a bar on a side street half a block

off Broadway," she said urgently. "It's not far from here. We need to go there right now. Nick is waiting."

"What's with 'code red'?" Sam asked.

"It was the old signal that the three of us used when we were in the Summerlight Academy. It means what code red always means. Something very bad has happened."

32

Lander Knox studied the back-cover photo on his copy of *Families by Choice* while he waited in line. The smiling faces of the Radwell family stirred the deep wellspring of hot acid inside him. It was all he could do not to hurl the book at the author's head. *Just one big happy family.*

He took out the small bottle of acid-reducer pills and popped one into his mouth. The picture was deceptive, he reminded himself. Things were no longer quite so perfect for the Radwell clan, thanks to his financial games. The knowledge that he had caused some serious collateral damage soothed him.

Acquiring the lab book and a psychic who could break the code that protected his inheritance was still his primary objective. But the loss of the Strickland money was starting to send shock waves through the family. It was obvious that not everyone in the clan knew what had happened yet. But during their last lunch together, he had sensed the panic and helpless anger that seethed inside Orinda Strickland. The old woman was terrified. And tonight he had glimpsed the strain in Diana Radwell's eyes. *Not much longer now,* he thought. Soon they would all be forced to confront the enormity of their impending financial doom.

It would be interesting to see what happened when the bankruptcy ax fell. The old lady would probably have a heart attack, for starters. And it was a known fact that major financial problems often caused divorce. The Radwells' marriage would no doubt be the next casualty. Dawson was already awash in guilt and viewed himself as a failure. There was no telling where that might lead. It was not unheard of for a man who had lost everything to commit suicide. The pretty blond twins would no longer be able to afford the sky-high tuition at the private college they attended. In the end, the picture-perfect Radwell family would be devastated.

The hot acid sank back into the bottom of the well. Lander suddenly felt much better. The person ahead of him in line thanked Radwell for the signed book and moved out of the way. Dr. Brandon C. Radwell smiled.

"How would you like the book inscribed?" Brandon asked.

"Would you mind making it out to 'Lander, who will one day choose a family of his own'?"

"Certainly." Brandon wrote quickly and signed the book. "Good luck to you, Lander. Remember, family is everything. Choose wisely."

"I'll do that, Dr. Radwell."

33

From the outside, the nightclub looked like a low-rent dive. It resembled a lot of the other clubs in the Capitol Hill neighborhood. The door and the street-front windows were painted black. But when Sam ushered Abby inside, they were greeted with a comfortable, upscale space warmed by a large stone fireplace. The back bar gleamed with polished wood and glass.

A grand piano occupied one corner of the room. A middle-aged woman dressed in a beaded gown, her blond hair piled high, played a classic show tune. Her makeup was elaborate. Rhinestones dripped from her ears and draped her throat and wrists.

The clientele was a surprising mix of male and female, but the body language made it clear that the men and women at the tables were friends, not dates. The dress code was eclectic, tending toward high-end designer jeans, shirts and slouchy jackets for the men. The drinks were mostly variations on martinis and cosmopolitans.

A few heads turned when Sam and Abby walked into the room, but after a brief, discreet scrutiny, everyone went back to their drinks and conversation.

Nick sat alone in a booth at the back of the room. There was a blue martini on the table in front of him, but it appeared to be untouched. Abby slid onto the seat across from him. Sam sat down beside her. Nick gave him a bored look.

"I see you're still hanging around," Nick said.

"Sure," Sam said. "I live in hope that one day you and I will be friends."

"Don't count on it."

"I'm crushed, of course," Sam said. "But I'm sure I'll get over it."

Abby leaned forward. "What's going on, Nick?"

"As of five-thirty this afternoon, I am no longer your competition," Nick said. "I fired my client, and I stopped looking for that hot encrypted book. If you've got any sense, you'll quit looking for it, too."

"What happened?" Abby asked.

"Benny Sparrow had a heart attack and died in his shop last night."

"Not Benny, too," Abby whispered.

"Yeah." Nick took a small taste of his drink and set the glass down. "I was willing to overlook Webber's heart attack. He was an old man and in bad health. Stuff happens. But now that Benny has checked out the exact same way, we're looking at one too many coincidences."

"Who was Benny Sparrow?" Sam asked.

"One of the three or four deep-end dealers most likely to be using the alias of Milton," Nick said.

"The killer must have gotten Benny's name from Thaddeus," Abby said.

"Looks like it," Nick said.

"Do you think Benny had the notebook?" Sam asked.

"If he did, the killer has it now," Nick said. "We won't know one way or another until we find out if the auction is still on. So far, there hasn't been any update." He turned to Abby. "This thing is way beyond a deep-end deal. We're talking the Mariana Trench. Time to bail, my friend."

"I can't, Nick," Abby said.

"Listen to me, Abby. You need to dump Coppersmith here, and get the hell out of Dodge. Like right now. I'm leaving town tonight. You can come with me."

"If the book is locked in a psi-code, then leaving town won't do me much good,"

Abby pointed out. "If the killer does have the book and decides he needs me, he'll come looking. I can't run forever."

"I can set you up with a clean ID," Nick said. "I made new, updated sets for you and Gwen a while back, just in case."

"Thanks, but it would be hard for me to disappear permanently," Abby said. "My family may not be close, but trust me, a lot of my relatives would notice if I just up and vanished tonight."

"Not to mention me," Sam said. "I'd notice, too."

Nick glared at him. "You still think you can take care of her?"

"I'm in a better position to protect her than you are," Sam said.

Abby gave Nick a worried look. "Where are you going?"

"To Hawaii to join Gwen. Got a reservation on a red-eye. I'm taking an extended vacation until this auction is over."

"Who was your client?" Abby asked.

"Mr. Anonymous," Nick said. "I've done other jobs for him. Look, are you sure you don't want to come with me tonight, Abby?"

"I can't," Abby said.

"You may be in real danger here."

Abby sat back against the cushions. "I'll be okay."

Nick gave Sam a dismissive look and turned back to her. "You're sure?"

"Yes." Abby smiled. "I'm sure."

"You'll call me if you change your mind?" Nick asked.

"I'll call," Abby said.

"In that case, I'm gone."

Nick downed the rest of the blue martini and pushed himself out of the booth. He looked at Sam.

"Remember what I said, Coppersmith. If anything happens to Abby, you'll answer to me."

"I'll take good care of her," Sam said.

Nick turned on his heel and disappeared through the doorway marked *Restrooms.*

Sam looked at Abby. "I'm assuming he didn't just go to the men's room?"

"That hall leads to the alley exit," Abby said. "Nick must really be running scared if he was afraid to go out the front door."

34

The icy-fingers-on-the-back-of-the-neck sensation hit Sam when they stepped out of the elevator on Abby's floor a short time later.

"Give me your key," he said quietly.

"Something's wrong, isn't it?" Abby whispered.

"Yeah."

She looked at the closed door of her apartment as if she expected to find a cobra on the other side. "I'm not sure this is a good idea."

He took the key from her. "Stay here," he said.

"Sam?"

"I don't think there's anyone inside now," he said. "Whoever was here is long gone."

He slipped the pistol out from under his jacket, just in case, and opened the door.

Shadows and a disturbing energy spilled out, but he did not pick up the subtle vibes that indicated the presence of someone hiding inside the apartment.

"Whoever was here is gone," he said.

"Ralph, the doorman, maybe."

"I don't think so."

He moved into the short hall and turned the corner. The city lights illuminated the chaotic scene in the living room. There was nothing professional about the search. The small condo had been ransacked by someone who must have been in a fit of rage at the time.

Books had been pulled off the shelves and dumped on the floor. The intruder had taken a knife to the cushions of the sofa and the reading chair. The contents of the desk drawers were scattered across the floor.

Sam did a quick tour of the bedroom and bath. Both rooms looked as if they had been hit by a tornado.

He headed back toward the living room, trying to think of a way to break the bad news to Abby. The hushed cry from the front hall told him that she had seen the disaster for herself.

He walked around the corner and saw her. She stood in the hallway, staring at her vandalized living room in shock and disbelief. Sam righted a lamp and switched it on.

"Why would anyone do such a thing?" She

clenched her hands into small fists. "This was my home."

He did not miss her use of the past tense, but he decided not to comment on it.

"The question is, what was he looking for?" he said gently.

"Obviously, he was searching for that damn lab book or something that would tell him who has it." She walked slowly through the wreckage and looked into the bedroom. "Dear heaven, he even went through my lingerie drawer. How *dare* he do such a thing?"

"We can call the cops," Sam said. "But I doubt if it will do any good. To them, it will be just another low-priority burglary. Not even that, because I doubt if anything is actually missing."

"Because what he wanted wasn't here for him to find. You're right. The cops will put this down as vandalism. They'll ask me if I know anyone who has a reason to be mad at me. How am I going to explain that some crazy guy with a paranormal ability to commit murder is after a forty-year-old lab notebook that's encrypted in a psychic code? They'll think I'm crazy. Then they'll find out about my time at the Summerlight Academy, and they'll know for sure that I'm a nut."

Sam walked to the sliding glass door and examined it. "Still locked from the inside. That means he got in through the front door. That settles it, this building definitely needs a major security upgrade."

"I can't stand it," Abby said. There was a strange tremor in her voice.

Sam turned quickly and went back to her. "Can't stand what?"

"I can't stand the fact that he was here, inside my home," Abby said. "I'll never be able to sleep here again. I'm going to list the condo with a real-estate agent tomorrow." She looked around. "No, wait, I'll have to get a professional cleaning firm in here first. I'll tell them to gather up everything and haul it to a charity."

"Hey, hey, hey, take it easy." He drew her into his arms and tried to think of something soothing to say. "It'll be okay. The bastard ripped up a few cushions and made a mess, but there's not a lot of serious damage."

"He touched my stuff." Abby was stiff with tension. She seemed unaware of his arms around her. "He was in my bedroom. My bathroom. My kitchen."

"I know. He'll pay for it, I promise you."

"This isn't about money, damn it."

He winced. "Bad choice of words. I didn't mean that he would pay financially. I meant

I'll get him for you."

Abby took a deep breath and straightened her shoulders. "Okay, then. Thank you." She stepped out of his arms and went toward the door. "Let's get out of here."

"Don't you want to take some fresh clothes with you?"

"No." She did not look back. "I won't be able to wear anything that was here when he broke in. I won't be able to use any of the dishes or the silverware or the sheets or my new towels ever again. He contaminated everything."

She was already outside, punching the button for the elevator. Sam switched off the lamp. He stood for a moment, contemplating the violated space.

"Whoever you are, you just bought yourself a one-way ticket to nowhere," he said to the shadows. "You should never have touched her stuff."

35

Abby walked out of the elevator into the dimly lit dungeon that was the underground parking garage. Her emotions were in turmoil. All she could think about was getting into the car and putting as much distance as possible between herself and her violated home. *No, not my home, not anymore.* Anger burned so hot within her that she did not register the ghostly prickle of awareness on the back of her neck until it was too late.

By the time she realized there was something wrong with the atmosphere in the garage, Sam's powerful hand was clamping tightly around her upper arm. She turned her head to look at him.

"What — ?" she began.

"Quiet," Sam said, directly into her ear.

He drew her swiftly behind a massive SUV that was parked in the corner. The gray walls of the garage formed a barricade on two sides. The big vehicle provided additional cover.

Ominous energy whispered in the shadows. Abby was suddenly chilled to the bone. Parking garages were always unnerving at night, and in spite of the condo's security measures, this one was no exception. Footsteps echoed eerily. There were too many dark spaces between the parked cars. She always walked through the gray concrete underworld as quickly as possible, keys in hand, all senses on high alert. But tonight she had been distracted.

The garage was far too quiet. There were no footsteps or voices, but her intuition warned her that she and Sam were not alone. Someone else waited in the shadows. Sam released her. She watched him take his pistol and a small chunk of silvery quartz that looked like a crystal mirror out from under his jacket. She wondered what the quartz was for but decided this was not the time to ask questions. There was the stillness of the hunter about Sam now. He was very focused, very intent. Very dangerous.

She did not know what to expect, a threat or a command from an armed gunman, perhaps. But there was only a strange, unnatural silence that seemed to deepen by the second. It was wrong. The pale glow of the fluorescent fixtures overhead was growing fainter. The garage was taking on a weird, dreamlike quality.

"Go hot," Sam ordered softly. "All the way."

She was already on edge, all of her senses, normal and paranormal, flaring in alarm, but she had made no effort to focus them. The problem with concentrating psychic energy for a prolonged period of time was that the exercise had a downside. The unpleasant jitters and, ultimately, exhaustion that followed a heavy burn were the least of her concerns. She could deal with those. What scared the daylights out of her in that moment was that the garage was starting to resemble the dreamscape of the Grady Hastings nightmare. It was bad enough to wake up and find herself standing beside her bed. What if pushing her talent too hard plunged her permanently into the dream?

Sensing her hesitation, Sam gave her an impatient glance.

"Do it," he ordered.

The garage was undergoing a bizarre transformation. The space around them was assuming an increasingly unreal aspect, as if it was sliding into another dimension. The rows of cars grew longer, stretching away into infinity. The concrete columns morphed into Möbius strips.

"Is it just me or is this starting to look like a bad dream?" she whispered.

"Looks that way to me, too."

She took comfort from that news. She wasn't in this alone. She wanted to explain the reason for her reluctance to follow orders, but this did not seem to be the time or place for an extended conversation. She had hired him as a consultant for situations like this. There was no point employing high-grade talent if you didn't follow up on the recommendations. Cautiously, she elevated her senses into the red zone.

Sure enough, the otherworldly distortion faded significantly as her para-senses took over. But the garage did not return to what passed for normal. When she was in the zone like this, she was able to perceive light from beyond the visible range of the spectrum. The scene was now illuminated in the radiance of ultralight.

In this eerily lit environment, human auras could be more easily perceived. The hot energy flaring in the shadows between two parked cars confirmed what she had already sensed. Someone waited in the darkness.

The senses-dazzling energy exploded out of nowhere. It was as if someone had lobbed a paranormal grenade directly in front of the SUV that protected them. Abby instinctively shut her eyes, but that did little to reduce the terrible glare. The explosion of searing ultralight affected her para-senses far more than it did her normal vision.

"Don't waste your time and energy trying to fight it, Coppersmith." The dark voice came out of the shadows. It was masculine but strangely distorted. *"My little flash-bang is crystal-powered. It generates more energy than any human can. It will soon overwhelm your senses. My advice is to shut down your talent before you burn out."*

"Too late with the flash-bang gadget," Sam said. "I've already got the fix on it."

"It won't do you any good. But go ahead and try to overcome it if you like. When you're satisfied that the device is stronger than you are, we can get down to business. Assuming you're still awake, that is. I'm sure you are aware of the downside of a serious psi-burn."

"I'll try to stay up late tonight," Sam said.

Abby sensed another rush of hot energy in his aura and knew that he had done something with the mirrored quartz. She realized that he was pushing an enormous amount of energy through the stone.

There was a reverberating clang as an object struck the concrete floor. The ultrawhite-hot glare that had filled the space abruptly winked out of existence. When her dazzled senses cleared, Abby realized that the garage had returned to normal.

"Shit." The epithet was accompanied by a harsh gasp of pain.

The stranger's voice was no longer distorted. It was, however, clearly annoyed. "You're a real son of a bitch, Coppersmith. How the hell did you do that?"

"A tuned crystal can generate more steady-state energy than a person, but it takes a human mind to activate it. I didn't take the fix on your flash-bang device. I took it on you." There was a short pause before Sam added politely, "I got it while you were chatting about the cutting-edge wonderfulness of your gadget."

"Fortunately, I brought backup."

"A real gun?" Sam said. "Good thinking."

"I assume you have one, too?"

"What do you think?"

"That you've got one." There was resignation and irritation in the stranger's voice. "You destroyed my flash-bang. It was a prototype, the first and so far the only version that actually worked."

"PEC technology?"

"Sure. Do you have any idea how long it will take me to produce another? It requires months to grow a single crystal large enough to power the damn thing, and that's assuming nothing goes wrong in the process. You know how delicate para-crystals are."

"What kind of seed crystal did you use?" Sam asked.

"I might give you that information if you tell me what you're using to power that weapon you brought to the party."

It dawned on Abby that the conversation had veered off in the wrong direction.

"For Pete's sake," she hissed. "This is no time to get into a technical discussion."

"She's got a point," Sam said.

"Yes, she does. I hate to admit it, but I may have underestimated you, Coppersmith. My own fault. I was warned that you might be a problem."

"I try hard," Sam said. "Sometimes I succeed."

"So I see. The thing is, I need Miss Radwell. I give you my word she will not be hurt."

"Then why are you trying to take her by force?" Sam asked.

"Because, unfortunately, you are in possession of her at the moment, and I doubt that you'll give her up without a fight."

"Good guess."

"All right, then, let's try this in a business-like fashion. Name your price for her. I'll top it."

"She's not for sale," Sam said.

Abby wanted to throttle both of them. "Stop talking about me as if I was a rare book up for auction, do you hear me?"

"In my own defense, I would like to point out that I did try to go about the business in a civilized way, Miss Radwell," the stranger said. "I heard rumors of your unusual talent, but it was made clear that you only work by personal referral. I was unable to approach you in the usual manner, because I'm not closely acquainted with any of your other clients and Thaddeus Webber declined to recommend me. So I tried an indirect approach."

"The herbal," Abby said. "You sent it to me."

"It was a gift intended to assure you that I was qualified to become a client. But you never responded."

"I've been a little busy lately."

"I understand. I tried hiring my own freelancer to find the book. He's good at his job, but he can't break codes. I decided I would try to hire you to handle the encryption after the book was in my possession. But this afternoon I got a message from the freelancer saying that he was resigning. I can only assume he was put off by the recent murders. I concluded I had no choice but to take drastic measures."

"Yes, well, as you can see, your drastic measures aren't going to work," Abby said.

"Out of curiosity, did Coppersmith come to you with a proper referral?"

"Yes, he did," Abby said coldly. "And by the way, he is not only a client. I hired him to protect me while I look for a certain book."

"The forty-year-old lab notebook that is coming up for auction. Yes, I know. Your choice of a bodyguard is an odd one, to say the least. Rather like hiring the wolf to watch the sheep, isn't it?"

"Sam and I have an agreement."

"I will double whatever he is paying you."

"Sorry, I have to consider my reputation in the business," Abby said.

"I give you my word that you will be in no danger from me."

"Right," Sam said. "That's why we're standing around this garage in the middle of the night, holding a conversation that includes a couple of para-weapons."

"It would appear we have a standoff this evening," the other man said.

"Who are you?" Abby demanded.

"I think we'll wait on the formal introductions. Maybe we can do business together some other time."

Anger flashed through Abby. "You're the one who invaded my condo and contaminated it, aren't you? Just so you know, I will never, ever forgive you for that. And I definitely won't work for a bastard who would do that to a person's personal space. I'm going to have you arrested."

"Calm down, Miss Radwell. I admit that I took a quick look around your condo earlier this evening, but it was obvious that someone else had been there first. Either that or you are a very poor housekeeper."

"Why should I believe you?"

"If I had searched your condo, Miss Radwell, I would have been far more discreet about the process. I would not have left any obvious indications of my presence."

Sam shifted slightly in the shadows. "Any idea who did go through the condo tonight?"

"No, but it looked like whoever did it was in a tearing rage, probably mentally unbalanced. For Miss Radwell's sake, I suggest you assume that the intruder is the same person who murdered Webber and Sparrow. You do know that both men are dead, don't you?"

"Yes," Abby said. "Are you going to tell us

that you're not responsible for those two killings?"

"Yes, that's exactly what I'm telling you."

"Both deaths were by paranormal means," Abby said. "It looks like you have the talent for designing the kind of gadgets that could be lethal."

"So does your bodyguard. While we're on the subject, Coppersmith, I don't suppose you would care to tell me what you used to destroy my flash-bang?"

"Sure. Right after you tell me what you used to turn this garage into a dreamscape."

"Sorry, proprietary secrets. You know how it is in the business world. Cutthroat. You can't trust anyone. To return to the subject of Sparrow and Webber, any idea who killed them?"

"There's a guy named Lander Knox running around in this thing," Sam said. "We've been trying to find him before he gets to the lab book."

"Webber and Sparrow were both very good at what they did. I will miss their professional services. But my chief concern at the moment is for Miss Radwell. I do not want to lose her, as well. Her talents are quite unique. But, then, you already know that, don't you? Take good care of her, Coppersmith."

"I'll do that," Sam said.

"Nice to know so many people are so concerned about my wellbeing," Abby grumbled.

"There are very few who can do what you do, Miss Radwell," the stranger said. "If for any reason you find yourself in need of a new bodyguard or a new client, please do not hesitate to contact me."

"Don't hold your breath waiting for me to get in touch," Abby said.

"You never know. Things have a way of changing. But since it appears that change is not going to happen tonight, I will say good-bye for now. I'll look forward to a future meeting."

"I suppose you want the herbal back?" Abby asked tentatively.

"Keep it as a souvenir. I'm not really into perfumes. But I would be interested to know if the Cleopatra recipe works."

Footsteps echoed in the shadows. Abby sensed Sam revving up his nearly exhausted talent. She knew that he was trying to catch another glimpse of the stranger's aura.

The alley door closed with a heavy metal clang that reverberated through the shadows. The garage went silent.

Sam got to his feet. "You asked him if he wanted the herbal back? What the hell was that about? Abby, that damn book was a bribe. You don't have to return bribes."

She rose quickly. "I told you, I have to think about my reputation."

"And you got upset with me because I talked a little shop with him."

"Are you okay?" she asked. "You took the brunt of that flash-bang blast."

"I'll survive."

"It must have been a very heavy burn. I can't even imagine how much energy you had to use to do whatever it was you did with that quartz. Are you sure you're okay?"

"Stop fussing," Sam said. "We don't have time. I'm going to crash soon."

"Right. Yes. Sorry. I suppose that was Nick's Mr. Anonymous."

"Probably, but he's not Mr. Anonymous as far as Coppersmith Inc. is concerned. We have another name for him."

"What?"

"The competition."

"That was someone from Helicon Stone?"

"Got a feeling we just took a meeting with Gideon Barrett, Hank Barrett's son. I told you that Dad and Hank have been feuding for years."

"Whew. Well, at least our side won tonight."

"Our side?" Sam sounded amused.

"Figure of speech," she said brusquely. "What now?"

"Now we find a place where I can crash for a few hours. Forget driving back to Anacortes. When I go down, I'm going to go down hard."

"I can drive."

"I know, but you'll be too vulnerable if I'm passed out on the backseat. I don't want to risk another carjacking."

Abby swallowed hard and braced herself. *Show no weakness.* Sam had used a lot of energy tonight. He would need to sleep, and soon. She had to be adult about this.

"We can go back to my condo," she said. "That's the nearest bed."

"No," he said, surprisingly gentle. "Not the condo."

36

He chose one of the big, anonymous hotels a few blocks away in the downtown core, and requested and got a room with no connecting doors. In the close confines of the elevator, he was intensely aware that he was not the only one experiencing the effects of a strong afterburn. There was a lot of edgy energy in Abby's aura. She had not taken the full force of the flash-bang blast because it had been focused on him, but she had caught some of the blowback. She was experiencing some of the downside, too.

"Are you okay?" he asked.

"I'll be fine," Abby said. "Just a little jittery. You know how it is. Probably just as well you didn't take me up on my offer to drive back to Anacortes tonight." She glanced at his duffel. "But if this keeps up, I may have to start traveling with an overnight bag the way you do. At least the hotel provided a few basics."

He looked at the small packet she clutched. The front desk clerk had given it to her. It contained a tiny toothbrush, toothpaste and a few other overnight essentials. She had refused to even take some of her underwear and a change of clothes from the devastated condo. All she had with her tonight was whatever she normally carried in her large tote.

The elevator doors opened. He followed Abby out into the hallway. He had to stay focused on getting her securely buttoned up for the night so that he could crash without having to worry about her safety.

"What was that flash-bang thing he used on you?" Abby asked.

"Damned if I know. The Barretts have their secrets, just like the Coppersmiths. I'd give a lot to know what kind of crystal he used to power that gadget, though."

Abby smiled.

"What?" he asked.

"In hindsight, there was a certain humorous aspect to that showdown in the garage."

"Yeah? I didn't notice anyone laughing, especially not me."

"Something about the way the two of you started to wander off into a discussion of crystal physics while you're both holding weapons on each other," Abby said.

"You think that was funny?"

"I guess you had to be there."

"I *was* there."

He concentrated on securing the room, but there was no getting around the fact that a part of him was consumed by the prowling tension that was the usual first phase of the post-burn syndrome. *You've been here before,* he thought. *You can handle it.*

The biochemistry of a heavy burn was complicated and not well understood. For males, there was a lot of adrenaline and testosterone involved, so the sexual arousal was predictable. But the hungry, urgent restlessness had never been this bad in the past. It didn't take a psychic to know why the sensation was so overwhelming tonight. It had a focus, and that focus was Abby.

He forced himself to go through the drill. He noted the location of the emergency exits and came up with two possible escape routes. His hand shook a little when he inserted the key card into the lock. If Abby noticed, she was too polite to say anything.

Inside the room, he secured the door and did a quick survey. No connecting doors, as promised. The sealed windows looked out over Sixth Avenue twelve floors below.

Satisfied, he unzipped the leather duffel

and took out two small crystals.

"What are those?" Abby asked.

"Think of them as psychic trip wires. If anyone tries to come in through the door or the window, I'll know about it."

"More PEC technology?"

"Yes."

"Do you always carry those gadgets and your gun in your overnight bag?"

"Yes."

When he was satisfied that he had taken all possible precautions, he turned around and looked at Abby. She stood, contemplating the bed, arms folded. Something about her obvious uncertainty irritated him.

"What?" he asked.

She cleared her throat. "Nothing. I, uh, thought there would be two beds, that's all."

For some reason, the knowledge that she did not want to share the bed with him hit him harder than the damn flash-bang had. And then he got mad; not at Abby, at himself. That was another problem with the burn-and-crash routine. It pushed everything, including normal, logical thought processes, to the edge. It made for a real roller-coaster ride.

"Sorry." He knew he sounded brusque, but that was a hell of a lot better than begging her to sleep with him. "This was all that was available in a room that had no connecting door. No problem. I'll take the chair or the floor."

"No, you certainly will not." Her brows scrunched together in a severe look. "You need to sleep soundly. You can't do that in a chair or on the floor."

"Trust me, the way I'm going to go down tonight, I won't notice where I sleep."

"Forget it. Sorry I raised the issue. I'm a little tense. You've had a very deep burn. I thought that you would sleep better alone."

"I'm not going into a coma." He took his overnight kit, a fresh T-shirt and a clean pair of briefs out of the duffel bag. "I just need some sleep." He headed toward the bathroom.

"By the way, what is PEC technology?" Abby asked.

"What?" It was hard to focus on her question. The urge to pull her into his arms and lose himself in her warm, soft body while the aftermath flames burned through him was growing stronger. What the hell was the matter with him? He had never been this close to the edge of control. Maybe Barrett's psychic flash-bang gadget had a few side effects.

"PEC technology," she repeated. "You and Gideon Barrett both used the term."

He stood in the doorway, staring into the white tile bathroom. "Stands for psi-emitting crystals. The paranormal equivalent of light-emitting diodes and liquid crystal displays."

"They're similar to LEDs and LCDs?"

"Yes, but the energy generated comes from beyond the normal range on the spectrum and has different properties. It's the kind of technology Coppersmith is working on in the Black Box lab." He moved into the bathroom and plopped the overnight kit down on the counter. "Do you mind if we save the science lesson for tomorrow? I'm beat. Not really in a good place to explain the physics of para-rocks right now. I need a shower."

"I was just curious."

That did it. Now he felt like a total brute. He closed the bathroom door.

He emerged a short time later wearing the clean underwear and the trousers he'd had on earlier. Abby was waiting, still fully dressed. She had the hotel vanity kit in hand.

It dawned on him that she did not have a nightgown.

"I've got a spare T-shirt," he said.

"Thank you." She looked relieved. "I'll take it."

He took a clean black T-shirt out of the duffel without a word and handed it to her. She slipped past him and disappeared into the small room. The door closed firmly. He heard water running in the sink. It ran for a very long time. He realized she was probably doing a little hand laundry. In the morning, he would probably find a pair of panties hanging on the towel rack. The vision heated his blood a little more.

He considered his options and went for the padded reading chair in the corner near the window. The sight of the ottoman cheered him in some macabre way.

"Damn perfect," he muttered. "Just doesn't get any better than this, does it, Coppersmith? You're in the middle of a burn. Abby is a few feet away, getting ready for bed, and you get to crash in a chair with an actual ottoman. You'll be able to prop up your feet. Wow."

The bathroom door opened a crack. "Sam, did you say something?"

"Just talking to myself."

"I understand. I do that sometimes, too. Well, actually, I talk to Newton. Maybe you should get a dog."

He realized that he was gritting his teeth. "I'll definitely have to think about doing just that."

The door closed.

He opened the minibar, chose two small bottles, the whiskey and the brandy. He yanked a pillow off the bed, turned off all the lights except the one by the bed and dropped into the chair. He propped his feet on the ottoman, twisted the top off one of the liquor bottles and swallowed some of the whiskey. He contemplated the closed door of the bathroom while he downed the medicinal alcohol. With luck, he would be unconscious by the time Abby came out.

The door opened quietly a few minutes later. Abby emerged wearing his T-shirt. It was much too big for her. The hem fell to her thighs. She looked sexy as hell in the shadows. An elemental thrill of possessiveness swept through him. He drank some more of the whiskey.

"Are you asleep?" she asked softly.

"Getting there."

"I told you to take the bed."

"I don't follow orders well."

"You don't have to be grouchy about it," she said. "I was just trying to make sure you'll get the rest you need."

"I'll sleep fine right here." *Eventually.*

"Are you drinking something?"

"Yeah." He opened the second bottle.

"Helps take the edge off the afterburn buzz."

"You got into the minibar?"

"Uh-huh." He swallowed some of the brandy.

"I could use a glass of wine myself."

"Help yourself. There are a couple of small bottles of wine in the bar."

She crossed the room, opened the minibar and studied the assortment. Then she glanced at the printed card that detailed the prices of the items in the bar.

"Geez, look at the prices," she said.

"Go for it." He saluted her with the miniature whiskey bottle. "Live large. I'm paying for the room, remember?"

"Okay, thanks."

She chose the little bottle of white wine, untwisted the cap and sat down on the edge of the bed.

They drank in silence for a while. He saw no reason to try to engage in conversation. It would only make things more complicated.

"How are you feeling?" Abby asked.

"Coming down. Finally." It was the truth, he realized. The alcohol and time were working. He would sleep soon.

"Before you crash, I just want to say thank you again. This is the second time you've saved me from someone who wanted to kidnap me."

He closed his eyes. "I've told you before, I'm just doing my job. But in fairness, I don't think Gideon Barrett would have grabbed you against your will. He just wanted to get me out of the way for a while so that he could talk you into accepting his offer. And he would have made you one hell of an offer, trust me."

"Looked a lot like an attempted kidnapping to me. It's sort of scary knowing that people want to kidnap you."

"I know," he said, gentler this time. She had good reason to be afraid, he thought. "You're handling it well. Lot of folks in your position would be basket cases by now."

"If I'm dealing with it well, it's because I've got you watching my back. So thanks, anyway."

He opened his eyes. "Even if I do have my own agenda?"

She smiled. "Everyone has an agenda. I can deal with that, so long as a person is honest about it. You've been up front about yours from the beginning. Well, almost from the beginning."

The last thing he wanted was her gratitude.

"Finish your wine, turn out the light and

go to sleep, Abby," he said.

"Okay."

She set the empty bottle on the nightstand, switched off the lamp and got into bed.

Sam contemplated the little brandy bottle and decided not to finish it. Too much alcohol might prolong the recovery phase of the crash. He set the bottle on the table beside the chair, leaned back and watched the shadows on the ceiling for a while. He thought about the array of people who were trying to grab Abby and the lab book.

"I'm missing something," he said after a while.

"What?" Abby asked from the shadows.

"Don't know. Can't think clearly tonight. But in the morning, I need to go back to the beginning of this case and look at everything from a different angle."

"You mean back to that first blackmail note?"

"No, back to what happened in Vaughn's library."

"You think that's where it all started?"

"The answer is there, somewhere."

"Maybe our chat with Grady Hastings tomorrow will give us a lead."

"I've never interviewed a crazy psychic,"

Sam said. "Should be interesting."

The deep sleep crept over him.

37

The woman walked down the endless basement hallway. He knew she was going to open the lab door, knew the killer was waiting for her on the other side.

He tried to go after her, but he was trapped in the shadows. He tried to call to her, desperate to warn her, but he could not get her name out.

At the door she paused, her hand on the knob. She looked back at him. For the first time, he saw her face. Not Cassidy.

"Abby."

"Sam, you're dreaming. Wake up. It's all right. I'm here."

Energy shivered in the atmosphere, summoning him from the nightmare. He came awake on a surge of adrenaline and psi, aware of the warmth of Abby's hand on his bare arm, aware of her comforting energy.

He opened his eyes and saw her bending

over him. Her anxious concern was a palpable force in the atmosphere. He had probably scared the hell out of her. Bodyguards weren't supposed to sleep on the job in the first place, and they definitely were not supposed to suffer from nightmares. There were rules about that kind of stuff somewhere.

He took his feet down off the ottoman and sat forward, scrubbing his face with his hands. He willed himself to full wakefulness.

"Abby," he said again.

"I'm here."

She was safe. She was not caught in the endless loop of the damned lab dream.

Automatically, he raised his para-senses and was relieved to discover that they responded instantly. He did not know how much time had passed, but it was clear that he had recovered from the heavy exhaustion that followed a hard burn. He glanced at his watch. The black crystal numbers glowed. He had slept for nearly three hours.

"Sorry," he said. His voice sounded rough, as if he had dragged it out of the fog of the nightmare. "Must have been dreaming."

"Yes. You called my name."

He tried to think. "It was the recurring dream I told you about tonight. But it was different this time. Sorry. Didn't mean to wake you."

"I was already awake."

He got to his feet. "Couldn't sleep?"

"No." She stepped back, out of his way. "Well, actually, I didn't try. I was a little worried after you fell asleep. You seemed feverish, so I decided to stay up until it looked like you were through the burn and sleeping normally."

First he had to deal with her gratitude. Now she was treating him as if he was an invalid. This relationship was going downhill fast.

"Just the afterburn fever," he said, trying to sound cool and in control, like a man who could handle his job. "I'm not ill. You've been through a burn. You know how it is."

"I know how it *feels,* but I've never been close to anyone else who is going through it, so I didn't know what it looked like. I didn't realize that it had some of the symptoms of a high fever."

"Aura heat."

"Yes, but you were giving off *a lot* of energy," she said. "I have to tell you it was a little unnerving. I was afraid that flash-bang gizmo might have caused some sort of delayed psychic stress."

"I told you, I'm all right." *Great.* Now he

was snapping at her again. “You don’t have to play nurse.”

“I was just looking out for you while you slept off the burn.” She was starting to sound annoyed. “I didn’t mean to offend your macho self-image. Do you always wake up in a bad mood like this?”

“No. But everything seems to be different with you.”

“Keep in mind that I had a bad day, too, and unlike you, I haven’t had any sleep yet. I am in no mood for sarcasm.”

He took a few beats to ponder that. “Does it strike you that we seem to be arguing over nothing again?”

“Yes, it does.” She folded her arms. “Any idea why that is happening?”

“Sure. I want to have sex with you, but every time I turn around tonight, you’re either thanking me or trying to take care of me. So I provoke an argument because it makes you mad. See, I’d rather have you mad at me than pointing out the fact that I’m a decrepit bodyguard.”

There was stunned silence for a few seconds. Abby finally got her mouth closed.

“Good grief,” she said. “That is . . . very insightful.”

“For a man, you mean?”

“For anyone. I’m impressed.”

She started to giggle. She covered her mouth with her hands and turned toward the window. The giggles turned into muffled laughter.

"Now you're laughing at me," he said, resigned. "You know, you can be hard on a man's ego."

She sobered, dropped her hands and turned back to face him. Her eyes sparkled with the tears generated by her laughter.

"Good thing yours isn't too fragile," she said.

"Every man has his limits."

"So does every woman. You were only half right, you know."

"Yeah?"

She smiled ruefully. "The arguments aren't all your fault. I may be pushing things a bit, too."

"Why?"

"For the same reason," she said.

He went still. "Yeah?"

"I want to sleep with you, but part of me thinks that is a very bad idea."

"Why?"

"Because something weird seems to happen when you and I make . . ." She broke off and coughed discreetly. "When you and I have sex."

"Define weird."

She spread her hands. "I don't know how to explain it, but it feels like something to do with our auras. It's as if my wavelengths are somehow resonating with yours. It's a very *intimate* sensation. Probably just my imagination at work. But I've been wondering . . ."

"Wondering what?"

She sighed. "If you must know, I'm wondering if it's some aspect of the psychic stress I experienced when I broke the code on that book in Mrs. Vaughn's library. Maybe some energy from the dreamstate is affecting my normal senses or something."

"Ah," he said. He smiled.

She frowned. "What is that supposed to mean?"

"You're wondering if having sex with me is making you crazy," he said. He was grinning now. "It's an intriguing question. One that will require a lot more research and experimentation."

"You're laughing at me, aren't you?"

"Yeah. That resonance thing going on with our auras? I feel it, too."

She brightened. "You do?"

"If you're going crazy, so am I. But unlike you, I'm not worried about it."

"You've experienced that kind of thing before during sex?" she asked, hopeful now.

"No." He smiled and moved closer to her. "Maybe that's why it feels so good. Personally, I've gotta tell you that I'm not going to lose any sleep over this."

"But what do you think is going on?" she asked. "The para-physics involved, I mean. It certainly isn't normal."

"You want the truth? I don't give a damn about the para-physics."

"You don't?"

"No."

He put his hands around her shoulders. Beneath the fabric of the black T-shirt, she felt sleek and warm and soft and like all that was feminine. Her scent clouded his senses, intoxicating and compelling. He tightened his grip on her and drew her to him. She did not resist.

Her lips were slightly parted. He jacked up his talent a little and saw that her eyes burned with a little psi-light. He could sense the heat in her aura, too. Sexual energy was so hot that it burned across the spectrum from the normal range into the paranormal. It was the raw energy of life. And he had never felt more alive than he did right now.

"Abby," he said.

"You're the scientist here," she said. "I guess if you're not worried, I should stop worrying, too."

"I like your logic."

He plunged his fingers into the storm of her hair and captured her mouth.

She wrapped her arms around his neck and kissed him back with a feminine heat that ignited a wildfire within him. It was all he could do to hold on to his control.

He wrenched his mouth free from Abby's and kissed her throat. Her hands moved down from his neck and slipped up under his T-shirt. Her palms felt good on his chest, soft and very warm.

"You feel feverish again," she said.

"No kidding. You're running a fever, too."

"Feels good."

"Yes," he said. "It does."

She pushed the T-shirt upward. He yanked the garment off over his head and tossed it aside. She kissed his shoulder, her mouth warm and damp on the phoenix tattoo. He took a step back and got rid of his pants and briefs. When he turned to her, she was smiling at him. He could already sense the intimate resonance pattern of their auras.

"Yes," he said. "Damn right, it feels good."

He tugged off the T-shirt she wore, scooped her up into his arms and fell with her onto the bed. He rolled onto his back, dragging her down across his chest. She made love to him there in the darkness, raining spicy wet kisses from his throat to his belly, and then she ventured lower. He groaned when her fingers closed around him. When she took him into her mouth, he sucked in a sharp breath and sank his hands into the thick, tangled curls of her hair.

She used her tongue on him, and he thought he would go mad. When she pressed gently against the ultra-sensitive place directly behind his testicles, he knew he had reached his limit.

"My turn," he breathed.

He eased her onto her back and came down on top of her. She was as damp as he was, slick with perspiration. He kissed her firm, dainty breasts until she was arching against him and clutching at him. Satisfied, he worked his way slowly down her body, savoring the taste and scent of her.

When he reached the tight little furnace between her legs, she cried out and dug her nails into his shoulders. He sensed the gathering tension in her and stoked the fires until she was fierce and breathless. He gripped her sweet ass in both hands and anchored her so that she could not escape his mouth.

She came undone in a storm of energy that dazzled all of his senses.

"Sam. *Sam.*"

"Right here," he breathed.

He shifted position, holding his weight on his elbows. He captured her face between his hands and plunged his tongue into her mouth at the same time that he thrust deep into her still-clenching passage. The convulsions of her release pulled him over the edge within seconds.

He gave himself up to the rushing freedom of the climax with a hoarse, muffled groan of satisfaction that seemed to echo forever.

A long time later, Abby became aware of the weight of Sam's thigh on top of hers. His arm was flung across her breasts. She turned her head on the pillow and saw that his eyes were closed. He looked to be sound asleep. Cautiously, she tried to edge out from under his sprawling weight. He tightened his arm around her, trapping her, but he did not open his eyes.

"You're awake," she accused.

"I am now." Reluctantly, he rolled onto his back. "You know, we should do this more often."

"What? Meet weird guys in parking garages who try to whack you with psychic flash-bang gadgets so that they can kidnap me?"

"Must you always focus on the negative? I was referring to the hot sex."

She smiled. "Oh, that."

He folded his arms behind his head. "Yeah, that."

She turned onto her stomach and levered herself up on her elbows. "How was it different tonight?"

"The sex?" He gazed up at the ceiling. "Let me count the ways . . ."

"Not the sex. The dream."

"The one you interrupted?"

"That's the one, yes." She paused. "You called my name."

"Probably because you weren't supposed to be in it."

"What was I doing in it?"

"Scaring the hell out of me," he said.

"Explain."

"It's the same dream that I told you about."

"The one in which poor Cassidy walks down the hall to open the lab door?"

"Yes. Usually, it's like some damned video loop. It keeps repeating, over and over again. Always the same. Until tonight."

"What was different about tonight's version?"

He looked at her, his eyes burning a little in the shadows. "Tonight you were the woman walking down the hall, about to open the lab door. I called out to you. Tried to stop you. But you couldn't hear me."

"You're worried about protecting me, and that concern came through in the new version of the dream." She leaned over and brushed her mouth against his. Then she pulled back. "But it's okay. I'm not Cassidy. If you called out to me or tried to warn me, even in a dream, I would hear you."

"Would you?"

"Yes," she said. "I heard you tonight, didn't I?"

He stroked her cheek with the back of his finger. She turned her head and kissed his palm. He wrapped one arm around her and drew her back down to him.

38

"What did you mean last night when you told me that we needed to go back to the start of this thing?" Abby asked. "You said you were missing something about the incident in the Vaughn library."

They were eating omelets and drinking coffee in the hotel restaurant. Abby was feeling surprisingly well rested. Which only went to show that if you had clean underwear, a toothbrush and a sexy bodyguard, a woman could handle anything, she decided.

For his part, Sam showed no signs of exhaustion. He looked sated and satisfied. He also appeared energized.

"You told me that the day of the home invasion, Grady Hastings specified that he was after a particular encrypted book," Sam said.

"Yes. Morgan's *The Key to the Latent Power of Stones.*"

"According to what little there is about

him online, there's no indication that Hastings was in the hot-books market. He doesn't have the money for it, for one thing."

"He told me that he needed *The Key* to help him with his research. Evidently, he's really into crystals."

"Like me," Sam said.

Abby smiled. "Like you without the Coppersmith money to fund his work."

"And without the Coppersmith connections in the rare-books market. And yet he somehow discovered that an obscure, psi-coded book on crystals was in the library of a private collector. How would that be possible if he wasn't tapped into the underground book world?"

Abby put down her fork and thought about it. "He said a voice in a crystal had told him how to find the book and that it was encrypted."

"Did the voice tell him about you?"

"Yes."

"Think we can safely assume he is delusional? He may have fantasized about hearing a voice in the crystal, but the information about you and the book was accurate. He got it from some source. Any ideas?"

"I don't know. I certainly don't advertise, and Mrs. Vaughn didn't put the contents of her library online. She is not dangerous, but she is as secretive as every other collector I've ever worked with."

"But serious collectors, dealers and freelancers like you would be aware of at least some of the more valuable books in her collection, right?"

"Oh, yes. That kind of gossip is always floating around. All of us who work that market keep close track of auctions, sales and rumors about recent acquisitions. What are you thinking?"

"Your dream intuition has been right all along. I'm thinking it is past time to talk to Grady Hastings."

39

"It was the voice in the crystal that told me that *The Key* was in Mrs. Vaughn's library," Grady Hastings said. "I couldn't believe it at first, but I heard it over and over again, so I knew it had to be true. I didn't mean to hurt anyone. At least, I don't think I meant to hurt anyone. Can't remember, exactly, to be honest. The doctor tells me I have to remember that part, but I can't."

"Why did you want *The Key* so badly?" Abby asked. "Do you remember that?"

They were sitting in the spare, utilitarian room the psychiatric hospital reserved for meetings between visitors and patients. An orderly stood some distance away, surreptitiously checking email on his cell phone. *Or maybe playing a game,* Abby thought. Whatever the case, it was obvious that he was not interested in the conversation. The woman who had led Abby and Sam to the visitors' room a short time earlier had explained that they were the only people who had come to visit Grady since he had been admitted.

Abby and Sam were on one side of a wide table. Grady sat across from them. He was no longer radiating the wild, chaotic energy that had swirled around him on the day he had invaded the Vaughn home. He still gave off the vibes of an individual who marched to his own drummer, but he was not scary today. Abby found herself feeling sorry for him. He seemed very worried, very young and very lonely. He was dressed in hospital-issue garb, a loose-fitting shirt, trousers and slippers.

"I needed *The Key* to complete my experiment," Grady said. His expression became animated for the first time. He straightened in his chair. "I was so close to the final step, you see, and the voice told me that the answer was in *The Key.*" His enthusiasm faded as quickly as it had materialized. He sagged back in defeat. "I can't believe I thought I was hearing a voice in one of my crystals. I must have been crazy, just like everyone says. I screwed up, and now I'll never know if I was on the right track or not."

Sam looked at him. "What was the nature of the experiment?"

"I was trying to grow crystals that could

be used as hearing aids. My mother was deaf. I used sign language from the cradle. When I was still a kid, I told her that one day I would find a way to help her hear. She believed in me. She died when I was fourteen, but she made me promise that I would never give up my goal of inventing a new kind of hearing technology. But they won't let me have a lab in here. When I asked them for some of the crystals that I was working on at home, the doc said that the fact that I believed crystals had some kind of special powers was another indication that I needed more treatment."

"Your doctor doesn't think there is power in crystals?" Sam asked.

"Nah." Grady grimaced. "He thinks it's all woo-woo stuff."

"Did you remind him that it's crystal technology that makes it possible for him to have a personal computer and carry a phone that can access the Internet?" Sam asked. "Did you mention lasers? LCD screens?"

"Sure," Grady said. "But I was working with crystals that have some paranormal properties, and the doctor can't grasp the concept."

"He's not alone," Abby said.

Sam folded his elbows on the table and fixed Grady with a deeply interested expression. "You were working with crystals to invent hearing devices?"

"Yeah." Grady came alive again. "According to my theory, almost anyone could use them. You wouldn't have to have a lot of talent. If I'm right, it will take very little psi to make my hearing devices work. Everyone produces *some* energy. But I was missing a critical element. I knew there was a problem, but I couldn't get at it. Do you know that feeling?"

"Yes," Sam said. "I know it well."

"One day I started hearing this voice telling me that I needed *The Key.*" Grady rubbed his forehead. "It sounds freaky, I know. But I just got this feeling that if I could find that book and the woman who could crack the encryption, I could make the breakthrough that I needed."

"You said the voice came from a crystal?" Sam asked. "One in your collection?"

"Yes." Grady frowned, bewildered. "I think so. But I can't remember which one. I don't understand why I can't remember that, either."

"What color was the crystal?" Sam asked.

"I don't . . ." Grady stopped. "Wait. It was green. I'm almost positive that it was one of my green stones."

"The voice in the green crystal told you

that *The Key* was in the Vaughn library?" Abby asked.

Grady gave her a plaintive look. "I guess so. I told you, I can't remember exactly. But how else could I have known that?"

"You had never met Mrs. Vaughn before you went to her home to get *The Key?*" Sam asked.

"No." Grady snorted. "Get real. How would a guy like me meet someone like that? I don't know anyone who has that kind of money."

"Where did you get the gun?" Sam asked.

"Huh?" Another troubled frown came over Grady's face. "I'm not sure."

"Did you buy it?" Abby asked.

"No." Grady rubbed his forehead. "I think I found it somewhere. Maybe on the front seat of my car. Can't remember."

"Did the voice tell you where to find the gun, and that you had to use it when you went to get *The Key?*" Sam asked.

"Maybe." Grady Hastings winced. "I'm sounding crazier by the minute, aren't I?"

"No," Sam said. "You're sounding more and more like a man who was set up."

Abby looked at him. "You think Grady was somehow hypnotized to go to the Vaughn house that day?"

"That's what it feels like," Sam said.

"But why? *The Key* is an interesting book, but the only thing that makes it really valuable is the psi-encryption."

"The contents of the book weren't important," Sam said. "The idea was to test you to see if you really could break a psi-code."

"Good grief," Abby said. "This is starting to make some sense."

"You and Grady were both unwitting participants in someone's experiment," Sam said. "The experiment was a success. Whoever conducted it is now after you."

"The blackmail notes," Abby said.

"Wait," Grady blurted out. "I don't understand."

"Neither do I," Sam said. "Not all of it. But I think I'm finally getting close."

Abby looked at Grady. "Sam is an expert on paranormal crystals."

Grady nodded. "I was starting to figure that out." He looked at Sam. "You're one of those Coppersmiths, aren't you? You're connected to the family that owns Coppersmith Inc."

"That's right," Sam said.

"Your labs must be awesome," Grady said wistfully. "State-of-the-art and then some."

"And then some," Sam agreed. "We do a little R-and-D work with hot rocks, too."

"You mean paranormal crystals, right?"

"Yes."

"*Awesome.* I'd give anything to have access to a lab like that." Grady looked around the bare visitors' room, his gloom deepening. "But I'll be lucky to get out of here someday, and even if I do, there won't be anything left of my lab. I'll have to start over."

"Why do you say that?" Abby asked.

"My equipment and my crystals are in the shed in back of the house I'm renting," Grady said. "Lease is up next month. I don't care about my furniture and clothes, but as soon as the rent comes due, the landlord will clean the place out. He'll probably put my crystals and lab instruments into a yard sale. All my stuff will be gone."

"I know exactly how it feels to have someone else mess with your stuff," Abby said. She sat forward. "If you like, Sam and I can pack up your rocks and your lab equipment and store it for you."

Grady looked startled. "You'd do that for me after I pointed a gun at you?"

"Yes, because I don't think you ever really meant to point that gun at me. By the way, Sam is not just a crystal expert, he is also a security expert."

"Yeah?" Grady was curious now.

"He's investigating what happened to you

and me at the Vaughn house," Abby explained. "He's been working for me for a few days, and as of now he's working for you, too. Isn't that right, Sam?"

Sam looked at her, brows elevated. "Well."

Abby turned back to Grady. "Consider yourself one of Sam's clients."

Grady processed the new data. For a few seconds, he looked hopeful. Then his eyes went flat. "I can't afford to hire a private investigator."

"Lucky for you I work cheap," Sam said. "Like Abby said, consider yourself a client."

"Yeah?" Grady started to look hopeful again. "Just like that?"

"Just like that," Sam said.

"And you'll pack up my lab stuff before the landlord sells it?" Grady asked urgently.

"Don't worry," Abby said. "We'll take care of your stuff."

"All part of the service," Sam said. He got to his feet. "I don't suppose you still have the key to your house?"

"No key," Grady said. "They took that away, too. But the lock on the porch door is nothing special. You shouldn't have any trouble getting inside the house. The hard part will be getting into the shed out back. I installed my own door and security system, mostly to keep my landlord out."

"Give me the code," Sam said.

"See, that's the tricky part," Grady said. "It's not an off-the-shelf system. It's PEC-based."

"Yeah?" Sam looked intrigued.

Grady glanced around the room and then lowered his voice. "You'll need a crystal to work it."

"What kind of crystal?"

"Doesn't matter. You just have to be able to generate a little energy through it. Find a resonating frequency, and the lock will open."

Sam moved his hand, calling subtle attention to the fire crystal in his ring. "Will this do?"

Grady studied the copper stone. Abby felt energy hum briefly in the atmosphere.

"Sure, that will work," Grady said. "Nice stone. I don't recognize it."

"Synthetic," Sam said easily. "It was grown in one of the Coppersmith labs."

"Awesome."

Abby rose before Grady could ask any more questions. "We'll report back as soon as we have some information."

"That would be cool," Grady said, brightening. "I don't get many visitors. In fact, you're the only ones I've had."

Abby frowned. "You don't have any family?"

"Not that you'd notice. I think there are some people on my mom's side somewhere, but I never heard from them after she died."

"What about your father?" Abby asked.

"He skipped out before I was born."

A chill of intuition twisted through Abby. "Did you go into the foster-care system after your mother died?"

"For a while," Grady said. "But everyone decided that I was on the crazy side, so I ended up in a special school for wackos."

Abby stopped breathing for a couple of heartbeats. Her talent flared. She was aware that Sam was motionless. His eyes were a little hot.

"Was the name of the school by any chance the Summerlight Academy?" Abby asked.

"Yeah." Grady widened his eyes. "How'd you know?"

"I'm a graduate, too."

"No kidding?" Grady sighed. "Well, I guess we both survived."

"Yes," Abby said, "we did. And when this is all over, I will introduce you to some other graduates. You can join our alumni club if you like."

Grady started to smile. The smile

stretched into a grin. "A club for graduates of the Summerlight Academy? That would be sort of cool."

Outside, in the parking lot, Abby got into the SUV and fastened her seat belt. She waited until Sam climbed in beside her.

"Given what we know of the laws of paraphysics, what are the odds that Grady Hastings and I both have the Summerlight Academy in common?" she asked.

"Realistically, the odds probably aren't all that bad, given your psych profiles and the diagnosis that you both got when you were in your teens," Sam said. "I doubt that there are a great number of boarding schools in the Seattle area that accept students with your unusual issues."

"Okay. What are the odds that both of us wound up together in Vaughn's library that day by sheer luck or coincidence?"

Sam started the SUV and snapped it into gear. "Zero."

"I was thinking the same thing. Where does that leave us?"

"Looking for a psychic who knows how to locate other genuine psychics in the Seattle area. Someone who has access to the Summerlight Academy records."

"If he has access to the records," Abby

said, "he would have a lot of information about the students' psych profiles and their personal situations. I'll bet that bastard picked poor Grady because he knew he was not only a talent but also alone in the world. There is no family to worry about him or to protect him."

"The son of a bitch would also know that you have a complicated relationship with your family. I'm guessing he would have preferred to use someone like Hastings, a loner, to break the psi-code, but he doesn't have much choice. There aren't a lot of sensitives with your kind of ability running around the Pacific Northwest. There are others who can find the lab book for him, but it would be almost impossible to find another code breaker."

"In other words, he was stuck with me."

"Something like that, yes."

"It's always nice to be appreciated for one's talent."

40

The house Grady Hastings had leased was a run-down bungalow in West Seattle. The rental looked as sad and depressed as Hastings had looked sitting in the locked ward at the psychiatric hospital, Sam thought. The place was in desperate need of a fresh coat of paint. The small lawn was patchy and studded with weeds. Yellowed shades were pulled down to cover the grimy windows.

Sam went up the concrete steps and set down the stack of packing boxes he had picked up at a container store. He checked the lock. Grady was right. It was standard-issue and probably original to the house. It took less than thirty seconds to open it.

"Doesn't look like Grady's landlord has put much money into upkeep," he said. He twisted the old-fashioned knob and opened the door.

"No." Abby followed him up the steps.

She had a large roll of Bubble Wrap tucked under one arm. "Why bother? I doubt if Grady was a demanding tenant. All he cares about is his work with crystals."

"True. As long as he had his lab, he was probably content."

Abby smiled a secret smile.

He eyed her with suspicion. "What?"

"Nothing. It just occurred to me that Grady isn't the only person around who is content so long as he has his lab."

"Yeah, well, I'm not the one sitting in a psychiatric hospital."

"There is something to be said for that." Abby followed him into the house, put down the roll of Bubble Wrap and closed the door. When she turned around and saw the nearly empty space, she froze. Outrage heated the atmosphere around her.

"There's hardly any furniture left," she yelped. "Someone stole Grady's stuff."

"It's possible," Sam said. "Empty houses are magnets for thieves. But I think it's more likely the landlord jumped the gun and started clearing out Grady's things."

"Bastard. I hope he wasn't able to get into the shed in back. Grady will be crushed if his lab stuff is gone."

Sam walked through the kitchen and opened the back door. The shed sitting in the yard looked like a ramshackle wooden fortress. The one window was boarded up. The gleaming new metal door was closed.

He walked across the weed-infested yard and examined the lock on the door. Abby followed him.

"Doesn't look like anyone has gotten inside yet," he said. "But it's probably a good thing we're here. Got a hunch the landlord will be taking a blowtorch to this door when he figures out that a regular locksmith can't open it."

He raised his ring to the dull, gray crystal embedded in the metal on the wall next to the door. Cautiously, he focused a little energy through the Phoenix stone. He sensed the familiar tingling current of power. The lock crystal began to heat with violet-hued ultralight.

There was a sharp click as the lock disengaged. Sam opened the door.

"The kid's good," he said. "Very, very good."

"And certainly not as crazy as everyone, including me, believed," Abby said.

"Maybe not."

He found a switch on the wall. The lights came on, revealing a battered metal workbench and a number of old metal cabinets. The concrete floor was bare.

He examined the lab with professional interest. The small space did not gleam with steel and polished equipment like the Coppersmith labs. There were no state-of-the-art computers. The chemistry equipment on the workbench looked as if it had been assembled from various do-it-yourself science kits and then seriously modified. An old burner designed for heating the contents of test tubes sat on one corner. A cumbersome, obviously hand-built laser occupied the far end of the bench.

"You know," Abby said, gazing around the crowded room. "If anyone else, members of the media, say, or the shrinks at the psychiatric hospital, saw this place, the first words that would spring to mind would be *mad scientist.*"

"I was just thinking that this lab looks a lot like mine," Sam said.

Abby cleared her throat. *"Mmm-hmm."*

He went to the bench to examine the laser. "Not as high-end, but most of the basics are here."

"Mmm-hmm."

He glanced back and saw that her eyes were sparkling with amusement. He sighed. "Go get the boxes and the Bubble Wrap. I want to take a look around before we pack this equipment."

"Okay." Abby turned and hurried back up the steps.

When she was gone, he went slowly, methodically, through the shed, opening cabinets and drawers. He discovered a number of stones and crystals, most of which would have been overlooked by the average rock hound. But with his senses mildly jacked, he could tell that several of the stones were hot.

He was holding one half of a split geode, studying the glittering crystals inside, when Abby reappeared.

"Find something interesting?" she asked.

"Nothing yet that would explain the voices that Grady heard." He put the geode down and took another look around. "He said the voice came from a crystal."

"A green crystal."

"I found several varieties of green quartz, a small piece of green tourmaline and some green andradite, but none of it was giving off enough energy to explain the voices he was hearing."

"Shall I start wrapping up the equipment while you look around?"

"All right. But I'd better dismantle the laser for you."

She smiled. "It looks like he found it in a scrap yard."

"He probably bought the various parts online and assembled them himself."

Sam started back to the workbench. A faint hiss of energy made him pause in midstride. To his slightly heightened senses, it sounded as if a small insect was buzzing somewhere nearby. He turned on his heel, searching for the source, and caught a flash of green out of the corner of his eye. When he tried to take a closer look, he discovered he could not focus clearly on the object that was giving off the energy.

"What is it?" Abby asked.

"I'm not sure yet." He stopped trying to see the object with his normal vision and raised his talent to the max. The dull gray of the concrete floor and the faded paint on the walls were abruptly transformed. The basement was now lit with ultralight. The rocks and crystals in Grady's collection glowed, bathing the space in a paranormal rainbow.

The buzzing-insect sound grew louder but not more distinct.

"Got it," Sam said.

"What?" Abby asked. "Where? I don't see anything except the rocks and equipment that you've already checked."

"Go hot. You'll hear it, too."

Energy warmed the atmosphere as she

went into the zone.

"Good grief," she said. "You're right. It sounds like a scratchy old audio recording of some kind."

"That's exactly what it is." Sam went to the filing cabinet and examined the array of precision-cut objects on top. "A recording. It's emanating from one of these."

"Those aren't crystals or rocks. They look like modernistic glass sculptures."

"They're prisms," he said. "Very special prisms. Grady probably used them to focus energy as well as light."

"There's a recording inside one of those prisms?"

"That's the only explanation that fits," he said. "It must have been laid down with psychic energy, and probably tuned to Grady's wavelengths. That's why we can only detect a faint buzz but not distinct words."

He picked up a heavy green glass prism. The shiver of energy got a bit louder but not much. "It's very weak to our senses, but it was probably a lot louder, stronger and clearer to Grady."

Abby moved closer. "I've never seen a prism like that one."

"It's called a retroreflector, a trihedral prism. It's designed to reflect energy or a beam of light back to its source, regardless of direction. Standard equipment in labs. But this particular prism focuses paranormal energy, not the normal kind. If it was tuned to Grady's aura, it would focus on him whenever he was in the vicinity."

"Once it acquired the fix, it activated the recording?"

"I think so, yes. The prism detected our presence and triggered the psychic message when we entered the room, but since it isn't tuned to either of us, we can barely sense the recording. Grady was never able to tell where the voice was coming from, because every time he tried to look at the prism, it reflected his own psychic wavelengths right back at him, blinding him while simultaneously playing the message."

"Sheesh. Over time, that would have driven anyone nuts."

"I think it would be more accurate to say that it had a hypnotic effect on Grady. Let me have some of that Bubble Wrap."

Abby picked up the scissors she had brought and cut off a length of the wrap. "I've never heard of a psi-recording. I didn't know such a thing was possible."

"The technology is in the experimental stage. This prism came out of a very sophisticated, cutting-edge R-and-D lab."

She handed him the Bubble Wrap and glanced around the room. "What about the gun? Where do you think Grady got that?"

"Whoever recorded the hypnotic message in this thing probably made sure the gun was conveniently at hand when Grady went to Vaughn's house that day."

"Poor Grady. That thing looks valuable."

"It's worth a fortune to certain people."

Abby frowned. "Think it came from your competitor's labs?"

"No." Sam peeled off a strip of packing tape and secured the Bubble Wrap around the prism. "This didn't come from the Helicon Stone labs."

"You're sure?"

"Trust me."

"So who else is running a hotshot R-and-D lab that could turn out something like that prism?"

Sam looked at her. "Take a wild guess."

"Oh, yeah, right. Coppersmith Inc."

"Yes."

"Oh, geez. This is not good."

"No," Sam said. "It's not good."

"You said the prism was valuable. Wonder why the guy who gave it to Grady didn't come back for it?"

Sam picked up the bundled prism. "Maybe because he couldn't get through the crystal lock on the door of this shed."

Sam stowed the last taped and sealed box in the cargo bay of the SUV.

"Where are we going to store all of this stuff?" Abby asked.

"We'll take it back to the Copper Beach house for safekeeping until we figure out how to spring Grady from the hospital."

Abby looked at him. "We are going to get him out, aren't we?"

"Yes. But right now he's safer where he is."

"What do you mean?"

Sam closed the cargo door. "As long as everyone assumes he's crazy, he's not a threat to whoever set him up."

"Oh," Abby said. "I see what you mean."

Sam started toward the shed. "I'll be right back."

"Where are you going?"

"I want to see if I can remove the crystal from the lock that Grady used to secure his lab door. It's a nice piece of engineering. I'd rather not leave it behind."

"Good thought."

She followed him back around the house and checked her email while he studied the lock. He would have to dismantle the whole mechanism, he concluded, which meant using a screwdriver and some other tools.

He was in the process of removing the lock when he heard Abby's sharp exclamation.

"Sam, we got it."

He eased the lock out of the door. "Got what?"

"The lab book."

"But the auction was set for two days from now."

"Not any longer," she said. "Our preemptive bid has been accepted."

He gripped the lock in one hand and looked around the edge of the door. "Are you sure?"

"Not until I actually see it." Abby was aglow with triumph and excitement. "But I just got a message from Milton, who claims that he wants to unload the lab book as quickly as possible and he's giving my client first crack. Actually, we're getting first and last crack. He wants to know if we're still interested."

"Why did we get lucky?"

"In a word, me. I told you, my reputation is good. The bottom line here is that Milton is running scared and wants to unload the lab book as quickly and safely as possible."

"He figures I'm the safe bet, because you wouldn't be working for me if you thought I might be untrustworthy."

"That's pretty much what it comes down to," she said. "He's decided to trust you because he trusts me. But he wants to move fast. I get the impression that he is very nervous. Believe me when I tell you that it takes a lot to make someone like Milton nervous."

Sam pulled the lock mechanism out of the wall. "Get the details. Tell him the money will be wired into whatever account he wants as soon as we have verified the authenticity of the journal."

She sent the message. A moment later, she looked up from the screen.

"Done. Milton just sent the code for the pickup location and his bank-account information."

Sam headed for the door. "Where is the pickup point?"

"A place where no one ever thinks twice about someone collecting a package."

41

"I left a shopping bag here a couple of hours ago," Abby said. She held up the claim ticket that she had found in a sidewalk planter in front of the museum.

The woman behind the coat- and package-check desk smiled. "I'll be right back." She took the ticket and disappeared into a back room.

Sam glanced around. "Isn't this a risky way to conduct business?"

"Beats the old locker routine at the bus station," Abby said.

Sam surveyed the monumental glass-walled forum in which they stood. There was art everywhere, some of it hanging from the high ceiling. "Definitely more upmarket."

The woman reappeared. She held out the shopping bag with the familiar department-store logo on its side. "Here you are."

"Thanks," Abby said.

She took the bag and opened her senses a little. Currents of energy swirled in the atmosphere. The object inside was hot. She looked at Sam and knew that he had picked up on the heat. Without a word, he took the shopping bag from her. They walked through the front doors onto First Avenue and turned right toward the Pike Place Market.

"This better be the right lab book," Sam said.

"I'm sure it is."

"Wonder where Milton is? Think he's watching us?"

"No," Abby said. "I think he's on a plane out of town as we speak. I told you, he was scared."

"Like everyone else involved in this thing."

"Except us, of course," she said proudly.

"Speak for yourself."

"Hah. Nothing scares you, Sam Coppersmith."

"You're wrong. I've been running on the edge of panic since that first day you came to see me on the island."

"I don't believe that for a minute."

"Believe it," he said.

"Why?"

"Because I've known from the start that you were in danger."

She glanced at him. "And that scares you?"

"Like nothing else I've ever encountered in my life."

"Oh," Abby said. She was not sure what to do with that information. "I've known some people who were scared *of* me but not *for* me. Except for my mom, of course. But she's been gone a long time."

"Trust me, I'm scared for you. That's why we're headed back to the island."

"Okay," Abby said. "For now, I mean. I appreciate it. But I can't stay there forever. After I break the code on this book for you, my job is done. I've got things to do. I have to find a new place to live, someplace that will take dogs. Got to put my old condo on the market. Then I have to get back to work."

"We'll take it as it comes."

A brisk wind whipped Abby's hair. She could see a bank of ominous dark clouds moving in over Elliott Bay.

"It's going to rain soon," she said.

"I understand it does that a lot around here."

It was clear that Sam's mind was not focused on the weather.

"How will we know?" Abby asked after a while.

"What?"

"How will we know when this thing is over? It will be easy to get the word out that the lab book has been acquired by a new owner and that the code has been broken. Heck, I'm sure it's already out in the underground. But we can't be sure that will be the end of the matter. What if whoever tried to kidnap me decides to try to steal the book from you?"

"I don't think the killer will risk trying to steal the lab book from my vault. He knows that he can't get through my lock."

"You're still convinced that whoever is after the book is the person who murdered Cassidy, aren't you?"

"I'm sure of it."

"Now what?"

"Now we go home. Can't miss the annual tech summit and the big barbecue."

"I didn't realize you were looking forward to it."

"The weekend is going to be a lot more interesting than usual this year."

"Why?"

"The killer will be there."

42

The Coppersmith family compound was ablaze with fiery grills. The annual Black Box technical summit was concluded, and the big barbecue was in full swing. The weather had cooperated, with plenty of sunshine and temperatures in the mid-seventies. The long summer day was drawing to a close, but there was still some light in the evening sky.

Abby stood at the edge of the crowd, a glass of sparkling water in her hand, and tried to shake off the chill that was lifting the hairs on her neck. Everything looked normal. There was a line in front of the open bar set up under a large tent. Elias and Willow Coppersmith were mingling with their guests. The sound of laughter and conversation rose up into the trees. All appeared as it should, except for one thing. A few minutes ago, Sam had disappeared.

Earlier that afternoon, he had given a

series of tours of his lab, answering an endless string of questions. Abby had been amazed at his patience with the children and teenagers. Afterward, he had done his duty, socializing with the employees and their families. But now he was gone.

She took a sip of the sparkling water. She hadn't had anything stronger to drink all afternoon, even though she could have used something to calm her nerves. A strange darkness was gathering at the edges of her senses. Every time she tried to focus on it, the eerie shadows flickered out of sight. But the sense of wrongness was intensifying. The only thing she knew for certain was that it was linked to Sam. He had set his trap, and now he was waiting for the killer to walk into it.

She had assumed the snare involved catching the killer on camera in the lab. But now she was having doubts.

Jenny O'Connell materialized out of the crowd. She had a glass of wine in one hand.

"I've been looking for you, Abby," she said. "I wanted to apologize for my behavior the other day, when you and Sam came to the Black Box library. To be honest, I was a little taken aback, or maybe just plain insulted, that Sam Coppersmith was using a freelancer to go after a hot book for his family's personal collection."

"I understand," Abby said. "It's okay. I know what librarians and academics think about those of us who work the underground market."

"It's hard enough having serious academic degrees and just enough talent to know that the paranormal is real. Most of us in that category have to pretend that we don't really believe in the existence of extrasensory perception, psychic energy or any of the rest of it. We tell people that we study the sadly deluded folks who do believe in it and examine the effects of such bizarre beliefs on culture and society."

"I understand," Abby said again. She couldn't think of anything else to say.

"Unlike many of my colleagues, I was lucky enough to get a job in a scholarly collection like the Coppersmith company library, where the paranormal is taken seriously. And what did I do? I treated you the way my old academic colleagues would have treated me if they had realized that I actually do believe in the paranormal."

"I get that," Abby said. She smiled. "My father has spent a lot of time in the academic world. I have a sense of how things work there. Please don't worry. I accept your apology."

"Thank you." Jenny sounded grateful and relieved. "I really would like to know more about your end of the field. I have to admit that I've always had a great curiosity about the private collectors' market. It's such a mystery, and so intriguing. Perhaps we can talk shop one of these days?"

"Sure," Abby said.

"Wonderful. I'll look forward to it."

Jenny wandered off in the direction of the bar. Abby watched her go and then turned to search the crowd once more. There was still no sign of Sam.

There was something else that was bothering her now, as well. Jenny O'Connell had been in the company of Gerald Frye for most of the evening. Now she was alone.

43

Sam sat in the chair, ankles stacked on the corner of his desk, and listened for the sound of footsteps in the hall. His gun was on top of the desk. So was the green prism.

It was just a matter of time. He had seen the killer make his way to the edge of the crowd a few minutes ago. Sooner or later, he would show up in the lab.

The desk lamp was switched off, but Sam was jacked. The crystals and stones in the display cases glowed in the darkness, casting the strange shadows that could be created only by ultralight.

The footsteps he had been waiting for echoed in the hallway at last, faint at first and then louder as they neared the door. There was a short pause.

The door opened slowly. A figure appeared, silhouetted in the opening. A toxic mix of fear, panic and desperation burned in the atmosphere.

The intruder hesitated, then moved quickly into the room and closed the door. There was a sharp click. A penlight beam arced through the darkness and came to rest on the packing boxes in the corner.

"You don't have to go through the boxes, Dr. Frye," Sam said. "I've got what you're looking for here on my desk."

Gerald Frye froze. "Sam."

"I had a feeling you would be the one who came here tonight, but I had to be sure."

"I was looking for you, Sam. Your mother noticed that you had disappeared from the party. She's worried because you've been so depressed lately. She asked me to see if you'd retreated here to your lab. I told her that you probably just wanted to get away from the crowd for a while, but that I'd make sure you were okay."

"Skip the bullshit," Sam said. "You're here to get the prism that you used to manipulate Grady Hastings. Must have come as a shock today when I mentioned during the tour that I had packed up the contents of the lab of a small-time researcher named Hastings."

"I don't know what you're talking about."

"The prism is the one thing that connects you to Grady Hastings. You realized that if I ever examined it closely, I would know that it had probably come from the Black Box lab. You were right."

"You're not making any sense," Frye said.

"I recognized the para-engineering immediately. Knew it could only have come from our facility. But there's a large staff in the Black Box. It took me a while to go through the list of suspects. I had a hunch you were the one who had created the hypnotic recording and tuned it to Grady Hastings's aura, though. You're one of the very few people in that lab with the technical expertise and the talent to do it. But that didn't mean that you were the killer. There was always the possibility that someone else had used your device. Trust me, I know how it feels to be set up. I didn't want to make a mistake, so I ran this little experiment tonight."

"I don't know what you're talking about." Frye edged toward the door.

"There's no point trying to run. It's over. Just a couple of things I want to get clear. Whose idea was it to try to steal the crystals? Yours or Cassidy's?"

"I'm not going to answer any of your questions. If you lay a hand on me, I'll scream bloody murder. There are a couple hundred people outside."

"We're in a concrete basement. No one will hear you scream." Sam took his feet down off the desk, sat forward and rested one hand on the glowing green prism. "But I'm not going to touch you. We're just going to talk."

"Why would I do that?"

"Because you want me to know how brilliant and how talented you are."

There was stunned silence. A great calm descended on Frye. He moved to the nearest display case and examined the cut geode inside. The blue ultralight from the glittering crystals embedded in the rock etched his face in eerie shadows.

Frye grunted. "Everyone said you were heartbroken, but I knew you were just pissed off because you had let Cassidy get so close to your family's secrets."

"That was part of it." Sam got up and walked around to the front of the desk. He leaned back against the edge and folded his arms. "So whose idea was it to try to steal the crystals?"

"Mine. I recognized Cassidy Lawrence for the opportunist she was the first time I met her. We were two of a kind. I dropped a few hints about the Phoenix stones. Imagine my surprise when I found out that she was already aware of them. That's why she set out to seduce you at that gem-and-mineral show."

"Guess that explains a few things."

"Cassidy, of course, thought she was using me. She was accustomed to being able to manipulate every man she encountered. She certainly dazzled you."

"How did she learn about the crystals?"

"The rumors of the Phoenix Mine have had forty years to turn into a legend. Cassidy came from a long line of crystal talents. She paid attention to that kind of chatter. She picked up the whispers of the Phoenix a year ago and started doing some serious research. She arranged to meet you at that gem-and-mineral show. The next thing you know, you're giving her a tour of the lab and she's filling out a job application."

"You started working for us before Cassidy did. How did you learn about the Phoenix Mine and the crystals?"

"Ray Willis filled up more than one lab notebook with the records of his experiments," Frye said. Cold triumph rang in his words.

"I'll be damned. Willis kept more than one notebook?"

"There were two, the one he showed to your father and Knox, and a second one in which he kept his own private records. Shortly before the explosion in the mine, he sent the second one to my mother for safekeeping."

"Why would he send it to your mother?"

"The two of them were lovers at the time that your father and the others discovered that vein of crystals," Frye said. "He realized the true value of the stones immediately, and wanted to conceal some of the results of his experiments from his partners."

"Did your mother have any idea of how dangerous the stones are?"

"No, of course not. The first lab book wasn't encrypted, but it might as well have been, as far as she was concerned. The notes are all written in the form of para-physics equations and technical jargon. I found it when I went through her things after she died a few years ago. But there was nothing in the notebook concerning the exact location of the Phoenix Mine."

"But after you found the lab book you knew who did have that information, though, didn't you? Your father's partners, Elias Coppersmith and Quinn Knox."

"I managed to track down Knox," Frye said. "He was deep into the booze and the pills by then. I tried to question him, but I couldn't get much out of him. His brain was mush. He told some very tall tales about the Phoenix Mine, but he had long since forgotten the coordinates, or pretended that he had forgotten. All I got from him was that it was somewhere in Nevada."

"Lot of desert in Nevada."

"Knox did let slip one other interesting bit of information. He told me the story of how he and your father had escaped from the mine after Willis tried to murder them. He said that they both nearly died because your father insisted on carrying out a sack of rocks."

"You realized that my family probably still had the crystals."

"I decided my best bet was to get a job with Coppersmith Inc.," Frye said. "With my talent, it wasn't hard to work my way into the Black Box facility."

"You became a trusted employee, but you couldn't find what you wanted most, the location of the Phoenix. And there was no record of the geodes that my father had carried out of the mine the day of the explosion."

"Since the stones were not housed in the lab vault, I knew they were most likely either here on the island or down in Sedona," Frye said. "Couldn't see the Coppersmith family letting the crystals get too far out of sight. After a couple of visits here, I realized that your private lab was the most likely place."

"But my security is good, and you didn't

even know where the vault was located. You needed to get someone inside. And then Cassidy came on the scene, and you saw your opportunity. How did she find the vault in the wall?"

"There aren't that many firms that specialize in high-end vaults and safes here in the Northwest. I eventually tracked down one that had a record of an installation here on Legacy a few years ago. There weren't many details, but a contractor had left some handwritten notes that made it clear the safe had been installed in a basement wall."

"Cassidy had the freedom of the whole house when she stayed here with me. But I still don't know how she found the vault. I never showed it to her."

"Finding it wasn't that hard," Frye said. "I knew there had to be a phony wall somewhere, and that the vault would be behind it. I gave Cassidy one of the high-end metal detectors we use in the lab. It didn't take her long to find the lever that opens the wall."

"After that, the two of you figured you were home free. You weren't concerned about your ability to crack the vault. Given your lab equipment and your talent, you assumed that would be a piece of cake. You chose a night when you knew that I was going to be away from the island on a consulting trip."

"When you go off on one of those trips, you're generally gone for several days," Frye said. "We knew we'd have plenty of time."

"You and Cassidy came to the island in a private boat. You anchored in one of the small pocket beaches to make sure no one in town witnessed your arrival. You made your way here and managed to disarm my house security system."

"I've always had a talent for locks, and yours had come straight out of a Coppersmith lab," Frye said. "That part was easy. Cassidy and I came down here to the basement. She showed me the mechanism that opens the fake wall."

"You got the wall open, but then you discovered that there was a new lock on the safe, one you couldn't hack."

"That damn crystal lock is your own design, isn't it?" Rage flashed in Frye's voice and in his aura. "I realized immediately I wouldn't be able to open it. The only option was to blow it. That's what Cassidy wanted me to do. But I hadn't come prepared for that. I knew enough about the crystals to know they were volatile. The last thing I wanted to do was use an explosive device. She was screaming at me."

"So you cut your losses and murdered her."

"I had to kill her," Frye said. "I had no choice. She was raving mad, furious with me for failing to get into the safe. She said I was a screwup. I'm pretty sure she intended to kill me. I acted first."

"Plan B, stealing the crystals, had fallen apart. You went back to plan A, trying to find the Phoenix Mine. This time, you decided to go at it using a research approach. You spent a lot of time in the Coppersmith company library. You even started a relationship with the librarian, Jenny O'Connell."

"Jenny knows a great deal about the hot-books market," Frye said. "Between you and me, she's fascinated with it. She even hangs out in some of the underground chat rooms. I asked her to help me search for a forty-year-old lab notebook rumored to contain some experiments performed on some rare earths from an old mine in Nevada. She got a real kick out of the challenge."

"Does she know why you wanted to find that notebook?"

"No. Of course I didn't tell her anything about the Phoenix or my connection to it. I had to be very careful. Jenny's a true-blue company employee. She would have gone straight to someone in the Coppersmith family if she had suspected that she was prying into your family secrets."

"Good to know," Sam said.

"Jenny suddenly caught nibbles of a forty-year-old book that was rumored to be coming up for sale in the private market. The underground chatter was that the book was a notebook containing records of some crystal experiments and that it was encrypted. I knew I had to get hold of it. But Jenny didn't have the kind of connections required to do a deal deep in the underground market."

"Her lack of connections didn't matter, anyway, because you didn't have the kind of money you needed to go after an encrypted book. They're expensive. You had to find another angle."

"Yes," Frye said. "I needed someone in the underground market who could not only find the book for me but also break the code."

"So you set out to find your own freelancer. You got lucky and came up with Abby."

Frye rocked a little on his heels. "How did you put it together?"

"You made one critical mistake. You used the Summerlight Academy student records to find the local talent you needed."

"You know about that? I admit, that does surprise me."

"You were obviously aware that the Summerlight Academy had more than its share of talents among the alumni, because troubled teens with certain para-psych profiles often ended up there. How did you discover that? Were you a student at the academy?"

"No," Frye said. "My mother was one of the counselors at Summerlight for years. She had some talent herself, enough to realize that several of the so-called troubled teens in the school were actually psychically gifted. She wanted to follow them and study them over time. She even went so far as to shape the admissions criteria to ensure that families dealing with teens who displayed certain kinds of psychological issues were encouraged to enroll their kids in the academy."

"In time, she created a very handy database of talents throughout the Pacific Northwest."

"For all the good it did her," Frye said. "Most of the real talents at the school either dropped out of sight after they graduated or refused to cooperate in her research study."

"But you were able to use the records to

trace Abby."

"The files were very complete," Frye said. "I found family names and addresses, and the name of the college she had attended. With all that to go on, the investigator I hired had no trouble locating her. After all, she had never left Seattle."

"Before you contacted her, however, you wanted to be certain that she could actually deal with serious psi-encryption."

"I certainly didn't want to risk another disaster like the Cassidy Lawrence fiasco," Frye said.

"So you set up an experiment to test Abby's abilities."

"When she took the job cataloging Vaughn's library, I saw the opportunity to conduct my test. Thanks to Jenny, I knew that Hannah Vaughn was rumored to have a small collection of encrypted books in her collection, including *The Key.*"

"To run your experiment, you needed another talent, someone you could manipulate with the prism. You chose Grady Hastings out of the Summerlight files, too. How did you get the prism into his lab?"

Frye snorted. "That was simple. I mailed it to him, explained it was a free sample from an online company that made scientific and research equipment. Miss Radwell passed the test with flying colors."

"But you knew that you couldn't afford her, even if you could get someone to refer you, so you started sending blackmail notes. Abby, however, immediately contacted Webber. By then he had heard the rumors about the lab notebook. He realized that Abby might be in danger. He sent her to me."

"I couldn't believe it," Frye hissed. He slammed a fist on the nearest workbench. "It was as if there was a conspiracy against me."

"It was a classic example of the oldest law of engineering. Anything that can go wrong will go wrong, and at the worst possible moment."

"No, it was your fault, you son of a bitch," Frye snarled. "When luck breaks, it always breaks in your favor. You should have been arrested for murder after you found Cassidy's body. But you walked away. When the rumors of the lab book started circulating, who does Abby run to for protection? *You.* I set up a careful, controlled experiment, and you figure it out because you believed the wild story of a kid who has been declared certifiable."

"For the record, Grady hasn't been declared crazy yet. He's still undergoing observation. But yeah, I figured it out. What are the odds?"

"Don't you dare laugh at me, you bastard," Frye said. "I have as much claim on those crystals as you or anyone else in the Coppersmith family."

"In that case, maybe you should have been up front about those claims instead of hiding your true identity, infiltrating Coppersmith Inc. and murdering an innocent young woman."

"Cassidy Lawrence was no innocent, but that aside, I had no choice. I knew that you would never give me my share of those crystals or tell me the location of the mine."

"Because the stones are dangerous."

"I'll be damned." Frye was amused. "You're afraid of them, aren't you? You and the rest of the Coppersmiths are prepared to let them sit in that vault forever, rather than discover their properties and find out what they can do."

"We're not afraid of them. We're being cautious with them. We need more advanced technology and instrumentation before we risk running experiments on them."

"Your family doesn't deserve those crystals." Frye reached into his pocket and took out an object. "So I'm going to take them. Now."

"A gun, Frye? That's a little over-the-top."

"Not a gun. Something a lot more interesting. A weapon that only I can use, because I'm the one who constructed it. One that won't leave any evidence. You Coppersmiths aren't the only guys who can work crystal."

Dazzling energy flashed from the object in Frye's hand. An icy shock wave lanced through Sam's senses. He tried to move and discovered that he could not even unfold his arms. The glowing stones and crystals in the cases did not dim, but the atmosphere took on an eerie, foglike quality.

"What made you think that I created only one prism?" Frye asked. "The one you found in Grady Hastings's house was a simple version I designed to deliver hypnotic commands. But this one is far more sophisticated. It throws the subject into a trance that is more like a true dreamstate. You will know what you are doing, but you won't be able to resist my orders. You will open the vault for me, and then you will take your own life using your own gun. For the record, this is what I used on Cassidy. While she was trapped in the dreamstate, I gave her an injection of a fast-acting drug that stops the heart but leaves no trace in the body."

The crystals and stones in the display cases were drifting in and out of the paranormal mist now. Sam fought to focus his para-senses and discovered that he no longer had any control over them. He could hear every word Frye said, but he could not respond.

"The difference between a true dream-state and your present condition is that under the influence of the prism, you are aware that you are locked in a dream." Frye walked slowly through the maze of glowing specimens. "Aware that you are powerless."

Sam watched one of the glowing rocks in the gallery burst into flames. The fire wasn't real. He knew that. But in his dreamstate, it seemed very real.

"I did bring a gun," Frye said. "But this time, we'll use yours."

He went behind the desk and picked up the pistol. Sam watched, helpless to stop him.

Frye's words echoed in his head. *You are aware that you are locked in a dream. . . .*

That was the definition of a lucid dream. According to Abby's friend Gwen, strong talents were especially good at manipulating lucid dreams: they just had to focus.

With an effort of will, he succeeded in pulling his attention away from the burning stone. The paranormal flames were abruptly extinguished. But now the darkly glittering interior of one of the geodes summoned him into an endless black hole in the universe. In the distance, he heard a labored *thud-thud-thud.* His heart. He was using a harrowing amount of energy to overcome the effects of the prism.

A spark of fire caught his eye. He managed to look down and saw that the stone in his ring was burning. *Real energy. Not part of the dream.*

"You will open the vault for me now," Frye said.

Slowly, painfully, Sam began to unwind his arms. Each tiny movement required enormous effort. It was like moving through quicksand.

And then he heard the light footsteps in the outer hall. A woman.

Abby.

"That will very likely be Miss Radwell, come to see what's keeping you," Frye said. "I didn't plan this, but it's going to work out well. When your new girlfriend walks through that door, she will be silhouetted against the light, a very easy target. You will kill her, and then you will open the vault. Afterward, you will turn the gun on yourself. Given your recent history of depression, no one will be terribly surprised."

The footsteps drew closer. Now he could

hear a familiar clicking sound. Dog nails. Abby had Newton with her.

Sam tried to call Abby's name, but he could not get the words out.

It was the damned recurring nightmare made real.

The footsteps and the clicking stopped. Frye moved out from behind the desk and aimed the gun at the door.

Sam pulled hard on his senses. This dream was going to have a different ending.

And suddenly he knew intuitively how to shatter the trance. He focused everything he had left through the Phoenix stone. It was all he had to work with, his only chance to save Abby.

He found the resonating frequency buried deep in the heart of the stone, the latent power that he had always known was there. In that moment, it was his to command.

The Phoenix crystal blazed with dark fire, swamping the energy that Frye was using to maintain the dreamstate. Sam came out of the paralysis on a wave of raw power.

Paranormal lightning arced from the ring, igniting Frye's aura. Psi-fire blazed around him, enveloping him in flames. He opened his mouth in a silent scream. His body stiffened, as if electrified. The gun and the prism fell from his hands. Violent convulsions racked his body.

He crumpled and collapsed without making a sound. The paranormal fire winked out. So did Frye's aura.

The door of the room slammed open. But it was not Abby who stood silhouetted in the doorway. Newton charged into the shadows, low to the ground, silent and dangerous. He locked his jaws around Frye's right ankle.

"Abby," Sam said. "Call off your dog."

Abby appeared. "Newton. That's enough."

Newton released the ankle and trotted back to her.

"See?" Sam said. "He goes for the ankles every time."

Abby ignored that. "Everything okay in here?"

Sam glanced down at his ring. The crystal was no longer burning.

He looked at her. "It is now."

44

"Well, of course you should have known that I wouldn't do something dumb like open the door and make a perfect target out of myself," Abby said. She patted Newton's head. "I watch TV like everyone else. You don't charge into an unknown situation. But Newton is a lot shorter than me. I knew that no one would be expecting a dog to be the first one through the door."

Newton licked her hand. She fed him another treat, his fourth or fifth, Sam thought. He had lost count.

Sam raised his glass. "Here's to Newton."

"To Newton," Willow said.

"To Newton," Elias repeated.

The four of them were sitting in the living room of the big house. A fire burned brightly on the wide stone hearth. The Coppersmith employees and their families had returned to their island lodgings, preparing to leave in the morning. The county sheriff and a deputy had come and gone, taking Gerald Frye's body with them.

Everyone seemed to think that Frye had died of a heart attack. There was, Sam thought, nothing to indicate otherwise. He looked at his ring and thought about the raw power he had pulled from the small Phoenix crystal. So much energy from just a tiny stone.

"Not to take away anything from Newton's act of derring-do," Abby said, "but it's obvious that Sam had the situation under control before Newton and I arrived."

"Don't be so sure of that." Sam swallowed some of his whiskey and set the glass down on the arm of his chair. He gazed into the flames. "In a weird way, I think it was knowing that you were coming down the hall and that you would open the door that gave me the juice I needed to break through the trance."

"You would have escaped from the dreamstate with or without me," Abby said, with conviction.

Willow smiled. "You have a lot of confidence in my son."

Abby raised her glass. "Another professional."

Elias studied her with keen interest. "How did you know?"

"Know what?" Abby asked.

"That Sam was in danger?"

Abby rubbed Newton's ears. "I just knew. And there was a huge sense of urgency about the knowing. I knew he had set a trap in the lab, so that was the logical place to go first." She glared at Sam. "I thought you had set up cameras to photograph the killer when he went after the prism."

Willow frowned. "Yes, that was the plan."

"I changed the plan," Sam said. He took his attention off the flames and looked at Abby. "Did you know that Frye was in the lab with me?"

"I wasn't certain, but I had a feeling he might be there, because Jenny O'Connell was alone. Frye had been with her most of the day, but suddenly she was on her own. When I realized the door was unlocked, I flattened myself against the wall, just like they do on the cop shows, and sent Newton in." She smiled, not bothering to conceal her pride. "And it worked great. Except that you had already taken out Frye, so in the end, it was something of a nonevent."

"Trust me, it was not a nonevent from my perspective," Sam said. He drank some more whiskey. He was still riding a post-burn buzz, but he was going to crash soon.

Elias scowled at him. "Why didn't you tell

us that you suspected Frye was the one who would walk into your trap?"

"He didn't tell you because he didn't want to get it wrong," Abby said quietly. "Sam knows what it's like to be falsely accused."

Willow sighed. "I understand. So does Elias. It's just that you took such a risk, Sam."

"A calculated risk," Sam said. He drank some more whiskey. "What I did not factor into the equation was the possibility that Frye might have another prism weapon. Also, I didn't factor in Abby."

"Or Newton," Abby said.

"No," Sam said. He smiled and rested his head against the back of the chair. The exhaustion was starting to seep through him. "I didn't make allowances for Newton, either."

Elias shook his head in disgust. "There were a few things that I failed to factor in, too. All these years I've been watching for a single lab book to surface. Knox and I were aware of only the one notebook containing the record of the experiments. It never dawned on us that Ray Willis had filled up a second notebook with the results of experiments that he ran in secret."

"The question now," Sam said, "is where did Gerald Frye stash the other notebook?"

"With luck, it will be among his personal possessions," Elias said. "We need to get someone inside his house as fast as possible to search the place."

"I can do it after I've had some sleep," Sam said.

"Forget it," Elias said. "I'll handle the search first thing in the morning. According to Frye's personnel records, he had no close family. No one will think it strange if his employer takes charge of his personal possessions until someone arrives who is authorized to claim them."

"Which may be never," Sam said.

Elias shook his head. "I still can't believe that we spent the past few days thinking that the threat was coming from Lander Knox. When all along, Gerald Frye was right there in the Black Box lab, plotting against us."

"I think we've still got a problem with Lander Knox," Sam said.

"You're right," Abby said. "There are a lot of unanswered questions here. Did Gerald Frye kill Thaddeus Webber and that other book dealer?"

"No," Sam said. He steepled his hands and contemplated the fire. "He didn't have the connections in the underground market to identify those dealers, let alone locate them. Someone else murdered those two people."

"What about the thugs who tried to kidnap me? Do you think Frye hired them?"

"No. Whoever murdered Webber sent that pair to keep watch for you."

"Lander Knox," Elias said grimly. "He's still out there."

"I agree with you," Sam said. "We'll find him. But the process of connecting all the dots will have to wait until morning. I can't think clearly enough to do that tonight."

"You need sleep," Willow said.

Abby nodded. "Yes, you do."

"I'm not arguing." Sam pushed himself up out of the chair. "If you will all excuse me, I'm going to crash."

He started toward the bedroom stairs.

"One more thing before you leave," Elias said.

Sam paused and turned back. "What?"

"You said Frye told you that his mother had an affair with Ray Willis and that Willis entrusted her with that other notebook."

"Yes," Sam said. "Willis didn't want you and Knox to know about those experiments."

"What about the missing crystals?" Elias asked. "The ones he used in the field tests? Knox and I searched for them after the explosion, but we never found them."

"I don't have the answer to that question," Sam said. "All I can tell you is that Frye made it clear he did not have them. That was one of the reasons he was so desperate to get his hands on the Coppersmith crystals. He felt that he had been deprived of his inheritance."

"His *inheritance?*" Willow's eyes widened. "You mean . . ."

"Of course," Abby said quietly. "It all makes sense now, including the psychic genetics. Ray Willis was Gerald Frye's father, the father he never knew."

45

Abby awoke to the knowledge that Sam was no longer in the bed. She opened her eyes and saw him standing at the window. His strong, bare shoulders were silhouetted against the moonlight. His hard face was in shadow. He was not alone. Newton was beside him, front paws braced on the windowsill. Together, both males contemplated the darkness.

Abby sat up against the pillows and wrapped her arms around her knees.

"Did you have another one of your nightmares?" she asked.

"No." Sam looked at her. "I woke up a while ago and couldn't get back to sleep."

"You had a rough evening. We all did, but you endured that dreamstate experience and nearly got killed. That kind of stress takes some time to get over."

"That's not why I couldn't sleep. I started thinking about some of the missing answers."

"You said they could wait until morning. The main thing to focus on tonight is that you solved Cassidy Lawrence's murder. That should give you some closure."

"Closure. Good word," Sam said. He turned away from the window and moved back toward the bed. "It does feel a lot like a door has been closed somewhere, this time for good. But there is another door still ajar. I think your stepbrother is standing on the other side."

"Dawson?"

"We need to find that investor, the one who is pressuring him to acquire the lab book."

"You think the investor is Lander Knox, don't you?"

"I think there's a strong possibility of that, yes."

"Even if you're right, Knox has to know the chase is over and that he lost. The lab book is no longer on the market."

"If he's killed two people to get it, he's unlikely to stop now. We need to find him."

Abby shivered. "I can call Dawson in the morning, tell him what's going on. Maybe he'll believe me and cooperate with us to help find the investor."

"Yes."

Newton dropped his front paws to the floor and trotted to the door.

"He wants to go out," Abby said.

"And then he'll want to come back in."

"It's the way of all dogs."

Sam went to the door and opened it. "Remind me to install a dog door this week."

Abby watched Sam and Newton disappear into the darkened hallway.

Remind me to install a dog door. She smiled. A gentle warmth spread through her. Installing a dog door sounded like a long-term plan, as if Sam was envisioning a future that included her and Newton.

She listened to the kitchen door open and close. Sam came back to the bedroom alone, got out of his pants and got into bed. He reached for Abby and drew her across his chest.

"Tonight, in the lab," he said, "when I heard you coming down the hall and realized that I could not stop you, I think I went a little crazy."

She framed his face between her palms and kissed him firmly on the mouth, silencing him. "No, that's not what happened. You need to remember events correctly. What *happened* is that, in an emergency, you pulled on psychic energy that you did not know you possessed because you've never had to use that much of it before. You broke free of the trance in time. If I had been dumb enough to open that door, I would have been okay, because you clocked Gerald first."

He put two fingers over her mouth. "You didn't let me finish."

She sensed his amusement and winced.

"Sorry," she said. "So what were you going to say?"

"That when I went a little crazy trying to break free of the trance, I suddenly realized that I could use the ring to do it."

"Really?" She pushed herself up on her elbows and peered at his ring. She could not see it in the shadows, so she jacked up her talent a little and studied the tiny aurora of energy that leaked out of the stone. "You figured out what it can do?"

"I think it acts as a kind of psychic laser." Sam raised his hand and examined the ring. "At least that's what happened tonight. I was able to channel my own energy through it and focus it in a way I've never been able to do before. I could feel the currents overwhelming Frye, setting his aura on fire."

"You didn't say anything to your parents tonight about using the ring."

"Because I'm still not sure what happened. I'll talk to Dad in the morning, though. We need to run some experiments." Sam paused. "Very careful experiments. And I need to contact my brother and sister, warn them that the rings appear to have laserlike properties and that they can be deadly."

"Maybe you'll know more when I break the code on the lab book."

"Yes." Sam thrust his fingers into her hair and wrapped them around the back of her head. "There's something we need to talk about."

"The lab book?"

"Not the damn lab book. The real reason I was able to pull the extra energy I needed to break the trance tonight was you."

"Me? But I was out in the hall."

"I knew you were there. And you were running hot. There's a connection between us, Abby."

"I know. It's weird, isn't it?"

"No, it's love."

She froze. Her mouth went dry. *"Sam."*

"I needed some additional power, and I drew it from the link between us."

"I realize there's some kind of psychic vibe going on here. But there might be a very straightforward explanation involving the resonating frequencies of our auras. Or something."

He touched the corner of her mouth. "I'm the expert here. If I wanted a para-physics explanation for what's going on between us, I'd have come up with it. But I don't need one. I love you. I have from the moment you stepped out of Dixon's water taxi. It was as if I'd been waiting for you all of my life and you had finally decided to show up."

Warmth and wonder sparkled through her. "Oh, Sam."

"You were like some fabulous new crystal, glowing with unknown fire and mystery. And you were in danger, and I had so much damn baggage."

"Well, to be fair, I had a lot of baggage, too."

"I know. Someone was trying to grab you."

"That wasn't the kind of baggage I meant," she said. "I'm talking about more serious baggage."

"What the hell is more serious than someone trying to kidnap you?"

She cleared her throat. "I have never been one to take risks when it comes to romantic relationships."

"Oh, yeah, right. The commitment-and-trust-issues thing."

"Yes. But I've always suspected that the shrinks and the counselors were wrong. I was pretty sure that I was just waiting for the right man to walk into my life. I knew I'd recognize him, you see."

Sam traced her bottom lip with one finger. "Did you?"

"The instant I turned and saw you coming toward me along the dock that first day. I recognized you, but I told myself I had gotten it all wrong. There was so much drama going on all around us. Everything was happening way too fast. For Pete's sake, we had sex the first night that we were together. I never do things like that."

"We made love that first night. Big difference."

"Sure, but at the time all I could focus on was the weird feeling that there was some kind of psychic connection forming between us. It was very confusing. I was afraid to trust what my senses were telling me. But now I know that what was really going on was that I was falling head over heels in love with you."

He drew her mouth down to his. Abby felt him open his senses. She responded, heightening her own talent. The kiss was dark and profound, the kind of kiss that sealed a vow.

The heat built quickly. Energy burned in the room. Sam rolled Abby onto her back and came down on top of her. She pulled him close, savoring the weight of him crushing her into the bedding. The power that charged his aura challenged and aroused and thrilled her in ways that she could not begin to explain or understand. She knew on some level that he was as compelled and captivated by her energy as she was by his.

Sam raised his head so that his mouth was only an inch or so above hers. In the shadows, his eyes heated.

"You and me," he said. "Forever."

She wrapped her arms around him. "Forever."

He took her mouth again. The night burned. So did the Phoenix ring.

She awoke to the muffled whine of an impatient dog.

"Newton," she said.

"Your turn," Sam said into the pillow. "I let him out."

"Okay, okay. But definitely a dog door."

"For sure. This week."

She got out of the warm bed, wrapped her robe around herself and slid her cold toes into her slippers. She left the bedroom, went downstairs into the kitchen and opened the door.

Newton trotted over the threshold and paused, radiating a hopeful air.

"All right," Abby said. "You're a hero. I guess you deserve a snack."

She opened the bag of doggy treats, took out a goodie and tossed it to Newton. He seized it out of midair and crunched with enthusiasm.

When he was finished, they both went back upstairs. Abby heard the chimes of her phone just as she arrived in the bedroom doorway.

"What in the world?" she said.

Sam levered himself up on one elbow. "Your phone."

"Yes, I figured that much out all by myself."

She grabbed the phone off the bedside table and looked at the glowing screen.

"I don't believe it," she said. "It's Diana."

"At this hour?" Sam grumbled. "It's four o'clock in the morning."

Abby took the call.

"If this is about Dawson and that book he wanted me to find for his client . . ." she began.

"Abby, shut up and listen to me." Diana's voice rose to a near-hysterical pitch. "Dawson has been kidnapped."

"What?" Abby's stomach clenched. "Please tell me this is some kind of really sick joke."

"I just got a call demanding a ransom."

"Let me guess. The lab book?"

"He's going to murder Dawson if you don't give him that damned book. Dawson's life is in your hands."

"You said we needed a plan," Abby said. "I just gave you one."

"It's a lousy plan," Sam said.

"Got a better one?"

"No. And yours just might work if we tweak it a bit."

46

Dawson was slumped in a chair in the yacht's main cabin. His wrists were fastened behind him. His legs were bound to the legs of the chair. He looked up when Abby walked on board. Disbelief flashed across his face.

"What the hell are you doing here, Abby?" he said. "I told him that you wouldn't come."

The good-looking, sandy-haired man with the gun chuckled. "But I was sure she would. She's your sister, after all."

"Stepsister," Dawson said dully. "I explained that she's not a blood relative. She doesn't even like me."

"But you're all part of Dr. Radwell's modern blended family, his family by choice. I admit I don't get the family-loyalty thing, but it can certainly prove useful."

Abby stopped just inside the cabin, the package containing the lab book in her hands. She looked at the man with the gun. He was polished and well groomed, the kind of a man who was at ease with money and the sort of people who possessed a lot of it. His open, classically handsome features invited trust. He was dressed from head to toe in iconic yachting attire, a dark blue polo shirt, well-cut white trousers and deck shoes. The ring on his hand was set with a large diamond. The watch was gold, the kind of timepiece that, according to the ads, was meant to be handed down to the next generation. The ads did not usually mention that in a pinch the watch could be pawned to buy a ticket to a no-name island if the Feds came to the door.

"You must be Lander Knox," Abby said.

"So you figured that out, did you?" Lander looked amused.

"Sam Coppersmith is the one who worked out your real identity."

"I see. Well, no harm done. When this is over, I will disappear again, just like I did a few years ago, when I wanted everyone to think that I was dead."

Dawson shook his head. "You shouldn't have come, Abby. He's a total psycho. Now he'll kill both of us."

"No," Lander said. "I'm not going to kill either of you, not unless you force me to take extreme measures."

"Bullshit," Dawson muttered.

"Why should I kill you or your sister?" Lander asked, in a voice of perfect reason. "She followed all the rules today. She came alone, as instructed. Paid a private charter service to drop her off at the cabin. She knows what will happen if I hear or see another boat or if there's any sign of a floatplane, don't you, Abby?"

"Yes," she said. "You'll kill Dawson."

"Exactly right." Lander gave her an approving smile. "But if everyone sticks to the plan, you both will walk away from this meeting, and I will sail away. You won't ever see me again."

"Why the gun?" Abby asked. "You've already murdered at least two book dealers by paranormal means, and I'm betting that you've killed others the same way."

"I have discovered that people tend to take guns more seriously than they do the paranormal. A gun concentrates the attention."

"Sam said something similar."

"And those people you say I murdered were all victims of cardiac arrest. There is nothing to tie me to their deaths." He glanced at the gun. "Certainly not this device."

"Device?" Abby took a second look at the

weapon in his hand.

"It looks like a gun, but it isn't a traditional pistol. It's crystal-powered. Kills without leaving a trace."

"He's lying about letting us go," Dawson said wearily. "He's a damned psychopath. He lies as easily as he breathes. He's been stalking you for months, using Grandmother and me. He's the one who set up the Ponzi scheme and suckered Grandmother and me into investing in it."

Lander gave Abby a warm, charming smile. "I don't want to have to kill anyone. All I want is the lab book. Once you've broken the encryption and I've verified that it's the right book, we'll take a short cruise. I'll put you and Dawson ashore on one of the uninhabited islands here in the San Juans. It may take you a while, but sooner or later you'll manage to flag down a passing boat. Plenty of time for me to disappear."

"What if we go to the police?" Abby said.

Lander shrugged. "They wouldn't believe you. There was no ransom paid. No money changed hands. At best, the kidnapping story will be viewed as a publicity stunt designed to help your father sell more books. Speaking of books, let me see Willis's notebook. I want to be sure you brought the right one."

"Afraid of being scammed the way you scammed Dawson?" Abby asked.

"You wouldn't take the risk," Lander said. "You know that it would cost your brother his life, and your own as well. But after going to all this trouble, I want to be certain that the book you found is the right one. You know how it is in the collectors' market, so many frauds and forgeries out there."

"True." Abby put the package down on the desk and started to peel off the tape she had used to secure the wrapping paper. "How will you know if this is the right lab book?"

"I'll know," Lander said. He moved closer to the desk to get a better look at the package. "In fact, I can already sense some energy around it."

"Encryption energy." Abby finished unwrapping the book. The atmosphere inside the cabin heated a little, but she knew that it wasn't all coming from the lab book. Lander had heightened his talent. He was powerful. The strange gun in his hand was suddenly a luminous green. A new chill went through her.

"You used a crystal from the Phoenix Mine to power that weapon," she said.

He followed her gaze to the gun and gave

her another approving smile. "Very good observation. My father thoughtfully kept one crystal as a souvenir. I ran a lot of experiments on it before I finally realized what it could do."

"That's what you used to kill Thaddeus Webber and the other dealer."

"Yes. I know the East Coast hot-books market quite well. I've been dealing in it anonymously for some time now. But sadly, I lacked connections here in the Pacific Northwest."

"But your contacts back east knew how to find Thaddeus."

"It took some doing, but once I located him, I was able to get the names of the most likely auction dealers from him before he suffered his heart attack."

"Before you murdered him, you mean. You sent those two men to kidnap me."

"I had hoped to avoid violence, but when it became clear that you had another client and that your dear brother was not going to be able to convince you to work for him, I realized I had to take more drastic measures. I wasn't absolutely certain that you would show up at Webber's house, but it seemed likely. I didn't have time to watch the place myself, so I hired that pair to pick up any female seen leaving his place. Obviously, they did a very poor job of grabbing you. I assume you had Coppersmith with you that day?"

"Yes."

"That explains why you got away," Lander said. "Never mind, what's done is done, and it's all ending the way it's supposed to end. Let's have a look at the lab book."

He opened the leather cover and examined the first page.

"There's Willis's name," he said. "The dates are correct." He turned one page and then another. His eyes tightened. "This is a record of experiments conducted on rare earths and crystals taken from a mine, but there's no mention of paranormal properties or the location of the mine."

"The book is still encrypted," Abby reminded him. "It won't make any sense to you until I break the code."

He closed the book with a snap. "Do it now."

"You promise you'll let us go?"

"I promise," Lander said. Anger flashed in his cold eyes. "I told you, I have no reason to kill either of you."

"He's lying, Abby," Dawson said.

Lander aimed the gun at him. "It occurs to me that now that I have your sister, I don't have any more use for you."

Dangerous currents swirled in the atmosphere. Dawson started to sweat. He gasped for breath.

"No." Abby grabbed the lab book. "You said you wouldn't hurt him. I'll break the code for you."

"Do it," Lander snarled.

She jacked up her energy, found the frequencies and held out the lab book.

"Okay," she said. "It's done. Here, take the book and let us go."

Lander reached for the book, ignoring her plea. His fingers closed around the spine. Abby seized the energy of the encryption and sent it into his aura.

Lander stiffened. His eyes widened in dawning horror.

"No," he screamed. He tried and failed to let go of the book. "You can't do this to me. I'll kill you first, I swear it."

His left hand was still frozen to the book. Abby sensed that the energy of the unlocking code was channeling straight into his aura. But he was so much stronger than she had realized. He managed to let go of the lab book. Gaining strength, he turned the pistol toward her.

"Bitch," he screamed.

The barrel of the pistol glowed hotter. Icy currents flowed around her heart.

Sam came through the doorway, the Phoenix ring on fire. Paranormal lightning crackled across the small space, igniting Lander's aura. Ultralight flames blazed. Lander jerked and twitched and writhed.

He stared at Sam from the heart of the inferno. "*No.* It can't end like this. The crystals are *mine.*"

In the next instant, he crumpled to the floor. His aura and the psi-fire winked out with a terrible finality.

Sam scooped up the crystal gun and looked at Abby.

"I told you this was a bad plan," he said.

"I thought it all went quite well," she said. Her voice sounded far too high and thin.

She hurled herself against Sam's chest. His arms closed fiercely around her.

47

"I don't get it," Dawson said to Sam. "How did you manage to sneak up on Knox? He watched Abby's arrival with his binoculars and made sure that she was the only one who came ashore from the floatplane. That island wasn't much larger than a big rock. We would have heard even a very small outboard engine."

They were back at the Copper Beach house. Sam had used his phone to summon the floatplane that had been standing by to pick them up. The pilot was a resident of Copper Beach. He had asked no questions about the unusual charter.

Abby sat in a chair near the hearth. Newton was on the floor at her feet. Willow had made coffee for everyone. She and Elias were following the conversation with sharp-eyed attention.

"I came partway out on one of the whale-watching charters," Sam said. "Figured

Knox wouldn't be overly concerned if he happened to catch sight of a boat full of sightseers in the distance."

"I understand," Dawson said. "But how did you get the rest of the way to the island?"

"Kayak," Sam said. "They make almost no noise. I came ashore on the far side of the island and walked the rest of the way. I stayed out of sight and kept an eye on things from the trees. The plan was for me to move in as soon as Abby started to unlock the psi-code. We knew that even if she couldn't take him down with encryption energy, she would probably be able to distract him long enough for me to get on board."

Dawson shook his head. "I still don't understand this whole code thing. Knox kept talking about how he'd need Abby not just to get the book for him but to unlock it. At first I assumed he meant a real code, one with secret meanings for certain letters and numbers. When I realized he thought the book was encoded with some kind of psychic energy, I figured he was just flat-out crazy."

"I think he was, in a way," Abby said.

"But you aren't." Dawson looked at her. "You never were. The family is wrong about you. There is something to this whole paranormal thing, isn't there?"

Abby smiled. "What makes you believe that?"

"I felt something weird happen when Knox turned that strange gun on me, and again when you gave him the book. It was as if there was some kind of invisible storm inside the cabin. The air seemed somehow charged." Dawson looked at Sam. "When you came in, the sensation got a thousand times worse. I've never experienced anything like it. Except maybe once."

"When was that?" Abby asked.

"The day you burned the book in the bathtub and Mom decided that you had tried to set fire to the house."

"In hindsight, I have to admit that she had some reason to be concerned," Abby said. "I was just coming into my talent. I had no idea what I was doing."

"What really frightened Mom was the fact that you seemed to believe you had set fire to the book with some kind of mental energy. But that's exactly what happened, wasn't it?"

Abby sighed. "Pretty much."

Elias looked at Sam. "We need to find the missing crystals. We've got one lab book, a good shot at getting the second one if it's with Frye's things, and we've got Knox's crystal gun. That will give us a lot to work with."

"Still got a long way to go," Sam said. "We're going to need Judson's and Emma's help. They are the only ones we can trust, the only ones who have a sensitivity to the Phoenix crystals."

Willow picked up her coffee cup. "What did you do with Lander Knox's body and his yacht?"

"I made sure there was nothing on board that tied any of us to the boat, and then I sank it," Sam said. "The water is very deep off that island. I doubt that the wreckage or the body will ever be discovered, but if they are, it won't cause much of a stir. Just one more tragic summer boating accident in the San Juans."

Abby looked at him over the top of her cup.

"What?" he asked.

"I was just thinking of what Dixon told me about you the first time he brought me here to the island."

Sam raised his brows. "That would be?"

"I was given to understand that if you ever had to get rid of a body, it would disappear for good," she said. "Something to do with all the deep water around these parts and the cleverness of Coppersmiths in general."

"Damn straight," Elias growled.

Sam let that go. He turned back to Dawson. "Are you going to tell your grandmother that she was giving out details about the family finances to a killer?"

"I don't think that I'll mention that he was a killer." Dawson tapped one finger on the arm of the chair. "That gets complicated."

"Yes," Sam said. "It does."

"I doubt that she'd believe me if I did tell her the whole truth, anyway," Dawson continued. "But I do plan to let her know that the guy she was doing lunch with on a regular basis for the past few months was the architect of the Ponzi scheme that she insisted I invest her money in. I'm also going to make it clear that it isn't Abby's fault that Knox was a fraud and a scam artist."

Willow exchanged a look with Elias. Abby was sure she saw some unspoken message pass between them. Willow looked at Dawson.

"It might be possible to recover whatever is left of the money that you invested with Knox, assuming he didn't spend all of it," she said.

"He didn't have time to go through that much money," Sam said. "He was focused on acquiring the lab book and getting the encryption broken. Depriving the Stricklands of the family fortune was merely a means to an end, collateral damage."

"In that case, I'll see what I can do," Willow said.

Elias grinned proudly. "My wife has a real talent for following the money," he said to Dawson. "If your grandmother's fortune is out there, she'll find it."

Dawson looked at Willow. "That's very kind of you. I might be able to help. I've got a little talent in that arena myself."

"Excellent," Willow said. "We'll work the project as a team."

They finished the coffee in silence. The flames crackled cheerfully on the hearth. Outside, the long summer day came to a close. Darkness settled on the island.

"I told Knox that he had miscalculated," Dawson said to Abby. "I explained that he had misjudged the family dynamics. I said you had no reason to risk your neck for me. But he was convinced that you would come. For a smart psychopath, he sure had a blind side. He actually bought into the image in that photo on the back cover of *Families by Choice.* Thought the happy Radwell family was the real deal."

Abby smiled. "Like Dad always says, family is everything."

48

Abby stood with Sam on the bluff above the small cove. Sam was on his phone. Newton was exploring some nearby rocks.

Sam concluded the call and slipped the phone into the pocket of his leather jacket. "That was the lawyer I had looking into the status of Thaddeus Webber's estate. Turns out there is a will."

"So Thaddeus did take steps to make sure his most valuable books went to a library?" Abby smiled. "That's great."

"He didn't leave his collection to a library. He left everything, including the contents of his book vault, to a single individual."

"He had some family after all?"

"According to his will, he left his collection to the person he looked upon as a daughter, although, given the age difference, maybe he should have said granddaughter. He left it all to you, Abby."

"What?"

Sam smiled.

It took her a few seconds to find her tongue. "But some of the volumes in that collection are worth a fortune."

"They're all yours now. The lawyer is making certain that the collection is guarded until it can be packed up and transported here to Copper Beach. You'll have to open Webber's vault, though. You're the only one who knows the code."

"This is amazing. I can't believe it. First your mother and Dawson track down the bulk of the Strickland fortune in that offshore bank and arrange to get it back. Then one of your fancy lawyers manages to spring Grady Hastings, who is scheduled to start work in the Black Box facility on Monday."

"Good talent is hard to come by," Sam said. "Don't like to see it wasted."

"And now I find out I'm inheriting all of Thaddeus's books. On top of everything else, I actually got a phone call from Orinda Strickland today, informing me that she intended to make provision for me in the Strickland family trust."

"You told her you didn't want to be named in the trust, didn't you?"

"How did you guess?"

"I know you, Abby. The money isn't

important to you. All you've ever wanted was to be part of the family. Don't worry, when you marry me, you're going to have all the family you can handle."

The late summer sun was setting, streaking the clouds with fiery light and turning the water to a sheet of hammered copper. Abby watched the spectacular sunset, aware of a glorious sense of happiness and certainty.

"Now I know why they call this place Copper Beach," she said.

Sam drew her into his arms. His eyes heated. "I told you that you would understand one of these days. Think you can call this island home?"

"Home is wherever you and I are together," she said. "Well, and Newton, too, of course."

"Newton, too," Sam agreed.

He kissed her there in the warm copper light of the summer evening. Abby opened her senses to the powerful energy of the love that she knew would bind them for a lifetime.

The Phoenix crystal burned.

ABOUT THE AUTHOR

Jayne Ann Krentz is the author of more than fifty *New York Times* bestsellers. She has written contemporary romantic suspense novels under that name, as well as futuristic and historical romance novels under the pseudonyms Jayne Castle and Amanda Quick, respectively. She earned a B.A. in History from the University of California at Santa Cruz and went on to obtain a Masters degree in Library Science from San Jose State University in California. Before she began writing full time she worked as a librarian in both academic and corporate libraries. Jayne Ann Krentz lives in Seattle.

The employees of Thorndike Press hope you have enjoyed this Large Print book. All our Thorndike, Wheeler, and Kennebec Large Print titles are designed for easy reading, and all our books are made to last. Other Thorndike Press Large Print books are available at your library, through selected bookstores, or directly from us.

For information about titles, please call:
(800) 223-1244

or visit our Web site at:
http://gale.cengage.com/thorndike

To share your comments, please write:
Publisher
Thorndike Press
10 Water St., Suite 310
Waterville, ME 04901

Earlier Events in Elizabeth's Life

1533 Henry VIII marries Anne Boleyn, January 25. Elizabeth born at Greenwich Palace, September 7.

1536 Anne Boleyn executed in Tower of London. Elizabeth disinherited from crown. Henry marries Jane Seymour.

1537 Prince Edward born. Queen Jane dies of childbed fever.

1541 Unlawful Games Act bans sporting activities and some Yule customs at Christmas.

1544 Act of Succession and Henry VIII's will establish Mary and Elizabeth in line to throne.

1547 Henry VIII dies. Edward VI crowned.

1551 Holy Days and Fasting Days Act. Strict Sunday and worship laws passed.

1553 Queen Mary (Tudor) I crowned. Tries to force England back to Catholicism; gives Margaret Stewart, Tudor cousin, precedence over Elizabeth. Queen Mary weds Prince Philip of Spain by proxy.

1554 Protestant Wyatt Rebellion fails, but Elizabeth sent to Tower for two months, accompanied by Kat Ashley.

1558 Mary dies; Elizabeth succeeds to throne, November 17. Elizabeth appoints William Cecil Secretary of State; Robert Dudley made Master of the Queen's Horse.

Earlier Events in Elizabeth's Life

1558 Elizabeth crowned in Westminster Abbey, January 15. Parliament urges queen to marry, but she resists. Mary, Queen of Scots becomes Queen of France at accession of her young husband, Francis II.

1560 Death of Francis II of France makes his young Catholic widow, Mary, Queen of Scots, a danger as Elizabeth's unwanted heir. Elizabeth names Earl of Sussex Lord Lieutenant of Ireland.

1561 Now widowed, Mary, Queen of Scots returns to Scotland. In London, St. Paul's Cathedral roof and spire burn.

1564 Earl of Sussex returns from Ireland to royal court in May.

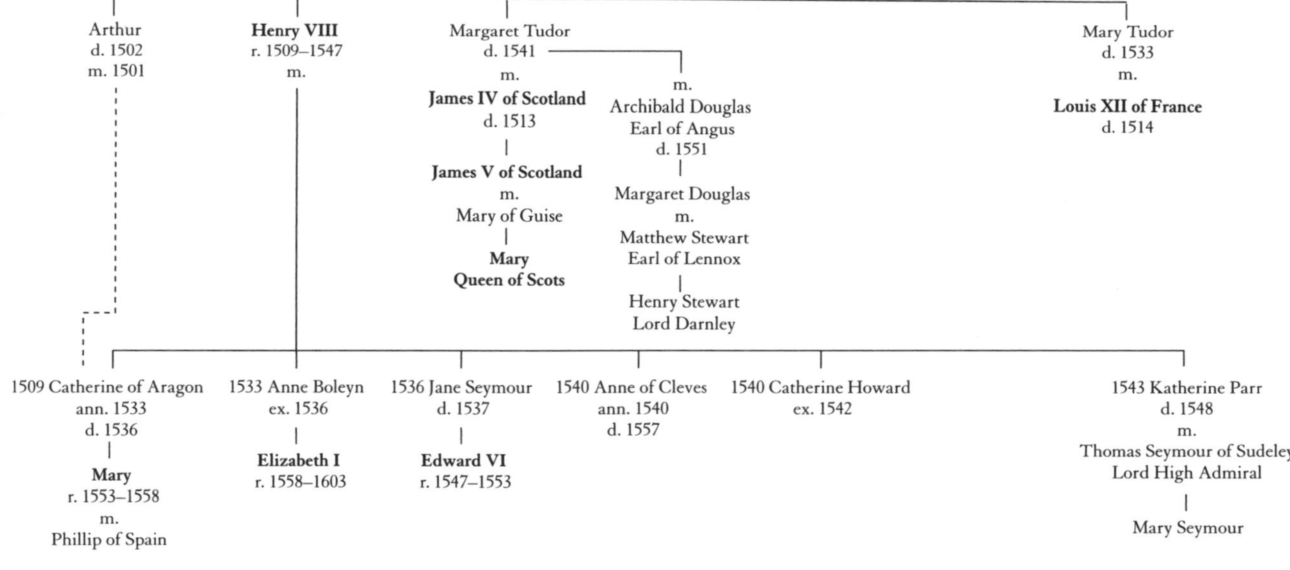
House of Lancaster
Henry VII
r.1485–1509
m.
House of York
Elizabeth of York
HOUSE OF TUDOR
Arthur
d. 1502
m. 1501
Henry VIII
r. 1509–1547
m.
Margaret Tudor
d. 1541
m.
James IV of Scotland
d. 1513
James V of Scotland
m.
Mary of Guise
Mary
Queen of Scots
m.
Archibald Douglas
Earl of Angus
d. 1551
Margaret Douglas
m.
Matthew Stewart
Earl of Lennox
Henry Stewart
Lord Darnley
Mary Tudor
d. 1533
m.
Louis XII of France
d. 1514
1509 Catherine of Aragon
ann. 1533
d. 1536
Mary
r. 1553–1558
m.
Phillip of Spain
1533 Anne Boleyn
ex. 1536
Elizabeth I
r. 1558–1603
1536 Jane Seymour
d. 1537
Edward VI
r. 1547–1553
1540 Anne of Cleves
ann. 1540
d. 1557
1540 Catherine Howard
ex. 1542
1543 Katherine Parr
d. 1548
m.
Thomas Seymour of Sudeley
Lord High Admiral
Mary Seymour

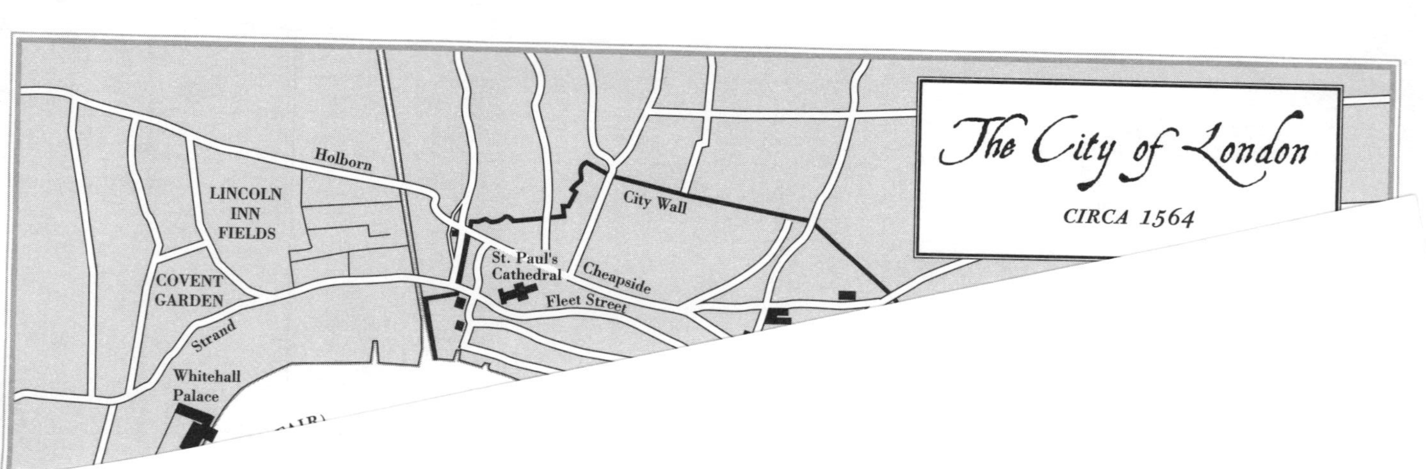

The City of London
CIRCA 1564
Holborn
LINCOLN INN FIELDS
COVENT GARDEN
Strand
Whitehall Palace
City Wall
St. Paul's Cathedral
Cheapside
Fleet Street

The Queene's Christmas

The Prologue

Cardamom Christmas Cake

Cream 1 cup country butter and blend in ⅔ cup brown sugar, beating with a spoon 'til frothy. Stir in 1 beaten egg. Stir ½ teaspoon grated lemon peel, ¾ teaspoon crushed cardamom (having been dearly imported from the Portuguese), ½ cup ground almonds, and 1 cup of currants into 2½ cups of fine white flour. Beat the dry ingredients into the sweetened butter. Pour into a greased cake pan or two layer pans and bake in a brick oven mayhap some three-quarters hour or until toothpick inserted in center comes out clean. Yon cake can be frosted with brown sugar icing. Dress cake with holly sprigs.

SEPTEMBER 29, 1564
ST. JAMES'S PALACE, LONDON

"I SWEAR, YOUR GRACE, THAT MAN WILL BE THE DEATH of you yet!"

"Robin Dudley, my Kat?" Elizabeth asked. She forced herself to stand still as the frail, elderly Kat Ashley, First Lady of the Bedchamber, and Rosie Radcliffe, her favorite maid of honor, pinned the ermine mantle to her shoulders over her russet velvet gown. If anyone but these two had spoken such impertinence to her, the thirty-one-year-old Tudor queen would have rounded on them soundly.

"Of course, that's who I mean," Kat pursued, fussing overlong with a jeweled pin. "Lord Robert Dudley, alias your dear Robin, about to become Earl of Leicester by your hand. I fear he'll think he's king in waiting."

"Or at least your main advisor, if not heir apparent," Rosie muttered as she fastened a diamond brooch.

"You too, Rosie?" Elizabeth asked of the pretty young brunette. "*Et tu, Brute,* and you with that sharp object in your hand?"

The queen kept her voice light, but her heart was heavy. Today she was creating Robert Dudley, her staunch ally and longtime court favorite, the Earl of Leicester despite the resentment of the court faction that detested him—led by Rosie's cousin, the Earl of Sussex.

"Your kith and kin had best not be saying I will name Robin my heir," Elizabeth warned.

"But you did name him Protector of the Kingdom when you were sore ill with the pox," Rosie replied.

"Those were desperate times. I've said I will not marry him nor name him, or anyone, my successor. If he weds my cousin Queen Mary of Scots, as I have counseled, he shall rule through her."

"But you've said you'll not name her heir, either," Rosie added, "though she's your nearest royal kin."

"They shall rule Scotland, not England. If I named an heir," Elizabeth said so sharply that both women stepped back, "disgruntled courtiers and conspirators for my crown would latch on to that heir like leeches, and my life could be more at risk than it already is. As for Robert Dudley, he is being created a peer not to make him worthy, for he already is.

"I'm ready," she announced with a toss of her red head that

rattled the pearls on her jeweled cap. "Let's brighten this dreary day outside with a fine old ceremony inside."

"It's still pouring cats and dogs," Kat observed as if they could not all hear the drumming of raindrops against the mullioned windows. "However wet the weather in the olden times, it never seemed so chilling. How I long for the good old days!"

"In the good old days, I was not queen but likely locked away in sundry country houses in tawdry gowns," Elizabeth reminded her. She took the old woman's mottled hands in hers. The skin felt as dry as parchment. "You said the other day, dear Kat, you longed for an old-fashioned Christmastide. Perhaps we shall have one."

Kat's flaccid features lifted a bit. Suddenly, she seemed younger, stronger. She had been withering like one of the brown chestnut leaves on the trees in the park, and Elizabeth had been deeply distressed at knowing no way to halt her slow slide toward a deathbed. Elizabeth's first governess and longtime companion, Katherine Ashley had been the only mother she had ever known, since her own had been beheaded when she was but three.

As the women left the privy chamber and her other attendants fell in behind them, Elizabeth glanced out the corridor windows. In sodden clumps, Londoners were gathering along the parkside lane, hoping for a glimpse of their queen. Once when she'd ridden into St. James's after hunting, a crowd of ten thousand had greeted her, shouting, "God save Elizabeth!" and throwing flowers.

That was one of few happy memories of the place, for St. James's had little to commend it to Elizabeth Tudor other than its being set in a fine hunt park on the edge of her capital city. It was an outmoded, small palace her half-sister, Queen Mary, had favored and died in. Here "Bloody Mary," as the people called her, had confined Elizabeth before having her hauled off to prison in the Tower; that hardly endeared this russet pile of bricks to her, either. She came only for particular ceremonies she did not want to seem overly grand and for respite from her favorite city palace, Whitehall, when the jakes needed to be cleaned. As soon as this investiture was over she would ride back there, muck and mire on city streets notwithstanding.

When the queen's crimson-liveried yeomen guards swept open the double doors to the presence chamber, her sharp eyes scanned the crowd. As handsome as ever, though he'd managed a humble demeanor today, Robin Dudley awaited amidst his little entourage of loyalists. He was attired sumptuously in blue and gold; for good reason had his rivals given him the sobriquet of "the peacock"—among other names.

Her dear, brilliant chief secretary, William Cecil, bearded and thin, looked hardly happy about this necessary charade. In truth, he was no friend of Robin's either, though the two tolerated each other for the sake of queen and kingdom. The clusters of courtiers included Rosie's cousin Thomas Radcliffe, Earl of Sussex, who would rather, no doubt, skewer and roast Robin than honor and toast him.

The queen's gaze settled on the two men she wanted most to impress today, so that they would report Robin's elevation to their Scottish queen. As diplomats, both spoke several languages including their native lowland Scots, but they were rapt in whispers now as they went down on their knees before her.

The queen wanted everyone, especially her too clever Catholic cousin, the Scottish Queen Mary Stuart, to know Robin was eligible to sue for Mary's hand. At least that is what Elizabeth and

Cecil had publicly promoted. Their actual plan was, of dire necessity, much darker and deeper.

"Ah, my lords, you must tell your queen, my dear cousin," Elizabeth announced so everyone could hear, "how greatly my court honors Lord Dudley, soon to be Earl of Leicester."

"Indeed, we shall tell her all," Simon MacNair spoke up.

"Of course you will," the queen countered quietly with nary a change of expression but a roll of her eyes toward the hovering Cecil.

MacNair was the younger and handsomer of these Scots, an aide to the seasoned Sir James Melville, who was Queen Mary's envoy to the English court. Melville was leaving for Edinburgh on the morrow, so Elizabeth would soon have only MacNair to keep an eye on. MacNair looked more the part of a braw Scot, auburn haired and big shouldered, while Melville seemed more polished and urbane. Elizabeth trusted them both in opposite proportion to how much Mary Stuart relied on them.

"Tell me, my lords," Elizabeth said, drawing herself up to her full height of five feet, six inches to peer down at them as they knelt, "whether your royal mistress is taller than I or not."

"Six feet tall, she is, higher by half a head," the black-bearded Melville said as she gestured for them to rise.

"Then she is too high," Elizabeth retorted with a set smile. "But not too high to take to herself as husband, consort, and king our illustrious Earl of Leicester. Come close and stand by me for this," she invited them and swept toward the throne awaiting on its dais under the crimson cloth of state.

As Robin knelt before her, the queen tapped his broad, fur-draped shoulders with the ceremonial sword and intoned in her clarion voice the traditional words creating him Earl of Leicester.

At her accession to the throne, she'd named him her Master of the Horse; she'd given him money, a wool monopoly, and Kenilworth Manor in Warwickshire—and her heart, though cursed if he would ever be sure of that while there was breath left in her body.

"And so, it is done," she whispered for Robin's ears alone and stroked his warm neck once with her left thumb. The ceremony was over. Her hand on the newly created earl's arm, Elizabeth preceded her entourage out of the crowded chamber. "I'll need my cloak," she requested as her women divested her of the ermine mantle. "With Ladies Ashley and Radcliffe and the Earl of Leicester, I am going in my carriage to Whitehall forthwith, and the rest of you shall come when you will."

The big, boxy city carriage was brought around from the mews. When Elizabeth was certain the rattle of its iron wheels on cobbles was not another deluge, she stepped outside. The rain had momentarily stopped. A roar went up from the hundreds of people who had waited outside the gatehouse.

"Come on then," she said to her courtiers, who she knew would soon be scrambling to follow her to Whitehall. "We shall walk a bit, as we've been closed in for days."

As ever, she glanced up under the arch of the stone and brick gatehouse at one of the few sets of the entwined initials, *H & A*, of her parents, which someone had failed to chisel away when her father wed his later queens. Ah, she did now recall a happy day here at St. James's during her father's reign; it must have been when Catherine Howard was briefly queen.

Elizabeth had been allowed to watch the Yuletide hanging of greens in the great hall, the decking out of the grand staircase, the bay and ivies being suspended in hoops from this gatehouse. At the banquet table that night, her father had smiled at her and shared with her a mammoth piece of his favorite Cardamom Christmas Cake. And Kat had been there, smiling, ever watchful and protective.

Elizabeth of England climbed the carved mounting block just outside the gatehouse, but she did not get into the carriage, which had followed her. She turned to her people and held up her hand. At first the crowd cheered and waved until someone realized she would speak. Slowly, the roar became chatter, murmur, then silence, while her guards held their halberds out to keep back the press of people.

Just when she was ready to speak, Robin, frowning, whispered up at her, "Your Most Gracious Majesty, it's going to rain again. Your coach is here, so—"

"So it will wait for the will of its queen even as the earls of her realm must," she told him. "My good people!" she called out. Men doffed their wet wool caps; children popped up, hoisted onto shoulders. "On this Michaelmas holiday honoring the archangel Michael, I wish to give to all an early gift for our next and grandest holiday, the Twelve Days of Christmas."

She glanced down at Kat. For once, she seemed avidly intent, excited, almost young again.

"This year, by order of your queen," she continued, "London shall have a Yuletide festival of old, even with mummings, setting aside the more recent strictures. And when these sodden skies turn to crisp, clear ones, we shall have a Frost Fair again, if, God willing, the Thames freezes over. Then all may frolic, wassail, give gifts, and cast off their common trials and woes for a few days, rejoicing in our Lord's coming to the earth to save our souls."

In the silence, she heard a man's mocking voice behind her, a courtier she could not name, hiss, "At least we'll have that, because we'll never frolic over Dudley's coming to the peerage, damn his soul." If anyone else heard or said aught, it was drowned in the shout of the crowd and patter of new rain.

Elizabeth saw how happy Kat looked, as if her queen had already given her an olden Yule with all its golden memories. She would simply hang the naysayers, the queen told herself, right along with the mistletoe and holly. Surely no one, in court or out, could argue with a good old-fashioned Christmas.

Chapter the First

To Make a Kissing Bunch

The size depends upon the span of the two hoops, one thrust through the other, which form the skeleton of the hanging. Wrap the hoops in ribbon, lace, or silk strips. Garland the hoops with holly, ivy, or sprigs of other greens, even apples or oranges. If at court, for a certain, string green and white paper Tudor roses from the hoops. Lastly, a sprig or two of mistletoe must needs be centered in the bunch for all to see. In the spirit of the season, hang the bunch where folks, high and low, may kiss beneath. Include enough mistletoe that men who kiss under its greenery and claim a berry for each kiss do not denude the bunch and ruin all the fine preparations.

DECEMBER 24, 1564
WHITEHALL PALACE, LONDON

"NOTHING BETTER THAN A YULETIDE HANGING," MEG Milligrew, Elizabeth's Strewing Herb Mistress and court herbalist, said as she came into the queen's privy chamber with a basket of white-berried mistletoe.

"The decking of halls is not to begin until the afternoon," the queen remarked, looking up from her reading. "I want to be there to see it, mayhap to help."

"It is to be later, but your maids were trying to snatch these to make a kissing bunch when I need them for Kat's new medicine."

In the slant of morning light, Elizabeth sat at the small table before a Thames-side window, frowning over documents Cecil had given her to read. She could hardly discipline herself to heed her duties, for the palace was already astir with plans and preparations. This evening began the special Twelve Days of Christmas celebration she had promised her people, Kat, and herself, though December 25 itself was always counted as the first day.

"Kat seems to do well with that mistletoe powder in her wine," the queen observed, sanding her signature. "Using it has been worth the risk, and heaven knows the royal physicians haven't come up with anything better."

"I'll never forget the look on your face, Your Grace, when I told you that taking too much of it is poison. But just enough has calmed the heat of Kat's heart's furnace and given her new life."

"I knew to trust your knowledge on it, and pray I will always know whom to trust," Elizabeth said as if to herself. She rose and turned to the window. Scratching the frost off a pane with her fingernails, she gazed out. Though a small stream of open water still flowed at the center, the broad Thames was freezing over from both banks. She took that for a fortuitous sign that a Frost Fair on that vast expanse was a good possibility.

As the queen returned to her work, the mistress of the herbs worked quietly away, and the mistress of the realm was content to have her here. Since before she was queen, Elizabeth had gathered about her several servants as well as courtiers she could trust. She and Meg Milligrew had been through tough times together, and Meg was a member of what the queen dubbed her Privy Plot Council. Should some sort of crime or plot threaten the queen's court or person, Her Majesty assembled her covert coterie to look into it and work directly with her to solve the problem.

Meg greatly resembled the slender, red-haired, pale queen and so could stand in for her, at least at a distance, if need be. Kat Ashley had been a valued member of the secret group before her faculties began to fade, and the brilliant, wily Cecil had ever served his queen as well privily as publicly. Stephen Jenks, Meg's betrothed and a fine horseman, had been the queen's personal bodyguard in her days of exile and now was in the Earl of Leicester's retinue, though ever at the royal beck and call.

The queen's cousin Henry Carey, Baron Hunsdon, a courtier she relied on, had served in her Privy Plot Council, too. Edward Thompson, alias Ned Topside, a former itinerant actor and her Master of Revels at court, was invaluable whether working overtly or covertly. Ned, the handsome rogue, was a man of many faces, voices, and personae and rather full of himself at times. But however witty and charming the blackguard could be, she would scold him roundly for being late this morning.

The queen had sent for Ned to hear of his preparations for the holiday traditions and tomfooleries. For the six years she had been queen, Ned had served as Lord of Misrule, the one who planned and oversaw all Yuletide entertainments, both decorous and raucous. She wondered if Meg had appeared because Ned was coming. Elizabeth knew well that the girl might be betrothed to the quiet, stalwart Jenks but had long yearned for the mercurial, alluring Ned.

"It's a good thing for you," the queen clipped out the moment Ned was admitted, "that the Lord of Misrule's whims can gainsay all rules and regulations in these coming days, for your presence here is long overdue, and I must leave soon."

Ned swept the queen a deep, graceful bow. "Your Most Gracious Majesty," he began with a grand flourish of both arms, "I will be brief."

"That will be a novelty. Instead, write out what merriments we shall see each night, for I want no surprises. As penance for my own frivolity, I must meet with the Bishop of London's aide, Vicar Martin Bane," she added with a dramatic sigh that would have done well in a scene from one of the fond romances or grand tragedies Ned staged for the court.

"That Puritan's presence here these next days will be enough to throw a pall over it all!" Ned protested.

"Keep your impertinence for the banquet tonight, or I will put a lighted taper in your mouth to keep you quiet," she retorted, but they exchanged smiles, and Meg giggled. Ned's eyes darted to the girl; it was evidently the first he had noted her here.

"Ah, but that's only for the roasted peacock," he recovered his aplomb, "and I intend to skewer with barbs and roast with jests everyone else. But there is one thing, Your Grace, a boon I would ask which will enhance, I vow, the entertainments for the court."

"Say on. Some new juggler or more plans for that mummers' morality play?" she asked, moving toward the door.

"To put it succinctly, my former troupe of actors is in town. Lord Hunsdon, patron of the arts that he is, tells me the Queen's Country Players are performing at the Rose and Crown on the Strand. I'm surprised they have not sought a family reunion yet. Of course, compared to my work here at court, theirs is rustic and provincial, but I thought," he went on, pursing his lips and shrugging, "if I went to see them, we could arrange a special surprise for Twelfth Night or some such—"

"A fine idea," she cut off his rambling. "Is your uncle still at their helm, and that other popinjay, ah . . ."

"Randall Greene, Your Grace. I know not, but will inform you as soon as I discover the current state of their affairs."

"But don't be gone long to fetch them. You're needed here, is he not, Meg?"

"Oh, yes, Your Grace," came from the coffer's depths where it seemed Meg hid her head as if to keep Ned from seeing her. "For all the responsibilities on his shoulders for the Twelve Days, that is," she added.

Elizabeth pointed to her writing table, and Ned hastened to take a piece of parchment. He dipped one of the quills in her ink pot, though he dared not plop himself in her chair, at least not until he began his reign as Lord of Misrule. That so-called King of Mockery could get by with anything, however much he was the butt of jokes in return for his own wit.

"At least you didn't say you'd stuff an apple in my mouth as if I were the roast boar," Ned mumbled without looking up as his pen scratched away. "I'd much prefer the lighted taper."

She had to laugh. However full of bombast, Ned always made her laugh.

Meg hoped Ned didn't realize she was watching every grand and graceful move he made.

"What are you doing in her coffer?" Ned asked her when the queen left the room. "You seem as busy as I truly am." He didn't even look up from his scribbling, although when the door closed behind the queen he scooted his paper before her chair and sat. The man, Meg fumed silently, was always busy at something or other, including chasing women, but never her. Yet there had always been something between them. Ninnyhammer that she was, Meg scolded herself, now that she was wedding Jenks just after the holidays, she'd never know what it was.

"Just hiding some mistletoe," she told him. "It's for Kat's potent medicine and not for the kissing bunches. Her Grace's ladies are making them now, and I've seen her Lady Rosie go through her coffers more than once."

"Fancy fripperies, kissing bunches. But, you know, one thing I remember about my mother," he said with a sigh, "is that she'd always hang little cloth figures of Mary, Joseph, and the Christ child in the hoops, so she'd never let my father kiss or pinch her under them, mistletoe or no. She'd have made a good Puritan, eh?"

"Unlike her son," Meg bantered, always striving with Ned to give as good as she got.

"Maybe you should make a kissing bunch just for Jenks."

She looked across the chamber at him when she had been trying not to, and, silent for once, Ned glanced up at that moment. Their gazes snagged. Silence reigned but for the crackle of hearth flames and the howl of river wind outside.

"I hope you're happy, my Meg, and make him happy."

"I intend to be and do so. And I'm not your Meg. Not now and never was."

"As prickly as holly, aren't you? Who taught you to read and walk and talk to emulate Her Grace, eh?"

"You did because she commanded it. And who used to chide me all the time that I was clumsy and slow?"

"God as my judge, not anymore. You've grown up in every way."

"But," she said, her voice tremulous, "I will make a kissing bunch for Jenks, a special one with sweet-smelling herbs like dried heartsease and forget-me-not, lovers' herbs."

"Alas and alack the day," he murmured, his heavily lashed green eyes still on her. He started to put his hand over his heart and hang his head most mockingly—she could tell that was what was coming—but he stopped himself. Instead, he gave one sharp sniff and went back to his writing.

"Always jesting, even when you're not the Lord of Misrule!" she scolded, surprised at her sharp tone after sounding so breathless a moment ago.

Ned had always been the Lord of Misrule in her life. He'd turned her emotions topside more than once, but she was certain, she told herself, that she was right to accept Jenks's suit. Now *there* was a man to be trusted.

"I've much to do and can't be wasting time with you," she added and threw a stray mistletoe berry at him as she slammed the coffer closed and hurried from the room.

The queen found Secretary Cecil and the Bishop of London's aide Vicar Martin Bane awaiting her in the presence chamber. At age forty-three, Cecil looked thin, pale, and careworn, but even compared to that, Ned was right: Bane could cool a room quicker than anyone else she knew.

"You requested a brief audience, Vicar Bane," she said when both men rose from their bows. "How does Bishop Grindal at this most important time of the Christian calendar?"

"It's of that I've been sent to speak, Your Most Gracious Majesty," Bane began, gripping his hawklike hands around what appeared to be a prayer book. Ordained in his own right, Bane served as liaison to her court from Lambeth Palace across the Thames, the traditional home of the Bishops of London, both in Catholic times and this Protestant era. Yet in the winter months, when Grindal was often in residence at his house on the grounds of St. Paul's Cathedral in the city itself, Bane spent even more time here at the palace.

Despite his somber black garb, the man was good-looking, with classical features and a full head of graying blond hair to match his neatly trimmed beard. But he was of stringy build and always seemed to be shrinking within his clothes. His cheeks were hollow, as if something inside his head sucked in his face and sank his icy blue eyes beneath his jutted brows.

"You see," he went on in a clear, clipped voice when she nodded he might continue, "there is some concern with all this coming merriment. The bishop and I did not realize at first you meant to flout your own family's statutes."

The queen felt her dander rise. "You refer, I assume," she clipped out, "to the Unlawful Games Act of 1541, banning sporting activity on the twenty-fifth day of December, and the Holy Days and Fasting Days Act of 1551, prohibiting transport and merriment, laws enacted in my father's and my brother's reigns."

At that rapid recitation, Bane's Adam's apple bobbed, perhaps in danger of also being sucked inside the dark void of the man. Did he not think she had a brain in her female head? She knew full well that both Bishop Edmund Grindal and his right arm, Vicar Martin Bane, favored the rising Puritan element in her country. They were men who saw the Catholic Church as nearly satanic but also viewed the Church of England, of which their queen was head, as dangerously liberal and in need of severe reform.

"I did not know you would be so . . ." he stumbled for a word, "current on those laws, especially seeing that your promise to your people on Michaelmas, in effect, Your Majesty, appears to have rescinded said laws—"

"Suspended them for this year alone, after which they will be assessed anew," she interrupted, her voice as commanding as his was cold. "The Tudor kings allowed such statutes to be enacted for specific reasons which are not pertinent now, in *my* reign, Vicar Bane."

"Yes, of course, I see," he said, his voice noticeably quailing as he shuffled a wary step back. He glanced askance at Cecil, only to find no help from that quarter. "Perhaps I was a bit wide of the mark," he added, "but we of the bishopric of the great city of London believe that even snowballing is a profane pastime, and if you encourage a Frost Fair on the Thames after all these years, London's citizens will be buying and selling on holy days, let alone running hither and yon on the ice."

"But we are leaving that all up to the Lord God, are we not?" Elizabeth inquired sweetly. "If the Thames freezes over by His will, when it has not in ages, I shall take it as His most gracious sign that my housebound and hardworking people may truly enjoy this holy season by holding a fair on the river. I myself recall earlier Frost Fairs with great fondness after not having seen one whit of profane behavior."

"But do you not live a rather sheltered life, Your Majesty? And we must consider your reinstituting of mummings. The earlier laws were partly passed because crime rose so severely when everyone was going about willy-nilly masked in playacting of sundry sorts."

"Yet my father himself, who cast off the excesses of the Catholic Church, loved masques and mummings at court and more than once played Lord of Misrule himself. I repeat, the decrees are for this one year, Vicar Bane, to see how things go. I assure you the precious, holy aspects of Christmas will be made dearer if they are not stifled by poor, plain rituals. We must have joy in this season of the year, for the Lord's gift to us and even for our gifts to each other. I am certain you will convey my words to Bishop Grindal and bid him come to court tomorrow to lead us all in prayer at the morning service. And you, of course, are welcome always to increase our happiness here."

When Bane saw he was beaten and bowed his way out, Cecil's stern face split in a grin. "The man doesn't know what hit him, but I warrant it feels like a jousting steed at full tilt," he told her, rubbing his hands in glee. For once those capable hands were not filled with writs or decrees, so perhaps even the diligent Cecil was ready to slacken up a bit at Christmas.

"He'll be back, lurking in corners," Elizabeth said, "but I refuse to let him or anyone else overthrow my hopes for these holidays. My most important tasks of the day are to present the new livery to my household staffs and to oversee the hanging of garlands and greens—and the Earl of Sussex has asked for some time, no doubt to warn me against listening to Leicester again."

A sharp knock on the door startled them both. At her nod, Cecil went to open it. Two yeomen guards blocked the way of the agitated-looking Scot Simon MacNair, brandishing a letter. Behind him, looking even more distressed, was Robin Dudley, whom everyone now, except the queen in private, addressed as Leicester.

"Your Gracious Majesty," MacNair clipped out, "forgive my intrusion, but I have a message of utmost import."

"What import, man?" Cecil demanded, plucking the letter from his hand as the guards let both men enter and they bowed.

"From Edinburgh, I see," Elizabeth said, noting well the familiar large, crimson wax seal the Queen of Scots employed.

"From your royal cousin to you, Your Grace," Cecil said. She saw him skim the letter even as he handed it over.

"Tell me what it says, Sir Simon," Elizabeth ordered MacNair. "Or, by the look on your face, Leicester, should you tell me?"

"Very well," Robin said. "The Scots queen has flat refused my suit for her royal hand."

"*Your* suit? *Mine* rather!" Elizabeth cried. She hoped that MacNair not only thought she was shocked and distressed but would report it forthwith to his royal mistress. Mary Stuart had taken the bait, though she was not yet hooked. If she rejected the Earl of Leicester, as Elizabeth had hoped, she might bite all the quicker and harder on the tasty Henry Stewart, Lord Darnley, whom Elizabeth intended to dangle before her.

Both royal Tudor and Stuart blood—for *Stewart* was the Scots' version of Queen Mary's Frenchified *Stuart*—ran in Darnley's veins. At the prompting of his parents and without Elizabeth's permission, the comely twenty-year-old Darnley had courted the newly widowed Queen Mary in France, before she returned to Edinburgh. Distantly related to Elizabeth, Darnley was a dissolute weakling. If he were king, he would sap the power Mary of Scots would need for any bid to seize her rival Elizabeth's crown and kingdom.

Elizabeth lowered her voice and tried to look morose. "I am deeply grieved the Scots queen, my dear cousin, does not think to take that which I have so lovingly offered and advised."

"How could she, Your Majesty," MacNair put in, "when the earl wrote privily to her he was not worthy of her?"

"What?" she demanded. "I have made him worthy of her, said he is worthy of her!" She felt her skin flush hot. Over anyone else, friend or foe, she could remain calm, but not over this freebooting blackguard she had long loved. Now Robin had defied her again when she had told him to keep clear of this business, that she and Cecil would handle it. But no, he had gainsayed her and jumped in with both feet as if he were bidden to make royal decisions here.

"You wrote her privily, in effect warding off her affections?" she cried, striding to Robin and hitting his shoulder with her balled fist. The wretch stood his ground.

"I was surprised, too, Your Grace," MacNair went smoothly on, "since it has long been noised about that the earl has a curtained painting of Mary Stuart he dotes on. I hear 'tis in his privy rooms at Kenilworth, near the corridor on which hangs a smaller one of Your Most Gracious Majesty."

Elizabeth was so furious her blood rang in her ears, thumping with the beat of her heart. She steadied herself as she had countless times ere this and said in a well-modulated voice, "Thank you, Sir Simon, for delivering this letter and for your additional information. I assure you I shall read most carefully my cousin's thoughts and respond to her in kind. Farewell for now. Leicester, you may stay."

When the door closed on the Scot and the queen heard her yeomen guards move back into their positions outside, she said calmly to Cecil, "Please ask Ned Topside to join us for a moment, my lord." He nodded and complied instantly, going out the back way by which she had entered.

"Topside?" Robin said, fidgeting and moving toward the other door as if he would flee. "What has he to do with any of this?"

"I won't even ask you about the portrait of *her* you have hanging in your rooms while the smaller one of *me* is in the corridor. I am wearied to death with your caperings, to put it prettily, my lord. I give you an earldom, but you presume to play king."

"Hell's teeth, Your Grace," he exploded, "you've been using me as a pawn to be taken by a foreign and enemy queen, so I thought I'd at least ascertain what the woman looked like. It's a poor portrait of her, especially next to any of you, including this one!" he cried and yanked a locket on a chain out of his doublet. He tried to pry it open with some difficulty.

"Never mind trying to make amends," Elizabeth insisted. "It's probably rusted shut from disuse if it hides my likeness!"

"If it is rusted shut, it is from my tears. You no longer love me as you once did—at least said you did!"

"And now I want nothing but silence from you! You were to keep to the side in my dealings with Mary Stuart, not get your sticky, greedy fingers into the Christmas pie like Jack Horner in the corner," she told him, wagging her finger as Cecil knocked once and entered with Ned.

"You called for me, Your Grace?" Ned said. He and Cecil looked almost as nervous as Robin.

"Master Topside, I regret to inform you that there is someone else I must appoint as Lord of Misrule this year, one who believes he can go his own way, so he will be perfect for the part. And you shall be his aide."

Ned looked confused, hurt, then angry. "But I—things are already greatly planned, Your Grace, and I was just about to visit my former colleagues, the Queen's Country Players, at the Rose and Crown, as you said I might, to invite them to help me with a play."

"You may still do so, but you will be assisting the new Lord of Misrule, especially at the Feast of Fools, where he will rule indeed."

She glanced at Robin, then away. He had gone from deathly white to ruby red. And he had not yet learned when to keep his mouth shut.

"You first raise me to the earldom, then offer me to your cousin queen, then make a laughingstock of me?" he demanded.

"When people remark that I keep my friends so close, Cecil," she said, turning to him, "I merely smile and nod, but the unspoken truth is, of necessity, I keep my enemies even closer. Ned, you may fetch your players, but be certain, if you stage a play, that the Earl of Leicester as the new Lord of Misrule takes the part of buffoon—or villain!"

"Holly and ivy, box and bay, put in the house for Christmas day." The queen's maids of honor and ladies in waiting chanted the old rhyme as they decked the halls where kissing balls hung from rafters and lintels. *"Fa, la, la, la, las"* echoed in the vast public rooms of the palace. But the queen's mood was still soured as she watched all the frivolity. Truth be told, she'd like to feed both Martin Bane and Robin Dudley a big bowl of mistletoe berries.

"It's not really true, is it?" Rosie's voice pierced the queen's thoughts. Four of her maids were standing close, looking at her on the first landing of the newly garlanded staircase.

"What was that again?"

"It's only a superstition about the holly berries, isn't it?" Rosie prompted.

Anne Carey, wife of Elizabeth's cousin Baron Hunsdon, came to the queen's aid. "Obviously," Anne said, "it's pure folk custom that these more pointed holly leaves are male and the more rounded ones female." It was traditional to count whether more sharp-leafed or smooth had been gathered each year; whichever kind was in the majority supposedly decided whether the husband or wife of the house ruled the roost in the coming year.

"I shan't leave to chance," Elizabeth said, "who commands this dwelling or any other palace for the entire year. I don't give a fig how many sharp leaves of holly are hauled in here, a woman rules."

She basked in their smiles and laughter. They made her feel better, and she was greatly looking forward to the awarding of the new liveries to the kitchen staff. Finally, she began to buck up a bit.

With her main officers of her palaces, the queen processed toward the vast kitchen block. Behind her came the four chief household officials, the Lord Chamberlain, Lord Steward, Treasurer, and Comptroller, with some of their aides, laden down with piles of new clothes. She had sent for her former groom and favorite horseman, Stephen Jenks, because anytime she chose to leave her yeomen guards behind, she felt better with him in tow.

The royal kitchens of the Tudor palaces actually held three staffs that occupied separate areas. The hall kitchen served minor courtiers and household servants who ate in the Great Hall; the lords' kitchen provided for the nobles who sat just below the dais in the Great Hall; and the privy kitchen fed the queen and whomever she chose to have dine with her. This particular set of liveries was going to her privy kitchen staff.

The mere aroma from the open hearths and brick ovens pulled the queen fully back into the mood for Christmas. The bubbling sauces, spitted roasts, and plump pillows of rising dough being kneaded for pastries and pies made her nose twitch. In a long line stood her staff, Master Cook Roger Stout to lowest scullery maid and spit boy. The fancy livery was for those of the highest echelons and those who served at table, but everyone would receive at least a piece of cloth or a coin. Most gifts were given on New Year's Day, but the household staffs needed their new garments now to look their best these coming Twelve Days.

Elizabeth went down the line from pastry cooks to larders, confectioners, boilers, and spicers, giving a quick smile and word of praise to each with the varied gifts. "Is that everyone?" she asked the beaming Stout as he sent his staff back to their tasks. "I see there's a doublet left."

"I reckon it's for Hodge Thatcher, Your Most Gracious Majesty, as I noticed him missing. If he's nodded off, I'll skin him."

"More like poor Master Hodge is busy putting the skin and feathers back on the peacock for tonight," Elizabeth countered.

Hodge Thatcher was Dresser of the Queen's Privy Kitchen, which meant he "dressed" or ornately arranged the fancy dishes, especially for the feasts. It was no mean task to garnish and decorate soups, meats, and pies. On occasions when she entertained foreign ambassadors, he'd turned out many a finely refeathered roasted swan with the traditional tiny crown upon its head. For this evening he must reaffix the roasted peacock's iridescent coat and prop up the fan of feathers. She'd seen Hodge at that task once years ago, when he first came to serve in her father's kitchens. She glanced over at the hatches through which he inspected all food before it was carried upstairs to her table, whether she was eating in public or in private.

"His workroom is by the back door near the street, is it not?" she asked. Carrying the doublet herself, she strode down the crooked corridor while Stout and her entourage hurried along behind.

"Ah, yes, what a fine memory you have, Your Majesty," he cried, sounding out of breath, "for his is the last door before passing through to the porter's gate and so outside the walls. Allow me to ascertain if he is within and announce you," he added, but the door was narrow, and the queen poked her head in ahead of the others.

"He's not here," she declared at first glance into the dim room, lit by a single lantern on the cluttered worktable. She saw that the small area served also for storage; pots and kettles, spits and gridirons hung aloft on hooks and hoisting chains.

Then, amidst all that, the queen saw bare feet dangling head high. She gasped as she gazed up at a bizarre body, a corpse, part man, part bird.

Chapter the Second

Roast Peacock

Take a peacock, break its neck, and drain it. Carefully skin it, keeping its skin and feathers together with the head still attached to the skin of the neck. Roast only the bird, with its legs tucked under. When it is roasted enough, take it out and let it cool. Sprinkle cumin on the inside of the skin, then wind it with the feathers and the tail about the body. Serve with the tail feathers upright, its neck propped up from within, and a lighted taper in its beak. If it is a royal dish, cover the bird's beak with fine gold leaf. Carry said proud bird to the table at the head of a procession of lower dishes for to be sampled first by the monarch. Ginger sauce is best served with this fine and fancy bird.

AT THE SIGHT OF THE HANGING BODY SOMEONE CURSED; a few shrieked. The queen continued to stare up at the partly feathered corpse, which seemed to have grotesquely taken flight.

"Hodge? What the deuce!" Stout cracked out behind the queen as Jenks drew his sword and rushed past her. He looked behind the door and under the long table. As more people tried to enter, shadows from the single lantern danced and darted.

"No one's hiding here, Your Grace," Jenks said, standing at her elbow and sheathing his sword.

"Your Majesty," came her Lord Chamberlain's voice behind

her, "you must come out, and we will see to this—this great misfortune."

Ignoring him, the queen pronounced, "Master Hodge is dead, whether by his own hand or someone else's is to be seen. My Lord Chamberlain, send for Secretary Cecil and get everyone out of the room and doorway, for you are blocking what little additional light seeps in."

"Cecil, Your Grace?" the man repeated like a dimwit.

Elizabeth finally managed to pull her gaze from the terrible tableau. "Yes, send for Cecil, and now," she commanded, turning to face the wide-eyed, whispering group. "I do not want this noised about, to sadden or panic my people in court or city at this happy time of year. But leave me now, for I shall take a brief moment to mourn." Indicating only Jenks and Stout should stay, she closed the door herself.

"Let's get the poor wretch down first," Stout cried and reached for the crank on the wall that worked the chain pulley.

"Wait!" Elizabeth ordered. "Touch nothing yet, as there may be clues or signs of what has happened here, even in this grit under our feet."

"For some specialty like the peacock or boar's head, Your Grace," Stout said, staring at the floor, "he did some seasoning as well as dressing. It's probably just sugar or ginger."

"Jenks," she said, "fetch that lantern closer, and Master Stout, leave us and try to be certain untoward rumors of this do not spread—and keep your people at their tasks as best you can. I am relying on you." Nervously clutching the new doublet he had been given, her master cook hustled out.

Poor Hodge was attired, as far as the queen could tell by staring up into the shifting shadows amidst hanging vessels and utensils, only in his breeches and shirt. His arms hung at his sides; four neatly arranged, plucked peacock fantail feathers protruded from under each armpit. And, though the man's contorted face showed, his forehead and hair were covered by the sleek blue-green body and drooped head of a peacock whose roasted carcass sat yet upon the worktable.

The queen's neck ached from staring up, but she felt awestruck by the bizarrely dressed corpse. In lantern light, the feathers gleamed and glistened; the body seemed to sway. If it was not a reflection from the peacock's coloring, the little she could glimpse of Hodge's face and back was not only contorted but bluish. She wondered if, beneath the collar of his shirt and draped peacock skin, the man had a noose around his neck, which had choked breath and life from him.

She noted a tall stool tipped against the wall. Had Hodges hanged himself by stepping from it, or was there some other explanation—and hence a Yuletide hanging of a far different sort than she had hoped for on this day?

"I guess he could have committed suicide," Jenks whispered as if he had heard her thoughts.

"If he didn't," she replied in hushed tones, "in the strange way the body is displayed, we've got both a murder and a mystery. Someone may have meant to take not only poor Hodge's life but the joy of our court Christmas."

Ned Topside was glad to escape the palace to clear his mind and try to rein in his temper, but the cold air felt like a blow to his spinning head. No one had seen him lose control—at least only one, and that was settled.

"Watch where you're going, dolt!" he exploded at a man who bumped into him on the Strand. The lout was carrying a pitifully small Yule log and must already have drunk a good cup of Christmas cheer. Damn the capering numbskulls in the street who seemed so happy when he was at his wit's end.

He'd show Elizabeth Tudor a thing or two about replacing him as Lord of Misrule, and with her fair-haired boy Leicester, no less! He'd get back at her in spades for this last-minute trickery, after how well he served her. Now he was caught in the box of having to ask his old companions to play at court but admitting he was no longer the favored Lord of Misrule, and he had no idea how to save face by playacting any different.

And now, a pox on it all, he'd just learned his uncle and his troupe of players had left the Rose and Crown for a better situation at the Lamb and Cross, an old pilgrims' inn hard by St. Paul's, and that was a good walk in this cutting river wind when he'd told the queen he wouldn't be gone long. Hell's teeth, what did it matter now, since on a woman's whim she'd put the preening Earl of Leicester in his place to make all the final Yuletide decisions?

Ned tied his cloak tighter around his neck and heaved the last of the capon drumsticks he'd filched from the palace kitchen into the middle of the street, where two dogs leaped on it, growling at each other. Ned wiped his hands on his handkerchief and hurried on.

Meg Milligrew had vexed him today, too, he admitted, kicking at a pile of refuse, then cursing when it dirtied his boots. Well might she resemble the queen, because she was acting as haughty, and without the excuse of being royal.

"Out of my way there!" he commanded a group of unruly

urchins in his best stage voice. Why should they be allowed to bat their bladder ball in front of busy citizens as they passed through narrow Ludgate? Where were their elders? Did no one teach the youth of England to be responsible anymore? He used to have to toe his father's and his uncle's lines when he was a lad.

Ned could see the new roofs of St. Paul's in the distance. After a fire three years ago started by a lightning strike, the grand city cathedral had had its huge roof newly rebuilt. The Catholics, Protestants, and Puritans had all claimed it was God's warning to at least one of the other groups. The queen wanted "freedom of conscience" for her people, but she also wanted public loyalty to the Church of England. At least she didn't imprison folks and burn martyrs at the stake as her demented half-sister had. Women!

Still seething, he located the Lamb and Cross and entered the warm, crowded common room. As his eyes sought a familiar face, the mingled scents of food and fireplace assailed him. Why weren't people at home on this Christmas Eve day? Then, above the noise of talk and laughter, he overheard a snatch of conversation: ". . . and good speeches in tha' *Cloth of Gold* play today, eh?"

"Excuse me, my man," Ned interrupted the stranger, "but can you tell me where to find the actors of that play? Are they still hereabouts?"

"Being feted by the host, ri' o'er there," the man told him with a nod, sending a blast of garlic breath his way.

Despite his foul mood, Ned's heart beat harder as he made his way over to the table in the corner. Yes, his uncle, Wat Thompson, was there, and Grand Rand, as he used to call the pompous jackanapes Randall Greene, to whom his uncle inexplicably gave all the good parts—inexplicably until Ned discovered they were lovers. That was something no one could know, lest they be arrested and worse as sodomites. How Henry Stewart, Lord Darnley, got away with his male lovers at court was beyond him. The queen knew of it but for some reason looked the other way when ordinarily nothing escaped her notice.

"Ned!" his uncle cried, rising, when he saw him coming. "Well, I'll be hanged! My boy, it's been far too long!"

Ned felt his throat tighten. He'd come far from his rambling actor's days, but those times had not been all bad. He hugged his uncle and even shook hands with Rand Greene.

"I hear you did *Cloth of Gold* today," Ned told them and struck a pose as his voice rang out. " 'And can our dear English King Henry not make France's *Francois Roi* look the very shell of a man?' "

" 'For our fair English shall e'er outmatch any man with French blood in his veins,' " his uncle picked up the next line, and they clapped each other on the shoulders.

"And the lads?" Ned asked, referring to Rob and Lucas, who had played the girls' parts.

"This is young Rob grown from a stripling," Uncle Wat said, indicating a curly-haired young man, stuffing himself with bread sopped in gravy.

"No stripling but a strapping lad," Ned said, reaching over to ruffle his hair.

"Lucas left us when his voice changed, but we have a new lad, Clinton, from Coventry, who's always sleeping, that one. But how and why did you find us, my boy?" Wat asked, shoving over on the bench so Ned could sit, too. "Still in Her Gracious Majesty's Service, her principal player, are you not?"

"I am and more. These past six years she's held the throne, I've been her Lord of Misrule, too, though I've agreed to counsel my Lord of Leicester on how to handle the task, just for this year. So as not to humble his lordship, I've agreed to dub myself his aide, but the major decisions are all mine."

He looked from man to man as he spoke, trying to assess if they were following him—and believing him. They were the most rapt audience he had ever seen. And now, he thought, for the end of this little play, where he would summon the *deus ex machina* from heaven itself for their small-encompassed lives.

"And so, I've told Her Majesty—just for this special Twelve Days of Christmas—I'd like to try to work my old troupe into an entertainment or two for the court."

Amidst the smiles, cheers, and backslapping, Ned nearly cried. He knew how they felt. He recalled the elation of that day the queen, then princess, had invited him into her household because she favored his voice, wit, and charm. She always was one to take a fancy not only to talent but to form and face, so at least he felt safe asking these men to court—excellent players but no genius or Adonis here to usurp his place.

"Shall we come with you right now?" Uncle Wat asked. "We have but one more performance on the morrow, and they will surely understand we must leave by royal command."

"Come tomorrow after the play, uncle, and by then I'll have found a cubbyhole or two for you in the servants' wing. You understand, the palace is quite full up at Christmas. You must come to the servants' door off the street near the kitchen-block porter's gate."

"We will be there with bells on," Uncle Wat declared and stood, windmilling his arm to someone in the crowd. "In the excitement of seeing you and this thrilling invitation, I almost forgot."

"Forgot what?" Ned asked and followed his uncle's gaze to see a tall, square-jawed, blond man with clear blue eyes shouldering his way to them through the crowd. He was one of the handsomest men Ned had ever beheld, and at that moment, with a sinking feeling, he discerned who he must be.

"A new player in the troupe?" Ned asked, his voice catching. He'd learned, last time he'd heard from them, that they were searching for someone well turned out to take his place, but . . .

"Giles Chatam," his uncle said, talking out of the side of his mouth, "our new man from Wimbledon. All the ladies love him, and he's the consummate actor, too, if a bit ambitious. You know, refuses to be kept in his place."

The smile and welcome Ned gave the man was some of the most difficult acting he had ever done.

"But what's the dreadful message here?" William Cecil asked as he gazed up agape at the hanging corpse decked out in a fowl's coat and feathers. "Do you plan to summon the coroner, Your Grace?"

"I must, if only to have poor Hodge declared officially deceased and, on the official examination of the body, get a second opinion about whether this could be foul play."

At her inadvertent pun, the queen's gaze caught Cecil's. He shook his head as if in warning; she bit her lower lip.

"A second opinion?" Cecil said only. "Then you mean that in the midst of all your public activities, you, with our help, intend to investigate this? Your Grace, we have the Scots envoy MacNair hovering so he can report your every move to his Catholic queen, several ambassadors in town who will be at court, Bishop Grindal coming tomorrow for the service, a feast and public celebrations on which hangs the goodwill of the court and people . . ." His voice trailed off before he added, "In short, this seems a dreadful joke indeed, and much more than poor puns on hangings and foul play are afoot here."

"I'll fetch the coroner forthwith, Your Majesty," Jenks said so loudly behind his betters that they startled.

She had almost forgotten Jenks was here, but she could hardly ignore the fact that surely word of this would spread. They must act in haste to gather evidence before they sent for public officials. And she had an appointment soon with the ever disgruntled Earl of Sussex, which she wanted to keep. She intended to tell him she expected him to get on well with his rival, the Earl of Leicester, at least during this holiday season.

"You may send someone to fetch the coroner, Jenks, but not forthwith," the queen said. "We may eventually have to summon the constable, too, though their investigations aren't worth a fig unless they can find eyewitnesses to interrogate. They seem to trample some clues and ignore or misinterpret the rest."

"Which, I warrant," Cecil put in, "we'll need to search out should you decide to pursue this, or perhaps to summon the Privy Plot Council."

"When you came in, you, as usual," she told her trusted Cecil, "asked the right question first, my lord. What indeed is the message here? Though it is a mortal sin to take one's own life, and I am deeply regretful if Hodge was somehow so desperate he did so, I pray, despite the bizarre trappings, this can be proved self-slaughter. If not, the message, at the very least, is that someone dangerous and demented has come to spend Yule with us."

"These back chambers are close to the porter's gate and street door," Jenks said. "I suppose some stranger could have come in."

"We'll question the porter, of course, but random chance is highly unlikely. Jenks, fetch more lights in here," she said, and he hastened to obey. "Cecil, I have promised an audience to the Earl of Sussex and must keep that appointment. Besides, it will allow me to see how quickly news of this has flown about our court."

"Should I not be at your side with Sussex? His festering hatred of Leicester has made him difficult to keep in line lately. Military men like our illustrious Thomas Radcliffe, Earl of Sussex, don't know when to keep quiet or calm. They think life must be all assault, attack, and violence," he protested before his eyes darted to the corpse again and he shuddered.

"Ordinarily, I would take you with me, my lord, but I need you to oversee this dreadful situation. While I am gone, fetch Roger Stout back and have him survey this cluttered worktable. I pray you make careful notes of what is here and, more important, what may be missing. See that the coroner is summoned, then clear the table so he can examine the body here, while you are still in the room, silently making your own observations. After the banquet tonight, I will hold a Privy Plot Council meeting in my quarters, where you will report all you—and Jenks—have learned."

"Yes, Your Grace," Cecil said. "Leave it all to us, unless you can send Topside to help, too."

"He should be back by now, but I hardly intend to do nothing until the meeting. I will later summon Stout for more questioning. With his information and your close observances from this site—best send Jenks to speak to the porter, too—we shall decide whether to pursue the matter further or let the conundrum be buried with Hodge."

Jenks came back in with Roger Stout, each carrying two lanterns; the small room filled with light. Though the queen edged toward the door, she thought of two things she could not bear to leave unasked and went back to stand under the corpse again.

"Master Stout, what is that gritty material on the floor?" she asked, pointing. "I stepped in it, but I see other prints there, which I want well noted and drawn to size. It is not sugar or ginger, as you suggested before, for in this new light the grains look too dark."

Stout took a lantern closer and squatted to sniff at the fine reddish dust. "Yet it looks like a spice—cumin, I warrant, Your Majesty," he reported. "It's what the peacock's innards are always dusted with before it's served."

"And this stack of gold leaf?" she asked, moving away to lift from the table a thin slab of marble as big as her palm, upon which lay an inch-thick stack of fine sheets of beaten gold. She had seen it before even in the muted light of the single lantern but had been too distracted to pay it heed. Now it shone like a small, square sun.

"He must have stopped—or been stopped—in the very act of dressing the bird for your banquet table," Stout said, as he glanced at what she held. "You recall, Your Majesty, how the bird's beak is always covered with gold foil for Yule."

"So," she said, "whether or not Hodge killed himself, we do have another mystery. When such a small amount of gold leaf is needed for the beak, why did he have here enough to cover a rich man's effigy? And if someone killed Hodge, why was this pure gold not stolen?"

"Perhaps because, if a man kills himself," Stout ventured, "he is too distraught or despondent to care for worldly wealth. Or Hodge himself was going to abscond with it but in self-loathing at his planned evil—and for other reasons—took his own life."

"Or," Jenks put in, "the gold wasn't taken because the killer was in a rush to flee once he spotted it. He'd already taken time to hang the corpse and deck it out. And he didn't want to get caught with stolen royal property on his person."

"Or just the opposite," Cecil said. "Mayhap it was a murder well planned ahead of time, and the killer's motive has everything to do with the message, so he did not want to distract from that with what would be petty theft—petty not in what was stolen but petty compared to the murderer's true intent. Discern that and we have our killer."

The queen sensed her clever Cecil would say more, but he did not. Perhaps his deductions were for her ears alone. She too feared that this death did not just strike at Hodge but that, indeed, someone diabolically devious had killed the messenger in order to send the message.

Chapter the Third

Hippocras

(Used as a digestive or to sweeten one's stomach.

A worthy potion for after feasting.)

From the cellar take 2 pints red or white wine. Place ½ teaspoon each of ground cloves, nutmeg, and ginger and 2 teaspoons of ground cinnamon all bruised together in a mortar, and 1 cup of sugar into a conical bag of felted woollen cloth (in the shape of the sleeve of Hippocrates, the brilliant Greek physician, for this is as much elixir as drink). Add some rosemary flowers and let the concoction sleep all night. Pour 2 pints of wine through the bag, for as many times as it takes to run clear. Pour wine into a vessel. If it be claret, the liquid will be red; if white, then of that color also. Seal down the drink until called for.

ELIZABETH'S STOMACH FELT KNOTTED LIKE THE NOOSE that must have choked away Hodge Thatcher's life. With her Lord Chamberlain and other household officers trailing behind her, she beat a retreat from the kitchen block back into the corridors of the palace. The scent of suspended green garlands permeated the vast place, and servants were setting up the Great Hall for tonight's feast.

She was no doubt late for the audience she had promised the Earl of Sussex, but it wouldn't hurt to let him cool his heels. She was hardly in the mood for his rantings about Leicester's growing power at court and his influence over his queen. Had she not proved time and again that even those she favored would not be trusted overmuch?

"Oh, Your Majesty," came a woman's voice as Elizabeth ascended the grand staircase toward the royal apartments, "there you are!"

Margaret Stewart, Countess of Lennox, waited at the first landing, so she was trapped. That smiling face always looked like a mask to Elizabeth. Beneath it, the queen imagined, lurked the countenance of a woman who was at heart a treacherous harpy. Though Margaret was fifty, her former beauty still haunted her plump face, but now everything about the woman seemed overblown: her big body, broad mouth, large teeth, prominent nose, even the hint of red in her graying tresses, which peeked from her velvet cap—and her ambitions. Yet Elizabeth tolerated her, for the older woman was niece to King Henry VIII and so another of the queen's female cousins who were her cross to bear.

Margaret and Matthew Stewart, the Countess and Earl of Lennox, were Lord Darnley's parents, covert Catholics, and rapacious relatives of both the English and Scottish queens. Elizabeth knew the Stewarts were plotting to wed their heir to Queen Mary in defiance of her own apparent plans for Dudley. She had promised to let Darnley go to Scotland to join his Scottish father, then changed her mind more than once. At least that was how this web of intrigue appeared to everyone but Elizabeth and Cecil.

"Cousin, how are you on this Christmas Eve day?" Elizabeth asked, nodding but not stopping. Margaret lifted her skirts and charged, puffing up the stairs after her. Elizabeth waited at the top and held out her hand to stay Margaret where she was, four or five steps down. When Elizabeth was a girl and out of favor with her royal father, more than once Margaret had gloated to take precedence and to keep the younger woman in her place.

"Oh, did you wish to speak to me?" Elizabeth inquired.

"I will be brief, Your Majesty. May not my son go north after these holidays to visit his father in Edinburgh? You had said before that he could go. My dear husband is petitioning the Scot queen's council for the return of our lands, and Lord Darnley would be of great help in this endeavor."

Oh, yes, she'd wager, Elizabeth thought, that Darnley would be of great help there. Not only with those dour Calvinist Scots lords but with the pliable Queen Mary herself. Indeed, Elizabeth was planning on that very thing, but she wanted to be certain both the bait and the big six-foot fish were hungry for their reunion when the English queen finally let him go, apparently under duress.

But she said only, "I shall consider it, Margaret. You must excuse me, but we shall speak more of this later."

"I heard there will be no peacock on display at the feast," Margaret said as Elizabeth turned away. "That is, none but the one Leicester's rivals call by that sobriquet, 'the peacock.' "

In the shock of realization, Elizabeth could have tumbled down the flight of stairs. She was hardly surprised that word of her privy dresser's death was out and about, not even that Margaret too must hate Leicester, whom she perhaps still believed to be her son's rival for Queen Mary's hand.

A new thought struck the queen with stunning force. If Hodge Thatcher had been murdered and was intentionally decked out with peacock garb, the mockery and threat could be aimed at the controversial Earl of Leicester.

. . .

"If you intend to rant about my heeding Lord Leicester's advice upon occasion," Elizabeth began with Sussex moments later in her presence chamber, "I do not wish to take my time. You are beginning to sound like your own echo, my lord, but I would ask you one thing about that."

"Of course, Your Grace," he said. "Anything I can ever do to help with, ah, anything . . ."

Sussex was hardly an orator, but that did not keep him from commanding a large faction at court. And did the man not realize that his hand perched on his ceremonial sword always rattled it in its scabbard, and to a regular beat? It was like listening to a ticking timepiece until one became a lunatic. 'S bones, but the ache in her belly was growing, and in these precious holiday times.

"I am ever at your beck and call for all service," Sussex plunged on, sweeping her a bow with the offending sword lifted so it wouldn't scrape the floor.

Thomas Radcliffe, third Earl of Sussex, had been her Lord Deputy of Ireland and had led and fought bravely there if with little ultimate success, though it seemed no one made much headway in the Eire's fens and forests. His health had suffered, and he had petitioned to be brought back to court, a request she had granted. But since he'd returned, he'd spearheaded the anti-Leicester group more zealously than he had ever fought the Irish rebel Tyrone. If the queen had not been so fond of his kin, her lady Rosie Radcliffe, and had not had a soft spot, too, for his wife, Frances Sidney, he just might be heading back for another tour of duty.

Once bright blond but now graying and balding, Sussex still had fine military bearing at age thirty-eight. She did trust the man to keep state secrets and would not usually mind having him nearby—if he would only stop that damned sword rattling!

"Instead of your asking me whether I am heeding Leicester's words on such and such an issue," the queen said, "I wish to ask you some questions about him, and I ask you tell me true."

"About the earl—ah, of course," he said, hardly managing to cloak his surprise.

"As to those who speak ill of him—and I shall not mention nor request names—by what nicknames might they call him?"

"You don't mean like 'Robin'? I've heard you call him that."

"Hardly, my lord."

"Ah, I believe Your Highness knows he used to be dubbed 'the gypsy' because of his dark hair and eyes."

"And for his tendency to mesmerize certain people, namely me, I have heard."

"I suppose that could be part of why he was called so. Also, no doubt, the fact he came with little fortune to court but has managed to—ah, find such good fortune here, some might say through sleight-of-hand or even gypsy-like theft. Indeed, Your Majesty, those people of Romany are known for such."

"So I have heard, but that trait attributed to Leicester would be wrong. 'S blood, Sussex, the man loaned me money once when I was declared bastard by my father and did not have two groats to my name. When I was sent to the Tower, though I was innocent in a misguided plot to overthrow my sister, he was imprisoned there, too, and sent me flowers and kept my spirits up. I mention these things so that those who might dislike the earl will realize he is not some border reaver sweeping in to plunder something here."

He looked astounded at her passionate outburst. His sword in its scabbard even stopped its confounded clatter.

"Any other sobriquets?" she prompted, wanting to get back to the business at hand.

"Well—ah, you've heard, of course, he's widely called of late 'the peacock.' "

"Widely called? I won't ask by whom, but why?"

"Some observers think he tends to strut, Your Majesty. And no one—but the Tudor monarch, and rightly so, of course—tends to attire oneself as finely as he does. Certainly, I can't hold a candle to the gleam of his satins, silks, and gems. I heard Martin Bane, for one, say such display is, well—absolutely sinful . . ."

Though his voice had gone from a trot to a canter, when she narrowed her eyes at Bane's name, he stopped talking. "Forgive me if I overspeak, Your Majesty, but it was at your bequest."

"Yes," she said, almost to herself. "I myself have goaded Leicester with the term *peacock* when he vexed me sore. But I will not have sniping among my subjects in my court during this holiday time. Is that understood, my lord Sussex?"

"It is. Of course," he said and punctuated that promise with a brief rattle.

"Then what more do you have to say to me today?"

"Only that I am heartened to see how lovingly my dear cousin Rosie serves you as maid of honor, Your Majesty. That is all, for we Radcliffes are ever grateful for your leading and wise counsel."

"Who could not favor your Rosie?" Elizabeth responded, though she knew full well he'd hardly requested this interview for that.

"Ah, she is a lovely girl," he added lamely.

"Lovely in her heart, that is what I value," Elizabeth said as she moved toward the door to her privy rooms. "Those of us who were children of great loves—even if that love was lost," she added quietly, "are ones who care deeply for others, my lord. Perhaps I shall have Rosie tell her parents' story again during this Yuletide, for I refuse to let jealousies and hatreds so much as creep in at court right now. We shall have only camaraderie for Christmas, that is my decree."

But her words rang hollow in her head. She feared murder had been committed in the precincts of her palace. Whether or not it was aimed at the "peacock" Leicester, the attack on the queen's privy dresser could threaten her court or even her crown.

For the Christmas Eve banquet that would begin the Twelve Days of Christmas, the front half of the Great Hall was cheek by jowl with the most powerful nobles of the land. Larded in among them at the elaborately set trestle tables were ambassadors, envoys, church legates, and senior servants. For minor courtiers and, behind them, other household servants, the rear of the vast hall held similar tables, though not quite as sumptuously appointed.

At the front of the hall, at the dais table with the queen, sat those of most noble rank: Margaret Stewart and Lord Darnley; Leicester; Sussex and his wife, Frances; the queen's Boleyn cousin, bluff, red-haired Henry Carey, Baron Hunsdon, whom Elizabeth called Harry, and his wife, Anne; and, as a special honor, Sir William Cecil and his lady, Mildred. But anyone in the hall who believed such seating paired her off with Leicester was much mistaken.

At the queen's behest, the musicians in their lofty gallery were momentarily silenced, the hall was hushed, and Cecil stood to read the announcement they had decided on:

> HER GRACIOUS MAJESTY DECLARES THAT THIS TWELVE DAYS OF CHRISTMAS SHALL BE CARRIED ON AS PLANNED WITH SEVERAL EXCEPTIONS. DUE TO THE MOST UNFORTUNATE DEMISE TODAY OF ROYAL SERVANT HODGE THATCHER, DRESSER OF THE QUEEN'S PRIVY KITCHEN, THE COURT WILL HONOR HIS MEMORY IN THESE WAYS: TO WIT, THERE WILL BE NO PEACOCK SERVED THIS YEAR; SPECIAL PRAYERS WILL BE OFFERED FOR HIS DEPARTED SOUL AT CHURCH SERVICE TOMORROW; AND THE BRINGING IN OF THE YULE LOG TO THE CENTRAL HEARTH IN THIS HALL WILL BE DELAYED UNTIL AFTER THAT TIME OF REMEMBRANCE. ALSO, FESTIVITIES UNDER THE AEGIS OF THE LORD OF MISRULE, THIS YEAR THE EARL OF LEICESTER, ASSISTED BY THE QUEEN'S PRINCIPAL PLAYER AND MASTER OF REVELS, NED TOPSIDE, WILL BE POSTPONED UNTIL THE DAY AFTER CHRISTMAS, THOUGH LEICESTER WILL THEN NOT RULE BUT MISRULE FOR THE REMAINDER OF THIS YULETIDE SEASON.

Murmurings and whispers assailed the queen's ears. At the Lord Chamberlain's nod, lutes, shawms, gitterns, drums, and pipes began to play again from the musicians' second-story gallery.

"I believe this is a fair blend of mourning and yet letting life—and Christmas—go on," Elizabeth said to Cecil, raising her voice to be heard. "I suppose they're vexed about waiting for the Yule log, but everyone gets so giddy over that I couldn't countenance it, even if Hodge's body will be held for burial until after Twelfth Day."

Hodge's death hardly seemed to stem the eating and drinking, she noted, though the queen's own stomach had not settled since she had seen the corpse hanging as if it were another piece of Yuletide holly to be cast off after the revels. She merely picked at her favorite dishes and settled instead for the sweet fruit suckets she loved. Her mind wandered from the conversation, even from Robin's, whom she had more or less forgiven once again for meddling where he was not bidden.

"I believe I will take some hippocras instead of straight wine," she told her servers, "just to help with digesting all this. The food was fabulous, of course, even prepared and delivered under duress." She saw their eyes light with pleasure as bright as their new livery before they hurried away.

Elizabeth's gaze caught Cecil's. He had not missed that she had hardly tasted the array of dishes. When the hippocras was proffered to her, she downed it, then excused herself early, though she told her Lord Chamberlain to announce merely that she was tired and all could stay at their places. She only hoped, despite the exhaustion of this day, that her master cook, Roger Stout, would have something to tell her about Hodge Thatcher's motives for possible suicide. She was no doubt clutching at straws, but if she received only one gift for the holidays, she prayed it could be that no murderer stalked her court.

Cecil also excused himself early and joined the queen just as Roger Stout was escorted into her otherwise empty presence chamber. "Will you write down pertinent facts, my lord?" she whispered to Cecil as Stout stopped before the table where his two betters were seated.

He appeared to be both flushed with excitement and drained

by exhaustion; she noted well that the new livery she had given him today looked pleasing on him, but for a fresh splotch on the left shoulder.

"Clifford," she addressed her trusted yeoman guard as he was about to leave the room, "draw up a chair for Master Stout, as he has had a doubly trying day."

"You are most thoughtful, Your Majesty," Stout said as he rose from his bow, "and I am most grateful." When both she and Cecil praised the meal, he told them, "If the many dishes were garnished well, thanks be to George Brooks, Master Hodge's 'prentice of long standing. With your gracious permission, I'll elevate him to the position of dresser *pro tem* 'til you name another."

"That will be fine, Master Stout," the queen assured him as he sat in the chair Clifford brought from the back of the room. When Clifford went out, the muted sounds of laughter and music floated to them from below.

"And now," she went on, "will you tell us anything you know that might indicate—despite the bizarre garnishing of Hodge's body—that the poor man might have possibly done away with himself?"

" 'Tis mostly from knowing his state of mind, Your Majesty."

"Say on."

"Hodge Thatcher comes from a long line of thatchers, I mean, those who thatch roofs, you see. Not unusual for a name to come from a long-tended family occupation. The thing is, Your Majesty, his father expected him to take over the trade, especially when the old man, his sire, slid off a roof—out by Wimbledon, it was—and broke his back. Can't move from his waist down, the old man."

"So Master Hodge felt guilty over disappointing his father?"

she summarized. Glancing over Stout's head she could see a portrait of her own father hanging on the wainscotted wall; she had paid it little heed for months, but it suddenly seemed to be staring at her. When she first came to the throne, she used to be ever aware of it. Sometimes the eyes even seemed to follow her around the room. Though her royal sire had more than once declared a woman could never sit on England's throne, she was certain her father would be proud of her—wouldn't he?

"Aye, guess that would be part of it," Stout said, pulling her back to the present. "But, you see, 'twas Hodge's dream to be a cook and in London, and when he worked his way up in the Tudor kitchens, he never would go home. His mother missed him sore, their only child, I guess. She died last year, and after that his sire would never take the coins Hodge tried to send, a most bitter, unforgiving man, he was, e'en afore his tumble from the roof. But then he got turned out of his home, and right afore holiday time, but a week or so ago, it were."

"And all this weighed heavily on Hodge's mind," she said. "He told you so?"

"Not only that," he said, nodding vigorously, "but I was thinking about that stack of gold leaf. Secretary Cecil here had me talk to the guards at the larder, where we keep the leafing for special displays under lock and key. Seems Hodge told them he needed the entire amount of it on hand to do not only the peacock's beak but legs and feet, too, special for the queen's Christmas, he told them."

"But I saw the bird's body was roasted with the legs under it and not leafed as usual," the queen observed.

"So did I, Your Grace," Cecil put in, "not that Hodge could not have stretched the legs out after it was roasted and leafed them over then. But still that stack of leaf was far too much for what he needed."

Hardly able to contain her excitement, Elizabeth stood and started to pace. Both men jumped to their feet so as not to sit in her presence. "Are you thinking, Master Stout," she asked, "that Hodge might have been intending to take or send at least some of that gold leaf to his father so that he might keep his home, or be well tended by someone? Perhaps he contacted his father or heard from him and—even partially paralyzed and homeless—the stubborn man would not accept charity from his son, not even at Christmastide. Hodge rued letting his people down and killed himself? Do I jump too far afield?"

"My thinking exactly, Your Majesty," Stout said, " 'specially 'cause of this."

He felt in the inside of his new livery doublet first on one side, then the other, until he produced a grease-spattered scrap of paper he carefully unfolded. When he held it out, Cecil reached across the table to take it from him and offer it to the queen.

"Open and read it, my lord," she said as her thoughts raced.

It was possible that Hodge had been despondent over his family problems, she surmised, gripping her hands together. Perhaps when he decided to kill himself, on the spur of the moment, he decked himself out to show whoever found him that he had lived proudly in his place as royal dresser and garnisher, however much his father criticized his chosen trade. And perhaps he had left behind a suicide note.

"I am having this writ by the sexton of the church," Cecil read, squinting at the folded paper and tilting it toward the bank of beeswax candles on the table. *"Money cannot replace nor buy the time you did not spend with us, come to us, and help me in the proud trade of your forefathers. You*

made your fancy bed with cooking for the family that ruined the true church. You chose their table finery and all that, so lie in it, that bed you made. You cared not a fig for us, and naught can make up for that now your mother's gone and I be like this, not even half a man and that without a home."

"So cruel, for all of them, and at Christmas," the queen whispered, stopping her pacing so fast her skirts swayed. She felt a sudden chill and clasped her elbows in her hands. Hodge's family had hated hers, but Hodge had chosen loyalty to the Tudors. Though this was not the suicide note she had been expecting, sadly, self-slaying seemed entirely possible now.

"The note's not signed," Cecil said with a catch in his voice.

"I warrant it did not have to be," she said. "The way it is worded could have sent him off the edge of despair. To lie in that bed, which his father cursed, perhaps Hodge defiantly became that peacock, which was fine looking, though it was dead."

"Aye, he was always proud of how he dressed the peacocks, swans, boar's heads, too," Master Stout said. "But maybe how gay and glad we all were in the kitchens that day made him think how wretched he was, so he climbed up on that stool, brought the chain pulley down a bit, and did the dreadful deed right then."

The three of them stood silent until the queen thanked Master Stout. He bowed and left the room, saying no more.

"You're no doubt much relieved," Cecil said from the other end of the table.

"I am. My stomachache is even better. It all fits. Perhaps now I will not call the late meeting of my Privy Plot Council, and we can all get back to normal after the prayers for the poor man's soul tomorrow. He won't be buried in hallowed ground now, but I will have Stout send a message to that unforgiving father of his. What? Why are you looking at me that way, my lord?"

"I am tempted to tell you all is well, but you have not yet heard some other things I have learned from your commanding me to observe the coroner's work and the scene of the death."

Her hopes plummeted; her stomach cramped again, despite that hippocras she'd drunk after dinner.

"When I appointed you my chief advisor, Cecil, I charged you to always give me true counsel, whatever the risk or cost."

"Then you'd best call that meeting, Your Majesty. More than that booted print in the cumin under Hodge's body suggests that foul play was indeed afoot."

Chapter the Fourth

Maids of Honor

Make pastry enough for a double-crust pie. Preheat brick oven by burning wood or coals inside, then raking them out. Roll out pastry and cut in rounds, then fit in small bun or tartlet tins. Prick pastry with fork tines. Bring to near boil ½ pint fresh cow's milk with 4 level tablespoons of white breadcrumbs (2-day-old bread is best). Remove from heat and leave for a few minutes. Into that mixture beat 8 teaspoons butter, cut in cubes. Beat in 2 tablespoons sugar, grated rind of 1 lemon, and ¾ cup ground blanched almonds. Although the mixture has some texture, be sure it is not lumpy. Beat in 3 good hen's eggs. Half fill the pastry shells and bake for 15 minutes or until pastry has pulled away from side of tins and filling is golden brown. Carefully lift pastry from tins and cool before eating.

IT WAS NEARLY ELEVEN O'CLOCK THAT NIGHT WHEN THE queen opened the hastily called meeting of her Privy Plot Council in her presence chamber. "I am not certain that we even have a murder to investigate," she explained, "but considering the holiday season and all that depends on its going well, we'd best at least put our heads together on Hodge Thatcher's strange demise."

She glanced around the table. Cecil sat next to her, frowning at a written report under his folded hands. Across the table, Meg Milligrew was wide-eyed; Jenks, beside her, looked intent, too. At the far end of the table, Ned Topside seemed glum and distracted when he should have been happy, for he had told her he'd found his old players' troupe and they were coming to court tomorrow.

On Elizabeth's other side, Harry, Baron Hunsdon, was disturbed by being so suddenly summoned from the festivities, but then he was the one among them who knew nothing of these events yet. He was probably alarmed because each time her covert council had struggled to solve a murder, deceit and danger followed. The queen rued Kat's absence, but she needed her sleep and should not be disturbed by unrest. Elizabeth longed to invite her maid of honor, Rosie, to replace Kat in this company, but if a murderer were out to disgrace Robin, her little band would have to investigate Rosie's kin Lord Sussex—along with about half the court.

The queen concluded her opening remarks with "Now that I have summarized for you the case for the poor man's suicide, my lord Cecil will present the other possibility."

"Granted," he began, "some of the physical evidence at the scene of death could be attributed to a suicide. Hodge could have half undressed himself, for his breeches, doublet, and shoes were found under his worktable. The coroner informed me that, for some reason, suicides sometimes take off their shoes, and Hodge was barefooted."

"On the other hand," the queen put in, "his disrobing could mean he was getting ready for his new livery and therefore expected to live."

"After all," Ned said as if rushing to her aid, "Her Majesty's interview with Master Stout tips the scales toward suicide."

"I'd like to believe that, too," the queen said, "but you are not, Ned, writing the script for the meeting as if it were some play."

Ned frowned and shifted in his seat as Cecil went on. "Also, the man could have climbed on that stool and slipped the knotted noose around his own neck, having donned the skinned coat of the peacock and having stuck those tail feathers carefully under his armpits. However, to be fair, before I proceed, let's listen to someone who came upon the death scene before I did.

"Jenks?" Cecil said, turning his way. "Anything to add at this point before I list the evidence to suggest we are dealing not with suicide but with assault and murder?"

"I found it hard to believe," Jenks said, "that when that noose—made of twisted twine, more or less a thin but strong rope really, was the same sort he used to truss up birds or boars for roasting—now, what was I going to say? Oh, that I find it hard to credit, if Hodge hanged himself, that he didn't flail around in choking to death and ruin the way those feathers stuck out, spaced just so," he concluded with gestures.

"Another good point," the queen said. "If he didn't struggle, he must have wanted his own death—and to be arrayed like that."

"Or if someone hanged him," Cecil countered, "the culprit held his hands in place or rearranged those feathers after the final struggle. Neither I nor the coroner saw ligature marks on his wrists or arms to suggest someone had him tied while he died, then removed such ties. But wait—here is the report I had the coroner write out and sign, and it is most compelling."

The queen noted that everyone seemed to take in a deep breath and go as still as a statue. All turned toward Cecil.

"I won't read you all the petty details and the Latin medical phrases," he said, "but to put it briefly, Hodge was knocked hard enough on the head to fracture his skull. The four-inch-by-eight-inch wound on the top back of his pate," he went on, pointing at his own head, "was no doubt received before he either stepped up on that stool—or was lifted up to be hanged from a rope attached to the pulley chains."

"He hardly took a hit like that," Jenks said, "by bumping into one of those hanging kettles, however big some are. They all hang high."

"And," Meg added, "it's not likely he got a knock on the top back of his head accidentally falling. Not and then climbed up there, like he was out of his head, for such a blow would make him dizzy at least, stun or knock him out at worst. If someone hit him, someone must have helped him up on that stool."

"Agreed," Harry put in, as if coming to life at last. "It's highly doubtful that the man would hit himself to make it look like an attack. If it's not a crime of passion, it sounds like a crime of planning."

"I fear so," Cecil said. "He was probably hit by the man who left a boot print in the spilled cumin grit on the floor—his murderer, who helped him look as if he might have hanged himself."

The queen listened with a heavy heart; yes, it must be a murder, one she could hardly ignore. Literally from up his sleeve, Cecil produced a second paper and unfolded it to show the sketch of the boot print she had requested.

"To size as well as shape?" she asked, gripping her hands hard in her lap.

"It is. Though it may not belong to whoever hit Hodge, gave him a hoist up, and knocked over that stool, it's a place to start."

"Was there blood," Harry asked, "on his skull up under that peacock skin?"

"Indeed, though it seems the bird skin acted as a sort of bandage to mat and pool the blood," Cecil explained. "Yet I doubt that the skin was placed on his head as an afterthought to hide that blood. It all seems diabolically designed. I believe the murderer slipped into Hodge's workroom with the intent to kill and display his victim, but for what purpose or motive I do not know."

"That," Elizabeth said, "is what we must learn to find the killer."

"By the way," Cecil added, turning over the coroner's report, "I've sketched something here I believe is as significant as the boot print."

"What's that, then?" Meg asked as they all gazed at the strange shape.

"I warrant it's the circumference of the head wound," the queen answered for him.

Jenks leaned forward, frowning at the sketch of the oblong wound with rivulets of blood or some crude pattern roughly drawn in. Ned quickly rose from his seat and leaned close to see.

"Yet his face was bluish," Elizabeth went on, "which means he did indeed strangle or suffocate from the noose—but after he may have been stunned enough to be lifted up there and dressed with the peacock regalia. If he were dazed, that could also explain someone's being able to hold his hands at his sides while he weakly struggled and so died, but without disturbing the symmetrical arrangement of feathers under his arms or making ligature marks."

Cecil nodded. Harry seemed silently thoughtful, and her servants still wide-eyed. Only Ned looked as if he'd like to argue, but for once he said nothing.

"Then I must cut this meeting short," the queen said, rising and scraping her chair back. "Cecil, Jenks, and I must return to the site of the murder instantly to search for what could have caused this mark—the first of the two murder weapons, in effect, if we count the noose, too."

"I looked around as best I could while the coroner worked," Cecil said as everyone rose. "Whatever caused this blow, Hodge's murderer must have taken it with him."

"I suppose it has to be a him," Meg put in as Jenks squeezed her shoulder and hurried after the queen, "because a woman probably couldn't lift him, but she could wear a boot like that. Are we going to check the boot soles of everyone to see if one fits that shape or has cumin stuck in the cracks of it, Your Grace?"

"That would be fruitless with so many at court. The culprit could merely change boots, though the size of the foot may help us to narrow down possibilities later. Meg, I can't ask my maids for a cape this late, or they'll know I'm going out. Lend me yours, if you please. My lord Harry, best go back down to join your wife and keep an eye on things below. If anyone asks how I am, report that I am fine but resting until tomorrow.

"Cecil, Jenks, and I," she went on, stopping in the door to her chamber, "will go down my privy staircase to the river, out and around to the kitchen court, and in that way, to avoid everyone still lingering about the Great Hall or gadding about in the corridors. Meg and Ned, you will stay here and, if something demands my presence, Ned, hie yourself to fetch me, while Meg speaks for me through the door as if I am too tired to come out."

As the queen took Meg's squirrel-lined wool cape, Elizabeth realized her herbalist did not look as happy as usual to play queen, even if only for Ned's eyes. Perhaps, for once, she didn't want to be alone with him, she thought as she hurried toward her bedchamber, where her father's old privy staircase could be entered behind an arras. Jenks didn't look too happy to be leaving Ned and Meg behind, either.

The slap of chill night wind shocked the queen at first. Meg's cloak was thin compared to hers. She must give the girl one on New Year's Day to ward off the sting of winter. At least this had a hood to pull up and gather close about her neck.

They had not brought a lantern, for they knew the palace windows overhead would light their way, and a nearly full moon shone off thin snow and thickening river ice. The queen's stomach growled, as if in foreboding; she realized she should have eaten something more, however unsettled she'd felt.

"The Thames is near frozen clear across," Jenks said. "We'll have that Frost Fair for certain."

The lights of Lambeth Palace, home of the Bishop of London and Martin Bane, when Bane wasn't at court protecting their interests, shone across the expanse of ice. Lambeth had its own barge with oarsmen, but with the Thames gone nearly solid, Elizabeth realized that the churchmen must have been traveling rutted roads and crossing crowded London Bridge. They'd be happy enough to soon use a cart or sleigh. When ice must be traversed, horses wore studded shoes, and wheels had nails pounded through them for traction.

Before the river tidal flats began, though they were but frozen mud now, a small path wended its way around the palace's stony skirts, and they followed that. One more turn and they could see the torchlit porter's door that guarded the kitchen block from the public street on the other side of the walls.

"That reminds me," Elizabeth whispered. "Jenks, did you

inquire from the day porter if anyone unusual came in or out of the kitchen-block gate this afternoon?"

"Yes, Your Grace. No traffic for once. All the Twelve Days supplies were already in, he said, and no one wants to leave where all the good times are—that's how he put it. Except for Ned."

"Ned put it how?"

"No, I mean, Ned went out the porter's door this afternoon, looking most distraught, too, didn't even answer the porter's 'heigh ho' to him. The poor man—the porter, Your Grace—thinks Ned's really the hail-fellow-well-met he plays in the comedies."

"Why would Topside be going out this back gate today?" Cecil asked sharply.

"He learned his old troupe of players is in town," Elizabeth explained, "so I gave him permission to invite them for a performance or two before all this happened. And he was vexed because I named Leicester as Lord of Misrule. Cecil, get us past the porter, won't you, as I have no wish for him to know it's me."

He walked ahead and knocked on the bolted door; his words floated to Jenks and the queen. "My lady and I have been walking by the river with a guard, but it's far too cold. We want to get back in by the kitchens, get a bit of warmth from the big hearth fires."

"Oh, my lord secretary, certes," the man cried and rattled his keys overlong opening the gate. With Elizabeth holding her hood close to her face, the three of them hustled past before he caught a glimpse of anyone else. Icy wind even here in the courtyard swirled up Elizabeth's skirts, but once inside, it was warmer, almost steamy with mingled, succulent smells. Despite the work they'd come to do, the queen felt even hungrier.

"I told Stout to seal off the dresser's workroom and let the man who replaced him work elsewhere for a few days," Cecil said, "lest we should need to return like this."

"Good planning, my lord," she said. "Jenks, go find Stout and tell him that we're here and why—and bring back some lanterns again."

He hastened to obey while Cecil unwrapped the thick twine stretched across the door from latch to hinge. Neither rope nor string, it looked to be the same sturdy stock that had been used in multiple strands to make the hangman's noose. Cecil opened the door. The darkness within seemed profound, almost a living, breathing being. In the pale slab of light from the hall sconce, the queen's eyes adjusted slowly. She imagined she could see the corpse still hanging amidst the pots and chains, a man sprouting feathers as if he could swoop at them.

She jumped as light leaped in behind her and Cecil. Jenks held one large lantern, and her master cook two more.

"Your Majesty," Stout said, "I had no idea you'd be back and at this hour. The staff is yet cleaning up and having a bit of our own feast, though there's a pall on things from what happened here. Still, you said, Yule will go on."

"You are doing what is right, Master Stout. I simply wanted you to know we are here. Please return to your people without divulging my presence, and I'll send Jenks for you if I need you further. By the way, did you hear the coroner say Hodge had a head wound?" she asked as he set his lanterns on the table and started for the door.

"I did," he said, turning back, "but assumed it was made by his bumping against or falling on something—a corner of his work-table or a fancy bowl, though I overheard the coroner say it seemed to resemble a fancy sword hilt, one molded or sculpted, but I deemed the latter quite impossible."

"I appreciate your help and discretion in this delicate matter. There will be nothing more right now," she told him, as she recalled the constant rattle of Sussex's ceremonial sword. The problem was, Elizabeth thought, not so much that Master Stout was clever only in the kitchen but that he could not conceive of evil in his narrow realm as she could in her broader one.

The three of them thoroughly searched the room for what might have been used to hit Hodge. They found nothing telltale or unusual on the floor, worktable, or shelves, or even aloft in the hanging kettles and pots she had Jenks peer into while he stood on the very stool the murderer had perhaps used to tie the noose and hoist Hodge.

"What was that low, growling sound?" Jenks cried, looking under the table again. "Not the wind?"

"It's my stomach," the queen muttered. "I should have eaten more at dinner, and that hippocras helped me not one whit."

"This search is a dead end," Cecil said, "if you'll excuse the pun."

"We must conclude that the murderer took the weapon with him," Elizabeth said with a sigh. "If we find it, we may find our man, but exactly what are we looking for? If only we still had the body, I'd take a close look at that blow myself."

"If you're up to it," Cecil said, "we could go look, as the corpse is not far from here. You never asked me where we had the coroner stow Hodge, so I didn't think you wanted to know. The ground's so frozen, he can't be buried until it thaws, though, at least, it sounds now as if the poor wretch is headed for a grave in hallowed ground instead of some potter's field with self-slayers."

"Then where is he?" she asked. "Surely, not in the palace proper and not in my kitchens!"

"In the boathouse on the riverbank."

"Is it locked or guarded?"

"A guard would freeze out there. It's barred and locked, yes, with all your barges off the ice now, but I still have the extra key," he said and, with a taut smile, produced it on his jingling chain of them.

"Bring that largest lantern, Jenks," she said, redonning Meg's cloak, "and, my lord, we'll need another." As they went out into the corridor, Stout stood there with a laden tray.

"I've been waiting to offer you a late-night repast when you emerged," he explained, his eyes darting among the three of them in the light of the two lanterns they carried. On the tray were tankards of beer, no doubt much like the ones the staff was enjoying now, and a little plate of cheese tarts—no, they were those lemon custard ones everyone called Maids of Honor she'd passed over earlier this evening.

"I know you like these, Your Majesty," Stout said, "and you did not eat a great deal at the Christmas Eve feast."

She merely nodded and, despite their terrible task ahead, reached for a tart. Murder or not, she was famished, and it both annoyed and touched her that even her master cook knew that she had not eaten much this eve. Would she ever become accustomed to the way her people watched her every move as if she were the head of a massive family?

At that thought, a shudder swept her. Despite the fact that Hodge Thatcher's family had obviously hated the Protestant Tudors for "ruining the true church," as the note put it, Hodge had chosen loyalty to her. Since this was indeed a murder, she must try to solve it for the memory of the man himself and not only to assure the safety of her court or crown. Any crime that struck at one of her people, cook to clerk to courtier, must be solved and punished.

Cecil and Jenks also took a drink and downed a tart—actually, Jenks ate three. When Elizabeth indicated she'd have no more, Master Stout wrapped up the rest of the pastries in a cloth and handed them to Jenks.

"They say, you know, Your Majesty," Stout said, turning back to her with the hint of a bow, "that your mother when she was maid of honor made these tarts for your royal sire."

"I've heard that, Master Stout, but don't credit it a bit. More like they were concocted by some clever pastry cook who knew he could charge more for them if they could be tied to such a tale. My royal father only favored massive portions, so these are much too dainty and delicate for him—or most men," she added as Jenks's big paw managed to crush another tart to crumbs before he could get it in his mouth.

Meg stood at the oriel windows of the queen's bedroom and watched the moon glaze a path on the white Thames. "It looks pretty but so dreadful cold out there," she remarked to Ned, who was seated at the queen's table as he had been yesterday, once again writing furiously.

"Chilly in here, too," he muttered.

"With this hearth blazing?"

"I spoke metaphorically, Mistress Milligrew—ah, I mean, Your Most Glorious and Gracious Majesty," he said, looking up. "If you keep up the way you've been treating me, I shall dub you 'the Ice Queen' and write you as such into the Christmas entertainment I am planning for my troupe's arrival tomorrow."

"If I'm treating you cold, it's only because you've treated me that way."

"Really?" he said, tossing down his quill. "Did it ever cross *your* mind that I might have a few important and weighty things on *my* mind this season? And now, the queen's off on a hunt for a murderer, and who needs that complication?"

"You're just angry because you're not Lord of Misrule this year and can't get by with all your high-and-mighty decrees as you always have, going about masked, kissing all the girls, the ladies, too—"

"Aha! Do I detect green eyes?"

"You're the one with the green eyes, and you know well enough how to use them. No, I'm not jealous, just in love with a man who, by comparison, makes you look pretty bad. As for *your* foul mood, *you* ought to be happy the queen's taking your old fellows in for the holidays."

"Happy as a hawk in a windstorm," he groused. "One member of the troupe is new and untested, and a bit of a climber, I'm afraid, and I'm going to have to take some of my precious time to keep a watch on him."

"Hm," she said. "Takes one to know one, so—"

She stopped talking midthought as Ned rose and came quickly to stand behind her at the window. She spun to look out again so he wouldn't be pressing her, face to face, against it. He leaned a hand on the deep sill as if to block her in or embrace her, but she saw he was craning his neck to stare out the window at something down by the iced-in barge landings.

"Just keep an eye on him yourself, name of Giles Chatam," Ned said, his mouth so close it stirred the hair at her temple and warmed her ear.

"You mean he's a ladies' man, too," she goaded, "and you don't think I'd be safe around him?"

"I mean he's likely to be disguised half the time because I'm writing him parts where he's masked and cloaked, dark parts, the villains."

"While you play the innocents and heroes, I suppose," she said and managed a laugh. "Best be careful, Ned Topside, queen's master player, or all your friends will see right through you," she scolded and, most unqueen-like, pushed him back and darted to the table to read the playlet he'd written.

"I'm going out," he announced, hard on her heels; he snatched the paper before she could read it.

"But you're to stay here."

"I'll be back directly, but I've got to use the jakes and can hardly borrow Her Majesty's velvet close stool, now can I?"

"How do you know about something as privy as her close stool?"

"Let's just say," he muttered, "she's as good as dumped me in it lately."

"Ned Topside!"

"Stop fretting. My stomach's just upset by something I ate at dinner, and it's ruining my disposition, too."

Meg wondered if he actually had a wench to meet. He didn't look ill. She knew he was vexed with the queen, but that gave him no leave to ignore her wishes. Hands on hips, Meg watched Ned walk away, open the door, duck under the yeomen's crossed halberds before they could react, and disappear at a good clip down the hall.

The door to the boathouse moaned mournfully, but the interior provided shelter from the cutting wind as the queen, Cecil, and

Jenks stepped inside. The large wooden structure sat upon rows of sawhorses and four-foot stilts along the river bank, but the entrance was level with the smaller of the two barge landings. Not only were the valuable rivercraft being kept under lock and key; the thick double doors were barricaded by a large beam bar the two men had lifted to get in.

Their two lanterns illumined the queen's massive state barge sitting high on tree trunks where it had been rolled in. Two other passenger barges and several working boats were hulking shadows in the depths of the low-ceilinged building. The single small window at the back overlooked the frozen river.

"Over here, in this far corner," Cecil said and started away. Elizabeth followed, then Jenks with the second lantern.

Floorboards groaned under their feet; the entire edifice creaked from the cold like old bones. Elizabeth and Jenks slowed their strides when they approached the ten-foot wherry in the corner. A sliver of moonlight sliced across the boat's prow.

"I had him laid in here like a mummy in a sarcophagus, so we'll have to unwrap his head," Cecil said, leaning over the side of the boat.

As Elizabeth stepped closer and looked into the ribbed hull, she wished she hadn't eaten even one little tart. In this cold, no odor emanated from the body, but the sight of the shrouded form shook her deeply. Cecil's mummy comparison aside, Hodge was laid out lengthwise in the boat, as if he were about to be launched for a fiery Viking funeral.

"Your Grace," Cecil interrupted her thoughts, "if you can hold a light for us, we can unwrap the top of his head, keeping his face covered."

"Yes, good idea," she said, taking the lantern Cecil held.

Jenks put down his lantern and little bundle of pastries on the wherry's single seat and climbed inside the hull to support Hodge's shoulders while Cecil opened the shroud from the top; they worked together to turn the body so that the back of the head was visible.

"Definitely struck from behind and with a downward blow," the queen observed, her voice sounding as shrill as did the wind through the boathouse chinks and cracks. They all startled at a distant hollow boom followed by a crackling sound.

"Just river ice settling," Cecil said. "It will be solid soon, but back to business. Hopefully, he never knew what hit him."

"But we must discern exactly what did," she said, "for it is our best hope to solve this riddle. There—hold him a moment just like that. Yes, I see the shape of the blow." Holding the lantern in one hand, she rested her other on an oarlock and bent closer. "But his thick, blood-matted hair keeps us from clearly discerning whatever pattern was on the weapon," she observed. "The coroner at least should have washed his head there. I wish we had some sort of lather to shave that spot for a close look."

"I could go fetch some and a razor," Jenks offered.

"No, I think that won't be necessary. Since the coroner is finished with the body, and we are the ones who will bury him when there's a thaw, I don't think anyone will even notice what I intend. Jenks, let me borrow your knife and those Maids of Honor, if you please."

Both men held the corpse while Elizabeth proceeded to smear the custard filling over the area on Hodge's head obscured by blood and hair. Carefully but awkwardly, her hand shaking, she began to shave his matted hair away.

"I can do that, Your Grace," Cecil said.

"Just keep holding him. I'm going to use this cloth to wipe it off, and then we shall all see what pattern of murder weapon lies beneath."

Her belly cramped from leaning into the boat as well as from her stomach-churning task. At least Cecil's sketch had captured texture as well as shape: Whatever had hit Hodge from behind had dented in his flesh and skull in a pattern. Within the outer form, there was a sort of band or belt with what might be an insignia in the middle of the band.

"A coat of arms or design, even a short word?" she asked, shifting the lantern to try to make the contours of the wound stand out in shadow. "If only we could read it!"

"As the coroner suggested, made by a sword hilt?" Cecil said. "Or by a large kitchen utensil?"

"That brighter light's better," Jenks observed, and Elizabeth nodded until her stomach cartwheeled again.

"What light?" she asked. "No one's moved a lantern, and the moonlight can't shift that fast. Could someone have a light outside?"

She tore her gaze away from the corpse. Through the single window of the boathouse, moonlight flooded in. No, it could not be that, she reasoned, for this was golden, warm light, not that of the winter moon.

"Someone must have lit a fire outside on the ice," she said. "We'll be seen leaving here and going back to the palace."

Both men looked up as she hurried to the window, then scrubbed at the swirling frost patterns on it so she could see out. She suddenly recalled how Hodge, lying in the boat, had looked as if he were about to be launched for a Viking funeral.

"We must run!" she cried. "I wager someone's lit a fire under us!"

Jenks dropped the body and vaulted from the wherry. Grabbing a lantern, he ran to the door and rattled it. "It's locked or barred from outside!" he shouted. "We're trapped!"

Chapter the Fifth

Mince Pie Mangers

This Yuletide variation of mincemeat pie should be baked in a rectangular crust, in the shape of a manger to recall the birth of the Savior. But the following recipe for the filling must be made months ahead so it can ferment. Mixtures of spices and liquors well preserve perishable meats and fruits.

Grind or crush (some use large stones for this mincing) 1½ pounds boiled beef, ½ pound suet. Combine with 4 cups beef broth and the following: 1½ teaspoons salt; 2 pounds apples, peeled, cored, and chopped; 3 cups brown sugar, tightly packed; 2 cups raisins; 1½ cup currants; 2 teaspoons powdered cinnamon; 1 teaspoon each of powdered mace, cloves, and nutmeg; 2 cups finely chopped candied rinds; 2 lemons with rind, ground up; 3 oranges with rind, ground up; 1½ cups cider; 2 cups of red or white wine, such as Rhenish or sack. Seal and age at least 3 months.

"WILL ONE OF THESE SMALL OARS FIT BETWEEN THE doors to lift the bar?" the queen asked Jenks as she and Cecil rushed to join him at the entrance to the boathouse. "I doubt if someone has the other key to lock us in. It's probably just barred." But she saw that the crack between the doors would take nothing wider than a sword, and such would never lift that heavy piece of wood.

They could smell smoke now, curling through the floorboard

cracks; they could hear the crisp crackle of flames. Surely, the queen thought, on the open riverbank in the cold of night, a fire had not been set by vagabonds trying to keep warm.

"Someone will see the blaze and come running!" Cecil cried, then began coughing in the thickening pall of smoke.

"But maybe not in time!" Jenks shouted. "I can break the window, but it's high up from the ice."

"Yes, break it!" Elizabeth ordered.

The men lifted a large oar from the state barge and smashed the window. Cold air and smoke belched in but, God be thanked, no flames so high yet. The men ran the oar around the small window, knocking out the panes of thick glass and their diamond-shaped metal frames.

"I'll drop down first to be sure no one's waiting," Jenks said, ripping off his surcoat. She thought he would discard it to keep it from catching fire, but he laid it over the jagged sill of the shattered window. Just behind their feet, tongues of flames flicked through the floorboards.

Drawing his sword and using only one hand to drop, Jenks went lithely out the window.

"All clear!" he shouted up. "No one!"

"All at tables and revels," the queen muttered, but she sucked in smoke and began choking, too. Her skirts and cloak burdened her, so she threw the cloak out first, then divested herself of layers of petticoats and heaved them out. With Cecil's help above and Jenks's below, she climbed out, dangled, then dropped the short way. Jenks half caught her, but the bank was slick with frozen mud; she sat down hard and sprawled out onto the river ice. Jenks came sliding after her, but she told him, "I'm fine. Help Cecil!"

He was soon out the window, too. " 'S blood," she cursed as the two men helped her climb the banks with her gown hems dragging, "I'll have the head of whoever set that blaze. And, I warrant, we'll find it's a villain who's as adept with nooses as with firebrands."

Even the voices of the boys' choir from St. Paul's, echoing so sweetly in the chapel at Whitehall, could not calm the queen the next morning. At the beginning of the Christmas service, as she had requested, a prayer had been offered for Hodge Thatcher's soul, though it had not been announced that someone—perhaps someone here in the congregation—had killed the man.

Not only did Elizabeth have a murder on her hands, but she was blessed to still be alive herself. Last night, Jenks had summoned help to fight the fire while she and Cecil had beat a hasty retreat back to the privy staircase. But with the river frozen, water to douse the flames had been slow coming. The building, with Hodge's body inside, had burned to its footers. Only the state barge had been saved, rolled out at the last minute because it sat so near the doors.

A hue and cry had gone out for the vagabonds who were supposedly to blame, but the queen believed Hodge's murderer had set the fire, at best to warn her, at worst to roast her like the Christmas peacock or suckling pig. Unfortunately, the press of people trying to put the fire out had trampled any other boot prints they might have matched to the one Cecil had sketched.

Elizabeth shifted in her seat. The service had gone on for nearly an hour already, most of it with Bishop Grindal's droning sermon.

"The holy scriptures of this blessed morn are, of course," he intoned, "readings of the nativity of our Lord."

His shrill voice roused her from her exhaustion and agonizing. However did this man come so far with that voice, she wondered. There were many fine, deep-voiced ministers she had known, but this one had talents and powers to rise above his greatest weakness.

As if he were a politican and not a prelate, the silver-haired, portly bishop had a habit of seeming to smile no matter what he said; sometimes it seemed his plump face would crack open like a porcelain ball. It was ironic that Grindal always looked quite smug and jolly compared to his chief aide, Martin Bane. Thin and black-garbed as a raven, Vicar Bane stood beneath the pulpit as if he were some sort of enforcer of whatever his earthly master might decree.

Elizabeth felt hemmed in with the Earl of Sussex on her right hand and the Scots envoy, Simon MacNair, on her left, though she had invited both men to those seats. Margaret Stewart and Lord Darnley were also in plain sight, across the aisle in the front row. Behind her sat Kat and Rosie. Robin, fuming at not being asked to sit next to her, was on MacNair's other side. She must tell Robin, at least, what had really happened to Hodge. He and everyone else here today knew he had enemies at court, but not that one particular person had stooped to both mockery and murder—and perhaps even attempted a fiery assassination of the queen.

"So it was while they were in Bethlehem, the days were completed for her to be delivered. And she brought forth her firstborn Son, and wrapped Him in swaddling cloths, and laid Him in a manger.

"That humble manger," the bishop continued, looking up from his text, "must be a reminder to us of humility. It is wrong to pursue overly lighthearted practices at this season. For instance, I speak to those who allow your mincemeat pies to be fashioned in the shape of the manger and brought to your feasts and who then celebrate with great abandon. And is it not pure, pagan superstition that a person will have as many happy months in the upcoming year as mince pies one tastes?"

Mince pies, Elizabeth thought. Bane had called snowballing profane yesterday, and now Grindal was scolding about mince pies? Did they not see the important things in this holiday season? Did they not know the large political and social as well as religious issues she faced, which made snowballing and pies mere trifles?

"Have not some of you," he plunged on, "even decorated that pie with springs of holly or the pagan mistletoe? Have I not heard that some have placed upon such a pie the pastry form of a babe, which was then devoured with said pie?"

Elizabeth had given him no leave to scold her people for age-old traditions of the day. He and his spokesman Bane presumed far too much of late. Not daring to look her way, Grindal continued reading,

"Now after Jesus was born in Bethlehem of Judea, behold, wise men from the East came to Jerusalem, saying, 'Where is He who has been born King of the Jews? For we have seen His star in the East and have come to worship Him.' "

Though she was tempted to stand and order Grindal to stick to such readings and not his own rantings, the queen settled back in her seat again. She wanted nothing to ruin the beauty or sanctity of this day. Already the season had gone awry with Hodge's death and the Christmas Eve tradition of the Yule log being postponed until today. Still trying to find a compromise between mourning for a death and rejoicing in the Lord's birth, she had asked that a religious mystery play be performed tonight and had postponed the Lord of Misrule's antics yet again.

"That star was a sign to the wise men of that day," Grindal said. "And today, do not those who are wise read the signs of the times, too? When lightning struck the dome of St. Paul's three years ago and caused the fire, some said it was a sign that God Himself was displeased with the indulgent, extravagant way that some ornate, Catholic practices were yet clung to in this land while it is claimed such things are purged and purified."

"And," the queen muttered only loud enough for those around her to hear, "some said that fire was God's displeasure with a radical, Puritan-leaning bishop who can do naught but criticize and carp!"

Simon MacNair, despite the fact he represented the Catholic queen of Scotland, murmured his approval of her words.

"And have we not now had a like sign?" the bishop went on, while Vicar Bane nodded as if his head were hollow and set on a stick. "The fire which destroyed the royal boathouse last night seems a warning against too much levity or frivolity at court this time of year. And the death of the man in the kitchens who was to decorate the peacock—one wonders if we are not harkening back to the pre-Papist church days of yore when the pagans had a human sacrifice—"

"What?" Elizabeth cried. "We harken back to no such thing!"

Pews creaked and satins rustled as heads snapped her way. Bishop Grindal seemed momentarily cowed, though his lackey Bane looked furious at her interruption.

"I'll not have my London bishop prophesying or pronouncing

judgment on the court and Christmas!" she went on. "You are not here to cast a pall but to give your blessing. Choir, another song, something for a recessional. Let us have 'Good Christian Men Rejoice,' for that is what we should all do on these Twelve Days, beginning with the bringing in of the belated Yule log to the Great Hall forthwith. Though there will be no mumming this evening, we shall view a mystery play by a visiting troupe called the Queen's Country Players. Bishop, will you dismiss us with your blessing?"

Elizabeth of England stood, glaring at Grindal and Bane. Everyone else rose. His voice still defiant, Grindal pronounced a blessing on them all. The queen barely let him get out his *Amen* before she bade Robin escort her out.

Elizabeth cheered with her courtiers and servants as six men dragged the huge Yule log into the Great Hall. It vexed her that Bishop Grindal—who had, she'd heard, hastily departed the palace, leaving Bane to oversee things—had been right about one matter: She'd read in some history book that in olden, pagan days, this part of the festival had included a human sacrifice.

The log was actually a tree trunk, marked a year before, on last Christmas Day. Though the lengths of logs varied by the status of households and the size of hearths, any of the queen's palaces could take one of ten feet. Her arm around Kat's shoulders, Elizabeth watched it drawn along the floor to impromptu singing and some dancing to carols played by the musicians in the gallery overhead.

"Oh, prettily decorated!" Kat cried in her excitement and clapped her hands like a child. "I haven't seen one that gaily done with garlands and ribbons for years!"

"I am happy that you are happy, my Kat," Elizabeth told her.

Everyone followed the log as it was rolled and lifted onto andirons; burning brands were thrust under its middle.

"Wait!" Robin cried. "Who has the piece of it kept to light next year's log? As Lord of Misrule, it is my duty to keep it safe."

"I see you have studied your duties well," Elizabeth called to him over the hubbub. He did not look so angry at her now. Robin had always liked being the center of attention, and she did not mind sharing that with him today. It warmed her to see everyone so merry, though the smell of smoke and the sight of flames recalled too well her nightmare in the boathouse last night.

"I have indeed studied my duties well, Your Majesty," Robin said, suddenly kneeling at her feet. Sussex, evidently not to be surpassed by his nemesis, knelt, too, only to have his wife, Lady Frances, giggle and hook some holly behind his ear.

"All right," Robin said, rising and clapping, "let's hear more singing, not from the fine boys' choir this time, but the likes of you revelers!"

With Robin himself leading, the crowd broke into "The Yule Log Carol." Even Kat's trembling voice swelled, Elizabeth's bell-clear one, too, and several fine ones she did not recognize until she turned and saw Ned had brought his band of players into the hall with him. They were singing out strong from the dais that would soon serve as their stage:

Part of the log be kept to tend
The Christmas log next year.
And where 'tis safely kept,
The fiend can do no mischief here.

"The fiend," Cecil said suddenly in her ear, "may have not done his worst yet. Your Grace, have you told Leicester about Hodge, or do you want me to explain to him that he must have a care for himself?"

"I shall tell him as soon as this is over, but now I wish to welcome Ned Topside's friends."

She motioned for Rosie to stick close to Kat and, still smiling and greeting one and all, made her way to the dais. Ned saw her coming, elbowed one man and said something to the rest out of the side of his mouth. They all bowed grandly, one at a time in order, like pins going down on the bowling green.

"It has been some years since you have helped me with the poison plot which threatened our person," she told Wat Thompson and Randall Greene.

Ned introduced the others, including a fair-haired young man who radiated confidence to match his comely face and fine form. "Giles Chatam, Your Grace," Ned introduced him last, almost as an afterthought.

"Your Most Gracious Majesty," Chatam said in a deep baritone to rival Ned's, "I am neither of those traits my name might suggest. I am not chatty and have no guile, for only loyalty and hard work lie behind this smile."

"Stow the poetry 'til later," Ned muttered, but Giles's smile was nearly as bright as the Yule log flames now fanned to life.

"I did not realize others in your old company were as clever as you, Master Player Topside," Elizabeth said, still regarding Giles Chatam. "I look forward to the mystery play and other performances."

As they swept her bows again, she realized that Giles reminded her of Ned when she first took him in, but without that cocky nature. Perhaps she should talk to Ned about Giles joining him as court player, but then, she'd best see how well the young man did performing first.

As the afternoon wore on, the queen saw that Martin Bane still lurked about, like a harbinger of doom. She glimpsed him shove a paper up his sleeve when she looked his way; he was probably writing notes for the bishop about what everyone said or did. If Bishop Grindal had not been popular, especially for helping to rebuild the burned roof of St. Paul's with some of his own funds as well as hers, she might consider dismissing him and Bane, despite the upheaval that could cause. She was sorely vexed they didn't approve of her Christmas. Surely, churchmen would not stoop to something low and immoral to make their dire prophecies of Yule come true.

When she could slip away, she summoned Robin to her presence chamber from the festivities still going on in the Great Hall. "Is there some problem with the performance this evening?" he asked. "I've entrusted most of it to Topside, and I'll take over the events of the morrow with the traditional fox hunt on St. Stephen's Day."

"Yes, I'm sure planning that is far more to your liking. Will we be able to ride the ice to Greenwich Great Park?"

"For one last day, we'd best take the bridge," he told her, sitting beside her on the window seat as she indicated. "We can't be too careful, you know. But what is it then, my queen?"

"What you can do for me is to be very careful yourself," she told him, not protesting when he took her hands in his big ones. They were warm; Robin's hands were always warm, and hers, especially lately, were always cold.

"Careful as Lord of Misrule? In what way?"

"I'll not have you tell others, but I must warn you in good faith that your person, perhaps your life, could be in some peril. Did you hear how my privy kitchen dresser was decked out when he died?"

"Holding peacock feathers from the bird he was preparing?" he asked.

She wondered if such slight misdirection had been noised about or if Robin, enmeshed in his own cares and concerns as usual, had just not paid enough attention to take the full meaning. "Listen to me, Robin," she said, gripping his hands hard. "Hodge Thatcher was struck on the back of the head, then trussed like a peacock and hoisted up to hang by a noose. I believe he did not take his own life but it was taken from him. And since he was arrayed as a peacock, Cecil and I have construed the message may have been a blow at you."

"Aha." He went ashen, no doubt not realizing how hard he pressed her hands. "Could Sussex have hired someone?" he asked suddenly. "And, forgive me, my queen, but Margaret Stewart and Darnley both detest me, as no doubt Mary of Scots does from afar. I am not exactly the best-loved man in the palace. I was settling into the Lord of Misrule role, hoping some would come to see me in a more lighthearted way—to think better of me."

She tugged her hands free and stood; he jumped to his feet beside her.

"We could be reading too much in, of course," she said, "but I wanted you to know and guard yourself well."

"Yet I suppose," he said, wringing his hands most unlike himself, "you could be reading not enough in. If I were you, I'd have a care, too, for the murder was of one called 'the queen's dresser,' the man who decorated everything you ate. Christmas delights or not, best have someone watch and taste your food. And since the word *dresser* has a double meaning and Rosie Radcliffe sometimes helps you don your garments, tell her—unfortunately, Sussex's fond kin—"

"I'll not have Rosie disparaged, I don't care who her kin are. I trust her with my li—"

"That's exactly what you are doing. I beg you to at least have her and someone else search your gowns for venomous barbs or some such. Someone as devious as you describe could have all sorts of harm in mind. And I wouldn't put it past Vicar Bane to try to prove God's wrath on us, either."

"I've long known he bore watching, but your points are well taken. We must all be wary, but we shall not be frightened out of a happy Christmas!"

Just as the early winter's darkness fell outside on Christmas Day, they held the mystery play in place of the more raucous mummers' one with all its maskings and elaborate costumes. "Mysteries and moralities," the common folk called these simple dramas, which were once trundled about the countryside on carts or performed by trade guilds in the cities. The playlets seemed quite staid and old-fashioned now, but Elizabeth knew Kat recalled such with fondness. And the biblical message might serve to calm Bane and any other Puritan elements about the court, even though the plays had been popular under the Papists of England.

As these were traditional scripts with but a few variables in speech, costume, or staging, many people, at least those who had reached the lofty age of forty, knew the plots and words by rote. Though the queen had seen these done only in her sister's days on the throne, she too knew what was coming.

With Ned cast in the main role as the evil King Herod, the players presented the drama in which the three wise men went to the king's palace to ask for directions to the place where the Savior was born. King Herod, however, was a deceitful liar who wished to kill the newborn babe. So the angel of God appeared to the wise men in a dream and told them to avoid Herod on their way home. The result was that Herod gave orders for many children to be slain, though that was only told in speech, thank God, and never reenacted.

"Did they have to do a play where the ruler turns out to be a killer?" Elizabeth groused quietly to Cecil as he suddenly appeared beside her at the forefront of the standing audience. "I favor that new blond actor, and he's rightly cast as an angel, at least," she said with a little grin. "But I think Ned needs a dressing-down for playing the monarch that way. Forgive me, my lord, but, Christmas or not, everything seems a conspiracy to ruin my holidays."

They walked slowly off to the side of the crowd, so they could talk without whispering. "Then I hesitate to tell you what I've come for, Your Grace." Her belly knotted again as he went on. "There is someone come to court to see your chief cook, but I believe you will want to meet the visitor."

"Stop riddling, for I've had enough of that."

"Hodge Thatcher's crippled father, Wills, has been brought clear from Wimbledon on a cart with nail-studded wheels on the edge of the frozen river. It seems Roger Stout sent him a message of his son's sad demise."

"Why should I see him, the bitter man? Or do you mean he's asking for his son's body?"

"I'm afraid so. He's broken, grieving. Somehow the two men who brought him carried him into the corner of the hall back there," Cecil said, nodding toward the screened entry to the kitchens, "where he saw the mystery play being performed. But the thing is, he says he sent word to a friend visiting London who used to live in Wimbledon. He asked this friend to go tell Hodge in person that he regretted that cruel note he sent—the one we evidently read last night."

"Wait," she said, gripping Cecil's sinewy wrist. "You're saying Hodge was to have a visitor sent by his father, a man who might have arrived the afternoon he was killed and so could know something about his death?"

"That's it, though neither you nor Ned Topside will want to hear the visitor's name," Cecil said, raising his voice to be heard over applause.

"What does Ned have to do with that—or I, either?"

Cecil nodded toward the kitchen entry again. "It seems Hodge's visitor is the angel in the play. Hodge's father thought Giles Chatam was playing at an inn and was surprised to see him here at court, but there you are—perhaps a witness, a fallen angel fallen right in our lap."

She did not laugh at his wordplay as her mind raced. "Then, too, the visitor could have killed Hodge," she muttered, smacking her hands into her skirts. "I'll see this Wills Thatcher now," she added, starting toward the kitchen entrance, "and then the bright and shining Master Chatam after he ascends back into heaven in this mystery play."

Chapter the Sixth

Mulled Cider

For the universal benefit and general improvement of our country, our love for cider shows the Englishman's favoring of wholesome, natural drinks, even in a preference to the best beer from hops. To make, put 12 cups Kent cider in a large pan or kettle, add 1½ teaspoons whole cloves, 1½ teaspoons whole allspice, 6 sticks of cinnamon, and 1½ cups of brown sugar. Add 1 bottle of fermented cider, which can be strengthened also by freezing. Bring to a boil, stirring gently to dissolve the sugar. Simmer for a quarter hour to blend flavors, then discard spices. If possible, serve in heated pewter tankards. Makes at least 18 drinks. If served at holiday time, include slices of apples and a piece of toasted bread and drink the toast!

THE QUEEN SAW THAT WILLS THATCHER LAY ON A PALLET in the privy kitchen, his paralyzed legs draped with a woolen blanket. His carriers had put him on a worktable, so that he was easier to see and hear or to keep him off the cold flagstones. Her master cook, Roger Stout, spoke with the wizened old man, and someone had fetched him something to drink. Evidently no one fathomed the queen would come into the kitchens again, for no one so much as looked her way until Harry Carey, who escorted her with Cecil, cleared his throat.

Amidst a gasp or two and quick bows, the place went so silent she could hear something bubbling in its kettle on the nearby hearth. Only Master Thatcher could not bow; Elizabeth's gaze snagged his before his eyes widened. His face was wrinkled and ruddy, perhaps from being out in the cold all the way from Wimbledon.

"This is your queen, Her Royal Majesty, Elizabeth," Harry announced to the old man, "come calling with her condolences."

"Majesty," Wills gasped, raising himself on one elbow in an attempt to roll into some sort of bow. He lowered his gaze, yet when he looked up again, his eyes were wide as platters. "I—you, here?"

"Whatever you thought of your son Hodge's trade, Master Thatcher," Elizabeth said, loudly enough for all to hear, "he was of good cheer and of much service to me. And he was most loyal. Should I thank you for teaching him those fine traits?"

"I—Majesty—I heard he died. Since then I regretted each hard word 'tween him and me, I did."

"So it took losing him to make you love him?" she asked.

"More like, it took Christmas, Majesty, my first one alone. I rue each day I didn't take pride in my boy. Aye, it's too late to say so to him. But I come for his body now, to bury him at home, near as I can get him to his mother's grave, though he'll have to lie in unhallowed ground, a suicide."

Elizabeth's eyes met Master Stout's; few yet had heard that Hodge had been murdered or that his earthly remains were now burned bones and teeth Jenks had raked together and put in a small wooden box. Stout knew these things but had evidently not yet told Master Thatcher.

"Leave us now, all of you but Secretary Cecil and Baron Hunsdon," she commanded quietly. "Master Stout, see that the men who came from Wimbledon with Master Thatcher have hot cider."

When the kitchen was quiet and Wills Thatcher, propped yet on his elbow to turn her way, waited, she told him, "Several things I must say about your son, and ask that you keep these confidences—and steady yourself for a shock." Looking astounded, he nodded.

"Firstly, Hodge did not kill himself over your harsh note, though he did read it. Indeed, he did not kill himself at all."

"He—ill, or his heart failed? At his age?"

"The thing is, you see, you must not blame yourself for causing his death. Hodge did not die by his own hand. I regret to inform you that your son was murdered, why and by whom we do not know, but I—my people—will discover."

The old man sank back flat on his pallet. He sucked in a ragged breath and stared straight up at the lofty, soot-stained ceiling. Tears tracked from his eyes, but she sensed he was both relieved and grieved.

"Forgive me for asking such a thing now," she went on, trying to keep her voice controlled, "but Giles Chatam from Wimbledon—you and Hodge knew him, and you sent him to your son?"

She waited while he composed himself. He struggled to sit, so Cecil and Harry stepped forward from the shadows to help him off the table and into the only chair. Elizabeth sat on a bench facing him. Again, the old man looked stunned at her proximity.

"Aye," he whispered at last, after a swig of the mulled cider Cecil fetched him. "Friend of the family, Giles's parents were. His father a glover, kept the whole town in gloves." Wills sniffed hard, took another sip of cider, and went on, "I thatched their house, and the lads ran about together for years. Both of them had a fanciful side I could never fathom . . ."

"Take your time, Master Thatcher. So Hodge and Giles were longtime friends?"

"Aye, 'cept when they both fancied the same girl. Had a bad row over that, and she up and wed someone else. Then Giles's parents perished in a house fire—don't know how it started middle of the night."

"A fire? His parents were trapped and died in a fire, but he was safe?"

"He got out somehow, that's all. Took it terrible they were both lost in the blaze, he did."

Elizabeth looked at Cecil, but he merely raised his eyebrows; Harry remained unmoved, but she didn't expect him to follow all this as her brilliant secretary evidently had. Besides, Harry had not almost been roasted alive last night.

"Go on, please, Master Thatcher," she urged.

"After the fire, we took Giles in for a few years. Hodge had already gone to make his fortune in London. Then Giles left with that acting troupe to wander far and wide. But, aye, I had the sexton write a letter to the inn where Giles sent a note he would be in London. Always wanted to see London, that boy. I had the sexton write Giles to go visit Hodge here, try to patch things up—for him and me. I never should of sent that cruel letter, and it was Christmas . . ."

"So all should be forgiven at Christmas," the queen said, rising with a sigh. "Master Hodge, I shall see that you have food and a warm place to stay until your friends can take you home. But one blow more, I'm afraid. We stored Hodge's body in the royal boathouse on the river, and a fire struck there, too. I regret to tell you that Hodge's body burned with the edifice last night, but we have carefully collected his remains, and you shall have them in a box to take home with you to bury in holy ground near his mother's grave."

Wills had slumped, then straightened his shaking shoulders. "I thank you for doing your best for him, Your Majesty," he said, his lower lip trembling. "Is—is there anything else?" he asked, and she could almost see him cringe.

"Only that your son left you a purse of coins to keep you well. How much was that Hodge had lovingly saved from his wages working for me and my family, Lord Hunsdon?" she asked. She almost quoted to the old man from his spiteful letter about her family ruining the true church, but she held her tongue. After all, it was Christmas, and that's what had melted old Wills's heart.

"I'm not certain, Your Grace," Harry managed with a straight face, "but he'd saved a goodly amount." Cecil nodded solemnly.

"Then you must see to it," she told Harry, "that Master Thatcher receives Hodge's purse before he goes home on the morrow. I am sorry for your loss, Master Hodge, and wish you well."

She walked from the room back to her own problems, but not before she heard the old man say in a choked voice, "No wonder my boy served the Tudors so well. Aye, God save that queen!"

Elizabeth gave orders for Wills to be tended to and, with Cecil in her wake, cut back into the corner of the hall. The mystery play had ended, and everyone was eating and milling about again. Occasional laughter pierced the buzz of a hundred conversations.

"Harry," she said, "please send Ned Topside to me at once, over there in the corridor, then rejoin your lady and the others. I rely on you to help keep people happy and to keep me apprised if they are not. My lord Cecil," she said, turning to him as Harry bowed and departed, "we shall see what our new player Master Chatam has to say about his visit to Hodge yesterday—and about the fire that evidently trapped his parents while he himself escaped. Some people, I've heard," she said, rolling her eyes, "are fascinated by fire, and right now, I am, too."

"Oh, Your Grace," Meg Milligrew said as she came down the hall behind them, "there you are. I went upstairs to get a few more sprigs of mistletoe. Someone's been taking not only the berries but the entire little branches out of the kissing balls, probably intending to use them privily later. I wish it was Jenks, just lying in wait for me!" she said, and laughed. Her face flushed; she looked happier than the queen had seen her lately. In the new year, perhaps there should be a marriage, Elizabeth thought, and not that of the queen, the one her people and Parliament would like to see.

Ned appeared, still in kingly costume, holding his tin crown, and out of breath. "Your Majesty, you wished to see me?"

"Rather I need to see your mystery angel."

He looked surprised, then alarmed. "Giles Chatam? Why—what's he done, if I may ask?"

"Hopefully nothing, but it turns out he not only grew up with Hodge Thatcher, but they both loved the same girl."

She saw Ned's eyes dart to Meg, then back to his queen. "But he was with the players. You aren't going to ask him if he killed Hodge like some jilted, lovesick swain, are you?"

"Not directly, but Hodge's father has just informed us that he asked Giles to visit Hodge, and who knows it wasn't yesterday afternoon?"

"My uncle would know, the other players, too," Ned countered, his usually controlled baritone voice rising.

"Precisely, so you are to circumspectly and individually question them about Giles's whereabouts yesterday and anything else they might know of his doings, including whether there have ever been fires set near where they've been traveling with him."

"I'll do all you ask, of course, Your Grace," Ned said, turning this mock crown round and round quickly in his hands, "but I would not have brought the troupe to court if I could not vouch—at least my uncle will, I'm sure—for the whereabouts . . ."

"Ned," Meg cut in so stridently that everyone turned to her, "you know people can slip out sometimes and not be where they're supposed to be, and no one knows it."

Ned glared at Meg and spun back to the queen. "You'd like to see Giles first thing tomorrow," he asked, "before everyone leaves for Greenwich for the fox hunt?"

"I want to see him first thing right now. See that your friends are settled in for the night, then bring him up to my presence chamber—and don't tell him why."

Ned bowed and hastened to obey, but his words floated back to her. "This will go to his head, really go to his head."

"That's the pot calling the kettle black," Meg muttered.

"And to what were you alluding," the queen asked, "about Ned's not being where he should have been?"

"It was just what Ned calls a figure of speech," the girl said, looking quite caught in something.

"Meg, tell me now."

"I don't mean to tattle," she blurted, "but he slipped out last night from your chambers when he felt sick over something he'd eaten, that's all."

Robin could have been right, the queen thought. She had to have her food watched. She'd had a bad stomach, and evidently Ned had, too.

"How long after Her Grace and I left did he depart," Cecil asked Meg sharply, "and how long was he gone?"

Now Elizabeth stared him down. What was he thinking?

"Don't exactly know," Meg said, tilting her head and looking thoughtful. "He just ran to the jakes. Later he said he threw up his food, then stepped outside to clear his head. Came back up out of breath and looking all windblown and feverish after maybe a quarter of an hour, so I dosed him with a bit of the chamomile I keep for you, Your Grace, for your stomach upsets and to soothe your temp—I mean, in case you get upset—an upset stomach. And if you let on I told you all that, Ned'll skin me sure."

"Those of us in the Privy Plot Council must not keep secrets, at least not from your queen," Elizabeth said, patting her arm. "Best go tend to that mistletoe now."

Meg looked as if she'd say more but obeyed. "Cecil," the queen said as they started down the corridor toward the main staircase and her yeomen guards fell in behind, "what are you thinking about Ned Topside?"

"The same thing you should be thinking, Your Grace," he dared, "but probably won't admit."

"That he left the palace by the kitchen porter's gate the afternoon Hodge was killed, and so passed directly by Hodge's workroom?" she parried. "That he left Meg alone when he was bid stay with her last night about the time the fire was set?"

"The truth is," Cecil whispered out of the side of his mouth so even the guards would not hear, "we must suspect everyone in this."

"Ned? Ridiculous!" she cracked out. Motioning her yeomen to stay back, she turned to face Cecil halfway up the sweep of garlanded staircase. "You have always preached such rampant distrust to me, my lord. From the first, during the poison plot, you told me to trust no one. But haven't we learned the hard way that we must have faith in people like Meg, like Ned? When everything went wrong at Windsor the year Robin's wife died so strangely, you warned me not to trust Robin, either, but he was surely innocent of her death!"

"So it seems."

"Seems? And everyone thought I should suspect my dear Kat just last summer when the maze murderer stalked my gardens. Ned has been with us through thick and thin."

"Your love of and loyalty to your people are ever admirable, Your Grace. But remember what I taught you, the legal term *cui bono?*"

"Who profits for himself—who has a motive?" she translated before he could. "Do you really believe Ned would be so vexed by my replacing him with Leicester as Lord of Misrule that he would kill an innocent privy kitchen dresser of his queen to ruin the holiday season?"

"Hard to fathom, but I know one thing. Ned's a consummate actor—probably this Chatam you're about to question is, too. At this season of the year when love and good cheer should fill our hearts, it's hard to accept that bad blood could course through some, but that may very well be the way of it."

"I know," she said angrily as they started to climb the stairs again. "Curse it, but don't I know."

. . .

"But I never received Old Wills's message to visit Hodge," Giles Chatam told her. Unlike Ned when he talked, the young man stood very still with a minimum of flourishes and gestures to detract from his facial expressions. Somehow, that made him seem more sincere than Ned.

"May I not tell Master Thatcher so myself lest he blame me for not delivering it?" he cried.

"I believe he is departing at first light for Wimbledon tomorrow," Elizabeth told him, "but, of course, you may explain to him."

"I overheard whisperings about a servant's death but had no notion it was Hodge," he said, his voice earnest and his face crestfallen. "I was hoping to look Hodge up tomorrow—I just didn't think it could be him."

"Have you called on him when you were in London other times?" she inquired. Cecil sat at a table in the corner, supposedly absorbed in his own business but, no doubt, taking notes. She had sent Ned out of her presence chamber, much to his obvious dismay, so she had kept her yeoman Clifford in the back of the room as a guard for this interview.

"In truth, there were no other times, Your Royal Majesty, for this is my first visit. That's why I go out and about every spare moment I can. It's a wonderful city, and I want to see all the sights—London Bridge, St. Paul's, the Abbey. But to perform for you and see Whitehall from the inside—it's more than I ever dared to dream."

His eyes were clearest blue, his forehead flawless. His demeanor was deferential yet not menial, polite but refreshingly unpolitical. She liked him very much, his talents, too.

"I understand you have been an orphan for years, the result of a tragedy."

"Sadly, yes," he whispered. His gaze, linked with hers, did not waver. "As Master Thatcher may have told you, a fatal fire broke out, the result, I fear, of my mother's carelessness with the Yule log embers. That is why I thought you had summoned me here, Your Majesty—I mean, that I was nearly crying when the play began in the Great Hall, because everyone had fussed so over the log being brought in, and it reminded me of my Christmas losses. I thought you would tell me I did a wretched job tonight as the Lord's messenger angel when I was in truth so distraught . . ."

Those crystalline blue eyes teared; he bit his lower lip and sniffed once hard. She ached to comfort him. To have each joyous Christmas bring memories of tragedy was tragedy indeed. Especially considering how things were going during this Yuletide, she sympathized with this poor young man completely.

Elizabeth felt safer out among crowds of cheering people the next morning than she had inside her own palace. She had covertly appointed both Roger Stout and her cousin Harry's wife, her lady in waiting Anne, to keep a good eye on the preparation and presentation of royal food and drink. Just after daybreak, her gaily attired entourage set out for the traditional fox hunt for this December 26, St. Stephen the Martyr's Day.

They made their own music, for many had strung bells on their reins. The queen, riding sidesaddle on her white horse, had jingling rings on her gloved fingers and bells on the toes of her boots. Even the crunch of the hundreds of hoofs on a dusting of new snow and their mounts' snorting of frosted air seemed musical.

Twenty of her mounted guards with flapping pennants on poles preceded her, and twenty brought up the rear of the parade. Down the Strand, through Cheapside, and across London Bridge, the yeomen shouted, "Make way for the queen! Make way! Uncap there, you knaves!" When she heard the latter, she sent immediate word for them not to order her people to uncap today, for the wind was chill. Yet most men did, and women cheered, and everyone huzzahed her passage.

Robin rode just behind her bedecked horse, then Sussex and her other earls and counselors—though Cecil had stayed behind to work—then barons like Harry, mingled with her maids of honor and ladies who had chosen to brave the brisk day. Simon MacNair and, unfortunately, Martin Bane were in attendance; Margaret Stewart and her son Darnley, too. Kat had come along, though the queen feared she'd catch the ague and had ordered the old woman bundled to her nose. Her dear former governess was enjoying each event of the season, and that warmed Elizabeth as had little else since Hodge's corpse was found.

She had brought none of her servants this day, but for Jenks. Of course, some kitchen help had been sent with Master Cook Stout ahead to Greenwich with supplies to pitch tents and prepare food and mulled cider for after the hunt.

Elizabeth loved Greenwich, the palace where she had been born, and visited it often, especially in the summer. Graced by two hundred acres of pasture, wood, heath, and gorse, and stocked with deer and other game, the Tudor redbrick edifice lay but a short barge ride east of London on the Thames, or a longer, harder ride ahorse.

But for a few green firs, the trees of Greenwich Great Park stood bare branched, all the easier to ride through and see one's prey. For some reason, the fox was the traditional St. Stephen's Day quarry. Perhaps, someone had mused once, that was because its coat was Christmas red and easier than deer or boar to spot against the snow. And, in the tradition of goodwill at Yule and in honor of the martyr, unless the hounds had mauled the beast, the St. Stephen's Day fox was always let go.

"Were the packs of hunt dogs sent ahead, too, Your Majesty?" Simon MacNair asked, suddenly riding abreast with her.

"The royal packs," the queen said, pointing back across the river at an island, which was completely iced in, "are kept in kennels directly over there, Sir Simon, which, in this weather, are even warmed. The place is most aptly named the Isle of Dogs."

"Ah," he said, squinting into the sun off the snow. Robin and Sussex rode closer on her right side, perhaps to eavesdrop on what the Scots envoy and their queen could be discussing. "But, Your Majesty," MacNair went on, "to prepare myself for my stay here, I've been reading far and wide about your realm, and I believe I saw the Isle of Dogs was named for the ghosts which haunt it yet."

Elizabeth shook her head, but Kat's voice cut in. "I've heard that tale, too, a sad one of lost loves and lives. A young nobleman and his new bride drowned in a marsh there, and their hunting dogs kept barking, barking until their bodies were found. And even now, years after, the hounds still bay, and the ghosts still call them to the hunt."

"There, you see!" MacNair said.

"Kat, I did not think you'd be a purveyor of such stories," Elizabeth chided. "The night howls people hear on this stretch of river are my hunt hounds, not some phantom menace."

"But a better story, you must admit, Your Grace," MacNair said, and she noted that, for the first time, he had used the more familiar form of address for her. Fine, she thought. She wanted to win this man over, but even if she did, she knew his loyalties lay with his Scottish queen.

"Since you seem to have a fanciful nature, my lord," she told him, "after the hunt, I shall show you the old Saxon graveyard in the forest, for small mounds still mark the site. You and my dear Lady Ashley can keep an ear cocked for what those spirits have to tell us."

They all managed a laugh, and soon the hunt was on.

The hounds, which had been brought across from the Isle of Dogs in small caged carts over the ice, seemed to scent the fox at once. They took off in a brown streak of tails and barks with the hunters' horses following.

Fox hunts were truly about the ride and the chase, not the capture. Elizabeth loved to ride fast and free and all too seldom did so anymore, especially in the winter. How this custom of fox hunting on the day named in honor of the first Christian martyr, who was stoned to death, had gotten started she'd never know. But at least it got everyone out of the palace for the day. She was even hoping it would clear her head so she could decide whether to dismiss the Queen's Country Players or keep them around with Giles Chatam under close observation. Why not, since the others she suspected of trying to mock Dudley, burn her to bits, and ruin Christmas were all her guests?

She leaned forward, urging her mount on as others tried to stay with her through the trees. If she or someone just ahead—and few dared ride ahead—bounced branches, little cascades of snow flew in their faces. Her horse's hooves beat faster, her bells rang madly as she pursued the fox and hounds.

Her thoughts pounded just as fast and hard. The murderer and would-be murderer was surely someone who hated Robin and perhaps her, too. The Stewarts did, of course, and MacNair wanted Mary of Scots on her throne. Sussex hated Robin but surely would not want her or Cecil dead, though he could want to throw a good scare into her so that she would heed his advice to marry and produce a Protestant heir.

She could not believe that a churchman like Martin Bane would traffic in murder, though it was obvious he and Grindal wanted to warn her to stop her celebrations at any cost. They might think she was a bit of a pagan herself, but they could never stomach the Papist Queen Mary if Elizabeth were gone. And the handsome, talented Giles Chatam? He might have a motive to harm Hodge, but to sneak out and try to kill his queen, who just might make his career? Or had he learned where the body was and, without realizing they were inside, tried to incinerate even the remnants of his rival forever?

"There!" someone shouted. "There it goes! It's circling, trying to lose the pack!"

The hunters wheeled about and thundered back toward the river through thicker trees. As they burst into a clearing, they were nearly to the pavilion tents where food and drink were waiting.

The fox charged right through, and, though most of the horses were reined in, the hounds and several mounts snagged tent ropes and upturned tables and food. Servants screamed and scattered, then all was silent once again but the distant baying of the hounds.

Elizabeth could not decide whether to laugh or cry. She pulled up and surveyed the chaos.

"It seems even your portable kitchens are in disarray this season," Harry said, reining in beside her.

"Oh, oh, Your Majesty, sorry, just so sorry!" Roger Stout called to her. The man appeared to be actually pulling his hair out while others bent to retrieve roasts or bread loaves that had rolled into the snow. "And here the gift that boy left for you took a tumble, too!" Stout cried.

"What gift and what boy?" she said, urging her horse closer.

"A special holiday gift for the queen, that's what he said. Ah, here, a heavy box it is, too, over here where it fell off the table."

Elizabeth dismounted before Harry could help her down. Jenks suddenly appeared and slid off his horse; Robin on foot, Sussex, and MacNair came closer. Across the way, still ahorse, Vicar Bain watched at a distance as if he were hiding behind trees. Margaret Stewart and Lord Darnley reined in. Snow pockmarked from the headlong rush of fox, hounds, and mounts crunched under the queen's jingle-belled boots as she walked slowly over to the box, a plain wooden one, bound with a leather belt. It looked the mate to Meg's herb box she'd given up for Jenks to use as a place for Hodge's mortal remains.

"Shall I open it, Your Majesty?" Jenks asked.

"Of course," she said, smiling at the little crowd growing

around her as more hunters straggled back. "Nothing like an early gift for New Year's!"

Jenks pulled off his gloves, and his cold fingers were stiff loosening the leather belt. When he opened the box, so many courtiers crowded around that they almost shut out the light, and the queen put up a hand to hold them back.

A piece of paper lay folded across the box's contents with large-lettered words on it. *"HANGING MEAT, ROAST MEAT, MINCE MEAT,"* Jenks read aloud. "That's all it says. No, here in smaller words, *Stones for murdering martyrs.*"

"What?" the queen demanded, her voice shrill. She leaned forward to see what the box held, then gasped. It was filled with stones, just plain rocks, at least a dozen of them, rough and bumpy. No, one, near the bottom, was completely covered with gold foil.

"Find the boy who brought these here!" she commanded, and another hunt was on.

Chapter the Seventh

Christmas Tussie-Mussies

Not only do dried garden flowers keep the scent of summer in the dark and dreary months, but they may well help ward off diverse diseases and cheer one's spirit. In the growing months, gather and dry such sweet-smelling flowers as you favor, lavender and roses, of course, not forgetting to include those which have not only scent and color but curative powers. The latter may include sweet marjoram for over-sighing, basil to take away sorrowfulness, borage for courage, and rosemary for remembrance, especially of joyous Yuletides past. Gather the dried blooms into small bouquets adorned by lace or ribbons. Strew the crushed or unsightly petals about on floors or table carpets or in coffers for delightful odors during the Twelve Days and thereafter.

"PUT THOSE STONES HERE, YES, RIGHT ON THIS TABLE carpet so they don't get chipped," the queen ordered Jenks. Lugging the box of them, he followed the other Privy Plot Council members into the queen's chamber at Whitehall before dawn the next morning. Ned quietly closed the door on the yeomen guards as Jenks tipped the box on its side to dump them.

"No, pick them out carefully," the queen commanded, perching on the edge of her chair, "here where we can see them in window light. I'll not have mishandled what may have been used to kill Hodge Thatcher, especially that gold-foiled stone."

"Yet we may be foiled indeed," Ned whispered to Meg.

"I heard that," Elizabeth said, "and am in no mood for puns or jests. How I am to smile my way through the holiday festivities this night I do not know."

"On the other hand," Ned replied, "since this is St. John the Evangelist's holy day, we can hope to have our murderer's head on a platter instead of that boar's head tonight."

"If I were Salome," she muttered, "I would gladly cast off my veils and dance all night to have it so, but to the business at hand. Cecil, please take out your sketch of Hodge's head wound, then each of us must take two stones to study to see if one fits the approximate pattern of the drawing."

He did as she asked, also producing the boot-print sketch from the scene of Hodge's murder. Elizabeth took the gold-foiled stone, which was completely covered with what appeared to be the same thin foil that had been on the table at the scene of the murder. Jenks, Meg, Harry, Cecil, and Ned did as they were bidden with the others. Evidently hewn from a larger piece of rock, the stones were of rough, pitted texture about the size of a man's fist.

"You might know, the boy who delivered these to me at Greenwich escaped just like the fox," Elizabeth groused, "nor could Jenks locate a site on the grounds which could have provided them." She shook her head. She'd hardly slept again; a headache as well as a churning stomach sapped her strength and concentration. "But I vow that, whatever it takes," she added, looking at each of them in turn, "whoever is playing this clever game with our Christmas will be caught and punished."

"The number twelve here may be significant," Cecil mused. "Symbolic of the Twelve Days of Christmas?"

"Pray God," Meg put in, "there are not worse gifts to come."

"But what's the flowery smell?" Cecil asked. "It's not coming from the box, is it? It's not my papers," he added, lifting both sketches and sniffing at them.

Elizabeth nodded at Meg to explain.

"No, my lord," the girl said, patting the thick, brightly hued table rug. "After I make the queen's sweet bags, pomanders, and tussie-mussies, Her Majesty likes me to crush the rest of the herbs and flowers to strew about. They've got to be fine as powder but with a touch of ambergris worked in so's it won't blow away right off and lingers."

As if they'd exhausted conversation, they spent the next quarter hour hunched over stones, hoping they could match a contour or pattern, turning each rock to compare its rough facets from all angles. Most of the stones were smaller than the size of the wound drawn in Cecil's sketch, and the ones that were large enough had no texture to match it.

"I thought it would be this golden stone, but it doesn't fit, either," Cecil said, examining it after the queen finally put it down in frustration.

"Ned had best not say, 'Foiled again,' " she said, wishing she could lighten her mood. Here it was, she thought, the third day of Christmas, and, evidently having opened Pandora's box, they sat about like lunatics, staring at stones.

Sighing heavily as her gaze lingered on the other sketch, she reached for it and held it up. "I had originally thought we would use this boot print only when we'd narrowed our field of suspects, but I'm getting desperate to save these holidays from further mayhem. Meg, do you have more of the dusting powder from making tussie-mussies for all my ladies?"

"Two bags of it, one even in a coffer in your bedchamber, Your Grace, so things in it will smell sweet."

"Then if you will fetch it, we shall tread another path."

As the queen stood, everyone rose. Meg darted off and was back in a trice with a cloth bag as big as an open handkerchief. The powerfully scented dust within made them all sniffle or sneeze.

"What—choo!—are you thinking, Your Grace?" Harry asked and blew his nose.

"I am thinking that no one will suspect aught is amiss if I ask my strewing herb girl to place some of this here and there on palace floors. As I recall, Meg, you spilled a goodly amount last Yule, and we all stepped in it, tracking footprints in and through it."

"Aha," Cecil said. "A good idea if Meg can pull it off."

"But how are you going to get the men we're wary of to step in it?" Harry demanded, before sneezing again.

"I'll leave that to Meg," the queen said as he sneezed yet a third time. "Oh, Harry, do go over by the window and breathe fresh air through the cracks. My lord Cecil, please make a copy for Meg of that boot print. Jenks, place the stones back in the box and—oh, Ned, that leaves you. Meg, put some of that dust on the floor, and we'll test Ned's print in it to be certain this works."

She could tell that Ned—her dear, volatile, talented Ned—wanted to protest but dare not. Meg did as she was bid, strewing a bit on the floor before his feet.

"It's like the conquering hero cometh," Meg muttered, not looking up at him. "I warrant the Earl of Sussex, Sir Simon MacNair, and for sure Lord Darnley will like the idea of crushed rose petals being strewn under their feet."

"And what about Giles Chatam, if you suspect him, Your Grace?" Ned asked. "Meg can't follow him about all day, and I don't trust him not to harm her if he's at all suspect."

"Not to mention how she'll manage Vicar Bane," Cecil said, as he came to watch, holding out to Meg the copy of the sketch. "He'll think such as sweet smells at Yule is right up on the list of sins with snowballing and eating manger-shaped mince pies."

"Let's not spend our time worrying about what we can't do but what we can," the queen commanded.

"But since you are here now, my lord Cecil," Ned put in, "why don't you try your print here, as I'd best be off."

"Because I've got to talk to Jenks again about the porter's confession he left his post for a while the afternoon Hodge was killed," Cecil told him, frowning. "One of the carters Jenks questioned said he came in with barrels of fresh water and no one was at the gate. As for doing your print, man, just pretend this is the epilogue of some play, and in recognition of your talents, your boot print is being preserved for all posterity."

Clenching his jaw, Ned stepped into the small rectangle of pale powder. He expected it to be more gritty, but he hardly felt a thing except the continued undercurrent of Cecil's distrust. It had begun when the queen's wily chief secretary had questioned him, apparently nonchalantly, about why he'd left the queen's apartments the night of the fire and where he'd gone. It seemed everything Cecil said of late had a double meaning that he couldn't quite decipher but knew didn't bode well.

"Just walk away now, Ned, naturally, normally," the queen prompted. Was it his imagination that she too seemed to be watching him like a hawk? "Oh, yes," she said as he stepped out of the stuff, "that's a good one. All right, then, this may work. Meg, take what's left in that bag as well as the other you mentioned and go about your duties, appearing to strew crushed flowers but actually gathering specific prints."

"I'd best spread this near others we don't suspect, too."

"Good idea," the queen assured her. "It may be tricky, and, of course, the person who made the original may have changed footwear, but the approximate size may allow us to eliminate some from further surveillance."

"I'll sweep this up so she has enough powder," Ned said and moved toward his ghostly print.

"Stay!" the queen said, grabbing his arm. "Ned, you said your uncle admitted that Giles Chatam left the inn the afternoon Hodge was killed, supposedly to see the shops at Cheapside. Because of Giles's earlier rivalry with Hodge, he must be suspect, especially if the porter left his post for a while when Giles could have hied himself into the kitchens, confronted Hodge, and then killed him. Since you are concerned Meg not tip Giles off or get too near him, I want you to stick close to the company's new player, both openly, when possible, but also covertly."

"But I'm needed around h—that is," he tried to temper his tone, "the Earl of Leicester hasn't overseen all this before, and he expects my help."

"I know it irks you he's changed some of your plans for this evening," she said, obviously trying to soothe him, "and I'd never ask you to be skulking in shadows if it weren't necessary. By the way, I think the earl has quite a lovely evening planned for tonight."

"Right," he told her. "I've laid all the plans for that, though much of it will be raucous and impromptu."

"Ned, don't fret, for Leicester does seem to be getting things under control."

Hell's gates, Ned fumed silently, *he* was the one about to lose control again. Stalking chatty Chatam was all he needed, especially when he'd like to get rid of him—and of Leicester, illustrious Lord of Misrule—so that he could rule and reign again at royal Yuletide. And to protect his queen, of course, for Leicester had never been worth the powder to blow him up, and she was secretly besotted with the man, he was sure of it. Ned almost laughed at his own mental pun, for Leicester had long been fascinated by gunpowder and had invested heavily in its production. But he summoned up his best acting skills to appear serious and calm.

"Of course, Your Grace, anything to help, but what if Giles slips out on one of his city tours again?"

"Then, if possible, you must follow, for who knows to whom he might lead us."

Tours of London, in this damned cold! Ned wondered if she—with Cecil's complicity, of course—just wanted him out of the way. Or had that pompous peacock Leicester asked that she keep the man who knew exactly how to arrange the holiday entertainments out of his hair?

"Meg," the queen was saying, "after you've managed to get a print, and before anyone else can scuff it out"—here, Ned thought, Her Majesty glanced back at him again—"you must compare the print to Cecil's drawing. You are to try to make impressions from the Earl of Sussex, Lord Darnley, Simon MacNair, Vicar Bane, and my chief cook—just to eliminate the possibility the latter stepped in the cumin accidentally. All of you may go to your duties now, and my thanks as ever."

When Ned saw that Jenks dawdled, he went out with Meg and followed her down the servants' narrow back stairs. He'd often used the anteroom just off the last turn before the ground floor for quick liaisons. Hoping no one else was there this early in the morning, he snagged Meg's elbow, opened the door, and pulled her in after him.

"Hey-ho, what's this?" she cried as he closed the door behind them.

Fortunately, he thought, the room was deserted, but it was quite dark. Someone had left a single fat tallow candle on the table, nearly gutted out. Backing a few steps away from him, Meg stood with the sack of sachet dust held before her breasts like a shield.

"I just need to talk to you," Ned said. "I need your help."

"My help? What's the matter, then?"

"Meg, we're old friends. Those months you were not in the queen's good graces, exiled from court, I always believed you'd done no wrong—believed in you."

"Let's hear it, then, and never mind the buttering up. What have you done?"

"Nothing, I swear to God, that's just it. But because I just happened to leave the palace the afternoon Hodge died and because I was in a fit of anger that Her Grace had put Leicester in my place as Lord of Misrule . . ." Amazed his voice caught and cracked, he raked his fingers through his hair. "And," he added, more quietly, "because I had to use the jakes the other night when the boathouse burned, I think she's vexed at me."

"Don't blame me for mentioning you stepped out."

"I don't blame you for anything. But I can't believe Her Grace would suspect me of doing something so horrid to try to ruin her and Leicester's Yule—"

"There was a murder, Ned. A man's dead."

"I know, I know, but Cecil's been acting strange toward me, and you know how she heeds him. Meg, I'm telling you the truth," he said as he stepped forward and placed his hands over hers on top of her sack. Suddenly, the flowery scent was almost overpowering, yet strangely seductive in this little room. His pulse pounded, and his knees were like custard, when he'd never had any sort of stage fright, let alone quailed before a woman. And this was only Meg.

Her lips slightly parted, she stared up into his eyes. How could they look so luminous in this dim chamber? He'd long known he had sensual power over this woman and hadn't really cared. She'd been to him the younger sister he never had, one to tease and take out his temper on. He might be proud of her accomplishments, but he'd never say so. Yet now an alluring woman stood here, one of flesh and blood, and she wasn't like a little sister anymore.

"Help you how?" she asked so breathily he nearly had to read her lips. "Put in a good word for you with Cecil or Her Grace?"

"No! No, you mustn't let on that I'm suspicious that they're suspicious. But you must let me know if you hear anything, even if it's from Jenks, about their moving against me."

"Your footprint back there—the two of them set you up to make a print?"

"I fear so."

"I vow, I didn't know."

"Of course you didn't."

"But I can't betray the queen, Cecil either, certainly not Jenks, even to help you."

"I'm not asking you to betray anyone, my Meg, really."

She almost swayed on her feet. He moved his hands to steady her at the elbows. It was as if he embraced her, for the small, sweet sack was the only barrier between them.

"You didn't—do anything—did you?" she asked.

"Kill Hodge?" he exploded, loosing her and stepping back. "Hell's gates, it pains me sore you'd even have to ask!"

"Ned, I'll think on it and try to do what I can, but I cannot risk angering the queen again. And Jenks loves me, so don't ask—"

"So don't ask if there's anyone else but Jenks who loves you?" He stepped closer again and lifted three fingers gently to her trembling lips. She either pouted or lightly kissed his fingertips. It made him almost tilt into her like a magnet to true north.

"I must be off now," she said as she took two steps back. "You heard I have much to do."

"I too, sticking to that new playacting Adonis like a burr. Meg, please just think on what I've said, and I beg you not to betray my confidence, that is, both my fears and my utter confidence in you."

"My lips are sealed," she said, but they were still parted in the most becoming way. "Have a care, then, Ned."

"I will, I do," he whispered. He opened the door and stood back so that she could dart out before him.

At the feast of St. John the Evangelist that evening, Elizabeth found her deep-buried love for Robin Dudley, Earl of Leicester, Lord of Misrule, bubbling to the surface again. Perhaps it was simply the glow of the holiday season, but he was a charming host, regaling everyone with memories of Yuletides past.

He had people laughing as he conducted a lottery with prizes for small token gifts, blindfolding the queen before she picked out slips of paper with names from his fancy, feathered hat. Nor did Robin flinch when his archenemy, the Earl of Sussex, drew the lot to present the boar's head to the queen later this evening, a singular honor. Robin cajoled lords and ladies to be in their best voices for the later singing of the traditional carols. And, after an hour of dancing where he led the queen out onto the floor to stately pavanes and gay galliards, he announced that all would sit in a circle before the burning Yule log and share their best memories of Christmas.

"A delightful evening so far, Robin," Elizabeth told him as he sat her in the center seat before the hearth and took the big footstool at her feet, while others of the realm were given full-size chairs or stood in two rows behind. "So restful, and I needed that," she whispered and squeezed his hand.

"I heard," he whispered back, "you are having the preparation of your food guarded. And I shall protect you with my life, love, and honor—always."

Things were looking up, she thought, for who could ask for a better Yuletide gift than that?

Robin gestured for the ewers of mulled cider to be passed among them, but he poured his and the queen's from an embossed flagon he kept at his feet. Kat, at the queen's request, was the first to recall her memories; however forgetful Kat was these days, the past seemed ever present to the old woman. "But this Christmas is almost as fine as those of old," she concluded as Elizabeth blinked back tears. Through them, she smiled at Robin again and mouthed, "Thank you from Kat and me."

"Your Grace, will you grace us with a graceful memory of

your own?" Robin asked, and everyone chuckled at the way he'd put that. As the room grew hushed again, the crackle of the flames and hiss of sap from the huge log whispered to them all.

Elizabeth cleared her throat. Thank God, Christmas was *not* ruined this year. The good times were still within reach, and she felt protected here, despite the fact that in this friendly company could be the one who wanted to do her and Yuletide dreadful harm.

"I treasure the memory of the time my father went in a sleigh with my brother—Prince Edward—and me at Greenwich," she said. She hesitated, surprised that the long-buried memory had just lain in wait for Robin's invitation. She must have been barely six or seven then, Edward even younger. "The sleigh was a gift from the ambassador from Muscovy, where they have feet and feet of snow, my father said, and we laughed and sang, and then got out and made snowballs, but Edward and I knew better than to hit him hard with one."

Everyone laughed at that, the warm memory of a father merging with the reality of the huge, tempestuous king they recalled. But Elizabeth caught Vicar Bane's baleful gaze as he stood by the screen in the corner of the vast hall. The other day he'd claimed throwing snowballs was near sacrilege, so she glared back. "Someone else's turn," she said, her nostalgic mood now marred. "My lord envoy from your queen in Scotland," she went on, turning to Simon MacNair, seated at the end of the row, "will not you favor us with a memory of Christmas?"

"I shall be honored," Sir Simon said and stood, though no one else had done so. "Just last year," he began, "at Holyrood Palace in Edinburgh, it was, actually on Twelfth Night. One of Her

Majesty's maids of honor, Mary Fleming, found the bean in the Twelfth Night cake and so was declared 'Queen of the Bean.' Her Majesty ordered Mary decked out in a gown of silver and jewels, while the queen herself was appareled in mere white and black with not a ring or necklace or pin, so humble is our queen, so confident in any comparison with others. And how dearly her lowest servants love her for it—that is all of my memory."

As he dipped a little bow in Elizabeth's direction and sat again, she felt her dander rise. The man was subtly criticizing her for her elaborate dress. And did he imply that her own servants did not love her? 'S blood, how she hated all the mincing and maneuvering of court life when she would like to just have this jackanapes banished, along with anyone else who might wish her and her people harm.

"Thank you for that picture of your humble Scottish queen," she replied sweetly. "Rosie," she went on, turning to Lady Radcliffe, sitting two chairs down the other way, "pray tell us your story of how you came to court."

"I was a Yule gift fit for a queen," Rosie said, "the most lovely, gracious, and grand queen in all the world. My uncle, the earl," she went on with a nod and smile at Sussex, "said I should serve our new young queen and plucked me from my parents to meet the monarch—and here I am and likely to remain so, for who, high or low, would not be loyal to our queen?"

"I could not do without you. But tell, then," Elizabeth prompted, "the story of your parents, a great love story, and Christmas is the best time for those, both the sacred and profane."

Blushing now, Rosie began, "During the reign of Her Majesty's father, King Henry, the Earl of Sussex—the previous earl, this was—rode out of London to take part in a tournament.

As the cavalcade passed the little village of Kensington, people hurried to windows to see the parade. A beautiful merchant's daughter, Isabella Harvey, leaned out so far she dropped a glove just as Sir Humphrey Radcliffe, younger son of the earl, rode by. Sir Humphrey dipped his lance, picked up the glove, and returned it to Isabella most gallantly, so who dares say chivalry is dead in these modern times?"

"The Radcliffes yet cherish chivalry and loyalty," Sussex put in as if he'd been given leave to speak. "Well, continue, niece."

"The entourage rode on," she said, her eyes alight, "but Isabella had entranced Sir Humphrey. He doubled back and, calling himself a squire of the earl, made himself so agreeable that he was invited by Isabella's father to supper."

"I knew we'd get to food," Robin put in with a hearty laugh. "After all that dancing, let's have some pastries here—and suckets," he called to the hovering servers. "Marchpane and comfits! Go on, then, Lady Rosie."

"The friendship between Sir Humphrey, alias Squire Humphrey, and the maid Isabella, daughter of a mere merchant, grew to love. She came to marriage well dowered, but indeed they were wed for weeks before Sir Humphrey told her who he truly was, that her husband was the son, not the servant, of the Earl of Sussex, once Lord High Chamberlain of England. And I am their first child."

The courtiers applauded the charming tale. The queen noted even Simon NacNair looked pleased. But to everyone's surprise, Kat cried out, "It just goes to show you can't trust men!"

"What?" Robin said, looking half annoyed and half amused. "All present company, no doubt, excluded."

"To carry on like some player on a stage," Kat went on, "to

mislead Rosie's mother so! For a Radcliffe, brother of our earl, to pretend to be something he was not is—"

"Is not something we shall discuss this night," the queen concluded for her, rising.

"Time indeed for the bringing in of the boar's head," Robin added. "And yet," he whispered for Elizabeth's ears only, "Lady Ashley probably only spoke what she's heard you say more than once in private."

"Perhaps she only spoke the truth," the queen countered with a tight-lipped smile. She raised her voice to the crowd. "Let us all move back to the table, where the Earl of Sussex, surely a man to be trusted, has the honor of the presentation of the boar's head."

"Because I allowed him to do so," Robin groused.

Evidently, Sussex heard that as he walked on the queen's other side. "Don't you know?" he muttered to Robin behind her back, "that, ah, the point of lotteries is that the Lord God can actually choose who wins or loses, Leicester? In a lottery no man is rigging the results, though I suppose you'd like to try."

"Rigging?" Robin replied. "Rigging like that which tries to hold in the big-bellied sail of a ship, a ship which should take you right back to Ireland so you can cool your heels in the bogs there—"

"Leave off your slurs!" Sussex demanded. "Your vile temper is like the gunpowder you produce and then charge all of us outrageous prices for to match your sense of inflated importance, and—"

"Enough!" the queen commanded. She jerked Robin's arm and glared at Sussex. "Perhaps Kat was right about men being like actors in a drama. They may seem charming and chivalrous, but underneath they carp and cavil and can ruin more than my mood or even Christmas!"

A pall of unease hung over the company as everyone was seated. The queen took a deep breath to steady herself. To the blast of trumpets, in came four tall pages bedecked in red and gold taffeta, carrying the heavy platter with the silver cover over the traditional boar's head. For the first time, Elizabeth was aware Ned Topside was here, for his voice rang out to start the familiar song:

Tidings I bring you for to tell
What in wild forest me befell,
When I in with a wild beast fell,
With a boar so fierce . . .

Elizabeth smiled, though she felt on edge from Robin's and Sussex's arguing—and from Vicar Bane still staring from the corner as if branding them all pagans in need of strict Puritan salvation. Margaret Stewart, pippin red with anger, evidently that she had not been asked for a Yuletide memory, was whispering to her frowning son Darnley. MacNair looked maddeningly smug after his flaunting of Queen Mary. But at least, thank the Lord God, it had escaped Kat that she'd caused a row, and she looked happy.

The boar's head in hand bear I
Bedecked with bays and rosemary.
I pray you all now, high to low,
Be merry, be merry, be merry.

When the dish was set before the queen, the Earl of Sussex stepped forward to do the honors of uncovering the boar's head.

With a smirk sent Robin's way, the earl swept the cover from the platter with a flourish.

Kat screamed. Robin cursed. The queen stared agape not at the head of a boar with an apple in its mouth but at the decapitated head of a red fox with its snout adorned in gold foil.

Chapter the Eighth

Suckets

Take curds, the paring of lemons, oranges, pome-citrons, or indeed any half-ripe fruit, and boil them in sweet wort till they be tender; then make a syrup in this sort: Take 3 pounds of sugar, and the whites of 4 eggs, and a gallon of water, then swing and beat the water and eggs together, then put in your sugar, and set it on an easy fire, and so let it boil, then strain it through a cloth, and let it seethe again till it fall from the spoon, then put it into the rinds of fruits. One of the queen's favorite delights, especially the orange, all the year round, but for their hue, use limes at Yule.

"I THANK GOD NOTHING DIRE HAPPENED ON HOLY Innocents Day," Elizabeth told Cecil as she paced in her presence chamber two days later. She was eating orange suckets as she walked, for they seemed to give her the physical strength she desperately needed. "At least there was an entire normal day after the shock of that fox's head on the platter."

"If you call it normal," Cecil said as he stood at the window, sometimes glancing out, sometimes at her. "The upheaval of searching the kitchens and questioning the staff about how the switch from boar's head to fox's head had been made, and coming up with naught—"

"Naught but the discarded boar's head in Hodge's old work area," she said as she tossed her fruit and spoon back on the silver tray with a clatter. She stopped to look out the window, too. A swirling snowstorm had blanketed London with a good half foot of huge, heavy flakes yesterday. "You know," she went on, her voice calm at last, "Ned suggested that nothing happened yesterday because the culprit lives outside the palace and was snowbound, but I don't think so."

"I'm afraid I don't either."

"Even Vicar Bane has a chamber here when he wishes it," she went on, reasoning aloud, "and he's been here more than he's been with the bishop lately. The fact that nothing happened yesterday could be because our tormentor is matching his wretched surprises to each day. The human peacock was killed and displayed just before the presentation of the peacock on Christmas Eve, the box of stones came on St. Stephen's Day because the saint was stoned to death, the fox after our fox hunt . . . 'S blood, I don't know, Cecil," she cried, banging her fist on the windowsill. "If that's the pattern, can we predict what's coming next?"

"I thought the fox's head might be as if to say, 'The fox may be traditionally freed on the Yuletide hunt, but I killed him, because I'm breaking or damning all your traditions.' "

"Yes, but more than that, I think. Death, past or present, is suggested by each outrage, but what about the threat of a future death? It worries me that the fox is redheaded. Remember when we tried to solve the poison plot, a dead red fox was left in my bed with the note 'The red-haired fox is next,' meaning me? At least I am taking even more care than usual not to eat or drink anything that isn't guarded from start to finish or tasted first."

"That is wise, Your Grace, but you don't think there's a threat of poison here? The culprit seems obsessed with food as symbols, not as weapons."

"Oh, Cecil," she cried, covering her eyes with both palms, "I said I don't know what I think anymore. Perhaps nothing happened yesterday, even on a day that commemorates the biblical slaughter of young children by King Herod, because the name of the day is Holy Innocents. Because we have no babes at the court to harm, our tormentor gives us the day off, so to speak. But tonight—the Feast of Fools—I'm fearing something more bizarre than what we've yet seen."

"You could cancel everything."

"For what reason?" she demanded, smacking her skirts and starting to pace again. She took another sucket off the tray, a lime one. "Shall I announce to my court and city—so to all of Europe—that some specter, some phantom, stalks our court, and the queen is sore afraid and too stupid to stop it?"

She talked with her mouth half full as fear and anger—and sugar—bolstered her passion to solve this plot to kill Christmas. "Should I arrest all those we suspect, and on what grounds?" she railed. "Shall I send the powerful Earl of Sussex, my military commander from Ireland, to the Tower? Lord Darnley, whom I intend to send to tempt Queen Mary? Should I put some poor, possibly innocent itinerant actor on the rack? Imprison Vicar Bane, of my Church of England, however much I'd like to have his scowling face out of my sight? I won't have him and Bishop Grindal preaching that our traditional ways and my Christmas decrees are cursed. The river's frozen over, and the building of booths for the Frost Fair I've promised has begun, so I can hardly halt the holidays at the court or in the city!" In utter frustration, she heaved the half-eaten sucket and spoon at the tray. Both missed, and the sucket spun away on the floor.

"It's like a snowball rolling down a hill," Cecil muttered calmly, staring at her discarded lime. She saw he was so used to her outbursts he hardly flinched anymore. "But, Your Grace, we shall find who is behind it all, I know we shall."

"It's taken Meg too long to get some of the prints, though I realize she can't admit what she's doing. And worst of all, I'm worried about Ned. I can't bear the idea he's involved somehow, not Ned, a Privy Plot Council member, no less."

Her yeomen guards knocked on the door; Jenks was admitted, out of breath. "You sent for me, Your Majesty?"

"I did," she said as he straightened from his bow. "I'm afraid we must backtrack to find our villain. I'm sorry to send you out in this deep snow, Jenks, but I want you to ride back to Greenwich to question my steward and gamekeepers there. It's possible they saw someone poaching or hunting or some signs of the fox kill can be found."

Turning his cap in his big hands, Jenks nodded; despite her frenzy, she was touched he was ever willing to serve her. "With the new snow," he said, "finding tracks or blood will be hard, but maybe the men saw something. I can ask around more about where the lad that brought the box of stones could live. I'll ride the river, since the Earl of Leicester has ordered the blacksmiths to put studded shoes on the horses. But first, I want to tell you Meg's gone."

"Gone? Missing?"

"Not that kind of gone."

"Gone where?"

"Don't exactly know, spur of the minute, I guess." He pulled a piece of folded paper from his leather jerkin and extended it to her. "She left me this in our secret place we pass notes—private notes—out by the stables, so guess she went toward the city."

She didn't ask what it said, but opened it. "It's just the sketch Lord Cecil made of the boot print," she said until Jenks pointed to the back of it. Written small, around the edges, in a hasty scrawl were the words *E. of S.'s foot fit. He went out, I've gone after. M.*

The queen sighed and handed Cecil the note. "If Sussex's foot fit," he said, "it's not much, but it's a place to start. Yet I can't believe it of him."

"I can't believe it of anyone we suspect," she admitted, crossing her arms as she felt a sudden chill. "But then again, to what place is the Earl of Sussex heading in the snow this cold morning when he should be staying in with his wife and anticipating the festivities this evening? Jenks, do you know if Meg got all the other prints yet?"

"She was going to report to you this morning, but guess I'd best tell, then. Lord Darnley's boot print was narrow and too long, so's it's probably not him stepped in Hodge's seasonings."

"All right. Darnley's rather slight to be hoisting Hodge up into a noose anyway, though I still trust Darnley as far as *I* can throw him. Say on."

"Chief cook's feet are far too big, so he didn't step in the stuff by accident, sending us on a wild goose chase. That reminds me, the Earl of Leicester stepped in Meg's powder, too, and smeared out the first one she'd done of Sussex 'fore she could study it, and was she vexed at him!"

"I can imagine," Elizabeth said. "The man does have a way of tramping on the best-laid plans. But she obviously managed to redo Sussex's print?"

"She's clever, my Meg. She used the fresh snow to get prints from Vicar Bane when he left this morning, same for that new actor Ned doesn't like."

"But how did she know Sussex's boot print fit, as her note says?"

"He too went out somewhere's, I'd guess, since she followed him but managed to write this note on the way and stuff it in our spot—out by the stables, like I said."

"Yes, heading for the city. But you must hie yourself to Greenwich, my man."

"We're still clutching at straws in this," Cecil said wearily after Jenks left to fetch his horse and get more bundled up to face the weather. "Flower dust is frail, and snow prints melt."

"It's more than what we've had. My lord, let's go down to see the river and watch Jenks set out. I'm feeling cooped up in here. Besides, I want to see how a stud-shoe horse does on the river ice. I may be a fine horsewoman, but this may be something different. When I ride out to see the Frost Fair, I'll not have my horse go down to its knees, nor," she added, emphasizing each word, "but for praying for divine help, shall I go to my knees in this chaos of Christmas!"

Meg had to hustle to keep the Earl of Sussex in sight. He was on foot and alone, not even a servant or guard with him. If he'd been ahorse, she'd have lost him sure, for banked snowdrifts on one side of the narrow streets made for rough going. Some well-trod spots were slippery, and each breath of cold air bit deep inside her. At least the city seemed not as crowded as usual, since many folks had gone down to walk on the frozen Thames.

If she'd known Sussex would take off like this, she would have donned a better cloak than this thin one. She had no gloves and only the stout shoes she wore about the palace instead of the fine Spanish leather boots the queen had given her last New Year's Eve. Now Meg's stockings were wet, and her toes tingled.

But Sussex's foot fit Cecil's sketch so well she just had to take this chance. It was not at all like him to be leaving the comfort of the court, not after all he said he'd suffered in the chill bogs of Ireland, which had given him the ague. Unlike some courtiers, he doted on his lady wife, so Meg didn't think he was stepping out for a tryst. The proud, stern Earl of Sussex was in love with his family name and honor and possessive of his closeness to the queen.

Down the Strand, past her parents' old apothecary shop she'd finally sold after she was widowed, through Temple Bar, Meg kept the tall, thin earl in view. As she crossed the slippery humped bridge over the frozen River Fleet and trudged through Ludgate, St. Paul's Cathedral loomed straight ahead, and she wondered if he was going there. After all, many people did for many reasons.

Although religious services were held on a regular basis in the choir before the high altar, the vast outer nave of St. Paul's had become a marketplace. So much traffic moved past the many trading stalls set up around the cathedral's tombs and font that the covered nave had become known as St. Paul's Walk, an extension of nearby Cheapside Market. Lawyers received clients there, and horse fairs were held, though probably not at Yule. "See you at St. Paul's" was a common cry. But why was the Earl of Sussex, who had servants to do his bidding, evidently headed there?

As she neared the cathedral, looking up, Meg again felt awed by the magnificence of this sentinel of the city, though, after the fire, the roof had been rebuilt without the spire. The massive morning shadow of this largest building in all England swallowed Sussex and then her, and that chilled her even more.

Yes, Sussex was indeed heading into the precincts of the cathedral. She hurried past St. Paul's Cross, where speakers of any ilk were permitted to give sermons of their choice, as long as they did not slander church or queen. Cloaked with snow, it stood alone in the cold. The Bishop of London's house was a stone's throw away, and she wondered if Sussex had come to see Bishop Grindal. But Vicar Bane was always around the palace, so the earl could simply have done business with him.

Sussex, slowing his strides, passed the bishop's house and went directly in the great west door of the cathedral. So as not to lose him in the crowds, pressing her hand to the stitch in her side, Meg hurried even faster.

The queen and Cecil donned warm cloaks and hats and went down the privy staircase to face the buffeting winter wind on the frozen river. "It feels good," the queen insisted as her cloak flapped like raven's wings. "Cecil, I've been praying to God for a clue to save Christmas."

"A clue like a star in the sky hanging over the culprit, or angels singing to point the way to his next outrage?"

"I am still not in the mood for jesting. Tonight, as Lord of Misrule overseeing a raucous mumming, Leicester will do enough of that."

Squinting into the wind, she looked upriver to the charred

ruins of the boathouse. It would be rebuilt when the weather turned warmer, but she knew she should soon order the clearing of the debris and ashes. Her eyes watered and her cheeks stung, but it was a bracing cold. Out on the ice the wind had swept clear of snow, men were cobbling together crude booths for the Frost Fair. Children and adults alike were sliding and falling and laughing on the solid white river as if they had not a care in the world.

"There he is, my lord," she said, pointing to Jenks as he rode out onto the ice and headed east. "The horse looks a bit nervous, but they're managing."

"And with you as our queen, so shall we all," he said.

As they turned to go back in, she glanced after Jenks again, half wishing she could stay outside on some adventure and not be closed in with her thoughts and fears, waiting for the other shoe—or boot print—to fall. Her gaze caught the rough stone foundation of the palace, rising from the frozen riverbanks just before the brick facade began, now all etched with driven snow. Had God indeed answered her prayer?

"Cecil, look, there," she said, pointing again.

"He's almost disappeared into the growing crowd on the ice."

"No, look at the very foundations of the palace. Down that way, toward where the boathouse stood—that rough hole in the lower wall that's pockmarked and has caught the snow. I want to look closer at it, for I swear it wasn't there before."

They crunched through the carpet of snow toward the spot. On the corner of the foundation, almost directly under the royal apartments, someone had hewn out pieces of gray stone—twelve of them.

. . .

Meg had been right about no horse fair today, but, despite the lure of the frozen Thames for the first time in years, many Londoners were in the nave of St. Paul's. Hawkers screeched to buyers, selling everything from books to plateware to expensive sugar, which was imported on Venetian galleys when they could navigate the river. She heard cries for roasted pig's trotters, gingerbread, even lemon suckets. Like the queen, Meg loved those, but she hadn't brought a farthing with her and could snitch all she wanted off the queen's trays anyway.

She watched Sussex make his way toward a vendor of pewter and silver goods. "Oh, no," she whispered to herself in the echoing hubbub under the vast roof.

Her spirits fell. She'd braved the cold and got her hopes up she was onto something in this search for a murderer, and this powerful peer of the realm had merely come to buy a gift for his lady wife or even the queen? Though the wind didn't blow through here, she shuddered. Now she'd have to head back all the way to the palace to tell Her Grace she'd come up with nothing but a numb nose and toes.

She stayed to the side of the nave, keeping one of the elaborate tombs between her and Sussex. Yes, he was looking at what appeared to be a fine pair of silver filigreed flagons with a raised design. She bet those cost a pretty penny. On a crude plank cupboard behind the vendor were displayed tankards and ewers, pitchers, flagons, and rows of plates all flaunting designs in relief. She sighed. Though she and Jenks would share a room in the servants' wing of the queen's palaces over the coming years, would she ever own something as fine as those?

She gasped. Standing at the side of the cupboard as if waiting for Sussex stood that new actor, Giles Chatam. And if he was here, could Ned, who'd been told to keep on his tail, be far behind?

Ned almost shouted for joy. Now he could report to the queen that Sussex, who hated Leicester, was here whispering to Giles when, if his business had been on the up-and-up, he could simply have spoken to him in the palace. Ned's mind raced through all the possibilities: He could suggest to Her Grace that, although Sussex would not dirty his own hands to disgrace Leicester or ruin the festivities over which the peacock presided as Lord of Misrule, he could have hired Giles to murder Hodge and ruin Christmas. And Giles could have wanted to get rid of his old rival Hodge, so Sussex could have told him about making him look like the peacock . . .

But no, Ned realized, he'd never convince the brilliant queen that those men had by chance found each other early enough to connive to kill Hodge. Still, anything to muddy the water to take her and Cecil's scrutiny off himself.

Then, to his surprise, he saw Meg Milligrew, peeking around the corner of one of the tall, ornate tombs, looking the part of a skulking grave robber. Had he taught her nothing about trying to blend in with the surrounding cast of characters? She looked flushed, disheveled, and windblown, but it was somehow beguiling.

Ned scanned the crowd around her and then the booth where Sussex was paying coin for something he'd bought, which had now been placed in a velvet drawstring bag. The pewterer had taken off his cap to reveal such a bright red head that he looked more Irish than English. Carefully, being sure Giles didn't spot him, though the young man was craning his neck to look up at the lofty ceiling like some rustic cowherd who'd never seen a big building, Ned worked his way over to Meg and came around the tomb behind her.

"If you came to meet a lover," he said low, "I hope it's me."

"Oh, Ned!" she said, spinning toward him. "You scared me near to death, even though I was looking for you. When I saw Giles here waiting for Sussex, I thought you might be near."

"If there wasn't a connection between the two of them before Hodge was killed, there is now. I think we can make some hay with that."

"But can we get close enough to overhear what they say?"

"In this noise? Best just keep an eye on them. Look," he said as he took her elbow and propelled her around the next tomb with its stone figure of a knight staring eternally upward, "Sussex is not one whit surprised to see him and is giving him a slip of paper."

"With his new orders on it, I wonder?"

"Be sure to tell the queen that's what it looked like to you."

"And now he's paying Giles!" she cried as Sussex extended coins to the handsome young man, just as he had to the redheaded pewterer before.

"Seeing is believing."

"And so, I'll stay with the earl and you stick to Giles, but not together."

Her cheeks were roses, and the excitement of the chase seemed to make her usually pale beauty bloom, even in this big barn of a place.

"Why not together?" he challenged and squeezed her waist. "We'll be careful."

But their quarries separated, and Meg went her way, probably back to the palace, behind the Earl of Sussex. With Ned shadowing him, Giles walked out of the cathedral and strolled down the bitterly cold, broad and windy Cheapside, gazing at the ornate swinging signs of goldsmiths' shops as if it were the mildest June day. Giles had told his fellows in the actors' company that he wanted to walk the city whatever the weather, and that seemed to be the truth. Hell's gates, but Ned had no intention of gawking at this man while he gawked at London. He was heading home.

But as he strode back through the nave, then out into the wind again, as if it were a sign from heaven that he'd been ignoring Meg too long, there she was again, huddled behind the big gray hulk of St. Paul's Cross.

"What are you doing here?" he asked, making her jump again. He took off his cloak and wrapped it around her shoulders, however much he was trembling, maybe not only from the cold, but the closeness to her again.

"You won't believe it," she said, pulling him behind the cross, "but Sussex went inside to see Bishop Grindal, and that croaking raven Vicar Bane met him at the door to let him in. I've never seen Bane as much as smile, but he out-and-out grinned, and they started whispering right away!"

"The plot thickens," Ned said, "and plotting they must be."

Chapter the Ninth

A Christmas Fool

The curdled custard called "fool" is an excellent dish for all the year, but with the dates and caraway comfits, fit for a special Yule dinner for young or old, poor or rich or royal: Take a pint of the sweetest, thickest cream, and set it on the fire in a clean scoured skillet, and put into it sugar, cinnamon, and a nutmeg cut into 4 quarters, and so boil it well. Take the yolks of 4 hen's eggs, and beat them well with a little sweet cream, then take the nutmeg out of the cream, then put in the eggs, and stir it exceedingly, till it be thick. Then take fine white manchet bread and cut it into thin pieces, as much as will cover a dish bottom. Pour half the cream into the dish, then lay your bread over it, then cover the bread with the rest of the cream, and so let stand till it be cold. Then strew it over with caraway comfits, and prick up some cinnamon comfits, and some sliced dates, and so serve it up.

"I'VE BROUGHT YOU A STURDY MARE WITH STUDDED shoes for the river ice," Robin told Elizabeth as he bowed before her in her presence chamber early that afternoon. "I know, consummate horsewoman that you are, you would appreciate a grander mount, but this one's closer to the ground, and I'm sure you don't want your usual horse chancing a fall and broken leg."

"His or mine? Well, Robin, as you are Lord of Misrule by my

own hand this season, I had best ride out with you to see how my people are doing. I believe it will do me good."

Yet she felt torn as she went into her privy chamber to don warm boots, cloak, and hat. She wanted to stay here until Jenks reported from Greenwich and Meg returned from following Sussex. Cecil was down on the riverbank with her guard Clifford, ascertaining that the twelve stones were indeed hewn from the foundation of her palace. Kat was napping while everyone else went hither and yon, preparing gifts for the New Year's exchange or arranging their fantastical costumes for the mumming this evening.

But the queen refused to be kept prisoner in her own palace, and she did want to be out with her people and with Robin. She was taking no chances she would be made to look the fool or put herself in danger. She rode out between Robin and Harry with Rosie and three other ladies in her wake. Four yeomen guards were mounted, and ten others walked the ice, keeping their distance but also keeping her in their sight.

The cold and the thrill of riding on the river invigorated her. After yesterday's storm, the sky was a shattering blue, and the sunlight off the expanse of ice was almost blinding.

"It's like another world," she told Robin as they slowly walked their horses straight out from the palace. Her sometimes sooty, dirty city seemed to sparkle, as if she rode the gold, gem-studded streets of heaven. When the Thames was water, she thought, it never looked as wide as this. From the palace to the broad bend that hid distant London Bridge, she could see her people as busy as ants, working to build their Frost Fair. However cold, they looked happy and so festive that her oppressive mood lifted even more.

"Needless to say," Robin told her, "the closer you get to the city proper, the more activity there is. Oh, by the way, with your gracious permission, my queen, I thought I'd plan something special for New Year's Eve. I've ordered my men to explode small bits of gunpowder on the ice—much noise and flash to bring in the new year. We'll save the rockets and firewheels for Twelfth Night."

"As Lord of Misrule, you are in charge of all that."

The wind whipped their words away in puffs of breath. "Good day to you," she called to a group of men hammering to erect a stall. Amazed it was their queen, they cheered and huzzahed, which made others come running and sliding. Elizabeth saw that some citizens had built bonfires on the ice and were cooking food; one enterprising lad had cut a hole through and was fishing.

"Robin, look at that plug of ice he's pulled out. The river has frozen to at least a foot thick here! I don't think even your gunpowder blasts could break that ice."

Their gazes caught and held. Robin sucked in a deep breath, and his nostils flared. He was, she mused, like the powerful gunpowder he believed was the future of warfare. Like her, he was of volatile temperament; together they were match to saltpeter in a blast of heat and light. But gunpowder could blow everything apart.

Not wanting to be seen lurking outside the bishop's house, Meg and Ned hied themselves back toward Whitehall, rehearsing all they had to tell the queen. Meg was so excited to be with Ned she almost forgot to breathe. It had been so long since just the two of them had worked together.

"At least we've discovered something to pursue," Ned said.

"It will be your best defense if you think Her Grace and Cecil believe you could have been involved," Meg tried to encourage him. "Dreadful how being part of the Privy Plot Council soon has you suspecting everyone. Next, we'll be thinking poor Kat's in on this, and then I'll know we've taken leave of our senses."

"Let's stop off at this tavern to get warm," he urged and steered her toward the Rose and Crown.

Despite how she was enjoying her time with him, she almost panicked. This was hardly like old times when Ned taught her to carry herself like the queen, to talk properly, and to read in those heady days she came to care for him. So much had changed.

"But we're almost back," she protested.

"Just for a few moments. To warm up."

"I should return this cloak you so sweetly—generously," she amended, "loaned me. I can't be walking into Whitehall in it anyway."

"Jenks would understand."

"He wouldn't understand us spending time in a tavern, now would he?"

"But this is the very place my uncle's troupe played for a day or two, so I thought we'd best ask a few questions here, to be able to report to Her Majesty how Giles behaved then. Actually, if we weren't so chilled, we ought to visit the inn where I found them and inquire there, too. Meg, this won't take long," he wheedled. "Jenks will understand, as he's always devoted at any cost to Her Majesty's best interests."

Despite her better judgment, she went.

Shading her eyes in the blaze of sun on ice, Elizabeth turned her horse reluctantly toward the palace. Cecil and Clifford were no longer outside by the palace's foundations. Rather, a mounted man who looked familiar was there on the snowy bank.

"Robin," she said, pointing, "that man ahorse near the palace directly under my apartment windows. Is that not Simon MacNair?"

"I believe it is, my queen, for I recognize his Scottish border mare. He wanted studded shoes on it and on another fine beast he said belonged to Duncan Forbes, his messenger to the Scots queen."

Elizabeth turned to look Robin full in the face. "Have you ever sent notes to *that* queen by MacNair's messenger?"

"Never, I swear it," he vowed, hastily crossing his heart like a fond lad.

"You did not entrust to him a privy letter saying Queen Mary should not consider you for her husband?"

His cheeks colored, more than they had in the wind. "No, I sent my own man with that."

"I don't believe the Lord of Misrule must tell the truth," she said, looking away from him, "but then neither do most men believe it is a necessity."

"Your Grace, you wound me sore to imply such. I knew Kat was parroting your words the night before last when we told our stories and she denounced men."

"You like to tell stories, I warrant," she shot back. "I've not forgotten MacNair's mention of that large portrait of Queen Mary in your privy rooms, my Earl of Leicester. Come on, then," she cried, and urged her mount forward, "but I shall speak with Sir Simon alone."

Though he looked as if he'd argue more, Robin kept her entourage back as Elizabeth, still mounted, approached MacNair.

"There is great excitement in the air, Your Majesty!" the Scot called jauntily to her and swept off his feathered cap in a grand gesture.

She did not move her horse onto the bank itself but stayed at the edge of the ice. Staring hard at him, she replied, "Since the view is so lovely out here, Sir Simon, why are you studying this ragged hole in the wall?"

"I would never have noted it, but I saw Secretary Cecil trying to rebuild it, or, shall I say, fitting stones into these holes. Is he also head of your building repair office, Your Grace?"

"You were there the day of the hunt," she said, deciding to challenge this man instead of jest with him or put him in his place for his subtle impudence. "You saw someone sent me a box of stones, and, amazingly, they came from there. I must say, someone has a sick sense of humor—a fool's sense of humor, and here we are now on the Feast of Fools day."

She studied him closely, for she had positioned herself so that he must stare into the afternoon sun to face her. Not a flicker of guilt or even further interest crossed his broad countenance at that sally. She'd best try again.

"Where is your messenger whose horse you asked to be shod with studs?" she asked.

"I don't rightly know, Your Grace, as Forbes headed north the day before yesterday with a letter to Her Majesty in Edinburgh. Sad to say he probably was caught in the snowstorm, but he'll fight his way on northward. We Scots are a hardy lot, you know."

"I do know. And what did you report to your queen?"

"That I wished her the heartiest and healthiest New Year, and told her I would soon send her a fine gift. By the way, some Scots call New Year's Eve Hogmanay, you know, Your Majesty."

"A strange name and not, I warrant, because you have many roasted hogs on that day?"

"It's spelled Hog-m-a-n-a-y, Your Grace, though most north of the border can't spell worth a groat."

"Are you implying that since I misspelled it, I would make a good Scot?"

"But you could only be a queen, Your Majesty, and then we would have one queen too many in fair Scotland."

"When I became queen there in place of my cousin Mary, I would dub the day Queenmanay and order both roasted hogs and Christmas fool custards for all my loyal Scots subjects. I shall see you at the feast this Feast of Fools, will I not, my Scottish lord?"

He gave a hearty laugh at her wordplay, and at the moment she rather liked the man. "You will see me but not recognize me," he said, "for I will be with the group of mumming men performing for Your Most Gracious Majesty. And I hear we are not allowed to talk but only sing—or laugh."

Their gazes met and held. Apparently open and honest, seemingly bluff and good-natured, Sir Simon MacNair appeared to be a hail-fellow-well-met. But the queen knew better: Like all political creatures—actually, like all men—he bore watching. She'd known that from the first Christmas she could recall, when her father had called her his little dearest on one day and named her bastard of a whore the next.

Once Ned convinced Meg to go into the Rose and Crown with him, he felt very nervous, and that wasn't like him. Was it suddenly because it seemed as if he were courting her, or because he had so much at stake convincing the queen to believe Giles was not to be trusted? Whether or not Giles was guilty, Ned needed him to look guilty. Not that he'd want the pretty boy to be arrested, of course, for if it began to look bad for him, he'd tip Giles off and suggest he flee London and never return.

"You're frowning something dreadful," Meg said as he seated her on a bench in the back corner of the common room near the hearth. Unlike the other day, the place was nearly deserted.

"Just thinking too much," he told her, squeezing her shoulder. "Shall I buy you ale or beer?"

"Mulled cider, if they have it. Hot!"

"I intend to bring back the tapman I talked to the other day about Giles."

He walked through the smoky common room with its mingled smells of wet wool, burning firewood, and four chickens sizzling on a single spit over the flames. His stomach growled in anticipation of the feast tonight with its roast suckling pig. It was not half as crowded here as it had been the other day, and he spotted the tapman easily at the counter amidst the few customers. The fat, jolly man went by the sobriquet of "Duke" since in his youth he'd been footman for the Duke of Northumberland.

Ned ordered two mulled ciders and tipped Duke extravagantly before the man realized who he was.

"Eh, you again, then? Still looking for your actor friends?"

"Looking for some information, if you've got the time," Ned told the nearly bald man. Duke had such a bull neck it looked as if his head were set directly on his huge, rounded shoulders. Every time he nodded it seemed to be in danger of rolling off.

"Why not?" Duke said and left his fellows to follow Ned. "If a man can't take a whit of a respite at holiday time, however much debt he has or problems, too, what's the point of things?" Duke guffawed as if he'd said something hilarious. "This your wench, then?" he asked as he saw Meg waiting on the bench. "Red-haired like the queen herself, eh?"

"Meg's a close friend of mine," Ned told him, and Meg nodded vigorously. "And we're here," he went on as the three of them huddled on the bench, Meg squeezed in the middle, "to inquire if you can give us any information about the handsome, young blond actor who was with the players."

"Wet behind the ears, he was, I could tell, but smooth."

Hell's gates, Ned thought, that wasn't much help and seemed slightly contradictory.

"Clever like," Duke tried to explain, rubbing his bearded chin, "and real int'rested in everything 'bout Londontown, that's what he called the city."

"Yes, I've seen he was interested in everything."

"Good 'nough actor, I warrant, but kept running out and 'bout between the short plays they did, used this hearth right here for a stage, they did."

"But how was Giles clever?" Ned pursued.

"Tried to make a good impression, least 'bout one thing. Boasted he was going to see Whitehall Palace soon, not only from the outside but inside, too. Had a friend who could get him in, leastways far's the kitchens."

Ned and Meg gave each other a pointed look. "Did he say who his friend was?" Meg spoke up before Ned could.

"No, and wasn't like to be the queen, was it? Why, I could of thrown the Duke of Northumberland's name at him—see, I was once his footman, missy," he said to Meg, "looked fine in liv'ry, too, 'specially new liv'ry at Yule, I did."

"Yes, I'm sure you did," Meg told him.

"But I was too busy that day, not like now," he added with a nod at the sparsely populated common room. " 'Sides, I been in a few fancy kitchens myself. Naw, just give me the small hearth here with the spit aturning at Yule, my wife in our warm room upstairs, and I'm content, no more court life or fetching and scraping for my betters in a rabbit warren o' rooms, e'en castle or palace, not me."

Duke leaned contentedly back against the wall behind the bench and belched as if to punctuate his thoughts. This time, Ned's gaze snagged Meg's and held. He wondered if she was thinking what he was, that there was some lure to the life this man described, even so crudely.

"We'd best get back," Meg mouthed.

Ned nodded. They finished their cider and thanked the man; Ned donned his own cloak this time, and they started out. But in the small entry hall, before they stepped into the cold world again, Ned blocked her in against the closed door.

"I've got a sprig of mistletoe in my jerkin," he said, amazed his voice was so rough.

"You already got what you came for," she countered, "more goods on Giles. Are you the one who's been taking the mistletoe off the kissing boughs I put up?"

"Not I—just this one. Do I need to get it out? I can't be seen giving you a Christmas kiss back at Whitehall if I don't want Jenks's fist in my face, peace on earth and goodwill to men this time of year, or not."

"No, we can't have that," she said with a sigh.

He moved quickly before she changed her mind. It was just a way of thanking her for sticking with him in this, he told himself. Just a cheery, holiday, one-time thing . . . a sort of good-bye since she was to marry Jenks, and the queen sometimes talked about having a wedding for them soon. It was just . . .

Meg gave a little moan and seemed to sink into him. His hand left the door latch to tighten around her waist; his other hand steadied her chin. They melded together, for much longer than he'd intended or expected. And yet it seemed to go so fast, the deepening kiss and the way they clung to each other, mindless of the place or time or who they were.

It was another loud guffaw from Duke, talking to someone in the common room, that brought Ned back to reality. He lifted his head, and Meg stepped quickly away from his embrace. Though no one was so much as looking at them, another man laughed at something Duke had said, and "That's a good one!" floated to them.

Quickly, Ned hustled Meg out the door. The queen would not think it one bit humorous if they didn't get back soon.

"My lord Harry," Elizabeth said to Baron Hunsdon the moment she'd heard all Ned and Meg had to tell, "please find the Earl of Sussex and escort him to my presence forthwith!"

She felt somewhat relieved that Giles Chatam's suspicious activities might help exonerate Ned, but her principal actor still bore watching. It seemed to her he was trying too hard to make Giles look bad. Meanwhile, the Privy Plot Council members still sat around the table in the queen's privy chamber. Cecil had reported that the twelve stones had indeed come from the palace's foundation, Jenks had said he'd turned up no sign or word of a fox killed at Greenwich, and Meg and Ned had come back brimming with news from their joint investigation.

"But what about Giles?" Ned asked now. "I thought, that is, Meg and I thought—"

"I will look into his actions, too, I assure you," Elizabeth interrupted, "though I don't think a frontal assault is the way to deal with him. On the other hand, Sussex understands the old saying, 'Might makes right.' "

"Sussex may head a powerful court faction," Cecil said, "but he dare not defy his queen."

"Let us hope," she muttered.

"Perhaps," Ned put in, "just removing Giles Chatam from among the mummers tonight and sending him away from court—"

"Ned, enough!" Elizabeth commanded and sat in the chair at the end of the long table so fast her skirt whooshed air. She intentionally did not bid the others to sit again. "And," she added, pointing at him, "don't be confronting Giles Chatam on your own until we at least arrange for someone to overhear what he may say."

"But I would report back faithfully what he said and—and I ask your permission to take my leave now," he added hastily, no doubt, she thought, when he saw the look on her face.

"All of you but Cecil may leave," she said, "but remember to keep a good eye out at the Feast of Fools for anything untoward. And if I manage to shake any confessions out of Thomas Radcliffe, Earl of Sussex, I will let you know."

When everyone did as bidden, Cecil said, "I note you didn't tell them you've secreted Clifford and Jenks in the kitchen for this evening. Do you still mistrust Ned?"

"I cannot afford to trust anyone—present company excepted, my lord—until we find and stop this Christmas-plot culprit. I cannot believe Ned would stoop to murder, though he is entirely capable of the cleverness of the assault on our traditions. He was livid when I named Leicester Lord of Misrule. Perhaps in passing through the kitchens that day he happened upon Hodge, they argued or there was an accident—and then he's been forced to hide what he's done ever since. In my heart I cannot fathom Ned a killer, even accidentally, but as queen I must be ruled by my head."

Instead of tempestuous Ned, she pictured her volatile Robin again, so handsome, so intense. She wearied of holding him at arm's length. She cherished the ride on the frozen river with him today, even though they'd argued. Sometimes she thought that if only she had a husband to help bear her burdens—but if she had a husband, then England had a king, and kings had a way of ruling over queens, too, so . . .

A sharp knock on the door shattered her musings.

"The Earl of Sussex awaits," Harry announced, sticking only his head and shoulders in. "And," he added, whispering now, "he's just returned to the palace."

Sussex had obviously come in great haste. When he swept off his cap to bow, Elizabeth saw that his boots—those boots that were the exact size of the probable murderer's—were mottled with melted snow. His hair was still mussed, and he nervously smoothed it more than once. His gloves were yet stuck in his belt, and his cheeks were burnished like two autumn pippins.

"Your Majesty, ah, what is the cause, and what may I do to help?" he inquired as he rose from his bow.

"Perhaps much. I have it on good authority you have been abroad this day, and as I've been no farther than the river, I'd like to hear all you've seen and done in my city."

"Ah, all I've seen and done in the city."

"Cecil, is there an echo in here?" she asked. Sussex shot Cecil a sideways glance. 'S blood, the queen fumed, but Sussex looked guilty of something, like the boy who stuck his thumb in a pie and pulled out a plum. But whether Sussex was a good boy or not remained to be seen.

"Someone saw me, I take it," he said, shifting from one foot to the other.

"Perhaps a little bird told me," she said, glaring at him.

"And you want to know if people are in a festive mood, or the condition of the snowy streets, or—"

She smacked the arms of her chair with her fists and jumped to her feet. Sussex stepped back so fast he nearly tripped. "Don't fence with me, my lord," she commanded, pointing her finger at him. "I may be a woman, unskilled in the military maneuvers you have practiced and perfected, but I am your queen. And I want to know why you went out today to meet someone you could well have spoken to in the warmth of this palace!"

"Ah—Vicar Bane? I stopped to wish good Yuletide cheer to Bishop Grindal, and Bane happened to be there, that's all. Is Bane back already—and, ah, mayhap mentioned he spoke with me?"

"Yuletide cheer was it? You stopped to wish Bishop Grindal good Yuletide cheer? I suppose you were simply shopping for New Year's gifts at St. Paul's Walk, too?"

"I—yes. You had me followed, Your Majesty? But what have I done to deserve—"

"I am asking the questions, Sussex, though you are doing a pitiful job with the answers."

His ruddy glow went white as bleached linen. Damn, but she'd be distraught if a powerful peer of the realm had caused this upheaval at court, let alone committed or ordered a murder. And all because he so hated his rival Leicester, his promotion and position?

"Did you see anyone else I would know on your goodwill jaunt, Sussex?" she went on. If he lied about seeing Giles Chatam and passing him a note and money, she must have Sussex more thoroughly questioned.

"Ah, yes, I saw someone else, but it's a private affair."

"Shall I tell your lady Frances of that? A private affair?"

He blanched again. "Not that sort of thing, Your Majesty, I swear it."

"And I swear to you that this is serious business to me and I must know it all."

"I saw the new actor, Giles Chatam," he blurted.

"Aha. A private affair. Meaning?"

"It's a sort of Yuletide secret, Your Majesty."

"Cecil, this is a man who can command an army but cannot command himself in my presence!" she cried, looking to her chief secretary and then back at the shaken but defiant Sussex. "I cannot afford secrets, man! Why did you meet and bribe and pass orders to an itinerant young actor you surely could not even have known before a few days ago?"

At last, Sussex looked shocked. "Is—is something wrong with him? I overheard he was going to be at St. Paul's. Ah, he loves to wander the city, Your Grace, and I said he should look me up."

"Obviously! Because?"

"I had a poem for him to recite to someone special on New Year's Eve, a poem I wrote myself, for, as you know, speaking is not my *forte*. I can fetch you the rough copy of it from my chamber where I have it hidden. A gift for my lady wife, as were the finely wrought flagons I bought from a vendor who was highly recommended to me."

Elizabeth sank into her chair again. The anger ebbed from her; she felt deflated. All that could be true, of course. She wanted to believe him. Still, he could have handed the poem and money to Giles Chatam here at court. And since when was he in so tight with Bishop Grindal, or was it Bane he really went to see where they would not be seen talking—perhaps plotting—together? She supposed neither of the churchmen could stomach Leicester's growing power any more than Sussex could.

"Shall I fetch you the poem for proof, then, Your Majesty?"

"My lord, as you know, there is someone skulking about our court, mocking our attempts to have a happy and holy holiday. The only proof I want from you is that you keep your well-honed eyes for enemies wide open and report to me should you note anything amiss."

"You—you suspected me?" he asked, aghast.

"I suspect anyone who acts suspiciously, my lord. Frankly, your foot fit the print of the one we believed murdered Hodge in the kitchens."

"M-murder? But—boots are made in such general sizes by so few boot makers and imported. These were," he said, frowning down at them.

"I realize all that."

"Who took my print, or did someone just eye my size? But why would I kill your privy dresser in the kitchen?"

"Never mind all that, Sussex, but heed my words to be watchful. I will not have another bizarre affront on me or our holidays here. And I charge you to keep this quiet."

"Because I detest Leicester, is that it?" he asked, evidently not knowing when to leave well enough alone, but the man's family pride was meat and drink to him. "And the corpse decked in peacock feathers mocked him? Ah—you asked me earlier, Your Grace, by what sobriquets he was known at court. But he has many enemies beyond me, I assure you, and some not so vocal about it who might sneak around to do something vile and sordid, which I would not."

"You may go, my lord, but I do thank you for your testimonial about how many others hate him and about your innocence in the matter of murder or general mayhem."

He looked as if he would argue more, but he bowed and left.

"I've done something I don't usually do, my lord," she told Cecil when the door closed.

"Anger an important courtier?"

"No, I've actually confronted two of the possible culprits today, three if you count Ned, and tried to put the fear of God—or of queen—in them. But MacNair and Sussex have both stood up well."

"So you're discounting them?"

"If I'm not discounting my dear Ned, I'm discounting no one. Keep a good eye out tonight, my lord, for at the Feast of Fools everyone will be disguised, not only the man we must unmask."

Despite being strung tight as a lute string, Elizabeth enjoyed the evening. The roast suckling pig was good—the first solid meat that had appealed to her in days—and naught appeared under silver serving lids on platters that should not be there. She had a double helping of the rich date-and-cinnamon Yule fool, the music pleased her, and everyone seemed happy to be wearing splendid costumes, Kat especially. Vicar Bane was the only one not so attired, though he did deign to don a plain half mask with huge eyeholes, the better to spy on everyone, she thought. But evidently the fun and gaiety were too much for him, for she saw him rip his mask off and depart in a huff after dinner.

She soon began to breathe even easier. At Robin's sign, while the ladies waited, the men who would return as the mummers slipped out to prepare their grand entrance. For some reason, the audience waited for an inordinate amount of time. She supposed she should have kept Ned as Lord of Misrule, for Robin was surely a novice at all this.

But everyone oohed and aahed when the men piled into the room helter-skelter, laughing and singing about "Good King Wenceslas," though the second time through they changed the chorus to "Good Queen Elizabeth." Along with everyone else, she tried to pick out who was who, but the mummers wore matching armored breastplates and helmets with their visors down. Identical bouncing white plumes made them look like knights ready for joust or battle. Yet everyone was soon laughing that their singing, echoing strangely, came from inside those domes of steel.

"I should think they would all go breathless and deaf in those!" Rosie cried, holding her sides she was laughing so hard.

Occasionally, two or more of the mummers would stage a willy-nilly sword fight between songs, or open a visor just enough to gulp down more ale or mulled cider. Cecil, nervous as a cat, came up to stand beside her chair.

"Ordinarily, they'd all be in the Tower for so much as drawing a sword in the monarch's presence," he groused.

"My dear Cecil, it's Fools day," she chided gently, "and the Lord of Misrule is in charge tonight, not me. Besides, my yeomen guards stand at the ready all around the room should someone step out of line."

Even though she was tempted to give a sign to Robin to stop the swordplay, she couldn't be sure which knight he was. Their tall helmets and feathers made them look the same height, the same build, and they all wore black hose and shoes. She supposed that was why her father finally halted the mumming years ago. Men got away with drunken or raucous deeds and were completely disguised. But she could tell the mummers were running out of strength and breath in those hot shells. Soon they would lift their visors and be done with this tomfoolery.

She was wrong, though, for they were leaving, being herded out by someone, though that knight didn't carry himself like Robin. Nor like Ned. Perhaps Ned's uncle or even Giles Chatam was taking charge of the scattershot exit.

But as all but one cleared the door, that man pulled out two small stuffed dolls from inside his breastplate. Everyone grew silent to see what was coming next. One doll had red hair and a wire crown; the other was a male doll with peacock feathers sprouting from his bum.

The queen gasped. Had Robin arranged to make light of his own nickname, or of what had happened to poor Hodge? It all happened so fast, in a blur.

The lone mummer held the dolls tight face-to-face, rubbing them together as if they were kissing—or performing a more lewd act. If that was Robin, she would kill him for this. Lord of Misrule or not, he had greatly overstepped.

Her ladies and the few men scattered throughout the audience remained silent but for a smothered snicker or two far behind her.

"Enough," Elizabeth declared, rising, "whether those poor

puppets stand under the kissing bough or not!" Appalled, she fought to keep from blushing. She didn't care whether Robin would plead Misrule's rights or Fools night or the end of the world, she was going to have his head on a platter, either for doing this or allowing this.

"Cecil," she whispered, "see that my guards detain that man, I don't care if it is Leicester."

"Yes, Your Grace," he said and disappeared into the crowd as her ladies prepared to follow their queen from the room. But when she glanced again at the door, it was empty, for the lone knight had disappeared behind the others.

Elizabeth went directly to her rooms and dismissed her entourage, saying Kat and Rosie would help her undress for bed. But the moment the back hall cleared, she asked Rosie to look after Kat and, with only her yeoman Clifford with her, headed for Robin's rooms. Good rooms, she fumed, warm rooms, she'd given him. Whether drunk with liquor or with power, he had gone too far.

Nearing his chamber, she came face-to-face with Ned, Jenks, and Meg, coming her way in a rush down the corridor, so she sent Clifford back to his post.

"What happened?" Ned cried.

"Were you among the mummers?" she asked him, not breaking her stride. They wheeled about to follow her.

"Yes, but I only heard something happened at the end I didn't see. Who did what?"

"I saw," Meg said. "I went to see how Jenks was doing guarding the kitchens, but I saw it. Jenks and I just met Ned in the hall."

"Wait here," Elizabeth said and pounded her fist on Robin's door. If he was not back, she'd post Jenks here to bring him right away when he returned. His title of Lord of Misrule was going back to Ned forthwith, and Robin was being banished from court.

"Guess he's not back yet," Meg said.

"If he has one bit of brain left, he'll just keep going, clear to Scotland or to hell!" Elizabeth declared. "I trust him to keep a lid on things, and he makes it all worse."

But as she turned to march back to her apartments, she heard a muffled sound. Had she knocked on the door so hard that she'd pushed it partway open? Had it not been closed or latched?

She gave the door a little shove, and it swung easily inward.

Trussed with a web of ropes, Robin lay belly down, stark naked on a table, with his lower legs bent up behind him. His blue face contrasted with the red apple jammed in his mouth. He was desperately trying to keep his ankles close to his head, for if he let them straighten, the noose around his neck cut off his air like a garrote. Stuck within the ropes were two crudely lettered parchment signs, which partly hid his nakedness. One read *YULE FOOL* and the other *ROAST SUCKING-UP BORE.*

Chapter the Tenth

Roast Suckling Pig

To roast a pig curiously, first tie the legs back. You shall not scald it but draw it with the hair on, then, having washed it, spit it and lay it to the fire so that it may not scorch, then, being a quarter roasted, and the skin blistered from the flesh, with your hand pull away the hair and skin, and leave all the fat and flesh perfectly bare; then with your knife scotch all the flesh down to the bones, then baste it exceedingly with sweet butter and cream, being no more but warm; then dredge it with fine bread crumbs, currants, sugar, and salt mixed together, and thus apply dredging upon basting until you have covered all the flesh a full inch deep; then, the meat being fully roasted, draw it and serve it up whole. Place an apple in its mouth and surround it on the platter with baked apples and onions, also sprigs of rosemary and bay.

"HELP HIM!" ELIZABETH CRIED, BUT SHE TOO RAN TO Robin. Ned held his legs to ease the strain on the noose as Jenks cut his cords. Forgotten for now, the two bizarre messages sailed away and were trodden underfoot. The queen loosened the rope around his neck as Meg seized his shirt from the floor and covered him.

"Jenks," Elizabeth said, "carefully cut the apple in half so we can get it out of his mouth. Robin, you're all right now, you're safe," she told him, plucking the fruit out in two pieces. While he heaved in huge breaths that shook his big frame, she grasped his shoulder, then rubbed his bare back as if she were comforting a child.

"He would have died for sure if we'd not come!" Jenks said as he finished cutting and tearing the ropes away.

Attempted murder! Elizabeth thought. What if she had lost Robin? Brushing tears from her cheeks, she felt flushed, but her skin was gooseflesh. To think that she'd blamed him for that rude affront downstairs when he was fighting for his life up here.

"You must have been tied before the mummers entered the hall tonight," she told him as Jenks pulled a sheet off the nearby bed to wrap him. "And the demon who did this could have taken your place among them."

With their help, Robin sat up slowly. "Would you prefer a chair or bed, my lord?" she asked. He nodded toward the bed Jenks had just ripped apart, and they helped him to it. However, he sat up in it, leaning back against the carved headboard, his face now livid, his neck red and welted where the noose had chafed him.

The queen fetched wine and held it to his lips. Weakly, he lifted one hand to hold her wrist. Though no doubt still shaken and shamed, he lifted his gaze to hers at last.

"I thought I would die," he whispered, "and never see you again. My last thoughts—of you."

"Meg, go fetch one of my physicians," the queen commanded.

"No!" Robin whispered, gripping her wrist. "No doctor. I do not want this all over the court and country. Please tell no one, my queen."

"Yes, all right. The three of you, wait just outside the door," she ordered, "and leave it ajar. I will speak with my lord alone a moment to hear what happened."

The three of them did as bidden; she could hear them whispering in the corridor. She lifted the heavily embossed flagon of wine so Robin could sip again and stroked his wayward tresses off his forehead, wet with sweat. Carefully, she sat on the edge of his bed, her hip next to his knee.

"I should have heeded your words of warning," he said. "Because of all we mean to each other, the love I bear you, someone wants to humiliate and kill me. I desperately need your help and protection, my queen."

"God as my judge, you shall have my help!"

"And your love, too? Just a bit?"

"You know I do—I have and do," she stammered. "But to keep you—all of us—safe, I must discover who did this."

He frowned and lifted both hands to his head. Rope marks marred each wrist. "Splitting head pain," he whispered. "I can't recall much. After the feast, I was in a flurry, getting the mummers ready. I realized I'd left my speech upstairs . . . here, in my chamber. My servants were downstairs, helping everyone into armor, so I ran up here to fetch it, up the back servants' staircase."

"So you weren't with the mummers," she repeated, feeling greatly relieved. "You were no part of what they did. But did you see anyone with two dolls?"

"Dolls? There were no dolls."

The sheet slid off one muscular shoulder, and she hastily reached to rewrap him. Now that her panic had ebbed, cold clarity and common sense set in: the Virgin Queen of England was alone with her so-called favorite on his bed, and he was naked under that sheet. It terrified her how much she wanted to stretch out beside him to comfort and be comforted. But she must plan her next move, though that was rather like playing chess with a phantom.

As for keeping this attempted murder quiet, she agreed with Robin. She did not want him privily or publicly mocked by his enemies. Such ridicule must be the motive behind Hodge's death and now this. But these were also affronts against her. She had no doubt Queen Mary of Scots would laugh herself silly if she knew the illustrious Earl of Leicester had been displayed as a boar, a pig. Those rag dolls so lewdly tumbled together were bad enough—but this . . .

"Meg, Jenks, Ned," she called as she stood, "enter!"

"Yes, Your Majesty?" Ned asked, as if he were spokesman for the group.

"First of all, I hold the three of you accountable to keep what happened here a secret. If our Christmas culprit wants to cause more chaos, he must fail at least in having this noised abroad, or if someone gossips of it, we shall trace the source and have our man. Meg and Jenks, stay here while I question my lord Leicester. It is obvious he may have beheld our murderer, though the horrid experience has made it hard for him to recall."

"The blow to my head," Robin explained, his voice much stronger.

Elizabeth set down the flagon of wine and stooped to look closer at his head. "You didn't say that before. Hodge was hit on his head, too, yet I see no blood on you. Will it hurt if I touch it?"

"Never. Not your touch," he whispered for her ears only.

Perhaps the real Robin was back now, she thought. He looked almost smug. She felt through his thick, glossy hair, her fingertips skimming his scalp. He flinched. "There," he said. "I was hit there with something from behind, that's all I know. I can't remember anything else until I heard your voice at the door and tried to call for help."

Elizabeth realized she did not want Ned to hear all this lest she had to question him later. "Ned," she said, turning toward him, her hands still on Robin's head. "Oh—I didn't see you take those insulting messages out with you," she noted when she saw the parchments in his hands. "Leave them here, and go make a list of all those who were among the mummers tonight. Then I will have you as well as Lord Leicester and his servants peruse the list and mark off which men they are certain were in armor, and perhaps which one came late to be costumed and was the last one from the room with those damned dolls."

"What's all this about dolls?" Robin asked.

"I'll explain later."

"So by process of elimination, you hope to discover who hit me and arranged this part of tonight's performance—ow!" he cried, jerking from her touch on his head. "That must be the very spot I took the blow."

Strange, she thought, but unlike poor Hodge, not a bit of blood, scab, nor so much as a bump marred Robin's pate. The tender spot she'd just touched was inches from the first place that had caused him to flinch. But the man was hardheaded in more ways than one; a lump would no doubt rise like a goose egg on the morrow.

"So the last thing you recall," Elizabeth prompted after Ned left, looking much dismayed, and Meg and Jenks stayed by the door, "is running up the back servants' stairs. Those twist and turn so someone could be close to you yet remain out of your sight, even if you turned around to look back down."

"Which I didn't," he said, then added, "at least I don't think so."

"And, pardon, Your Grace," Meg put in from across the room, "but there's a small room off those stairs someone could have popped out of."

"Yes, that's true," Robin said, frowning. "I regret to say that I'm going to be about as much help in this as poor Hodge was."

"Jenks," Elizabeth said, "take a torch and search the entire length of those stairs to see if something was dropped. Look in the anteroom Meg mentioned, too."

"Yes, Your Grace. Shall I take these two signs, then? Mayhap we can match handwriting like we tried to do with the murderer's boot pr—" he got out before he evidently recalled that Leicester knew nothing of their investigation.

'S blood, Elizabeth thought, perhaps he knew now, so she might as well tell him everything. "Yes, when you go, Jenks, put those signs in my rooms. They are clues indeed."

"Wait!" Robin said. "Your Grace, I didn't see the signs you speak of, though I have suspected that you were privily looking into what seems to have gone so awry this holiday. Let me see those, man," he ordered.

Elizabeth gestured for Jenks to show Robin the stiff parchments with the heavy slashes of dark lettering. "It's someone clever with words," Robin said, frowning at one message and then the other. "He's clever but so evil that he's actually enjoying this, making a game of it all. And he hates me with a passion."

"And therefore hates and defies me," Elizabeth added. "All right, then, Meg, remain with me, and Jenks, be off with you."

"Sit again, please," Robin pleaded, patting the bed.

Instead, she shoved the nearest chair close and sat, leaning forward to hold his hand. "I assure you, I have a list of those who could want to shame or harm you, Robin. Sussex at the top, for obvious reasons."

"I'd wager my entire fortune on that."

"But he is so obvious, we must not jump to judgment. The wily Scot MacNair obviously resents your slighting, and therefore insulting, his queen. Lord Darnley and his mother detest you, since they want Darnley to wed Mary and probably think you're simply playing hard-to-catch with her, though I have reason to believe Darnley did not harm Hodge. Some suspicion for Hodge's demise has been thrown on that new blond player, Giles Chatam, but I can't fathom he'd dare all this. Oh, and have you had harsh words of late with Vicar Bane or his master Bishop Grindal?"

"I have indeed. A fortnight ago Bane warned me in no uncertain terms to steer completely clear of you but for council business. He believes I'm a bad influence, of course, a libertine who draws you even farther from the stern Protestant faith."

"*His* version of it," she amended. "Cecil and his wife have Puritan leanings, yet they are hardly harbingers croaking doom for such things as snowballs and a little fun at Yule."

"Exactly. At any rate, I saw Bane huddled with Sussex, so he may have put Bane up to warning me off. As Bane snidely put it, our relationship, yours and mine, my queen, might look morally compromising if I had the queen's ear—and perhaps had even more of her than that."

"He said that? The weasel! Then he is to be watched even more than I thought. And I saw him throw down his mumming mask tonight as if it were a gauntlet and stalk out early. Pray God he didn't do this to you and then don armor to try to shame me with that crude mummery of the dolls. My father was right to outlaw mummery however much everyone loves the tradition."

"Speaking of the mummery tonight," he said, "pray tell me about those dolls."

"All right. The last mummer to leave the hall pressed together two small figures which mimicked us in a most lewd way."

"Or in a loving way?" he countered. "Lucky dolls."

Though his grin was more of a grimace, she at least knew she had her Robin back. But things were different now. She would allow him to help her in the investigation. Cecil might balk, but she could use the extra help, and Robin must now be protected at all costs.

"I don't want to leave you alone," she told him. "Why haven't your servants returned?"

"I gave them leave to watch the festivities in the hall, then take their leisure with the kitchen workers tonight," he explained, scooting down in the bed as if he'd take a nap, "but it's not of my servants I must speak." He squinted toward Meg, then added, even more quietly, "You see, now I do recall seeing a single person on that staircase tonight."

"Meg?" the queen whispered.

"No, Ned Topside."

The next day, December 30, was Bringing in the Boar Day, originally a time to replace the domestic hogs supposedly eaten so far during the holidays with fresh meat. But, despite wanting to cling to tradition, the queen canceled the hunt, claiming cold weather. The truth was she could not face some other dreadful occurrence.

She still was not sleeping well, for the same horrid dream had disturbed her more than once.

In it, she and Robin walked the riverbank after their wedding. The marriage was not the nightmare of it, for she rather relished that, at least until the horrid part began. Down they went, holding hands, their feet and legs, then bodies, sucked into the bog along the banks. And all around them, as river water rushed in to drown them, stood a pack of dogs howling at the skies and baying for their blood.

Even now, she shook her head to clear it. She must ignore such sick fancies and solve what crimes had already been committed. She must stop whatever dreadful deed her tormentor planned for New Year's Eve and the first day of 1565, the seventh year of her reign.

"You wanted to see me, Your Majesty?" Ned's voice carried from the door of her privy apartments. She had told her yeomen guards to let him in where she and Cecil sat catching up on writs and decrees that could not wait for the new year.

"We did," she said, gesturing him in. She could tell that he was not happy to see Cecil and that he took note when her favorite yeoman guard, Clifford, stepped into the room instead of simply closing the door behind him.

"Ah," Ned said, "Secretary Cecil here, too. I heard there was a Privy Plot Council meeting earlier this morning without me, so I assume you want to catch me up on everything now. Your Grace, must I really stick so tight to Giles Chatam? He's starting to think I favor him, when I want him out the door when the players head for the shires again."

"Would you like to sit, Ned?" she asked.

"If it please you," he said and sat across the table from her and Cecil.

"Anything else to report on Giles?" she asked.

"He's got the heart of a rustic but the brain of a courtier, I fear. Sad to say, if he can't win me over—which he cannot—he'd probably just as soon knock me on the head to get my post."

"Knock you on the head? An interesting turn of phrase. Are you hinting that he might have knocked the earl out and wants to do the same to you?"

"I would not go that far—yet," he said.

"Then how far would you go?" Cecil demanded.

Ned had seldom been afraid, but he was now. Surely Her Grace could not believe, after all they'd been through together, that he was guilty of heinous acts. Ned knew how she still cared for Robert Dudley, her damned precious Robin. Why, if Dudley hadn't been suspected of murdering his wife several years ago, he'd probably be in Elizabeth's lap in more ways than one, and Ned would give anything to counter that.

But now he was starting to be terrified he wouldn't be around to keep that from happening. A few years back when the queen had discovered Meg had defied and lied to her, there'd been hell to pay, and that wasn't even a question of murder. However much she cared for Meg and valued her skills, the queen had banished her from court.

"How far would I go?" Ned threw back at Cecil, knowing he was about to play one of the most important scenes of his life. "I'd go to hell and back to help Her Grace."

"Then tell us," Cecil went on as if he'd suddenly become the queen's inquisitor, "why the Earl of Leicester saw you on that staircase where he was struck and from which he was, no doubt, carried or dragged to his room to be trussed like a dead boar. Ned, you really should have volunteered that you saw him rushing up that back staircase, to help jog his memory."

Ned's insides cartwheeled, but he fought to remain calm. "I thought it best to let the earl tell his tale while things were fresh in his mind, and then the queen ordered me away. The plain facts are that I saw him run out of the mumming preparations last night and thought he might need help, so I followed him. Of course, I would have brought all this up later in a Privy Plot meeting—if I'd been invited to the meeting."

"You say you thought you'd be of help to the earl, but you haven't been, have you?" Cecil parried, folding his arms over his chest. "To him or us?"

Ned didn't like the staging here, sitting across a table facing both queen and Cecil, but too late to change that now. He'd have to carry this off with commanding eye contact. "I called to him," he explained, speaking slowly, "but he was a ways ahead of me on that twisting staircase. When I caught up to him, he said I should head back down and keep an eye on things. If he doesn't recall all that, I would attribute it to his head blow, which must have been delivered by someone else when I left him. I immediately did as he said, went back downstairs, got into my armor—"

"On your own?" Cecil interrupted. "It seems no one recalls helping you don your armor, and most remarked they needed aid with it."

"Yes, on my own, my lord," he said, trying to keep his rising dread in check. Cecil had just given away the fact that they'd been questioning others besides Leicester. "After all, I've been in and out of stage armor half my life, and that's what that was, most of it," Ned plunged on. "The weather was too cold to send someone to the Tower to fetch pieces from the royal armory, so some of it was the property of my uncle's troupe."

"Yes, we heard. But back to the topic at hand."

Ned swallowed hard. Cecil was too wily to give things away without intending to, so he must mean to make him sweat a bit. Now he'd let on they were asking the Queen's Country Players about his behavior. Ned had not tried to change the subject just now, and curse Cecil for implying that in front of Her Grace. He prayed they hadn't questioned Meg about his trying to get her to vouch for him, because she'd said she wouldn't lie to the queen or even to Cecil.

"Ned," Her Majesty put in, "several of the mummers say you planned the activities for last night, though I take it the speech Leicester left in his chamber was his own. People have said that you planned the similar armor that made everyone look so alike. Furthermore, I recall that in a jesting way you mentioned to me both a peacock and roast boar shortly before Hodge Thatcher and the Earl of Leicester were attacked and horribly displayed as such."

He shifted his gaze, carefully, not dartingly, from Cecil's hard stare to the queen's worried countenance. Desperately he hoped she, at least, could be convinced to be on his side.

"Mere circumstance, Your Grace. As for the earl being named Lord of Misrule, frankly, it's been entertaining to help him. I'm happy to do it, for all the detailed planning is really not his strength, you know." He managed a slight smile and little shrug.

"What is his strength, then?" Cecil pursued, leaning over his clasped hands on the table. "Leicester seems to think you, like several others at court, might resent Her Grace's friendship with him."

"I'm just an actor, my lord, a servant, and not some peer of the realm to be dabbling in political or personal matters."

"Can you deny," Cecil said, narrowing his eyes, "you were especially annoyed that Her Grace named the earl Lord of Misrule in your place, when, indeed, so much of the work and planning for the Twelve Days has been yours in the past—let alone how all your preliminary work this year was simply assumed by him?"

Yours *in the past*—the words seemed to echo in Ned's stunned mind. What if the queen dismissed him and his career at court was in the past? What if he was forced to go on the road again, or worse, if she kept the handsome Giles to replace him? God forbid, what if she had him arrested for further questioning?

It was then that he made a gut-wrenching decision. All life was a gamble, wasn't it? He opted for being insubordinate and defiant rather than proper and cowering.

"Your Majesty and Secretary Cecil," he said in such a clarion voice that they both blinked and sat back a bit, "I see no reason such insinuations and slights should be aimed at one who has served Her Majesty well and would give his very life for her, indeed, for both of you. If you think I've done aught amiss, or am behind the dreadful deeds which I have been proud and vigilant to help you probe, say so and let me deny it plain. God's truth, but I am guilty of naught but perhaps pride and a bit of bombast here and there, a necessity in my calling. And as for not favoring the Earl of Leicester, I believe you yourself, my lord Cecil, have had harsh words with him and even harsher feelings for him over the years. Am I dismissed or worse, Your Most Gracious Majesty?"

"A pretty speech, but—" Cecil began, his usually controlled voice aquiver with anger.

"You are dismissed," the queen cut in, "only from the Privy Plot Council for now, Ned, because I want you to keep a closer watch on Giles."

"I see," he said, not budging immediately. Actually, he did see. How like the brilliant queen he'd adored and studied for over six years. She would keep her true motives close to her chest, but she would also keep him close. Time and again he'd seen her do that with those she suspected of deceit or treachery before she cut them down.

"I suppose I should be grateful you are even willing to see me," Margaret Stewart, Countess of Lennox, told Elizabeth that afternoon. The countess gave her usual disdainful sniff as the queen walked the Waterside Gallery for exercise with her ladies trailing behind. You might know, Elizabeth thought, in this Yuletide season, when most wore merry colors, Margaret was cloaked in black velvet and satin. As they turned back along the vast array of windows overlooking the frozen Thames, Margaret sniffed yet again.

"Have you a cold or the ague, Margaret?"

"No, I have what goes beyond a physical complaint, Your Majesty, and I thought it best I tell you."

"Please do. I much favor honesty. And so I will tell you that when the northern roads clear, Lord Darnley may visit his father in Scotland and, of course, personally deliver my best wishes to Queen Mary."

"But you have said so before and changed your mind."

"What is that they say?" Elizabeth countered. "Ah, 'Do not look a gift horse in the mouth,' I believe. Consider it my New Year's gift to both of you. And what is it vexes you so sore, Margaret?"

"This holiday especially you have treated me as if I am of inferior or no rank, Your Majesty. Kat Ashley is not of royal blood nor of the peerage, and you favor her more than you ever have me, worrying whether she enjoyed this or did she see that. Best queens should heed rank if they want theirs heeded. You did not ask me to tell a tale of my memories of Christmas the other night, but Kat told hers. And do you know what my Yuletide memory would have been?"

"I believe you will tell me," Elizabeth murmured as they turned and walked back again. Through the windows, she kept her eyes on activities on the Thames rather than on Margaret's sour face. It looked so cold out there, but she preferred it to the chill she'd always felt with this distant relative who had been so cruel to her in her youth when she desperately needed friends at court. Besides, Elizabeth was in a wretched mood today and didn't need Margaret's carping. She had a meeting with Vicar Martin Bane soon, and the mere thought of that was ruining the whole day.

"I recall," Margaret plunged on, "the Christmases when I was treated as one of the Tudor family, which I am. I recall the times I was esteemed and honored, harkened to, and trusted for counsel—"

"Times before you sent your son to woo Mary of Scots in France, perhaps, in direct opposition to my royal wishes?" the queen interrupted, keeping her voice low and sweet. "Times before, once she returned to Scotland, you parlayed behind my back with the Scots lords, perhaps times before there were Christmases when someone tried to ruin things with a dead kitchen worker, a box of stones, and a fox's head in place of a boar's head on a platter." Elizabeth wanted to throw the outrage about Leicester in her face, too, so she could read her reaction, but she bit her tongue. Perhaps whoever was responsible would make some sort of slipup on that.

"Well," Margaret declared huffily, "I have no notion of why you're fussing about all that to me!"

"Good. Let us keep it that way by not talking about this anymore, or talking at all. You see, I have a Christmas memory of when I was ten and you intentionally ruined my gown with gravy and told me I was skinny and whey-faced and had freckles bad as pox marks and that your ties to the Tudors would always elevate you over a king's bastard, so that I must walk at least two steps behind you. But Margaret," she added, taking a breath and ignoring the woman's shocked stare, "thanks to my good graces, here you are in step with me—perhaps even several steps ahead."

Abruptly, the queen stopped walking. Margaret swished past before she could turn back, but Elizabeth had already headed for the corridor to return to the royal apartments where Kat was waiting.

"You know," Kat whispered when Elizabeth told her what

Margaret had said, "the countess was in a foul mood last night, too. Even though her son was to be among the mummers, she left the hall before they came in. She was probably upset she wasn't the center of attention or given some special honor."

"Kat, you never cease to amaze me," Elizabeth said and gave her a hearty hug. "Do you remember when you used to help the Privy Plot Council solve crimes, and you'd keep an eye on people for me?"

"I do, but I'm glad it's not those dreadful days again, even if we are having an old-time Christmas."

Elizabeth smiled grimly as she left her ladies to go alone into her bedchamber to use the close stool. There she startled Rosie Radcliffe, bending over the table, rifling through the stack of court documents she had yet to sign.

"Oh, Your Grace!"

"Rosie, whatever are you doing? Why aren't you with the others?"

"I—I was, but I seem to have lost a piece of your jewelry—a bracelet, the one with rubies and emeralds you favor at Yule—and thought it could have come unclasped or snagged in these while you and Secretary Cecil were working earlier today."

Rosie went red as a rose indeed; the queen knew the bracelet was missing, but she had thought she'd lost it on Feast of Fools night. Could Rosie, who cared for the jewelry cases now that Kat no longer could, have hidden it to give herself an excuse to snoop?

The queen's stomach knotted, and her head began to hurt again. Surely Rosie had not been sent by her uncle Sussex to discover how much the queen knew of his plotting against Leicester.

Lest that be true, Elizabeth knew she must keep an eye on her too. It was a sorry state of affairs, the queen fumed, that at this joyous season, she couldn't trust dear friends much more than she could her enemies.

Chapter the Eleventh

Christmas Candles

At Christmastide only, much delight of the season can be added to candles, and not only through dipping them to additional thickness. As ever, for making fine beeswax candles use linen rags to wax and roll, but with links or torches use coarse hemp. For the holidays, the wax can be scented with scents such as lavender, rosemary, or lemon verbena. Dye the molten wax red or green, expensive though it may be. Red hues can be achieved by adding ground imported sandalwood or brazilwood from East India, imported by galleys on the Thames and purchased from a booth on St. Paul's Walk. If used at court, a rich Tudor green can be made by adding juice of spinach or crushed green wheat. Of course, such are the colorings used to make puddings, sauces, and gravies bright at table the year round.

"STATELY AND LOVELY AS THE STURDY FIR, SO STANDS *our queen, who may bend to help her people but shall never break. And should cold winds of foreign discord buffet her, she shall shed her cares like melting snow and be our guide and sign of green and sunny springtide days and years to come . . ."*

Elizabeth heard the flattering words echo off the hammerbeam ceiling of the Great Hall. From behind the decorative screen that kept drafts from creeping down corridors, she stood listening to the Queen's Country Players rehearse their new drama.

She knew they were planning a play that Ned had written but

Robin had carefully overseen lest other disasters befall. People were yet whispering of the dead privy dresser and the severed fox's head. Cecil had said rumors were rampant that the insults were aimed not only at Leicester but at her for championing him. Vile gossips were insinuating that a queen who could not control a court Christmas could hardly command a kingdom.

Now she and Robin were determined that all other entertainments planned for this holiday season must throw favorable light on the queen, for well they knew that stagecraft could be statecraft. Beyond that, how she hoped that her once trustworthy Ned did indeed believe those flattering words of praise he had written for this play.

With Lady Rosie and Lady Anne Carey with her, Elizabeth stepped from behind the screen into the hall near the dais the players were using for a stage. She surveyed their scenery. A wooden ladder poked above the canvas backdrop of painted snow and frozen Thames.

The first to see her, Ned's uncle Wat, gestured for the rehearsal to halt. She was both annoyed and alarmed that Ned was not among his fellow players. She had expected to see him here and perhaps spot Jenks off in the corner, for she'd told him to keep an eye on Ned and Giles, even if Ned did catch on. Should Ned question Jenks, he was simply to say that the queen had put a second watch on Giles.

"Welcome, Your Majesty! We are most delighted to have you visit our humble efforts," Wat Thompson told her with a grand bow immediately aped by the other actors, including the two boys dressed and bewigged to play women's parts. The handsomer of the two was attired as richly as a queen; indeed, he sported a red wig and a crown. The curly-haired lad wore a Tudor green gown with white puffs of satin on his shoulders and atop his hat and very bushy skirts. Then Elizabeth realized he *was* a bush—a fir tree, at least.

"What is the plot of this play?" she asked, though she'd meant to inquire first where Ned had gone.

"Ah, Your Majesty, you are puzzled by the two lads' parts," Wat said and gestured the boys forward. "Rob is the personification of you, the beloved monarch of our realm, as the sturdy fir—though graceful, too. Look graceful, lad," Wat muttered *sotto voce.* "And Clinton, more slender and prettier of face, is to represent you at the end of the drama, Your Majesty, as eternal queen triumphant."

"I've been symbolized by a great oak once, but never by a fir."

Even as Wat opened his mouth to reply, Giles Chatam stepped from behind him and spoke. "The fir is ever green, Your Most Gracious Majesty, ever young, strong, and supple despite the burdens of snow, wind, or cold—"

"Or," she put in, noting a stuffed nightingale stuck on Rob's shoulder, "despite birds in her branches. I am certain it is a lovely play. Shall I lend you a tiara in place of that tin-looking one?" she asked, gesturing toward Clinton's head. She frowned at the sight of it. The thing reminded her of the wire one the mummer's doll had worn last night.

"We would be most honored, *most* honored," Wat declared, stepping in front of Giles in turn, "and will guard it most closely. The performance is for January the third, Evergreen Day, Your Gracious Majesty."

"Then it makes even more sense than I thought," she told them. "And what part do the others play?"

"Of course," Wat said, glaring at Giles as he sidestepped again to be in the queen's line of sight, "you perhaps heard my voice as narrator of it all. Randall portrays our mighty England, and Giles is the new year with all its blessings and bounty to come, later to be draped in garlands of apples and walnuts, *et cetera.*"

"And Ned?"

"The old year which passes," Giles put in before Wat could respond. "Being much older in appearance and outlook than I, he'll be weighed down by a garland of regrets, I don't doubt."

It was the first time the queen had disliked the handsome man. The slur against Ned had been subtle but sly. "But do we not all have regrets?" she asked, staring at Giles. "Do you have none, even recent rueings of mistakes or sins, Master Chatam?"

"I, Your Most Gracious Majesty? I rue that I did not come to see my old playfellow Hodge Thatcher before his untimely death, of course. And that I cannot continue to live in Londontown, however much I admire this company of players and enjoy the countryside of fair England. Frankly, I rue that Ned Topside has a place in your court and in your regard I would die for."

She almost asked the brazen boy if he would kill for it, too. Surely he had not somehow set up Ned to look guilty of something he himself had done. All the mummers from last night, including Giles, Wat, and Randall, had sworn to Baron Hunsdon that they did not leave the presence of the other players and had no notion of which disguised man had produced the two dolls at the end.

Unfortunately, Elizabeth thought, Ned's own actions kept testifying against him. Today he'd disobeyed her by leaving his post here, as he had several other times recently. "Where is Ned, then?" she inquired, as if it were an afterthought. "I believe the old year is just as essential as the new one in this rehearsal."

"Don't know why," Wat said, "but he had business outside on the riverbank and said he'd be back in a trice."

"But a trice has come and passed," Giles said.

However angry she was at Ned, the queen came to mistrust Giles then and silently scolded herself for being taken in by his fine face and form ere this. A long shot he might be in this search for the Christmas killer, but he bore watching, and that tricky Ned was not here to do it. This time she wasn't sending Jenks or anyone else to look for him but was going herself.

Trailing Rosie and Anne, the queen hurried to her apartments to don her boots and hooded, fur-lined cloak. Kat sat alone in the early afternoon sun slanting through the windows. But that was not what seized the queen's attention; she stopped dead still where she stood.

Earlier this morning she, Cecil, and Harry had been minutely examining the two parchment signs Robin's attacker had bound to him. They had left them on the window ledges here. Now, with sunlight streaming in, something they had missed stood out starkly.

The two large sheets of stiff parchment, which were obviously of fine grade, not only showed the slashing strokes of dark letters and words but, beneath that, revealed even more.

" 'S blood and bones!" Elizabeth cried, stomping over to the windows.

"What is it, lovey?" Kat asked from where she'd apparently been contemplating sunbeams.

"Rosie," Elizabeth said, turning to her startled ladies-in-waiting, "please take Kat for a slow stroll in the gallery, and I'll rejoin you here later."

"But I can stay here with you, if there's a problem," Rosie said, nervously plucking at the folds of her skirts.

"I'm not leaving if anything's amiss!" Kat cried.

"Neither of you is to worry," Elizabeth insisted. "Lady Anne will be quite enough company for now." When Rosie looked as if she'd balk, the queen began to panic that perhaps Sussex *had* told his niece to keep an eye on her queen. "Rosie, perhaps you can look for my lost bracelet while you are walking in the gallery," she added pointedly.

At that, Rosie hustled Kat out while Anne remained. "Whatever is it, Your Grace?" she asked.

"I want you to go fetch both your lord husband and Cecil for me, quickly," Elizabeth told her as she pounced on one piece of parchment and held it up close to her eyes in the sun.

When Anne hastened to obey, Elizabeth seized the second sign, then darted to her table, where a pile of documents still went unread. She scrabbled through her papers until she came to what she wanted. When Cecil and Harry came in with Anne, the queen had three pieces of parchment, the two large ones with big, bold lettering and a smaller one with regular script, set on the windowsills.

"A clue right under our noses we missed!" she said by way of greeting and pointed at the parchments.

"You are brilliant as always, Your Grace," Cecil clipped out as he hurried to the windows and stooped to get on eye level with each parchment in turn. "How could we have missed this? Sometimes it's the tiniest, most everyday thing that escapes us."

"It is indeed, my lords, but I've learned the hard way that is the important thing about solving crimes. Do you remember the old adage 'For want of a nail, the shoe was lost, for want of the shoe, the horse was lost, for want of the horse, the rider was lost'?"

" 'For want of the rider,' " Cecil added, " 'the battle was lost, and for want of the battle the war was lost.' "

"But you have not gone far enough, Cecil," she added, "and that's what worries me. 'For want of the war, the kingdom was lost,' and I'll not have that here!"

"But the clue you're speaking of here still escapes me," Harry said, shaking his head. "What in heaven's name are you two talking about? We already went over all that writing, but it was too big and crude to try matching to any of our possible villains' regular hand script."

"The watermarks in the papers," Elizabeth said.

"They all match," Cecil muttered, nodding.

"But those indicate only the place the parchment was made or purchased," Harry protested, though he too bent to look at the ghostly watermarks on the three parchments. "I've seen it done, Your Grace. A wire in a shape to identify the parchment's maker or seller is pressed into each piece of wet rag before it's dried."

"Harry," the queen said as Anne came up behind her husband to also peruse the papers in the sun, "some watermarks indeed identify the prospective buyer, if he or she is of great wealth or power—or of righteous reputation . . ."

"But what, exactly, does this watermark depict?" Cecil asked, turning the smallest parchment upside down. "I just hope we can trace its dagger-like shape."

Almost giddy with excitement to be getting somewhere in this labyrinth of leads—and to be outthinking Cecil—Elizabeth could not help but smile. "The watermarks are not dagger-like shapes, Cecil, but the now burned spire of St. Paul's."

"Aha," Harry said, sounding pleased to be following at last.

"Which," the queen went on, "was not replaced after the fire, because I would not allot the Bishop of London and Vicar Bane the money they wanted for it. As you recall, the city needed additions to St. Bartholomew's Hospital. Bane dunned me hard for the funds, but I have a duty to my treasury, to Parliament, and to my people. So I did not give in to building the steeple rather than helping the hospital when I had already donated much toward the rebuilding of the cathedral's roof."

"And revenge for tying the purse strings, which made Grindal and Bane look bad, could be a secondary motive," Harry declared. "Your Grace, perhaps your declaration of a festive Christmas is only rubbing salt in their already open wounds."

"Exactly," she said, hitting her fist in her palm. "Now look closely, my lords and Anne, at the small parchment which matches the others. That is an epistle charging me to 'clean up Christmas' which Vicar Bane sent me just yesterday."

"Aha!" Harry repeated. "But would an educated man like that be so stupid as to tie signs to Leicester with the bishop's watermark on them?"

"We didn't think to look for watermarks at first," Elizabeth argued while Cecil put the small epistle close to his face and sniffed at it.

"Remember, Your Grace," he said, "when my sketches of the boot print and of Hodge's head wound took on the scent of that flowery *pot pourri* of Mistress Milligrew's?"

"You mean you smell that there, too?"

"No, I smell smoke, as if the very pores of the paper have

soaked it in. Smoke and the faintest whiff of—something sweet, I think it is."

He extended it to her, and she sniffed at it. "I warrant you are on the mark, my lord," she told him.

"But those very scents could have come from this room," Anne put in. "Smoke from the hearth here, sweet scents from the strewing herbs or even the queen's fine-scented clothes."

"No," Elizabeth said, shaking her head so hard her pearl drop earrings rattled. "Unlike these larger pieces of parchment, this letter from Vicar Bane has been somewhere unique. He's hardly one to have sweet scents on his person, so perhaps it's a question of where he wrote this letter or kept the paper. Now where could this have been stored or written that these other, larger parchments were not?" She took up both of the mocking signs, sniffed at them, then passed them to the others.

"No," Cecil concluded, "it's only the epistle from Vicar Bane that reeks of that strange smell, not these two signs. So does that mean Bane did or didn't knock Leicester unconscious and truss him like a roast boar—or bore, as this sign says?"

"I believe," the queen said, "I shall now look forward a bit more to my meeting with Vicar Bane today, to discuss," she added, taking his letter and reading from it, " '*that signs from heaven are wreaking havoc on our pagan, impure court and city Christmas which could soon spread to all the kingdom.*' You know," she added, looking at each of her cohorts in turn, "the smoke of this letter reminds me of the burning of the boathouse. Cecil, I'd appreciate it if you could spare a man to keep an eye on Vicar Bane for me, after I speak with him—unless he gives himself away and I have him arrested."

"I've just the man."

"Harry and Anne, I was about to take a walk outside to find

Ned Topside, and I just had a thought that I may know where to look."

"Where's that?" Harry asked.

"Either where the stones were taken from this building's very foundation or, more likely, the place where Cecil, Jenks, and I were almost baked alive."

In the biting air on the riverbank, Ned Topside had no idea what he was looking for, but he knew he had to find it. The idea had occurred to him when he'd looked out the window of the Great Hall. He'd climbed to the top of a ladder from which two pillowcases of cut lace would be dumped, sending snowflakes from heaven onto their makeshift stage during their little drama on Evergreen Day. From the ladder, he could gaze out the high windows at the riverbank, where he'd seen four workmen raking up the rubble of the burned boathouse.

Being forced to leave off watching Giles and taking a chance on disobeying the queen's orders, Ned had made excuses and set out.

"Find anything unusual in this mess?" he'd asked the workmen, hoping the queen hadn't given them those very orders. He should have come out here ere this to look for evidence left behind.

"Metal oarlocks," the big-shouldered one told him as they raked through the ruins, which had finally stopped smoldering. "Fire started underneath and went up, so's not much wasn't charred real good."

"Charred bad," his loutish-looking fellow worker corrected him, as if they were tutors about to give a lecture on good grammar. " 'Course things that was dragged out, like the royal barge, was saved."

Starting to feel cold instead of warm in his excitement, Ned nodded as he gazed at the big barge, wrapped with layers of protective hemp like a massive mummy.

"Where did they get that much hemp?" he asked the workers. "I could use some of that for a court entertainment I have coming up."

"Don't know," the big-shouldered one said to him.

"I do," muttered the lout, who suddenly wasn't looking so loutish after all. "The boatmen good as robbed the chandlery of it, and there was a real fuss, 'cause hemp's needed to make extra torches for the holidays. You know, like the one I saw way over here," he added and shuffled to the very edge of the charred pile to lift the remains of a short torch called a link.

"Was that found in the charred remains?" Ned asked, walking through snow and ash to look closer at it. What was left of its wax showed it had been dyed red for Yule, so it must be a current one. "But why didn't it burn up, too?" he added.

" 'Cause it was over here a ways!" the man told him, vaguely pointing in the direction of the Bishop of London's Lambeth Palace. "It didn't come direct from this burnt pile," he added as if Ned were a dunce.

Ned knew link torches were made by pieces of hemp being dipped in precious beeswax and rolled together, then attached to a short pole, though little was left of this one but a red stub of waxed hemp and the shaft. The point was, Ned thought, as his pulse quickened, it was an expensive link only someone of wealth or position would use. And it had been evidently heaved out of the way of the burning building, or perhaps dropped when someone fled.

He'd take it to the chandlery in the back buildings of the palace and see if one was missing or if someone had asked for an extra, especially just before the boathouse burned. After all, individual types of lights were doled out by rank, and these colored Yuletide ones might be carefully counted. Most of the men the queen suspected could probably lay their hands on a fancy link like this, though Ned was around the palace enough to get his hands on one, too.

Sadly, this evidence did not bode well for him to throw suspicion on Giles Chatam: Besides the fact that a man of his station would not have access to such a link unless he stole it, Chatam had not been staying at Whitehall when the boathouse burned or when Hodge was killed. Although Giles might have burned his own parents alive in their house, Ned finally faced the fact his own goose was cooked unless he could link this link to someone else the queen suspected.

Holding it gingerly, Ned spun to hurry back into the palace. Standing in his path, Jenks waited not ten feet away, legs apart and arms crossed over his chest. But worse, slightly behind him stood Baron Hunsdon and the queen herself.

"I—I believe I've found a clue," Ned blurted, looking straight at Elizabeth as he rose from his shaky bow and held the link out toward her.

"Of . . . ?" she said, not budging. He thought she looked livid; surely the wind could not have polished her usually pale cheeks that red.

"A link . . . that is, a torch, no doubt a fairly recent one from the palace that appears to have been heaved aside in haste—from over there," he added, gesturing toward the general direction of Lambeth Palace. It was then, as rattled as he was, inspiration hit him. "The Thames was fairly well frozen that night of the fire," he plunged on, "so someone could have slipped across the ice from that direction, from Lambeth." Though his arm was shaking, he pointed directly at the Bishop of London's property and prayed the wily queen took his bait.

"But you just said it appears to be a torch from my palace," the queen countered, narrowing her eyes in the wind—or at him.

"Yes, but Bishop Grindal's emissary Vicar Bane is in and out of the palace like a specter day and night!" he insisted.

"Let me see that," she said, and Ned hastened to hand it to her.

"What if," Baron Hunsdon said, "its scent matches that of Bane's epistle and the stench of this burned boathouse? It's all circumstantial evidence, but it's starting to add up."

"Bane's epistle?" Ned declared. "I hope not more condemnations and threats against the queen's Christmas?"

"Let's not get off the subject of your behavior, Master of the Queen's Revels," Elizabeth said, her voice as cold as he felt. "I asked you to remain with Giles Chatam, and yet here you are out by the boathouse. It reminds me of the night of the fire when I commanded you remain with Meg in my apartments and yet you left her and went out who knows where."

"My stomach was indisposed. Yes, I stepped outside for a breath of fresh air. I—I simply wasn't myself that night."

Ned knew he was talking too fast. He hadn't dressed warmly enough; he was shaking, and his teeth were chattering. Jenks and Baron Hunsdon seemed to block him in now, as they all stood facing the queen. He hoped Jenks didn't know he'd been trifling with Meg, but both men would do anything for Her Majesty, even, no doubt, turn on one of their fellows of the Privy Plot Council. Her Grace had looked only worried when she'd questioned him before, but now she looked outright angry.

"You weren't yourself—so you said. You didn't come out here that night to torch the boathouse in your anger at me for naming Leicester as Lord of Misrule, did you?" the queen demanded.

"How can you even ask such of me, Your Grace?"

"Stow your flippant rejoinders for now, Ned! I'm not suggesting you thought I was in the boathouse at the time, so it could have been mere coincidence that you burned it in a sort of protest and now came out to destroy the link you pilfered—"

"No!" he shouted and stepped back only to bump into the solid strength of Jenks, who had somehow shifted behind him. To Ned's utter horror, he heard Baron Hunsdon scrape his sword from its scabbard.

"I want to believe you, Ned," the queen said, "but I cannot take that chance right now. You tried to sneak the two lettered signs from the Earl of Leicester's room last night, didn't you?"

"What? No! As for this torch—I was going to check in the chandlery to see if anyone had taken an extra. Since the stubs are collected and remelted, I thought I could tell, especially with one colored for Christmas, as surely they keep close track of those—this, I mean."

He was losing control of himself in this nightmare. How long had it been since he hadn't commanded a performance, hadn't known all his lines and just where to stand and move?

"The chandlery! Of course," she said, nodding at Hunsdon. "That could be the source of the combination of scents on the epistle. Ned, you are relieved of your duties for now. I am sending you to stay at Greenwich for a while because—"

"But no one's at Greenwich! Just a skeleton staff! No one's coming to Greenwich for the Twelve Days!"

He knew at the moment of his outburst that he should never have interrupted her. Worse, he should never have tried to cover his tracks or conceal his resentment and anger at her. He fought to get hold of himself, to stand up straighter, to keep his voice in check.

"You're exiling me to Greenwich for the holidays, Your Grace?"

"Yes, we shall put it that way. And when people ask where you are, I shall say—like that night I went to the kitchens and then the boathouse—you are indisposed."

"I was only trying to help, always," he said, his voice suddenly sounding very small.

"We shall see. I'm afraid," the queen was saying to Baron Hunsdon and his wife, Lady Anne, "that locking up everyone I suspect of not dealing straight with me may be the answer, but then there would be so few left for the New Year. Jenks, see that Ned gets inside, and then have my yeoman Clifford escort him downriver."

Accompanied by Baron Hunsdon and Lady Anne and carrying the burned red link, Her Majesty headed back toward the palace. Ned saw her sniff at the link again as if it were a bouquet of flowers some fond, departing lover had given her.

He stumbled as he turned away with the grim, stoic Jenks walking behind him, now not a companion but his guard. He craned his head to look back at Elizabeth of England, suddenly fearful he'd never be summoned or scolded and smiled upon, mayhap never see her again. He prayed that his years with her would not soon be mere memories. What if he would never again make her laugh, or trade puns with her, or help her privily to ferret out someone who would harm her people or her person? However could this Christmas and New Year, his favorite season of the year, have gone so dreadfully, deadly wrong?

Edward Thompson, alias Ned Topside, once called the queen's fool, Master of Revels and Lord of Misrule, only realized he was crying when his tears iced on his cheeks.

Chapter the Twelfth

Wassail

As the word wassail *means* drink hail *or* drink health, *it is the perfect libation for the Twelve Days. Heat 3–4 pints of ale or beer and add 1/3 cup of sugar and 1/4 cup mixed spices such as 2 cinnamon sticks, 1 tablespoon of whole cloves, and 1 tablespoon of allspice. Cut up 2–3 small, sweet apples, sprinkle with brown sugar, and bake in the oven for half an hour. After heating the liquid and apples together, beat egg whites until very stiff and float them on the drink so it looks like lamb's wool to help keep the tipplers warm. Place the drink in an outsized bowl, the more ornate the better. Sing wassail songs going from door to door, carrying the bowl, wishing all folk well, and hoping they refill the bowl so the merriment may continue all the night.*

THE QUEEN'S FIRST THOUGHT WAS THAT THE PLACE THAT made lights for her palace looked very dim indeed.

But for the kitchens, structures that employed open fires were set apart for safety, so the chandlery huddled among the back buildings near the smokehouse and laundry. The large room with its vent hole in the ceiling and pots of molten wax simmering over wood fires was one place at Whitehall she had never visited. It smelled of the soot that encrusted the walls and ceiling, but—her heart beat harder—there was also the faint hint of floral scents.

"All here within," Harry's voice boomed out from the door set ajar, "your queen is paying you a holiday visit!"

His voice echoed in the domed room; the three women stopped stirring and gaped. The only man in sight, bent over his desk writing, exploded to his feet and bobbed a bow while the workers, still holding wooden paddles dripping red or green wax, curtsied. Their full-length canvas aprons, stiff with wax, crackled.

As Elizabeth's eyes adjusted, she saw that ropes strung with different-size candles, links, and torches draped the stone walls. Great loops of woven wicks, ready to be cut to proper lengths, hung like wreaths on hooks; rolls of hemp and linen and stacks of torch poles were piled around the room.

"I can see you are all hard at work," she told them and threw back her hood in the warmth, though she kept her cloak wrapped tight to avoid splatters. "You are the master of my chandlery?" she inquired, regretful she did not know the man when she could rattle off the offices, titles, and names of so many in her service.

"Aye, Firk Bell, Most Gracious Majesty," the small, thin man replied. He looked as jumpy as if his feet were being held to a fire under the vats. "Ah, something wrong with that link, then?"

She handed him the stubby light. "I am wondering how much you can tell me about this and the person to whom it might have been allotted. It is from this chandlery?"

"Aye, made just a few weeks ago," he told her, squinting at it. "Melted us a new batch of the same Surrey beeswax Penny's been astirring, much demand for colored, scented lights for the rest of the Twelve Days."

"I can't tell if that link is scented."

He sniffed at it. "If 'tis, the odor's light, but with real good candles they only give out scent when they're burned, Majesty. As to who could have had it—pardon if I look in my books," he said as he scuttled over to his table, walking backward so he wouldn't turn away from her. "Hm," he said, then louder to his staff, "all of you, back to work or the vats will crust over. You know that, and I shouldn't have to tell you—pardon, Majesty.

"Links this length," he went on, bobbing up from his desk again, "shorter than the torches for your chambers and the Great Hall, go to many nobles and advisors, but I'm trying to recall who got the red and who the green, 'cause we didn't mix them, but I'm not sure we had a method, that is, we have a method and I keep good books, but not with colors, 'cept for Vicar Bane, of course."

At that, Elizabeth could have fallen into a vat of wax. She glared at Harry and shook her head to warn him from blurting something out. She'd been intending to work up to mentioning Bane.

"Except for Vicar Bane?" she said. "And why is that?"

"When he's here at Whitehall, a great deal lately, must say, won't accept scented candles—smacks of popish incense, he says, told us that several weeks ago."

"So you make special unscented and plain candles for Vicar Bane?"

"Unscented, of a certain, Majesty, but he wants red ones, picks them up himself, the color of martyr's blood, he says."

"Although lights are always allotted and then delivered to everyone's rooms, he comes here to pick them up himself, Master Bell?"

"Oh, aye, likes it here better than anyplace else in the fancy palace, he says, 'cause it 'minds him of where the scribes and Phar'sees of the day are headed, you know, to Hades, to burn forever, preached me quite a sermon on it 'bout a fortnight ago, said fancies and fripperies at Christmas was the devil's work. And sat here just a few days ago at my writing table to wait for his allotment of candles and links, working on his 'spondence."

She fought to remain calm while her heart nearly beat out of her chest. It must be Bane behind all this. "You mean his correspondence?" she asked.

"Aye, that's it. So other than the red and unscented—which this one might be," he added, sniffing again at the link in question, "not sure who got scented red ones."

She would burn it herself to discover if it was scented, the queen thought, as she took the link back from Firk Bell. And then she would await her once dreaded interview with Vicar Martin Bane today with great relish. He was all too obviously a creature of darkness, who was working hard to provide hell on earth for the peacock Leicester and his fancy Christmas queen.

"What do you mean you can't find him?" Elizabeth cried when Harry, Jenks, and her yeoman guard Clifford returned empty-handed. When Vicar Bane had not kept his appointment with her, she'd sent them to bring him here. Now, at her outburst, all three of them looked mute.

"Well?" she went on, jumping up from the table on which the unscented red candle still sat smoldering. Both Robin and Lady Anne were with her. Once again, Elizabeth had sent Rosie out with Kat, then had summoned Robin to explain to him all their efforts to discover who was behind the bizarre insults and crimes.

It was Robin who spoke before the others could. "You heard the queen, men. Clifford, did you look in the chapel as well as in

Bane's chamber? Jenks, has he taken a horse from the stables? He's not the sort to enjoy the Frost Fair, but for all we know, he's gone out to chastise those having a good time out there. Best we send guards, armed if need be, to both Lambeth Palace and the bishop's house at St. Paul's, should he be visiting his lord and master, Bishop Grindal!"

"We will keep searching, Your Grace," Harry said simply, in effect ignoring Robin's commands. He gestured to the two men to follow him out.

"Clifford, stay a moment!" Elizabeth called, and the tall yeoman came back in and closed the door.

"Robin," the queen said quietly so Clifford wouldn't hear, "I've found it best to treat all in my Privy Plot Council kindly and keep my temper on a low simmer so as not to insult or scare off assistance."

She hoped she hadn't made a mistake bringing Robin in on all this, but, after all, he had borne the brunt of the attacks and had a right to help defend himself. When she'd told Cecil that the Earl of Leicester was *pro tem* on their Privy Plot Council, he'd nearly had steam hissing from his ears.

"It's only," Robin muttered, "that no one but us seems to be able to think for themselves."

"Unfortunately, the Christmas killer seems to," she whispered. "Clifford, a question before you go," she said, speaking louder and gesturing for him to approach. "You delivered Ned Topside safely to Greenwich and put a watch on his door?"

"Just like you told me to afore you accused him down on the riverbank, Your Majesty. It's a decent-sized room on the second floor, that east wing overlooking the river, and I asked for some wood for the hearth there, like you said. The skeletal kitchen staff will be sure he gets enough to eat, though it'll be plain fare compared to here. And I told the visiting players he's indisposed."

"At least, in a riverside room, he can watch the activities on the ice," she mused aloud, strangely angry with herself that she regretted sending Ned away. A pox on the bombastic meddler and prevaricator—or worse, but she missed him already.

"There's nothing much on the ice outside of Greenwich," Clifford said. "The Frost Fair doings are mostly 'tween here and the bridge. No, he's looking out at not much but snow and your herds of Greenwich deer been wandering out on the river."

Poor Ned, alone with only deer to oversee at Yule. At least if the phantom struck again while she had him locked up, she would know he was not to blame and could release him. Despite her frustration and anger at her principal player and former Lord of Misrule, that was her hope.

"That will be all, then, Clifford, and my thanks."

"No thanks from you ever needed, Your Majesty. It's enough—the best New Year's gift of all—I can serve and help protect you. We'll find the vicar soon and have him back here for questioning."

"See that you do," Robin piped up, reminding the queen again of one reason she abstained from matrimony. Never would she entrust the power she now wielded or the care she bore her beloved England to a husband, especially one who not only thought he was, but truly was, king of his castle.

Wassail, wassail, all over the town,
The cup it is white; the ale it is brown . . .

New Year's Eve had always been Elizabeth Tudor's favorite part of Christmas. Not only the continuation of wassail caroling but the gift giving, the sumptuous array of food, the first foot custom, and the fireworks . . .

> The cup it is made of the apple tree,
> And so is the ale of the good barley.

But tonight she felt tied in knots so tight she could scream. Cecil was standing stiffly by, frowning despite the merriment. Meg had red eyes from crying about Ned, Jenks was testy, and Rosie was sulking over the queen's continually sending her on distant errands. At the head table elevated on the dais, only Kat seemed to be oblivious to twisted tensions.

So much in the queen's view annoyed her, but then, she must admit, she was easily annoyed of late. Among her courtiers and guests seated below the elevated dais, Simon MacNair was all smiles and smooth manners as he chatted with Margaret, Countess Lennox, while her son Lord Darnley amused himself by leaning against the wall near the wassailers and ogling Giles Chatam.

The hall was ablaze with red and green torches sweetly perfuming the air, so Vicar Bane, who was still missing, hardly had a shadow to lurk in, should he appear. The pompous prig had now become first on her list of culprits, though she still had devised a way to test Sussex tonight. He was vexing her this evening by whispering to almost everyone he met, all while glancing askance at his queen—or perhaps at Robin at her side.

Meanwhile, Robin was sticking too tight, with his hand on his ornate sword, whether to protect himself or her from the next onslaught, she was not sure. Worse, though the Lord of Misrule was expected to give commands for the festive evening, he seemed to think he could also order her about.

Robin rose to his feet and cued the royal trumpeters to herald his words. When their clarion tones died away, the hubbub in the vast hall, stuffed cheek by jowl with peers, nobles, advisors, ambassadors, senior household officials, and servants, slowly quieted.

"By my decree, the order of events this eve," Robin announced grandly, "shall be the banquet, gift giving, and then the first foot custom, followed by fireworks on the Thames—one of my gifts to you, Your Majesty—which we shall all view from the Waterside Gallery. Your Lord of Misrule commands you to eat, drink, and be merry!"

"Did you have to put it that way?" Elizabeth groused, though she forced a smile as he sat back down beside her. "You do know the next line of that, don't you?"

"We shall not die but live and love, my queen," he told her and reached under the tablecloth to squeeze her hands clenched in her lap. His heavy touch there jolted her, but she managed not to show it.

"Rest assured of your safety," he promised, "for I have ordered all dishes not only to be tasted but to be brought in uncovered tonight, even if we eat cold food. There will be no surprises this night but in the opening of gifts."

"And in that, I pray there will be no more shocks such as that box of stones with its note that said they were for murdering martyrs. Which reminds me," she said, tugging her hands free and folding them on the table, "that Vicar Bane told my master of the chandlery he wanted red candles because red represents the blood of martyrs."

"Then it must be Bane behind all this."

"If so, he's taken leave of his senses, though perhaps he at first simply ordered Hodge Thatcher not to gild the peacock—a frivolity, of course—and Hodge refused," she rushed on, thinking aloud. "They may have argued, and it went awry. If Bane can wander into the chandlery, he could certainly drop in on Hodge through that back door to the kitchens. Bane must fear I have ferreted out his crimes—his sins—and so he's fled."

"Then we are safe this night and can enjoy ourselves," he tried again to cajole her. "And if it's Bane, I should have insisted I be the first footer instead of Sussex, but you were so sure putting him on the other side of that door would prove something."

"I knew he would be in a like position to you the other night when you were attacked, that is, alone for a moment. If he goes unbothered, it means something. Besides, I'm giving him a second opportunity to bring in a strange item under that cover I must open, and if something is amiss there," she said, glancing at Sussex, "I can at least accuse him of complicity against us and have him further examined."

"And if the first foot custom goes awry, will that mean everyone will believe we face a dreadful new year?" Robin demanded, though his tone remained light and teasing.

"I know it's a risk, but I can't help that. We may not even reach the new year if I can't stop these outrages now!"

"My queen, cannot we have some joy of this day? To cheer you, I must tell you what one of your gifts is. I took to heart, as I do all things you say, your Christmas memory you shared the other day."

She felt her panic mute, her fears momentarily soften. "The sleigh ride with my brother and father?" she asked.

"I've had metal runners put on a small wagon bed and lined it with soft furs and pillows. Tomorrow I shall take you for a ride on the river with it, clear to Greenwich, if you'd like, to see the Frost Fair and greet your people, who love you dearly—but never as much as I."

Tears wet her lashes, and she longed to hug him. "Robin, I thank you. That is so thoughtful and so dear. But if someone's out to harm you or me, we must take precautions for our safety."

"Jenks, Clifford, others can ride along. Somehow, with this jackanapes who has been bothering us, I think the farther from Yule food and your royal kitchens we can get, the better off we will be." He threw back his head and shouted a laugh that made her wonder if he'd been into the wassail.

Though deeply moved by his thoughtfulness, she couldn't help but fret that Robin could joke about what had happened to him and call it mere bother when he had nearly died. And *jackanapes* was nearly a term of endearment, something you called a naughty, saucy child. It hinted at capering and jesting, when their enemy was a foul plotter and killer. She was probably just too on edge, she thought, but Robin's mood reminded her of that bump on his head. Neither was quite right.

Ned judged it to be nearly midnight, but he couldn't sleep. Unless those ghostly hounds on the isle across the river—and he wasn't superstitious—were yet baying over the legendary watery deaths of their master and mistress, the queen's hunt dogs should be silenced. He stopped pacing and looking out.

The full moon in the clear wintry sky shed silver dust on the scene out his second-story prison window. He was being held in a chamber usually assigned to the staff of important visitors in the east wing, which had a view of the forest and, if one looked far sideways, the river flowing in from London. Moonlight etched the skeletons of trees, ice weighed down the river, and snow blanketed the Isle of Dogs, the entire view as heavy and cold as his heart.

"Hell's gates!" he cracked out to the empty bedchamber they'd locked him in.

He began to pace as he had all day since he'd been left here to rot. At least the queen hadn't sent him to the Fleet, Bridewell, or some other prison, he thought, trying to buck himself up. He wasn't of lofty enough rank to be put in the dreaded Tower, but if he'd been any sort of lord instead of her Master of Revels, she probably would have sent him there. He fancied that, if he pressed his forehead to the frosty windowpanes and craned his neck to look to the left, he could see its cold gray stones.

As he passed his tray of bread and cheese and cold sliced duck, he kicked at the table it was on. The single fat candle shuddered but burned on. He could full well picture what queen and court were feasting on tonight under a hundred blazing lights. He could hear the raucous noise, the rollicking music, the jests, of which he was master. Her Grace would be accepting expensive, unique gift after gift and giving her friends and advisors sacks of coins or silver plate in return.

And for her closest servants—well, she'd given them all fine Spanish leather riding boots last year. How rich the creaking, pliant leather had smelled, how very opulent it had been, so what was she giving out, perhaps even right now?

Though his eyes teared up, he sniffed hard to keep from crying. He forced himself back to the window to survey the frozen world outside. Down below, on the ice, he was certain he saw someone move. And not the deer he'd noted earlier, nosing about for water on the banks before settling for eating snow. Was that not a man on a horse, way down here, far from the Frost Fair?

He prayed it could be Jenks or Clifford come back for him, but he knew better. That was the only New Year's gift he longed for, to have Her Grace forgive his lies and anger and all they had wrought and call him back. But why would someone sent for him dismount out there in the cold and dark?

When he looked again, he saw naught amiss.

He stared out, wide-eyed but no longer seeing. He did want something else besides Her Grace's forgiveness. He wanted Meg's smile, Meg's approval and trust, Meg in his arms again, opening her mouth to his, Meg in his bed.

"Hell's gates!" he repeated as if cursing would cure his pain. He thumped his fist against the window, then saw something else move outside.

Another rider—or the same—had come up into the trees, but he seemed to have dismounted, to be hunched over. Perhaps a messenger had become ill, or decided to walk the rest of his way in, or his mount had gone lame. Whatever could the man be doing while his horse stomped impatiently, a horse evidently fitted with studded shoes to traverse the ice? It was a little too late to be ripping mistletoe off those huge oaks.

Ned scrubbed at the mist his breath had made on the thick pane, blinked, and stared yet again. No, he must have been totally mistaken, for now no one was there at all.

Chapter the Thirteenth

Figgy Pudding

Chop ½ pound imported, dried figs, and mix with ¼ cup bread crumbs. White manchet bread, preferred by those of wealth or rank, is best, but a lesser bread such as yellowish cheat is fine. Do not serve, at least at holiday time, the coarser breads of black rye or especially oats, favored in rude or rural places. Lightly brown 1 cup of autumn-gathered walnuts and mix with other elements including 1 cup brown sugar, 3 tablespoons melted butter, 4 beaten hen's eggs, and spices: ½ teaspoon precious cinnamon and ¼ teaspoon nutmeg. To make special for Yuletide tables of rank and honor, add ¾ cup of sugared citrus peels, perhaps left from the making of suckets. Bake for at least 1 hour and serve with cream or hardsauce; the latter made from Madeira or malmsey is best.

ELIZABETH WISHED SHE COULD ENJOY ALL THIS AS MUCH as Robin seemed to. She noted that the marks on his neck and wrists had faded fast, as perhaps the terrible memory of his assault and attempted murder had, too. That was what made him so merry tonight, to have back his life, which could have been tragically cut short, she thought.

"It's most generous of you not only to give me the sleigh ride but to foot the bill for tonight's fireworks," she told him. "But then you have always adored gunpowder and explosions of all sorts."

"Especially the sort we could have between the two of us," he murmured, leaning close with his big, brown hand on the table beside hers. "Around you, I am but a burning match, my queen, waiting to ignite your—"

"Favorite fireworks on the river. Ah, the first course!" she declared, nodding at Master Cook Roger Stout as he made his appearance at the head of the parade of platters.

The queen tried to smile, to nod and even applaud with the others when a particularly spectacular dish came in. She took a hearty swig of wassail, hoping that would help to lighten her heart. But she still kept envisioning a bizarre peacock, a fox's head with a gold snout, and Robin trussed like a roast boar instead of the fineries of the feast that were set before the queen.

If the uncovered banquet food came cold, fine, Elizabeth thought, for cold food was the first of the ten traditional courses; the second was hot, the third sweet, and onward through a great array. The red gravies, blue custards, and yellow sauces looked especially festive against the layers of white linens covering the table, which glittered with silver plates and glass goblets. Huge saltcellars in elaborate shapes adorned each table. All the guests soon fell to with their personal knives and spoons.

Accompanied by the wail and beat of music from the elevated musicians' gallery, sallets came first, some boiled, some compound, followed by a flow of fricassees, boiled meats, stewed broths, and sundry boiled fowls. Then all sorts of roast meats, everything from capons to woodcocks. Wild fowl, land fowl, and hot baked meats such as marrow-bone pie arrived to make the table groan. Next came cold baked meats of wild deer, hare pie, gammon of bacon pie, then shellfish, though not so many dishes of that since the rivers were solid ice.

Among the sweets came candied flower petals, fat green figs from Portugal, dates, suckets, tarts, gingerbread, florentines, and spiced cakes, and the queen's childhood favorite, figgy pudding, though she merely picked at it now. At last came the annual massive marchpane masterpiece, rolled in on a cart. People stood at their places or even on benches to see a miniature frozen Thames with tiny booths upon it and a replica of Whitehall Palace on its bank side. All of this was washed down with a selection of malmsey, Gascon or Rhenish wines, beer, or ale.

As the tables were cleared and her courtiers lined up for the exchange of gifts with their queen, Elizabeth's spirits began to sink even more. This was the point at which Ned had always stepped forward to amuse and amaze her guests with quips, jests, or riddles. What a riddle these Christmas crimes had become, she agonized. She could not bear to believe Ned was a deceiver and a killer, and yet a parade of evidence suggested that very thing. On the morrow she intended to send guards out looking for Vicar Bane, but now a whispering Sussex, an ever watchful Simon MacNair, and a gloating Robin were driving her to distraction and—

She almost choked on the last bite of figgy pudding. She had just put her dear Robin in the list of possible villains when she knew he could not possibly be guilty. No, the attacks had been aimed *at* him, and he'd suffered greatly, being mocked and molested.

Putting down her golden spoon and nodding that her place could be cleared, she noted a smiling Simon MacNair working his way through the press of people to stand before her.

"Some happy news, I hope," she told him by way of greeting as she stood and was escorted to her throne under the scarlet cloth of state.

MacNair hurried behind her, chattering. "Although I have gifts for you from myself and from your royal cousin, the Queen of Scotland, Your Most Gracious Majesty, I wanted to give you another sort of gift, if you would allow it."

"What sort of gift?" she asked warily.

"Sleight-of-hand tomfooleries, Your Majesty. Queen Mary adores them between courses or entertainments, and I thought you might, too."

"I'm not in the mood for surprises, nor is our court like Queen Mary's."

"Of course not, Your Grace," he said, still smiling up at her most pleasantly. "I swear to you there will be no silly dolls or boxes of stones. I offer naught but blessings for the beautiful Queen of England at this start to the new year," he declared with a flourish as he produced a gold crown coin from midair, one with her likeness on it.

Elizabeth laughed as other crowns seemed to drop into his flying fingers from his nose, his earlobes, and then—with her permission—her chin. Ohs and aahs followed, until quite a crowd had gathered, watching raptly. Soon her lap was full of coins, and she was delighted at their bounty. Was this, she wondered, the gift from him or his queen? Cecil shuffled forward, and Robin leaned in with his hand still on the hilt of his sword, but this clever display seemed harmless enough to her.

"Sir Simon MacNair, you are a man of surprises and hidden talents," she told him, loudly enough for all to hear. "Imagine, tricks with crowns—and my very image—disappearing and then appearing."

He only laughed as he seemed to lift a coin from Robin's pouting lower lip. "And now," MacNair added as he flapped open a large linen handkerchief, "will not Your Grace wager these coins by allowing me to wrap them in this cloth?"

"Will I get them back with interest?" she demanded, as it seemed everyone in the room leaned forward, breathless to see what the Scot would do next.

"I do promise you it will be interesting."

All this made her miss Ned dreadfully. Even though voices in the crowd called out such things as "Never trust a Scot!" and "You've heard how tight they are with coins—and tight with their Scots whiskey, Your Majesty!" she put the crowns into his handkerchief.

Everyone, even the musicians in the balcony, went silent as MacNair knotted the handkerchief, then, holding the ties, swung the bundle once, twice, thrice over his head.

"And so!" he cried and untied it with a flourish. "See, Your Majesty, it still has crowns within!"

The queen saw the coins were gone, every last one of them. But within lay two gold-framed miniatures, each of a woman wearing a crown—herself and Queen Mary, only Mary was smiling and Elizabeth looked sober as a Puritan.

Everyone huzzahed and cheered and clapped as MacNair plucked them out and held them up for the crowd, turning so all could see. Elizabeth wasn't sure whether it was a slight or the miniaturist's failure that Mary looked far better, but she intended to pin MacNair down about it later. Yes, she was certain Mary's was more flattering.

"And so I ask Your Majesty's forgiveness for giving my gifts before those of loftier rank, but I could not contain myself," MacNair said with a deep bow as he produced a purse of coins from up his sleeve and offered them to her too. "I fear, Your

Grace," he added, his voice more intimate now, "that Ambassador Melville would have my head, my position at least, for this, but as he is not here, and it is holiday time . . ."

"When the cat's away, the mouse will play, my lord?" she countered, also keeping her voice low. "Do you find it difficult to answer to one who is not here to see the lay of the land, yet to whom you are responsible?"

"How logical and perceptive you are, Your Majesty. I fear that being at best the *aide-de-camp* to those greater than I is my lot in life, however high I rise. I began as the youngest of eight children and so must of necessity make my own way in life. I am envoy for an exacting master and an even more volatile mistress."

"My cousin Queen Mary?" she asked, fascinated. "And is she volatile, while you call me logical and perceptive? I give you leave to speak freely on this and would count it as a favor if you do so."

"Your cousin Mary Stuart, Your Grace, is sensitive and sensual, a creature of feelings and emotion. You, I have observed, may feel deeply, too, but your head commands your heart, for your intellect is most impressive."

Again, she found herself liking this man, though she could ill afford to. "I hope, though you are away from your people at this time of year," she told him, "that you will enjoy yourself among us. Is there aught else you would say before I proceed with the other gifts? For back in the array of them is a fine silver plate for you. And when your messenger Forbes returns from Edinburgh, I shall send him north yet again with a New Year's gift for my cousin and sister queen."

"You are ever gracious, and I am grateful," he said, shifting slightly so that he seemed to block Robin out for a few moments, though her Lord of Misrule was now giving orders for the exchange of gifts. "Just one more thing, Your Grace," MacNair said, whispering. "As the earl—" here he darted a look at Robin, then back to her—"proved he was not to be trusted by my queen, perhaps he should not be trusted by any queen, even one ruled by her head more than her heart, as queens indeed must be."

If he meant to say more, it was too late, for Robin turned back and clapped his hands to signal the highest-ranking peers to step forward first. By then Simon MacNair had melted back into the crowd.

As in every year since she'd been on the throne, New Year's gifts had been showered on the queen, including jewels, uncut or mounted in rings, pendants, or earrings. She received finely wrought saltcellars, ink pots of Venetian glass, and the traditional gifts of garments: ivory-ribbed fans, veils, sets of sleeves, bejeweled stomachers, embroidered smocks, cloaks, ermine muffs trailing silken ribbons, collars, and the new-style wider, stiffer ruffs. Lengths of russet and garnet satin, red grosgrain and taffeta, damask and camlet. Scissors, pinchers, penknives, fragrant filigreed or porcelain pomanders, bodkins, ear pickers, tooth pickers, hair crispers, and ornate seals. In turn, according to rank or service, for each presentation, Elizabeth's Lord Treasurer gave the giver the appropriate weight of coin or plate.

Many crowded even closer to see what the Earl of Leicester's gift would be. He held his presentation for last, a set of twelve gold forks imported from Italy.

"What are those?" Kat asked, leaning close.

"Ah, tiny pitchforks," Sussex put in, "to prick all of us when we misbehave."

Elizabeth looked up straight into Sussex's pale blue eyes. "And have you been misbehaving, my lord?" It was so unlike the man to jest that she took it for a clever if circumspect criticism.

"They are all the rage for spearing food," Robin said, his stance rigid and his tone taut as he and Sussex seemed to square off again. "However, they are so civilized that Ireland, where you've been, Sussex, or Scotland, for that matter, will never have them."

MacNair, political creature that he was, merely frowned from afar at that, and Elizabeth silently blessed him for not jumping into the coming fray. She put her hand on Robin's arm and smoothly poked him in the ribs so no one could see, while she said quietly to Sussex, "I believe it's nearly time for the first foot custom, so best you'd go before you put your foot in your mouth instead of over the threshold, my lord."

Swallowing his stubborn pride, Sussex went out the side entrance behind the screen. He would walk around to the front doors, which had been barred all day, and enter from there.

Cecil edged closer to the queen; by tradition, at ten minutes until midnight, he took out his timepiece and signaled the musicians. They began to play a fanfare. Heads turned toward the main doors. Although the queen felt the first foot custom was mere superstition, it was one many still clung to and one Kat dearly recalled.

The honored "guest" came in precisely at the stroke of twelve, carrying a large silver salver on which sat—under a cover—something traditionally green and growing, such as a potted plant, to symbolize the new year. At court, the first footer was admitted by the monarch, since he or she must accept the gift. Supposedly, all sorts of bad luck could befall if the first footer should hesitate or trip. Many English households followed the same custom, but word always spread throughout the kingdom of what had happened at the palace.

Now, in a way, Elizabeth thought as she rose to walk toward the doors, Sussex had become an actor in her play. She had set a possible trap for the molester and the murderer who terrorized her court and ruined her Christmas. She did not mean to make Sussex either scapegoat or sacrificial ram, but she hoped the villain might take advantage of this coming moment: Sussex stood alone with a covered tray. If he were assaulted—and surely, as a military man, he was on his guard—or if something insulting or shocking appeared on his salver, she would go on from there to link it to him or someone else she suspected.

And, but for Vicar Martin Bane, she knew exactly where all her possible candidates for the Christmas culprit were right now. Margaret and MacNair were in her line of sight, as was that damned Darnley, who was hanging drunkenly on an annoyed Giles Chatam, while Ned was safely stowed at Greenwich.

In the hush of the crowd as the new year approached, Elizabeth started toward the doors to open them. The crowd of courtiers parted for her as the Red Sea had for Moses when he was fleeing Pharaoh's murderous hordes. Though her yeomen guards lined the room, and Robin, Jenks, and Harry came behind, hands on swords, she clutched a fork she had seized at the last moment. Inspired by MacNair, she had it hidden up her sleeve, a personal if paltry defense against what might await her on the other side of those closed double doors. She was certain the villain would do something new on New Year Eve's.

. . .

During the gift giving, while the dishes had been cleared from the banquet tables and whisked by in the corridor between the Great Hall and the kitchens, Meg had easily lifted the remnants of figgy pudding off a passing tray. Morosely, she had shuffled into the kitchen and sat alone on the hearth and picked the figs out. She was expected to be in the Great Hall for the first footing, but no one would miss her in that crowd, and it wasn't Ned at the center of attention this year. He was as good as the queen's prisoner, sent to exile from court and Christmas, and Meg was both furious and fearful about that.

"You not going out for the ceremony, then, Mistress Meg?" Roger Stout asked her as he hurried past. "I'm going up to watch from the back of the musicians' gallery. It's in less than five minutes, I'd wager."

"Oh, yes, I'm coming," she lied and didn't budge, though she figured she was probably getting her lemon yellow best skirts smudged, perched on the bricks like this. But the silvery embers gave off a steady warmth that felt good. Since Jenks had told her Ned was taken away, she'd been as cold as ice, and she and Jenks had had an argument over that.

So she wasn't just moping over Ned's predicament but over her own. Meg felt half of her had been ripped away, and she'd never felt like that before, not even when Jenks disappeared into plague London earlier this year. He was always kind and sweet to her, which Ned seldom was, so why didn't she feel the same sweeping way for Jenks as she did for Ned? What in heaven's name was wrong with her?

One of the sturdy-legged dogs that ran in cages to turn the hearth spits somehow got back inside from the small kennel out back and slumped at Meg's feet.

"You too, eh?" she muttered and fed it sopped pieces of bread she fished out of the pudding. Though apparently exhausted, the dog devoured each morsel. "Least you're not one of those howling dogs the queen's been having nightmares about."

"Want a meat tart?" the sergeant of the pastry, who used to ogle her, asked. She figured he couldn't see the dog at her feet as he rushed by, so he must mean it was for her. "I've got some leftover fancies here much better than those cold puddings, sweetling," he said with a wink.

"I'd count it a high favor," she said listlessly. "Just leave it there on the table." The man picked one off a shelf in the shadows, left it where she'd said, and darted out, probably to see the first footing, too.

The thing was, Meg thought, as angry as she was with Her Majesty for sending Ned to Greenwich when Meg was sure he was innocent of any part of the attack on the queen's Christmas, she did know one way to maybe help him out. If she did, though, she'd probably get the queen vexed at her, and she didn't need that, especially if she had to plead with her to keep Ned on. And the Earl of Leicester would have her head, too, if she told the queen what she knew about him.

Sighing heavily, Meg got up and took the meat tart off the table. When she bent down to give it to the spit dog, he leaped up so fast she nearly tripped over him and had to grab the edge of the table to keep from falling. As the dog devoured it, Meg went out to watch Her Majesty open the Great Hall doors to the first footer.

In the sudden hush in the Great Hall, the single knock echoed. At least it sounded, Elizabeth thought, relieved, as if Sussex was not only present but right on time. She opened the doors herself, and there he stood, safe and alone, holding the covered silver salver. Though Sussex was sure of foot and in fine physical form, Elizabeth held her breath as he stepped into the hall itself without hesitation, or stubbing his toe, or falling.

Amidst the swelling cheers and corporate sigh of relief, he went down on one knee and delivered his little speech. "Ah—a New Year's gift for—Your Majesty, though the Lord of Misrule—asked me not to, ah, gaze upon it."

Elizabeth could only be grateful his stumbling words did not count as a curse for first footers.

"Robin?" she said, turning to him. "Is something special on that salver?"

"Very," he said only.

Yet after Sussex's presentation of the cutoff fox's head the other night, she was fearful of what lay beneath. As she reached for the handle of the cover, she could see, distorted and bizarre, her reflection in its polished dome. Holding her breath, she lifted it to reveal a fresh sprig of mistletoe. And before she knew Robin would move—or before she could give him the permission he did not ask for—he kissed her in front of them all.

Silence stretched out at first, then cheers and laughter bubbled up, no doubt from Robin's supporters, while Sussex—and Rosie, standing beside him now—looked quite vexed. The queen felt she was two women, the one who had long loved this irrepressible man and the queen who could afford to love and trust no man.

"And now," Robin hurried on, perhaps fearful of which woman would speak, "your Lord of Misrule commands you all on to the Waterside Galley for the fireworks."

"Seen a few of those here already!" a male voice in the crowd called out as, once again, her courtiers parted for her to pass through to lead the way. With a tight smile on her lips, which still tingled from Robin's kiss, she ignored his proffered arm and walked back into the heart of the hall alone.

Her usual retinue swiftly fell into step behind her; the others surged forward. But as she passed her now empty throne, she saw a wooden box upon it.

"What is that?" she whispered as her gaze swept past Robin and sought Cecil. Where were Harry and Jenks when she needed them? The box greatly resembled the one that had held the stones.

"And who leaves a gift without waiting to receive one in turn?" the queen asked, her voice ringing out to quiet everyone.

"Does no one come forward to claim this gift?" Cecil asked, blessedly stepping from the press of people to help her. "Did anyone see who placed this here during the first footing?" No one spoke up; hardly anyone, she noted, so much as moved. "Then," Cecil said, "we shall take it with us, and you may open it later, Your Grace." He picked it up before Robin could get to it.

At the top of the great staircase as she led her shifting, swelling entourage upstairs, Cecil appeared at her elbow, carrying the box.

"Is it heavy?" she asked, turning her head toward him, for Robin walked on her other side and Sussex with Rosie and Kat behind.

"Not quite as heavy as stones. I'll take it into your apartment and look lest it be something that would harm y—"

"I'm going, too," she cut him off. "Lady Anne," she called to her, "you and the Lord of Misrule may escort everyone to the windows in the gallery, where I will join you shortly. I bid you, Robin, stay your signal for the fireworks until I arrive. Rosie, as ever, keep near Lady Ashley."

Taking only Harry with them, then admitting Jenks, who came

and knocked on the door, the queen and Cecil placed the box on the table in her presence chamber.

"Now that I see it closer and in better light," Elizabeth said, "I fear it is a very similar box to the one which held the stones."

"A box we erroneously thought held a murder weapon," Harry added.

"Stand back, Your Grace," Cecil urged, "and I will open it."

Harry stepped forward to block her from it as if it might explode. Cecil lifted the lid.

"Well?" she demanded, stepping out from behind Harry. "What?"

"Perhaps we've been too on edge," Cecil observed. "It looks to be just another normal New Year's gift."

"But no one claimed it," she noted, peering down at six heavily molded and embossed flagons resting in nests of red velvet. "Oh, a lovely set, though rather heavy and masculine."

"Perhaps a man picked them out," Cecil surmised.

"Best I lift them out for you," Harry said, and Elizabeth let him, touched by the concern they all showed her.

"All made from the same mold, I'd wager," Cecil said. "Expensive, too. Someone must have forgotten his gift or been tardy with it, then stepped out after the first footing and didn't hear you ask who had left these."

"Ha," Harry put in. "A gift this fine, someone will want to take credit for it."

Elizabeth picked up the first of the flagons and examined it closely, including the maker's hallmark on the bottom, a *V* set in the middle of a *W,* so it almost resembled one of those imported Eurasian flowers called tulips. The molded design on the exterior of the deep cups did not look like something recognizable but more like a swirling river current. The design was vaguely familiar, but after handling all the gifts tonight, she could not recall where she'd seen such.

"Ugh, this one's not been washed," Harry said. "Dried grape juice or red wine on one entire side of it."

"Wait," she said, still staring at the design. "Clean or dirty, I've seen this pattern before."

As Harry set each flagon on the table, others took them, turned them, tipped them, and peered inside. Elizabeth put hers down and seized the encrusted one.

"Maybe it's like a set you already have," Harry said when all six flagons were out and he had searched beneath the velvet on which they rested to find nothing else.

"No," she said. "I think we're looking at the pattern Cecil drew, the pattern of the crushing blow to Hodge Thatcher's skull."

"One of these is a murder weapon?" Cecil cried. "Then that dried stuff . . ."

"Hodge's blood," she said as chills swept her. "The Christmas killer is mocking us, daring us again by giving us the murder weapon we could not find nor figure out. That's his gift to me for New Year's, and I'd bet a throne he's not finished with us yet."

Chapter the Fourteenth

Winter Sallet

Indeed a good Yule sallet, fit for winter months, as it does not demand lettuce or spinach leaves, which may well have rotted in the cellar ere the holiday season. Mix together 2 ounces each of blanched almonds (with your shredding knife cut grossly), raisins of the sun, thinly sliced figs, capers, and currants. Dress them with 6 tablespoons olive oil, 2 tablespoons wine vinegar, 2 ounces of sugar, and a few leaves of sage in a deep dish. Cover the mixture with slices of 1 orange and 1 lemon, peeled and sliced crossways and laid in a circle. Put a thin layer of red cabbage leaves on top in a circle, then olives, all arranged in circles. Excellent sundry forms of such sallet may also include parsley, sage, garlic, leek, borage, mint, fennel, and rue, but be sure they be washed and picked clean.

"YOUR UNCLE, THE EARL OF SUSSEX, SAYS THAT WIND'S howling like a banshee out there, Lady Rosie," Meg said as she entered the queen's presence chamber with fresh strewing herbs the next day. At least, Elizabeth thought, Meg's eyes weren't red this morning, and she was evidently no longer avoiding her.

Elizabeth looked up from her card game of primero with Kat, Anne, and Rosie, annoyed that Meg had come up with a word she did not know. But since Sussex had said *banshee,* she'd best pursue the comment.

"That must be Irish Gaelic," she told Meg. "What did he understand it to mean?"

"Overheard Lord Cecil ask him the same, Your Grace," Meg replied, coming closer, "but the earl claimed the word is Scots."

Anne discarded and said, "Funny that your military man sent to Ireland comes back with Scottish words."

Elizabeth frowned, wondering if Sussex, like Robin and, of course, MacNair, had been in communication with the Scottish court. "Perhaps Sussex heard it from Simon MacNair," she said, glaring at Rosie, who had yet neither found the missing bracelet nor convinced the queen she wasn't her uncle's spy. "Meg, did he say what the word means?"

"Oh, yes. It's something about a female spirit whose wailing warns a family that one of them will soon die."

"How dreadful a thought on this first day of the new year," Kat said.

"Especially with all we've been through," Elizabeth agreed and glared at Rosie to warn her not to defend her uncle. Could Sussex be intending that as a warning he was planning another murder, the queen agonized, or was it mere chance he said such?

Elizabeth frowned down at her hand of two queens—hearts and diamonds—and her lower-count cards. She would surely lose this hand. Worse, she'd tossed and turned all night and felt exhausted, so it was just as well her official visit to the Frost Fair and ride in Robin's sleigh was put off until tomorrow. The so-called banshee wind was buffeting the booths and scouring snow off rooftops to cascade it down as if it were snowing again.

At least the stiff wind had come up after the fine fireworks display Robin had presented last night, so it had gone off without a hitch. Ignited gunpowder had sent rockets, firewheels, squibs, and pikes of pleasure vaulting into the air from the frozen river. Folks at the Frost Fair had been able to enjoy it as close as the court, while others from the city crowded the banks of the Thames to cheer and clap. There had not been as many fireworks as last year, but she had not complained, for, with all that had been happening, she thought it best not to make a pompous show.

"Was there something else you wished to say, Meg?" Elizabeth asked, looking sharply up from her cards again as the girl hovered.

"I was just wondering if you have heard from Ned—I mean about him. Jenks and I are most concerned, that is."

"So am I," Elizabeth admitted, spreading her cards on the table, only to be beaten by Rosie's hand. The young woman squealed and scooped up the small pile of silver shillings as the queen rose. "Meg, come over here," Elizabeth said, and motioned for her to sit beside her on the pillows in the window seat.

"Yes, Your Grace?" She obeyed but looked poised to flee.

"There was much circumstantial evidence against Ned, and I have exiled him from court for his own good right now. If he is locked up at Greenwich and more dire events occur here, such as the box of flagons last night, then I shall know he is innocent and release him."

"Pardon, Your Grace, but what box of flagons?"

"Ones which may include the murder weapon used against Hodge."

"Oh, then you can call Ned back if they appeared last night."

"I choose to wait a bit longer to be very sure."

"No one told me about flagons," Meg said, lowering her voice. "Was it two of them in a velvet drawstring bag?"

"No—six, nestled in velvet. Why did you say two?"

Meg mouthed the words. "Because that's what Lord Sussex

bought at St. Paul's Walk that day he met with Giles Chatam. You know, when I was following Sussex, and Ned was trailing Giles."

"Ladies, I thank you for a lively game of cards," the queen said, rising, "and would be alone for a few minutes but will rejoin you soon."

"Is aught well with you?" Kat asked, rising and coming closer. "I know that look, lovey, and it means you're fretting."

"Nonsense. We've all just had too much Christmas and New Year to boot," Elizabeth teased as she hugged Kat, then shooed her women from the room. When the door closed, she said, "Meg, come over here and look at these flagons."

"Yes, much the same," she said, examining the one the queen handed her. "At least it's the general style and pattern of those displayed on the shelves of the pewterer at St. Paul's."

"And you and Ned witnessed Sussex buy two of them, then whisper to Giles?"

"These exact ones, I'm not sure. But, Your Grace, if Ned could be brought back, he could help to identify them, too, as I'm sure he got a much better look at them, so—"

"For his own good, Ned stays where he is right now, but you have indeed helped his plight. Meg, just as Kat can read my expression, I warrant I can read yours after all our years together. There is more that you would say on our investigation, is there not?"

"No, Your Majesty. I've said it all, and you have every right not to take my advice about Ned."

They stared each other down a moment, as if Meg were an equal who did not deign to drop her gaze. The queen felt they were fencing, but over precisely what, she was not certain. If only she could recall where she had seen plateware or drinking vessels with a design similar to what these flagons bore. She'd had Harry and Anne traipse down to the storage room and look through all her New Year's gifts to no avail.

"Then you are dismissed, Meg, and have Clifford fetch Sussex to me immediately."

"Ah, yes," Sussex said, turning one of the flagons in his big hands, "I've seen their like. Works of art, every one of them."

"Seen their like where?" Elizabeth asked, trying to keep both her excitement and temper reigned in.

"Fine work done by a, ah, Master Vincent Wainwright, who has a portable booth in St. Paul's Walk. Works at night, sells during the day, I've heard, and don't know where he lives."

"Are you his patron or some such that you know his name?"

"Merely a customer, Your Grace, but then so are others of your court and no doubt many in the city. Wainwright was in fact indirectly recommended to me, ah, by Leicester."

"What? Considering that you two cannot communicate without nearly coming to blows, am I to believe you were speaking civilly with Leicester, and he kindly suggested you buy from Master Wainwright?"

"No, rather, I heard him suggesting to Queen Mary of Scots's man at your court—MacNair—that he send some to her because they were fine work."

"Yes, I believe Leicester still has a soft spot for that other queen in his heart," she muttered and began to pace. After all, she fumed silently, she had not yet forgiven the wretch that he had Queen Mary's portrait closer to his bed than the one of his own queen. And who knew but that Leicester had told MacNair where to get an artist for those miniatures that made the Queen of England look sour next to the charming Scots queen.

"Giles Chatam told you, didn't he?" Sussex interrupted her agonizing. "I mean, ah, that I bought some of these flagons? But what is the import of all this, Your Grace? Yes, I bought two of them from the same pewterer—and sent them both to my heir for a New Year's gift. Those flagons greatly resemble this one of yours, but, ah, the pattern is different, God as my judge, it is."

Elizabeth sank into a chair at the head of the long table in her presence chamber. She felt she grasped at straws again when she'd thought at last she had a handhold on all this. But she still wasn't ready to have Sussex or anyone else arrested for murdering either Hodge or Christmas.

"You sent them to your heir," she asked slowly, "who is not at court, so you do not have those different ones in your possession?"

"Exactly, Your Grace."

It smacked too much to her of Sussex's earlier far-fetched claims he'd hired Giles to recite a poem he'd written. But he had told her he could produce that, at least, and she'd not made him do it.

"Describe this Vincent Wainwright for me," she said.

"Oh, easy as, ah, pie to spot in a crowd when he uncovers his head, Your Grace. His hair is brick red, real russet in the sun, brighter than your own or even that herb mistress of yours."

"But it's hardly sunny inside St. Paul's, even if he did doff his cap to you, my lord. Have you seen him elsewhere in the bright winter sun, perhaps when you bought from him some other time?"

"I have not. Sorry if my—ah, explanation didn't suit, but

smoothness of tongue is not my strength, as truth and loyalty are, Your Grace."

Elizabeth always felt safe and happy among the common folk of her realm. The next day—Snow Day, it was dubbed on the holiday calendar—dawned brisk but sunny, and the bitter wind had spent itself. At midmorning, driven by Robin in his makeshift but comfortable sleigh, and followed by her entourage of eight mounted yeomen guards, the queen went sleighing on the frozen river. She regretted only that her most trustworthy yeoman guard, Clifford, was not with them, for she'd sent him to locate and bring in the St. Paul's Walk pewterer, Vincent Wainwright, for questioning. She needed a list of the man's clients and news of anything he might have overheard. At least the ever faithful Jenks had taken Clifford's place in her retinue.

Cheers and caps thrown aloft saluted her. She smiled and waved back, called out greetings and questions, and patted the fat cheeks of babies tilted toward the sleigh by awestruck, beaming parents. Where small crowds gathered, the queen gave short speeches wishing her fellow Londoners and Englishmen a prosperous and happy new year.

Booths, which had hastily been put back shipshape after yesterday's gales, were strung out for nearly half a mile. She graciously turned down offers of drink or food but admired wares for sale. The royal sleigh stopped at some booths for her to shop; she passed purchased gewgaws and trinkets back to her guards until their saddle sacks bulged. Though her men kept close, she felt freer than she had since Christmas Eve, when all the chaos had begun.

"Look at that big fishing hole they've chopped in the ice!" she cried over the noisy chorus of huzzahs as Robin reined in the horse pulling the sleigh. Bundled up to their eyes, men and boys stood or sat fishing around a hole in the ice the size of a banquet table, through which the cold, black-green Thames lapped roughly.

"I have a confession to make," Robin said, tugging one of her gloved hands from her muff and squeezing it in his.

"What sort of confession?" she cried, turning to him on their single seat piled with pillows.

"My fireworks the other night—some were embedded too far into the ice and blasted that hole open. And, evidently, these fishing folk have kept it that way."

"But someone could fall in! The current's fierce, and that hole could weaken the strength of the ice."

"Your people, as you can see, my queen, deem it a great favor to be able to get fish for their holiday tables. Don't fret now, for the Bible says it only causes harm."

Robin, instead of Bane, she thought, quoting scripture, and about causing harm. "Of course I'm fretting," she argued, "because I don't like being so near that big hole in such a heavy vehicle. Horses especially should not get close. Drive on. Look, over there, not far, some sort of performance."

Near the site of the burned boathouse, someone was staging a drama before a makeshift set surrounded by a crowd of at least a hundred souls. As the sleigh drew closer, the queen realized the scene was the skeleton of a stable and the performance a mystery play, one depicting the Christ child's birth, for several sheep had been brought out near a manger filled with straw. The poor beasts were all having trouble standing.

"They've apparently just started, because here comes the holy couple toward Bethlehem," Elizabeth noted as Robin reined in. The lad portraying the pregnant Mary was bent over and helped along by the older man playing Joseph. When the crowd saw the queen, they whispered and elbowed each other, then parted to give her a clear path to see.

Elizabeth noted that quite a few of her courtiers had found the performance. Giles Chatam stood in the crowd with other members of the Queen's Country Players. She saw Sussex standing a bit apart with his wife, and Simon MacNair whispering to a burly-looking man.

"Who's that with MacNair?" Elizabeth asked Robin, pointing.

"Duncan Forbes, the courier he sends to Edinburgh with messages for Queen Mary and *vice versa,*" he said, then looked so glum she realized he wished he hadn't answered.

"Oh, yes, the messenger you supposedly never used for your own privy letters to the Scots queen."

"As your Master of Horse, my queen, and I've seen Forbes at the stables, that is all."

"He returned from Edinburgh in all this weather rather quickly, did he not?" she asked herself as much as him.

A man wearing cleric's garb under his cape ran, then skidded, toward them on the ice. At first Elizabeth thought it might be the missing Vicar Bane, but it was someone she did not know. Robin began to draw his sword, but Jenks stopped the man a few yards from the sleigh.

"I'm in charge of this drama and honored to see Her Majesty here," the cleric called out, and she nodded for Jenks to let him pass. Trying to bow, he nearly went sprawling again.

"Though Christmas itself is past, Your Gracious Majesty," the man said, evidently so excited he forgot to give his name, "we will deliver the message of this holy season every day here and are so honored by your visit. Far more souls are in attendance than in St. Paul's Walk, where we gave it other years with no Frost Fair."

That rather pleased her. Vicar Bane had insisted that no good could come of such frivolity as a Frost Fair.

"I certainly hope," Robin said with a chortle, "you don't intend to have wise men ride in on camels, or they'll look rather foolish sliding all over." All three of them glanced at the meager herd of three sheep huddled together to keep from going down, spread-legged.

"Those sheep and a turtledove later for the feigned temple sacrifice is all, my lord," the cleric said. "You did hear the donkey Mary and Joseph should come in with slipped in that big hole at dawn and drowned 'fore we could get him out, didn't you?"

"I'm so sorry, for the animal and you," Elizabeth said and took one of MacNair's magical gold crowns out of the pocket in her muff to give him. She caught her glove on the gold fork she'd forgotten she carried there, because it had been a gift from her dear Robin and seemed a weapon easy to conceal. "You see," she told Robin, after the man hied himself back to overseeing the mystery play, "holes in the ice can be deadly!"

"They're safe enough unless one makes an ass of oneself," he said and boomed a laugh that made heads turn just as the angel appeared, straddling the peaked roof of the stable to hold up a star in one hand and a trumpet in the other.

"Robin," Elizabeth said, thoroughly angry with him now, "drive on!" He turned the horse away, and her clattering contingent followed. They had just begun to wend their way eastward on the river when the queen saw a young woman, red-haired like herself, out on the ice waving and shouting. Meg. It was Meg.

"Robin, pull over there."

"What then, Mistress Meg?" his voice boomed out as she came closer. She was hardly bundled against the cold but flapped a pair of gloves in her hand. With an obviously uneasy glance at Jenks, Meg came around the back of the sled to the queen's side, instead of reaching over Robin.

"Your new ermine-lined gloves, Your Majesty, the ones Kat gave you for New Year's," Meg said. "Those you are wearing are not half so warm."

"What the deuce, girl, stopping us for that!" Robin cried. "Her Grace has a fox-lined lap robe and me to keep her warm."

If that was a jest, no one laughed. Elizabeth frowned but saw in Meg's gaze that the gloves meant something. Yes, when she took them from her, one crinkled. She gave Meg her other pair, and, as they pulled away, she managed to extract from the new one a folded piece of paper. She thrust it into her muff with her coins and fork until she could find a chance to read it without Robin seeing, then pulled on the new pair of gloves. As she glanced back, she saw Jenks doff his cap to Meg and Meg wave at him forlornly.

As they sleighed gaily past the rest of the fair, then under London Bridge, waving up at people who spotted them, the queen tried to relax and enjoy herself. She kept her eyes on Robin's handsome face rather than the Tower, where her sister had once imprisoned her and her mother had been beheaded. After following the broad curve around St. Catherine's Dock, they were out in the country. How often in the early years of her reign she had wished to be off with her dear Robin, alone—or nearly alone—like this.

But perhaps, she mused, not so near the Isle of Dogs. In a way, she would like to visit her kennels of hunt hounds there as she had several years ago, but the ghost tales of the place Kat and Simon MacNair had told on the fox hunt had stayed with her. The two lovers, who supposedly drowned near this spot in the river while their hounds bayed, had haunted her. She shook her head to cast off her sense of deep foreboding.

As they made the next turn and spotted Greenwich Palace upon its snowy hill, her stomach cramped. Perhaps she should not have switched from suckets to eating so much sallet, hoping that would stop her ailments and her nightmares. Just as her hounds were kept in their kennels, poor Ned was prisoner in that east wing she could see emerging from the trees.

Ned could not believe his eyes, which were aching from staring out at the sunstruck snow. The queen was coming. Coming here, to Greenwich! With only a group of mounted guards—Jenks among them—in a sleigh, the Earl of Leicester at the helm.

His insides cartwheeled. Could she be coming to see him? Release him? Perhaps that lone rider he spotted the other night was sent ahead by her to make sure it was safe for her to visit during this dangerous holiday season.

Their backs against piles of pillows, Leicester sat close to the queen on the narrow length of seat. He held the reins with one hand, for his other arm rested behind Elizabeth's back as if he embraced her. They were covered to their hips by the same lap robe as if it were a blanket on the bed they shared.

Suddenly, Ned recalled something he had overheard Leicester

tell Sussex last month, something he had not told Her Grace at first because it would have made her angry, and then it had quite slipped his mind. Ned figured it was just more of Leicester's bravado, but maybe it had meant more.

Ned had eavesdropped on the earl's bragging to Sussex that Elizabeth had elevated him to the peerage and promoted him as Queen Mary's betrothed because she wanted the world to know he was good enough, not for the Scots queen, but for the English queen, to wed.

"She'll have me yet, man, you'll see!" the earl had said smugly to the irate Sussex. "She'll come around the first time something really goes wrong to shake her plans and she realizes she couldn't bear to see me hurt or to lose me. Once Kat Ashley dies, but for Cecil, I'll wager you a kingdom no one will be her confidant and mainstay—and who knows what else?—but me."

No. Oh, no! The sleigh had stopped on the river. They weren't coming up onto the lawn or to the palace. Leicester was getting out and carefully walking the ice to talk to the queen's mounted guard while Elizabeth herself bent over something in the sleigh. Was she heartbroken? Ill?

Ned shouted and beat on the thick windowpanes until his fists turned cold and bruised.

As Robin walked away to speak to her guards, the queen quickly pulled Meg's note from her muff. He had proposed taking her just a little farther down the river, without the array of men behind them. The idea had seemed both romantic and foolish to her. Actually, she told herself, she would have insisted he head back immediately to the city had she not been eager to read Meg's note and needed him to get out of the sleigh for a moment.

I should have told you yesterday, but Earl of L.'s foot, just like that of Earl of S.'s, fit the bootprint of H.'s murderer. I didn't think a thing of it earlier, since we never suspected L. of anything. But he did say someone hit him from behind while he was going up the back stairs. But to hit him from behind, the person would have had to be so tall, and the earl's already tall. Forgive me, Your Grace, to implicate one you love dearly as a friend, but I swear by all that's true, if your loyal Ned could be at fault, could not someone else close to you need watching, too?

Meg

Elizabeth crumpled the note and stuffed it in her muff as Robin started back toward the sleigh and her guards turned to ride away toward the city. She almost screamed at them to stop.

For suddenly, certain clues fell all too perfectly into place. Robin had not only been hurt but had benefited from the recent dreadful events. The bizarre display of Hodge's body obviously mocked Robin, but could he have set that up to get her sympathy? She had felt protective of him but had not drawn him into the investigation, so perhaps he'd decided to make himself look even more threatened.

They had found Robin naked, tied, mocked, and apparently almost dead, but he could have had one of his servants or grooms from the stable tie him up. Perhaps it was not truly as bad as it had looked. He'd showed no signs of the blow to the head he claimed; his welts and marks quickly healed. Then, indeed, she'd realized she loved him. 'S blood and bones, she'd nearly climbed into his bed! She'd taken him back into her heart and her protection and trust as she had not in years.

And now he was coming toward the sleigh, closer and closer while her guards wheeled about and headed away.

And the most damning clue? Although she could not picture Robin as a murderer, some still believed he had arranged for his wife, Amy, to be killed four years ago so that he could wed Elizabeth. She had banished him from her court and life, but he'd been exonerated and fought his way back into her heart.

But when she'd tried to offer him as consort to Queen Mary and was so furious with him over heading that off, perhaps he'd gotten desperate again and decided on something brazen and bizarre to make her take him back in her arms and life for good.

True, she'd named Robin Lord of Misrule, but he had begun to presume, to order her around beyond those bounds. He'd kissed her before the court, as if he were a husband who had rights over her, as if he were the king.

Damn the man! He was to be trusted about as much as her father had been! She was tempted to stab him with his own gift of gold fork.

Just as Robin lifted his leg to climb back into the sleigh, she seized the reins and flapped them on the horse's back. "Ha!" she cried and turned the sleigh to go after her guards.

"Your Grace! Elizabeth!" Robin cried.

Jenks looked back and saw her. Her men turned.

"Jameson," she called to one of her guards as she reined in and climbed out carefully, "I want your horse. I will ride back, so you will go in this sleigh with the earl. Jenks and one more man, follow me, and the rest escort the earl back, coming behind. And

Jameson, you are to stay with the earl to be certain he arrives safely back at Whitehall and remains in his chamber."

"Yes, Your Majesty," he said and dismounted. "But you usually don't ride so tall a horse, and on the ice, and never astride with this sort of big saddle . . ."

She should have been touched at his concern, but he was just another man ordering about the woman who was queen. "I can ride anything in Christendom, man," she said, "sidesaddle or astride. Just give me a boost up. Jenks, to me, and bring another guard," she called, cursing silently as she realized her skirt would make her ride sidesaddle anyway.

She ignored Robin's frustration and fury as he walked mincingly toward her on the ice. Refusing to look back, she urged the big horse up on the bank along the river path toward London. As she did, she remembered something else that could incriminate him. The flagon she'd held to Robin's lips after his ordeal had been of a similar style to the flagon that had hit Hodge.

Though she had to ride on the ice again when she approached the city, trailing her two guards, Elizabeth set a good but safe pace back toward Whitehall. She felt even sicker than she had before, for she could not bear it if Robin had made a fool of her and staged all this to force her to openly care for him again. The contingent at court who hated him would be baying for his blood this time, even if the one murdered was a kitchen worker and not his own wife of noble rank.

Elizabeth left the river along the eastern edge of the palace boundaries and rode back to the stables. No more time could be afforded to keep things secret, to coddle reputations, or to avoid hurting someone's feelings. Even if she panicked her court and word got out to the city and kingdom, she was going to question the royal stable's grooms, curriers, and smithies immediately. She must know if Robin, her Master of the Horse and former master of her heart, had been spotted anywhere the afternoon Hodge was killed. Maybe one of his men had overheard or seen something.

"Shall I take your horse back to the stables for you, then, Your Majesty?" Jenks asked as her guards came to ride abreast.

"I need to see my stables," she said curtly. "I've visited the chandlery and the kitchens lately, but not the stables."

She was surprised to see the wide stable doors closed, but it made sense with the weather. Seldom had she come back here this time of year, and never had she approached the stables from the side walls of the palace boundary. Nor had she ever noted the circle lined with benches and knee-high watering troughs between the back of the building and the walls that ran along the Strand.

"That's a training ring for spring and summer foals when they're first weaned, Your Majesty," Jenks told her when she reined in and stared at it. "Hardly ever used this time of year."

"I can see that from so few footprints in the snow. Go inside and tell all present I have come to wish them a good new year. I'll follow in a moment."

But when her other guard dismounted and stepped forward to help her alight, her horse shied away and bumped into one of the stone drinking troughs. "There, boy, there," she said and patted his neck to calm him.

As she did, she glanced down at the bench and trough beside her. Jenks was right in saying they were not used this time of year, for the seat was covered with blown snow and the thigh-high trough held not water but ice. And the ice of the one closest to her looked a strange blue-gray hue, as if it reflected the sky.

Still mounted, she brushed a bit of snow off with the toe of her boot and peered down, wondering if she would see her reflection. She gasped and nearly fell off the horse. Staring up at her was a man, wide-eyed as if in surprise, encased in solid ice as if he lay in a stone and glass sarcophagus.

She had found Vicar Bane.

Chapter the Fifteenth

Rye Pie Crust

Rye crust is best for standing dishes, which must be stored or keep their shapes, for it is thick, tough, coarse, and long lasting, mostly for show and not for digestion. Also, dough made with boiling water will hold better for shaping. This is ideal for display pastries at court, even large ones, namely those which contain live birds to delight the ladies when the pie is opened and the birds begin to sing and take wing. How many pockets full of rye measured for the crust depends upon its size. Such crusts can be baked, then slit open with care to introduce doves, blackbirds, or larger surprises. A rye pie can bring much merriment, especially during the Twelve Days of Christmas.

SO AS NOT TO ALARM THE COURT, ELIZABETH ORDERED Martin Bane's body to be hewn whole from the water trough in one large piece of ice, wrapped, and carried by her guards into the chandlery to be thawed in a vat of water over a slow fire. When she saw it would take too long to clean wax from the vats, she sent for the largest old kettle in the kitchens.

She had realized there were only two possible places to thaw out Bane's body, and she was starting to fear the palace kitchens. After she sent the chandlery staff away, only Jenks, Meg, and the queen kept watch over the fire melting the block of ice in water in the biggest iron soup kettle the men could drag in. Perhaps it had not been cleaned well, for leaves and pieces of vegetables floated to the surface, or else the particles were from fodder spilled into the horse trough and caught in the ice, too.

Her orderly world was turned upside down, Elizabeth thought, as she personally oversaw the gruesome thawing. Robin, who had authority over her stables, where the drowning must have occurred, was being detained in his bedchamber. Cecil, whom she wanted at her side, had been sent to interrogate him, while Cecil's men had been assigned to thoroughly question workers in the stables. Vicar Bane, whose realm should have been the chapel, was dead in the chandlery. Ned, who had always been able to lighten her heart, was exiled to Greenwich.

"Of course," Jenks said as they huddled near the kettle, "the vicar could have tumbled into the horse trough, hit his head, and drowned. Still," he added, obviously, Elizabeth thought, when he saw her frown, "however slippery one of those benches might be, why would he be standing on it?"

"Precisely," Elizabeth said, frowning at the debris floating in the water.

"So," Jenks went on, "the same someone as knocked Hodge and the Earl of Leicester on the head could have done this. In that case, he meant for him to drown and become a block of ice."

"He was a block of ice anyway, if you ask me," Meg put in.

"We did not ask you," Jenks replied.

The queen noted how the two of them snapped at each other lately. Usually when they'd disagreed, it had been with calm respect, not bitter bile, though Meg and Ned had often fought with passion. She sighed and thrust such personal problems away for now.

"Meg, it's bad luck," Jenks added, "to speak ill of the dead."

"Which," Elizabeth said, holding her hands out not only to halt their bickering but to be warmed by steam escaping the vat, "is why I have sent Baron Hunsdon to explain this as pure mischance to Bishop Grindal and the city coroner. Grindal has every right to know his vicar is dead, but we shall call this an accident until we prove otherwise, and we must do so soon."

"A sad way to mark the vicar off our list of possible killers," Meg said, as Cecil came in from outside and stamped snow off his boots.

"Well, my lord," Elizabeth said, striding to greet him, "did you turn up any evidence against Leicester?"

"In questioning him, I did not," he said, walking over to peer into the kettle, then moving away again to join her nearer the door while Jenks and Meg watched over Vicar Bane. "The earl seems to have an answer, such as it is," Cecil said for her ears only, "for every question or accusation. He says he is outraged that I would suggest he did anything to coerce favoritism from you, for 'Her Grace is ever mindful of me as a man and subject and her adoring servant,' or some such wild words."

She shook her head and bit her lip to fight back tears. "Have your men finished questioning Leicester's men in the stables?" she asked in a louder voice.

"According to what they have discovered so far," Cecil reported, removing his gloves and no longer whispering either, "Leicester was in and out the afternoon Hodge was killed. Unfortunately, of course, it is not far from the stables to the back kitchen entrance near Hodge's cubbyhole."

"It can't be my lord Leicester," Jenks insisted, coming closer. "I've served under the man all the years you've been queen, Your Grace. He's smooth and wily and wants his way, but—"

"That he does," Elizabeth muttered.

"—he's not a murderer. Can't be."

Can't be echoed in her mind. Can't be Robin, can't be Sussex, can't be MacNair, can't be Darnley and Margaret, or Giles Chatam. This was all becoming a hideous nightmare in which she felt she slid and slipped upon the icebound river, edging nearer a huge hole of wild, dark water, which haunted her dreams.

"Let's go over exactly what we do know about the time of Bane's death," Elizabeth said. "Vicar Bane was alive at least until last Friday, when I saw him rip off his mask and stalk out of the Feast of Fools banquet. Did any of you see him thereafter or speak to anyone who did?"

"Not I," Cecil said. "But you received that epistle from him rebuking the court's Christmas festivities on Saturday."

"No, on Friday, but I didn't show it to you until Saturday. I believe he wrote it—at least dated it—Friday. I sent men to arrest Bane on Saturday," she went on. "They say they scoured the palace and inquired at both of Bishop Grindal's homes, but Bane was at neither place nor had been recently."

"So," Cecil concluded, stroking his beard, "he must have drowned, or *was* drowned, between Friday and Saturday."

"I have independent evidence," Elizabeth told them, as each turned her way, "that it was indeed on Friday, between four in the afternoon and eight in the evening."

"Of course, the water!" Cecil said, snapping his fingers.

"What about it?" Jenks asked.

"The one question," Elizabeth explained, "I asked the grooms before you and my other guards carried Bane away from the stables was when they last filled that watering trough. Obviously, Bane fell in or was put in when it held water and not ice. When the stable lads refilled it at four that afternoon, Bane was not in there yet, but was soon after, for he lay deep in the water and it iced downward from above. The grooms were sure the trough nearest the doors was solid ice by eight that evening, but they hardly went around in the dark peering into all of them."

"Brilliant, Your Grace," Cecil muttered.

"Once I realized my horse and those of my guards had stamped through whatever footprints might have been in the snowy circle," she added, "I had to make amends—discover something."

"But how about outside the circle, then?" Cecil asked. "The murderer's prints inside it might have been obliterated by your horse's hooves or even yesterday's wind, but what if Bane were killed elsewhere and then carried or even dragged to the trough?"

"You will yet keep me humble, my lord," she admitted. "Jenks, it's getting late, but take one of the torches from the wall and carefully search about where my lord Cecil suggests. Look for footprints or drag marks, and if you find such, ask the lads in the stables if they've been pulling sacks of grain or whatever."

"All right," he said, "but one other thing, then, Your Grace. Long as I've worked in those stables, the troughs are not used in the winter, so why did the water get changed at all that afternoon? You want me to inquire about that, too?"

"It seems," she answered, trying to keep her voice steady, "that my Master of the Horse decided that the weight of that much ice might crack the stone troughs, so he ordered the water changed, though more than one lad said they had a tough time chipping all the ice out."

"Oh, no!" Meg cried. Elizabeth turned, thinking Meg would insist that proved Robin was guilty, but she was pointing into the kettle. "He's thawed, and will you look at this!"

They rushed to the kettle. Bane's head had floated to the top of the water, though he'd turned facedown with his pale hair waving like sea grass above him. One thin hand had risen to the surface, the fingers curled as if they had just released the folded piece of paper that bobbed in the water.

The queen took it out and carefully opened the sodden piece of stiff parchment. Fortunately, it was folded tightly inward, or the water might have washed off the ink of the printed words.

"Is it in the same hand as his letter cursing the queen's Christmas?" Cecil asked.

"It's in block letters, hastily formed ones, not in script, more like the mocking signs tied to Leicester when he was trussed like a roast boar," she said and read aloud:

> *To all who truly worship the Lord High God—forgive me for stooping so low to physically fight the sinful frivolities which degrade true Christmas. I should not have taken things so into my hands, for " 'vengeance is mine' sayeth the Lord" and not that of a mere vicar in His calling. I have sinned, but then so did the queen's privy dresser, the peacock and boar Leicester, and, most of all, the queen. "In the measure that she glorified herself and lived luxuriously, in the same measure give her torment and sorrow." Amen.*
>
> *Martin Bane*

"It's turned treasonous now," Cecil whispered.

The queen gawked at the note, her mind racing.

"But it's over!" Meg cried, gripping her hands together. "Bane was behind it all! Ned can come home, and it wasn't the earl to blame!"

"But," Cecil said, "who left that package of flagons on the throne New Year's Eve, then—after Bane must have died?"

"Maybe he planned for that before his death," Jenks said. "You know, as part of his confession to the crimes. A servant could have left it there for him, Your Grace. He could have decided to give up the murder weapon, then drown himself in remorse."

"To atone," Cecil whispered. "Yes, the guilt could have eaten away at him as it did Judas Iscariot when he rushed out and killed himself. Your Majesty, are you quite well?" he asked and touched her elbow to steady her, for he must have noticed how hard she was shaking.

"I think," she said, her voice trembling, too, "that Vicar Bane would be less likely to commit the sin of suicide than Hodge Thatcher, let alone murder another. But if he were in that desperate state of mind to drown himself, would he trust his confession note to a trough of water? Yet, it is on the paper to which he would have access."

She stooped and held the note toward the fire as if she would toast it. They saw clearly that the familiar watermark on the parchment matched the earlier ones.

"But the wording sounds like him," Cecil argued. "The quote is from the Bible."

"It's from Revelations," she said, standing. "And, however much I want to believe this nightmare is over, my revelation is that our murderer has struck again, even more cleverly so. Meg, help me lift the poor man's head just a bit. There!" she cried.

Although Bane's silvery blond hair had hidden it at first, he had been hit hard on the back of his head. They saw no blood or scab, but a livid goose egg of flesh had raised there, and the ice had preserved it perfectly.

"Just like Hodge was hit—and maybe the Earl of Leicester, too!" Meg cried.

"Nor do I think," Elizabeth said, as she and Meg let Hodge sink into the water again, "that the leaves floating in the ice with Bane are from an unscrubbed kettle or horse fodder, especially not those which are common seasonings like sage and basil."

"Why, yes," Meg whispered. "That's what herbs they are."

"Our kitchen killer," the queen went on, "is amusing himself again by presenting a murdered man—one who served me—as food. I don't care what this cleverly worded note says, I don't think the killer is Martin Bane. He's just another victim."

"And so," Cecil whispered, "it's as if the murderer has given us a cryptic recipe and forced us to make vicar soup."

"Exactly," Elizabeth exclaimed.

The next morning, Ned saw that a man—one he didn't recognize—was doing something on the ice, near where the queen and her men had been yesterday. He was quite bundled and muffled up. It must be someone from the meager winter staff at Greenwich, but why would he have ridden a horse out there when he could have just walked?

Ned reckoned he might be pounding small stakes or spikes in the ice for some sort of sliding race. Yes, that must be it, for he was laying ropes from those stakes along the ice toward this riverbank. Would it be, Ned wondered, games only for local folk of the small village nearby, or would the city or court people be coming, too? At least he'd have a fine seat.

He smiled grimly as he pictured again how the queen had

driven the sleigh away from the Earl of Leicester and forced him to ride back with a yeoman guard while, mounted, she'd left him in her dust—or scattered snow. If he had not seen that she knew to mistrust her Robin, Ned would have written a note telling her what he'd overheard between Leicester and Sussex and insisted it be delivered to Whitehall. He shook his head and sighed. It had always amazed him how the queen and Leicester fought, yet still loved each other. Now, it had come to remind him of how he felt about Meg.

All these years he'd spurned her, but he admired her deeply. She'd been only a girl who'd lost her memory and her past until the queen had given her a future. When he'd been ordered to teach Meg to walk and talk correctly so she could emulate the queen if need be, how quick she'd been to learn royal demeanor and delivery. He'd never told her that, though, told her quite the opposite. But through Meg's tough times, Elizabeth had cared for her, Jenks adored her, and Ned Topside . . .

"Hell's gates, it's just because she resembles the queen I adore, a form of the queen I can touch and possess," he gritted out, hitting his fist on the wood-paneled wall.

The thought amazed him. Could it be that loving Meg was the only way he could have a bit of the volatile, brilliant goddess Elizabeth? Or did he love Meg for being Meg?

He jumped at the knock on his door. "Stand back, then, Master Topside," his guard, Lemuel, bellowed. Ned heard the familiar latch lift and the key scrape in the lock.

"Evergreen Day on the calendar, then," Lemuel said with a broad smile as he came in. "Traditional meat pie day, my mother always said," he went on as if Ned could care about his family or his damned good mood. "Capon pie, it is, still hot, too, so's hope you'll eat better than you been so far." The big-shouldered man, one of the groundskeepers here, not even a real guard, put Ned's noontide tray down. It also bore bread, some sort of pudding, and a fresh flagon of beer.

"Hand me that chamber pot, then, so's I can dump it and bring it back," Lemuel told him, and Ned sullenly did as he was bidden.

This single guard who came and went wasn't much security, Ned mused, so Her Grace must believe he wasn't really guilty. Or she thought him such a milksop she didn't worry he'd manage an escape. If he tried disobeying her again, he was done for good with her—was guilty—that must be her thinking.

When Lemuel went out, Ned sat down and began to eat the meat pie, a good one, though all food tasted like sawdust to him here. He wondered how the large, hollow, fancy pie at court this evening would look and what would pop out of it when it was cut. He'd seen everything from doves to blackbirds to frogs jumping all over the table, making the ladies laugh or scream.

Two years ago, Ned had hidden in the pie himself and leaped out to deliver a lengthy paean to the queen. This year, if he were in charge, instead of Leicester—unless she'd replaced him, too—he'd have something inside it to tie into the play the actors were going to present to her wherein Elizabeth of England reigned ever green and fresh as a fir tree in the snow and ice.

Frowning, he rose to look out the window again. The man on the ice was gone. When Lemuel returned with that chamber pot, he'd just ask him if it was someone from this palace, Whitehall, or the Frost Fair, and what in heaven's name he was doing out there.

. . .

"The Earl of Leicester is demanding to talk to you to convince you of his innocence," Cecil told the queen the moment he entered her apartments. "He's making quite a fuss."

"Then see that he is informed of two things. Firstly, I do not parlay with those who think they can usurp my authority. And secondly, if he does not just sit there quietly and wait until I have time to see him, he will be trussed and gagged, and I know he is quite familiar with the arrangements for that!"

"Yes, Your Grace."

"Cecil, I thank you for not gloating," she said as he turned away to deliver her command.

"Gloating?" he echoed, obviously surprised. "Whatever I think of Leicester privily, I can hardly relish that he might indeed have murdered, or ordered murdered, two men who serve you, even as I serve you with great pride and care."

She pressed both hands to her head as if to hold her wild thoughts and fears in. "Cecil, I think I'm turning lunatic. It can't be Robin behind all this any more than it can be Ned, yet I am constrained to keep them constrained, and all because some demon is amusing himself by serving up my people as Yuletide food!"

"And here we stand, as at the first, waiting for the other shoe to drop."

"No, I have had enough of that. I am not taking a defensive position but am going on the offense. It's the way Sussex says he tried to fight the wild Irish, but they kept just disappearing into their bogs and fens. But this enemy will not elude me, I swear it!"

"Other than interrogating Leicester personally and hoping Clifford returns with that pewterer to question, what do you intend?"

"Come with me, my lord. It is in the kitchens that it all began, so perhaps we can find some answers there. These events have put me off food, and I've been avoiding the place like the plague, but no more. The battle is enjoined!"

Cecil hurriedly gave a guard her order to keep Leicester quiet, then followed her—she already had Jenks with her—down the servants' staircase and through the back corridor to the Great Hall. Now empty, it had already been decked out for the play and feast tonight.

The queen noted that the painted backdrop for the allegory had been turned to the wall. She started at a good clip toward the kitchens again, then turned back so abruptly Jenks almost smacked into her.

"What is it, Your Grace?" he asked.

"I am sick to death of surprises and of someone perverting our beloved holiday traditions," she said as she hurried between set tables across the hall toward the scenery with Cecil and Jenks hustling to keep up. "Move this backdrop out, will you, Jenks? See, it's all on little wheels, Ned's idea and a good one."

"We all miss him, Your Grace," Jenks said as he complied, and Cecil helped him move the set out a bit from the wall. Again, as ever, she was touched by Jenks's loyalty, not only to her but to her Privy Plot Council members when she was certain he would like Ned out of Meg's life.

"Ugh," Cecil muttered, "the backdrop is still wet—and rather sloppily painted." He held up his hand, green as grass under his smeared cuff and sleeve.

"But that was finished three days ago, and prettily done, too she protested and, holding her skirts tight, stepped between tl wall and the backdrop to gaze up at the entire expanse of it.

Her mouth dropped open, and her pulse pounded like fireworks exploding. The scene had been hastily painted over: The fir tree symbolizing her now looked drooped and tattered and was ready to topple into a hole crudely painted in the ice. Her stomach churned, for she recalled that gaping cavity in the Thames ice with the dark current of water beneath.

" 'S blood and bones, he's struck again!" she cried.

"You don't think Giles . . ." Cecil began.

"I don't know what in Christendom to think. Jenks, see that the play is canceled and this backdrop taken down. Indeed, I may halt the rest of the Twelve Days so this marauding murderer cannot keep getting the best of me. Cecil, there is one more thing I must examine to keep chaos from tonight's feast."

"What?" he cried, then just hurried to keep up with her again.

"I'm finally learning to outthink him, I vow I am," she threw back over her shoulder as she rushed toward the kitchens. "Evergreen Day it is, and he's tried to twist the scenery of a play to mock me. It's me he's after, Cecil, not just my servants or even Leicester."

"Then you think the earl's not to bl—"

"Whoever is behind this could have help."

"From someone in the kitchens?"

"I don't know yet, but what's the other tradition of this day?" she asked, not breaking stride as the delicious mingled smells from the kitchen block assailed them.

"You mean pies?" he asked, sounding out of breath. "Especially the large one you cut open with the humorous surprises in it?"

"Exactly! Just as I lifted the platter from over the boar's head

only to find a fox with a gold snout, what am I to find when I slice into that pretty pie?"

They did not have far to look for the masterpiece that the pastry chefs had cooling on a wheeled cart in the hallway by Hodge's old workroom. The outside door was ajar to cool the pie as big as a card table and perhaps also to air out the smoky kitchens. Master Cook Roger Stout, evidently told she was here, soon appeared at her side.

"And what is being placed inside the queen's pie this evening?" she asked him as he rose from his bow.

"Are you certain you want to know, Your Majesty?" the man asked, repeatedly wiping his hands on his apron. "After all, for it to be a surprise . . ."

"What will it be?" she shouted, only to have the man and several pastry cooks who'd followed flinch as if she'd struck them.

"Doves, Your Majesty," Stout told her. "Twelve doves to symbolize not only peace, the Earl of Leicester told me several days ago. He said it also stands for God's approval on the kingdom, even as a dove flew down to give the Lord God's holy blessings at His own Son's baptism in the River Jordan."

Her thoughts scattered, and she tried to grab them back. How sweet of Robin to have planned that. He could not be behind this. If something were amiss in this pie, would it not clear him as well as Ned?

"Your Grace," Cecil said, taking her elbow, "you are not going to faint?"

"Of course not!" she declared, turning to Roger Stout again. "When you introduce the doves into the pie, you don't need much of a hole, do you, Master Cook?"

"No, Your Majesty, as they are carefully inserted one at a time, just over here, in this large vent atop the crust."

"Which," the pastry cook closest to her added, "is then stopped up with a decorative piece of crust." She ignored the fact that the two pastry cooks were muttering something about giving all their secrets away.

"Then why," she asked, "does it look as if there is a section already cut out over there by the door, a larger piece than the vent, one which looks as if it's been fitted back in place? See there?" she demanded, pointing.

Stout rose and hurried around the pie, but the pastry cooks beat him there. "I—don't know. What happened here?" he demanded, turning on his underlings.

"So skillful, it's nearly invisible," one said.

"Someone's been tampering with the best work we've done all year!" the other protested.

Elizabeth strode to the section she had seen in slanting light from the open door. Though she intended to demand a knife to cut into it, Jenks arrived just then.

"Jenks, hand me your sword."

"Your Majesty," Cecil said, "let me do it lest something dire leap out."

"I'll be careful," she insisted, taking Jenks's proffered sword. She cut carefully into the pie along the lines already there, while Roger Stout leaned close to support that piece of pastry from falling in and the pastry cooks wrung their hands. Everyone crowded close.

"You are in my light," she told them, and all but Stout and Cecil moved back.

She peered into the pie that would soon hold the flutter of doves. Within lay the two dolls that had been used to mimic her and Robin on Feast of Fools night. This time it was not Robin who was mocked, for tied to the queen doll's wire crown was a pair of authentic ass's ears.

Chapter the Sixteenth

Pancakes

Take 2 or 3 eggs, break them into a dish, and beat them well; then add unto them a pretty quantity of fair running water; then put in cloves, mace, cinnamon, and nutmeg, and season it with salt; make it thick as you think good with fine wheat flour. Then fry the cakes thin with sweet butter, make them brown, and so serve them up with sugar strewn upon them.

THE QUEEN, WITH CECIL, HARRY, ANNE, JENKS, AND MEG in attendance, paced her presence chamber, trying to decide what to do next. She knew she must act, and not just continue to rant. On the table where she often took her meals lay the pieces of paper with the murderer's mocking missives, which, she was certain, included Bane's so-called suicide note. Cecil's sketches of the boot print and the blow to Hodge's head lay there. The box of flagons and the box of stones, gold leaf from Hodge's death scene and from the beheaded fox's snout, the stub of torch, and the dolls with the peacock feathers and ass's ears also sat upon the table as if they could tell her who had used them to ruin lives and Christmas.

"At least, I believe I know where our clever culprit got those ass's ears," the queen said as she turned to walk past her friends, who lined her path. "When Robin and I were out in the sleigh yesterday, we heard that the donkey for the Frost Fair mystery play had fallen through the ice and drowned."

"Amazing he wasn't trapped under the ice," Harry put in.

"I think not," she said with a shudder. "I have no doubt the carcass was hauled off the ice, and our murderer saw the opportunity for more mayhem." She sank into the chair at the head of the table and covered her face with her hands.

"Are you ill, Your Grace?" Cecil asked.

"Only sick to death of all of this," she said as she heard the others slip into the chairs around the littered table. "I just recalled that Leicester made a joke of it, a pun. He said something like those too near the hole in the ice—which he admitted his fireworks caused—were 'safe enough unless they made an ass of themselves.' "

She nearly cried. Although she'd seen many courtiers watching that play who could have heard about the donkey's death, Robin had also jested earlier about peacocks and boars. Yet he was being held in his room, so he must have someone else working with him who had placed the dolls and ass's ears in the pie.

But Jenks was the only one she knew upon whom Robin had relied closely and continually over the last six years. She used to think that was because she favored Jenks so, and Robin saw the man as a bond between them. Since Jenks's wit was for horses, could Robin have used him somehow to pull the wool over her eyes?

She spread her fingers to stare at Jenks. He looked brooding, but no doubt only with concern for her. Unless she had suspected Meg or Kat herself, as she had Rosie, no one was more loyal to her than Jenks, and yet it had just crossed her mind to mistrust him. Who would she turn against next? She could not—would not—live in a world where she could not trust anyone.

At that moment Elizabeth Tudor could not bear her loneliness. How could she think that those dearest to her, who had been through hell to help her get her throne and protect it, would betray her? No, she would not let the whoreson bastard who was killing Christmas kill her trust of those she valued and loved.

They all startled when a knock rattled the door. The queen nodded to Cecil, who stepped out quickly and closed the door so that no one could see the mix of persons huddled in such familiar fashion around her table.

"Your yeoman Clifford's returned, Your Grace," Cecil said as he stuck his head back in.

"I have often thought we must add him to our little council, but until then, best we keep up appearances," she said with a nod to Meg and Jenks, who rose from the table and hurried out into the next room. "And leave that door cracked so you can hear," she called after them, then nodded at Cecil to admit Clifford.

Her favorite yeoman looked worn and windblown with beard stubble shadowing his cheeks, but then he'd been looking for the pewterer Vincent Wainwright for nigh on two days.

"Did you track him down, Clifford?" she asked as he rose from his bow across the table while Cecil stayed by the door as if guarding it.

"First I tried St. Paul's," he reported, sounding out of breath, "but saw no one, then found out the tradesmen had all gone to set up booths at the Frost Fair. He wasn't there, so looked high and low near Cheapside where he was supposed to live, folks saying he'd been around, that he was here or there. But finally learned he'd gone home for a few days, to his parents' home, that is, to Southwark, so finally found him."

"And brought him back with you?"

"Wainwright's sicker than a dog, Your Grace. I know you don't want someone like that here. His mother says he just ate too many Yule sweets, but he says it's the gripes, so—"

"Did you ask him about who bought at least six flagons from him?"

"Oh, aye, Your Grace, but you won't like what you hear."

"Just tell me, man."

As he spoke, he ticked off about twenty names on his big fingers, including, "The Earl of Leicester, the Scots envoy MacNair, Lord Northumberland, Lord Knollys, Countess of Lennox—for her son, she said. Also, he said the Earl of Southampton, and several other courtiers whose names he didn't know all bought from him. Sounds as if he's caught folks' fancies for gifts this year."

" 'S blood and bones!" she cried, smacking her palms on the table. "It seems, Cecil, we are still in the same stew, though this testimony might help clear Sussex, if he only bought two flagons. Clifford, my thanks. Take what respite you can, and I shall summon you if I need to go out."

Clifford accepted that with a bow and quick retreat, but Cecil had barely closed the door before he remonstrated, "Go out where?"

"I would speak with Ned Topside and then release him."

"But we can send someone to return him here in a trice. It's but an hour before the early dusk, and it's cold out there."

"I know the hour and the weather, my lord! It's just that I do not know the answers I must have, and the walls of the palace are closing in on me as if I were inside that dark crust of pie just waiting to fly! You see, now this wretched mess has me speaking in terms of food, when even that has been ruined for me lately."

Cecil, arms crossed, still leaning against the door as if he would block it, jumped away as another knock resounded. The queen indicated he should answer it.

"It's Master Cook Stout," Cecil said, not even closing the door behind himself this time. "He's most distressed at something he's found."

Her pulse pounded in foreboding. "Megs, Jenks, stay where you are," she called to them. "Harry and Anne, remain with me. Cecil, let the man in.

"What is it, then, Master Stout?" she asked as he nearly bounded past Cecil. "Something else about the pie?"

"I've tried to keep a good kitchen!" he burst out after a haphazard bow. "But since poor Hodge's death, it's all been topsy-turvy, and now this!" he cried, waving a piece of parchment.

The queen jumped up and moved around the cluttered table to snatch it before Cecil could. She held it up to the window light. "Yes, St. Paul's steeple!" she cried, which she saw only perplexed poor Stout more.

"Bane's hardly back from the dead," Cecil muttered.

"It's a recipe," Stout said, wringing his hands as if he were washing them. "Someone's been tampering with my recipes!"

"Indeed, Master Stout," the queen said, trying to keep calm, "someone's been tampering with your recipes and all our well-laid plans. When and where did this appear?" she asked as she bent to read the small script in good light.

"Don't know exactly, but since last night. I have my book of them in my office, known by heart, for can't see taking them into the fray to get them splattered and stained. I didn't write it, and few of the cooks can write. It's a mockery, I tell you that, but not in my hand or anyone's I know!"

"But it's just about pancakes, Master Stout."

"My recipe is labeled 'Pancakes,' not 'Christmas Pancakes for the Queen.' Read it, then, just read it, Your Majesty."

"Oh, I see!"

"What is it, Your Grace?" Cecil said and came to look over her shoulder as she read in a voice that went from wary to enraged:

Christmas Pancakes for the Queen

Take eggs from a wall and give them a fall, then beat them again and again. Add fast running water, spice as you ought to, then pieces of peacock or boar in their turn. Stir in wheat flour and butter fresh-churned, then fry the cakes carefully lest the topside burn. For all the queen's horses and all the queen's men can't put Christmas or court back together again.

"I've never, never," Stout protested, "put meat in pancakes!"

"A recipe for disaster," Elizabeth cried. "It's from him."

"It's from Hodge's murderer?" Stout asked, his voice now a mere squeak. "He's tampered with our peacock, boar, pies—and now this? But what are eggs on a wall?"

"He's using that old nursery rhyme, where the eggs are people," she started to explain, then realized she had no time for that. "Go back to your kitchens and lock the doors, Master Stout," she said, still staring at the recipe, "especially the one by Hodge's workroom that is near the back door."

"And near my office where this appeared."

"Go, now. I will send guards to help you."

"But the feast tonight? Is it still on?"

"You must prepare it as if nothing had happened, even put the birds in the pie, for I vow I shall be back by then to cut it."

"You're not still going out to release Ned yourself?" Cecil asked as Harry hustled Stout from the room and Meg and Jenks ran back in.

"I've felt guilty all along that Ned was locked up at Greenwich and Robin here, though someone's been making them seem guilty," Elizabeth explained as she threw the recipe atop the other evidence upon the table and hurried toward her bedchamber door with Meg behind her.

"Your Grace, I think they've done a good enough job of that themselves," Cecil protested.

"Read that recipe again, Cecil," she ordered, turning back at the door. "Read the words *lest the topside burn*."

"Oh, no! Oh, no!" Meg cried, and Elizabeth put a steadying hand on her arm while Jenks stood yet dumbfounded. "The killer's going after Ned!"

"I fear so," Elizabeth said. "Our clever murderer, who has not only walked on eggs at court but has broken and beaten them, has killed Hodge and my court vicar and tried to kill Robin—my servants all. The bastard no doubt lit the boathouse with me in it, unless he thought he was just attacking you and Jenks that time . . ."

The queen let her voice trail off. The killer had spoken in symbols before, so it didn't actually mean he would burn Ned, though she would make certain no harm came to him and warn her staff at Greenwich. But Meg, who had gone to school too long listening to both her sovereign and Cecil, blurted, "Your Grace, what if the killer's going to try to burn Greenwich with Ned in it?"

"We will ride there, to capture and stop him. I don't like the way the Christmas killer obviously knows the grounds of Greenwich to be able to poach a fox and leave a box of stones. Meg, stop sniveling, for I need you to help me into my man's riding garb. Jenks, fetch Clifford and saddle five horses ready to run the

ice and have them brought below to my privy staircase immediately."

"I'm going, too!" Meg insisted.

"You are staying here with Cecil to play queen busy at her desk," Elizabeth commanded.

"But five horses?" Cecil said.

"Myself, Jenks, Clifford, Harry—and Leicester. Cecil, spring the earl from his room and say his queen has immediate need of him—if he can keep his mouth shut on this ride so we can catch this Christmas killer."

"But it could be a trap," Cecil insisted.

"But one he himself will be caught in this time," she vowed.

She glanced at her dear people as she turned into her room. Cecil looked both frenzied and furious; Anne hugged Harry good-bye; and Jenks looked only at the distraught Meg with tears glassing his eyes.

The queen scrambled into warm hose and trunks, wool shirt, leather jerkin, cape, and riding boots. She grabbed two of the gold forks Robin had given her and slid one inside the top of each boot. Meg, who must now don the queen's garments, hastily handed her a pair of gloves, hat, and muffler.

"You're not thinking the killer's someone in the household at Greenwich?" Meg asked, blinking back tears again. "I mean like someone who comes and goes here through the back kitchen door, perhaps bringing in fresh game for the table from the forests there? If so, Ned could have been harmed long before this!"

"He'll be free within the hour. Meg, I've been wrong about Ned."

"Mayhap we all have."

Elizabeth had no time to pursue that. She squeezed Meg's shoulder and went to open the door to the privy staircase while Meg lit a lantern.

"It's been a while since you went out like this—and never for a better cause," Meg said as she rushed down the stairs behind the queen, holding the lantern aloft to light her way.

"We need Ned back here," Elizabeth vowed as her voice cracked with emotion.

"Yes, we need him here," Meg echoed as the queen opened the door to find Jenks waiting with the others.

Jenks and Meg simply stared at each other. He helped the queen mount. God help us, Elizabeth thought, to solve not only the murders but the mess Ned, Jenks, and Meg were in.

Having exhausted himself pacing and agonizing, Ned had begun to sleep irregular hours. It made the time pass and temporarily obliterated his fears. At least Elizabeth of England had consigned him to a prison with a fireplace, food, and warm bed. He snuggled down in it now, the counterpane and covers tight around his hunched shoulders.

As he inhaled deeply and sighed, he realized the ashes on his hearth, which he'd let burn down, smelled too strong. He'd just shovel them into his chamber pot and send them out the next time Lemuel came. The friendly lout seemed only good for carting food trays and emptying chamber pots, for the man hadn't even known who that could have been, both by day and night, down on the frozen river.

Ned sniffed again, for the scent was sharper now. It bit into his nostrils and his head so bitterly that his eyes watered and his throat felt sore. If he took sick here, he'd miss Meg's healing hand for certain.

He sat up and opened his eyes. Was it dusk already? It was as if fog, thickening, settling, had permeated his chamber. He saw a gray film of smoke creeping under the door, swirling and rising.

Only silvered embers lay in the grate and had sifted through onto the hearth. Yet a fire must be nearby, and he was locked in.

"Lemuel!" he shouted and began banging on his door. "Let me out! There's fire somewhere! Fire!"

This time, unlike the other day, the queen rode astride, bundled and muffled so no one would know who she was as she passed her people's Frost Fair. Harry and the newly freed Robin rode abreast, the two guards behind. Robin had evidently decided to obey her for once, since he said naught but to whisper he would guard her with his life. Their eyes had met, she had nodded, and that seemed to be enough for him right now. The queen quickened their pace as they passed under the arches of London Bridge.

As she did, she thought of the childhood refrain Kat used to sing for her: *London Bridge is falling down, my fair lady.* But worse, the innocent nursery rhyme the Christmas killer had perverted kept taunting her: *Humpty Dumpty sat on a wall, Humpty Dumpty had a great fall, and all the king's horses and all the king's men could not put Humpty Dumpty together again.*

There was no king in England, but a queen—who must be stronger than any man to hold her throne and keep her kingdom safe. Granted, her realm was ever threatened from without, but she must not have it threatened from within. She must right things. She must.

Now that they were away from people, Elizabeth was about to address her men. She intended to order them to free Ned Topside, warn her small Greenwich staff of danger, then accompany her and Ned back to Whitehall before darkness set in. And above all, to beware of tricks and traps.

But she could be too late, for she smelled something acrid on the wind.

Smoke! Dear Lord in heaven, not smoke! Fire and smoke had prepared many a dish for the table, so would suit a murderer who had a bizarre taste for displaying his kills.

Ned was appalled when he realized that burning material of some sort had been wedged under his door. It not only smoked but began to burn the door to his room.

He splashed his remaining ale and a ewer of wash water on it, but that changed nothing. Trying to keep low for the best air, through the thickening smoke, he glanced wildly about the room for something to shove the burning debris away.

He broke his wooden food tray into long pieces and poked, almost blindly now, through burgeoning smoke and the first flames, trying to dislodge the material jammed under his door. He was hacking so hard and his eyes were stinging so—he'd never get a breath to shout for Lemuel again.

It crossed his mind that the mysterious riders he'd seen outside might have come to survey the palace and set a fire. But why? Fires in palaces were usually the result of someone careless with a hearth or candle at night, or more likely an accident in the kitchens.

He was going to have to change his tactics here, he realized as his eyes streamed tears. His solid, narrow window would probably not break, and he was on the second floor, where a drop could cripple or kill him. He'd have to try to break down the door. If it was only weakened enough by the flames by now . . . if he wasn't too weak to lift this chair to pound at it . . .

The single chair in the room seemed to have the weight of the world atop it. Dragging it toward the door, thinking how distraught Her Grace would be if she lost Greenwich, for she had been born here and loved the place . . . thinking how he loved the queen and loved Meg but could never tell Meg so and hug her hard . . .

He tried to lift the chair, but he was hacking too hard. He had to get out of here to clear his name. Tell Meg something. Hugged hard by suffocating smoke, Ned crumpled against the heavy chair and slid to the floor.

Chapter the Seventeenth

Water for Cooking and Baking

Water is not wholesome, sole by itself, for an Englishman but is cold, slow, and slack of digestion. The best water is rain-water, so it be purely taken. Next to it is running water, the which doth swiftly run upon stones or pebbles. The third water to be praised is river or brook water, the which is clear. Standing water, the which be refreshed with a spring, is commendable; but standing water and well-water to which the sun hath no reflection be not so commendable. And let every man beware of all waters which be putrefied with froth.

ACROSS FROM THE ISLE OF DOGS, ELIZABETH AND HER entourage left the river and cut up into the trees surrounding Greenwich Palace, the same area where they'd begun their fox hunt over a week ago. From here they could see that flames licked inside at least one window on the second floor of the east wing.

"I know you are angry I've been ordering you about, Your Grace," Robin said and reined his horse in to block hers, "but you cannot go near a burning building. We must leave a guard here with you and ride in to rouse the staff."

"And to fetch Ned out, I promise, Your Grace!" Jenks cried and spurred his horse toward the palace before she could give him leave.

"Yes, all right. Go, Robin, but be careful. Harry can stay with me."

They gasped as a boom filled the air. Fireworks shot skyward to sprinkle sparks into the bare-limbed forest, as if it were New Year's Eve again. Their mounts shied or reared, and the distant dogs in the royal kennel howled. Robin wheeled back toward her.

"I must tell you," he shouted, "that I have learned someone stole some of the fireworks I had stored for the New Year's celebration. There weren't half the number I'd planned. I would have told you, of course, but I didn't want to be blamed for aught else—which," he added, emphasizing each word, "I did not do!"

"But gunpowder is in those fireworks," she cried, "gunpowder for firearms which could be used in an insurrection." She thought of Sussex, her military man, but surely he would not raise arms against her, however much he hated her reliance on Robin. No, it seemed as if the gunpowder thieves were using it for fireworks—and perhaps to start the fire at Greenwich.

"Harry, take Robin's place at the palace and help Jenks fetch out Ned Topside before I go after him myself. Robin, stay with me. If you don't know who took the fireworks, at least, how were they stolen?" she demanded as Harry charged after the others.

"I swear I don't know. I had men guarding them out by the gatehouse to the Strand."

"And so not far from the back way into the kitchens," she muttered to herself.

"My men didn't realize some of the fireworks were missing until they went to set them up on the ice that evening. They swore they weren't drinking or careless. Several courtiers came out to see how the powder was put in the rockets, they said, but that's not unusual. In truth, Your Grace, some of the fireworks seem to have vanished like—like that bracelet of yours Lady Rosie's been searching high and low for."

"I fear we've found the gunpowder at least," she said as another boom ensued and the rocket called a Pike of Pleasure hissed skyward. But it looked as if, she noted, it had been launched from back *in* the forest, not into it.

"Your Grace, perhaps this will bring folk from the village beyond, maybe even from London to fight the fire. Let's move away a bit, down on the river to direct help should it come."

Her leg brushed his as they urged their skittish mounts out of the trees to the riverbank. She realized that she could yet mistrust and suspect Robin, but she thought she now knew who the culprit was in this war he was waging against all she held dear.

His name—shouted in the distance—woke Ned. Was it his father calling him to come downstairs for Christmas or New Year's morn? His uncle Wat would be there, full of good cheer and good food, home from the road for a few days, presenting scenes from great dramas. Uncle Wat would let him play a soldier and speak a few lines, maybe carry a wooden sword while half the village crowded in and clapped and clapped . . . just like the crackling sound nearby now.

"Ned! Ned, where are you? Which room?"

He'd best heed Father and get up. He'd have to go outside to milk the cow and check under the hens for eggs before festivities began. Maybe Mother would be preparing pancakes today, with rich butter and cream or honey.

"Ned! Ned Topsi-i-i-de!"

He lifted his head and began to cough again. He slitted his eyes open. Why was he sleeping on the floor?

"Ned! Fi-i-ire!"

Fire! Had he nodded off in a fire?

"Here! Here!" he thought he shouted, but he was hacking so hard he wasn't sure he'd told his father where he was at all.

A rattling sound, a scrape. A bang and a whoosh of air. He tried to lift his head again but just wanted to sleep. His stage voice, that deep instrument that had served him so well, came out a croak, a wheeze.

More noise and someone's hands on him, lifting him. He tried to embrace his mother, shaking him to get up. Or was it Meg come to creep into his bed?

"Meg?" he whispered. "Meg, I love you."

"Jenks," a rough voice said, one hacking, too. "It's Jenks."

"Robin, you must do something for me," Elizabeth said.

"Anything, my queen."

"I'm certain those fireworks are coming from back in the trees and not being shot from afar into them. Can you ride back in to see who is setting them, get behind him, perhaps snare the wretch? It may be the killer—"

"My would-be killer. They told me about Bane's death, and to think it could have been me. Yes, I'll go, I'll get the whoreson murderer, if you'll swear to stay right here."

"I will, and send others who might come."

"I'll be back with the culprit who took my fireworks, at least!" he vowed and spurred his horse up the bank into the trees.

Elizabeth dismounted because her horse kept shying wildly at each blast and perhaps at the smoke smell, too. It was all she could do to keep from charging in to help oversee fighting the fire or from going after the villain in the forest herself.

She tied her horse to a tree so he wouldn't keep jerking her arm while she held the reins. It was lonely out here as darkness fell, but her anger overcame her anxiety for her own safety. Until she heard the baying of the hounds. And the nightmare of her drowning with Robin in the river came back to her.

"A pox on it!" she muttered aloud. She and Robin weren't together, and the river was frozen solid. Those foolish nightmares were the least of her troubles.

For she was sick over worry about Ned. If he died from this, she'd blame herself. And Meg would blame her, too.

Pacing to keep warm, Elizabeth counted three more rockets in the sky and heard the dogs roused again. She tried to reckon how long it would take people to come from the village or the city—or would they just think it was more of the Twelve Days celebration and merely gaze up into the sky in awe? The smoke was not drifting toward the nearby village. Would it dissipate before it brought someone from the city? The flames had not yet been visible from the roof of the east wing.

She was certain she heard hoofbeats. Too fast for Robin returning through these thick trees. No, the sound was that of studded hooves on ice, not on snow, and coming from the direction of the city.

She stepped back into the cover of the bankside trees. Though the twilight had nearly bled to night, she saw it was the Earl of Sussex, mounted and alone. But now that she was certain she knew who the killer was, she need not fear Sussex. What if he brought word of something amiss at Whitehall? She suddenly feared all this could be a diversion, and she had fallen for it. What if the Christmas killer had struck again?

"My lord Sussex!" she called out, and he drew his horse up sharply.

He looked shocked to see her, although that might be because she was in man's attire. His dismount was nearly a tumble as he came closer to stare at her.

"Your Majesty? I heard Leicester got out of his room and rode off in this direction with some men. I wanted to bring him back, could not summon my men in time, but I never thought to find you here—ah, like this."

"I remember you said we must learn to fight like those we fight, my lord," she said, coming back onto the ice. "A killer has been stalking me, so I am stalking him."

"Pray God, he doesn't disappear into the trees like the Irish into their infernal bogs and fens, but I've never seen them shoot rockets to call attention to themselves. I believe you no longer think I am to blame?" he asked, coming closer and gesturing as yet another rocket shot skyward. "Ah, those have caught something on fire at Greenwich, haven't they?" he asked, looking now at the demonic glow in the east wing. "Are you sure it's not Leicester behind this, then?"

"I am. I did think it might be you for a while, because the culprit so obviously hated Leicester." She realized then why she should have eliminated Sussex from the list of possible culprits long ago: Sussex was intelligent but not clever and had no sense of humor, perverse or otherwise, and the killer did. "But," she went on, "since you are going to vow to me now that you will not attack the Earl of Leicester anymore when we have foreign enemies we must fear, I will trust you."

"Enemies like your Catholic cousin Queen Mary?"

"And her minions who adore her. So will you vow to me as I have said?"

"Yes, Your Grace, most heartily, and, ah, pray you'll tell Leicester the same."

"I shall indeed. He's in the woods to hunt the man who has been shooting off those fireworks, and I'd like you to put aside all animosity and help him. Watch for the next rocket and try to trace its projection point. As for Greenwich, I've sent men to rouse the staff and put the fire out."

"I cannot leave you alone, Your Grace."

"Then I must help Robin myself."

"No, I'll go at once. And you have my word on, ah, peace on earth between me and Leicester." He mounted swiftly and urged his horse off the river ice to disappear between the black bars of tree trunks into the snow-laden forest.

As the night swallowed him, she heard again the distant, eerie baying of dogs from the isle across the river, like the fabled evil omen of hounds from hell. Yet they were her own animals, well fed and fit for the hunt. Perhaps she should have them loosed on the marauders in Greenwich forest. She recalled that Simon MacNair had recounted the strange story of ghostly hounds when he was new to his position and in London for the first time and would have no cause to know of her kennels unless he'd been out in this very area. Or perhaps his messenger, Duncan Forbes, who was his link to Mary of Scots, had told him.

She pictured again MacNair's brilliant sleight-of-hand tricks that could pull coins from the air or make them vanish, just the way Robin's fireworks had disappeared, and her bracelet. Had the canny Scot smiled and snatched it somehow off her arm so cleverly she did not notice it was missing? Had Vicar Bane found a stack of parchment missing one day and had no notion when it had gone—as well as a red, unscented torch? Yes, she knew now whom she must capture and imprison when she returned to Whitehall.

She startled as she heard a horse—no, at least two—coming at her from the forest. Robin and Sussex returning? Jenks with Ned? She had been about to mount and ride toward Greenwich to be certain Ned was safe.

Robin's distinctive black stallion broke from the bankside trees first, with him sitting tall in the saddle. Her shoulders slumped in relief. Back already, he must have met with success, but had not another rocket just raked the treetops? Since the second horse was being pulled behind, he must be leading someone out, though not Sussex, for he'd been on a mount with white fetlocks.

"Robin!" she called, relieved. "You've brought me either Forbes or MacNair, have you not?"

"Indeed, I've brought you MacNair," the man, not Robin, said with a harsh laugh. "And dare I guess I now address the Queen of England, the one who follows her head more than her heart?"

She saw that, though the man wore Robin's hat, his shoulders were broader. MacNair! It *was* MacNair. She had guessed it earlier but far too late.

"Happy holidays, Your Grace!" he said, his voice mocking. "And for the last course at the final feast of the Twelve Days, here is your Robin, fallen off his wall with a great fall, just as you tried to dump him on Queen Mary."

Elizabeth gasped and stepped back only to bump into a tree. Robin was slumped either unconscious or dead on MacNair's horse, for the Scot shoved him and he toppled limply to the snowy riverbank.

Ned knew now that it was Jenks who had dragged him out of his smoky room. It was somewhat easier to breathe here in the corridor, but now they faced worse than smoke. Crackling red-orange flames barred their escape in the only direction they could flee. He realized he'd called for Meg and Jenks had heard. Now Jenks knew how he'd felt about Meg and that his dying thought was of her.

Yet Jenks had pulled him out.

"How'd you get through those flames?" Ned rasped.

"They weren't big then—caught the carpet."

It was the Turkey carpets of the corridor that burned, belching flames and smoke, though fire also devoured the draperies and danced toward the ceiling. It must have been a carpet jammed under his door that was set afire to suffocate him.

"About Meg—I . . ." he tried to tell Jenks.

"Stow it. Let's get out of here."

Jenks thrust a piece of cloth at him, covering his face with it. For one moment, Ned thought he meant to smother him, but then he would have just left him to roast in his room. The cloth was cold and wet—melting snow packed in it, a wet cloth to breathe through, maybe to rub along skin so hot it seared the very soul.

"We'll leap through it together," Jenks told him, dragging Ned to his feet and grappling him against his side by an arm like an iron hoop. "Clear the carpet, then roll. And hold my shirt to your face, lest we're trapped by flames or smoke again."

His shirt, Ned thought. He'd tried to take Meg from him,

treated him like a dunce all these years, and he'd given him the shirt off his back to save him, maybe save him for Meg.

"Ready?" Jenks asked, coughing. "If we fall, roll!"

Ned tightened his arm weakly around Jenks's shoulder, hoping he knew it was meant as a hug.

"Now!" Jenks cried and lunged at the flames, dragging Ned off his feet with him.

"You've killed him!" Elizabeth accused and tried to break Robin's fall, though his weight took her down with him as MacNair dismounted.

"Merely hit over the head," he told her as he kicked at Robin. "My final Yuletide gift to you is his company, such as it is. Stubborn ass, he wouldn't die when I had him all trussed up, but I'll be sure of it this time."

When she was certain that Robin yet breathed, she rose slowly to her feet to face the wretch. "And all because I offered him as consort and husband to my cousin, your royal mistress, and you took offense to that?" She must stall for time. Someone would come. Sussex from the forest, Jenks from the palace, someone.

"*I* took offense at it, indeed, as do all braw, loyal Scots who know Mary Stuart is but a breath away from your throne—and that breath is yours."

"I suppose you think you've been terribly clever. But why murder innocents?"

"You've no right to a happy holiday—or happy realm, not the way you treat my dear queen," he claimed, crossing his arms over his chest and ignoring her question. "You cannot hold a candle to her."

"You said once her servants adore her. Meaning you?" Keeping Robin's prone form between them, she took a slow step out to clear the tree, though she was certain, even with the snow and ice, she'd never outrace him.

"To answer your first question," MacNair said, "your servants were eliminated to mock you and Leicester, though you owe me dearly for ridding you of Bane's Puritan presence. My poor queen is ever harassed by his like, John Knox, for one, and a host of priggish Protestant lords. Actually, Bane got in my way, preaching I should not serve a Catholic queen—popish, he called her. And then I saw how he could be part of the game."

"So once you killed Hodge Thatcher, you decided to make the most of mocking Yuletide traditions."

"Silly antics and fancied-up foodstuffs everyone fusses over," he muttered darkly, as if it were a curse. "I've always hated Christmas. In the charming chats you and I have had, I believe I forgot to tell you that my father was the master cook in King James of Scotland's kitchens at Holyrood. Like Hodge Thatcher, he thought he'd gone to heaven to work for royalty. My father ruled his kitchen realm, just as he lorded it over his family. Not a charming, warm bone in his body, not even at Christmas," he ranted on as his voice rose. "No sense of humor or tolerance of those with a clever tongue," he added and spat into the snow.

"But, somehow, under your father's tutelage," she surmised, "you became familiar with the way the royal kitchens worked."

"He insisted I follow in his steps when I found it all dirty and dull."

"But if your father served Queen Mary's father, you have followed in your sire's steps to serve her now. Do you not want to break free of his control over you by—"

"King of the kitchens, Father privily dubbed himself," he went on, as if he hadn't heard her. "I started as a wood and fire boy, then a pot scrubber. I knew nothing, he said, nothing. He wanted me to learn all he knew, but I observed things only to find a way out."

She tried another tack, uncertain whether to try to provoke or placate him. "Unless he was a trickster and murderer, you hardly followed in his steps, Sir Simon."

"I preferred magic, not daily drudgery, you see." He was speaking boldly and grandly now, as if he had a vast audience. "You liked my sleight-of-hand, I know you did. I learned that, too, at the Scots court, from a traveling magician and necromancer who slept in the kitchen. It turned my stomach to do the tricks for you which delight Queen Mary, so it was my pleasure to also abscond with other things under your people's noses."

"Bane's writing parchment?"

"And some of that stack of gold foil on your privy dresser's table. Not to mention these lovely fireworks for my special farewell display for you this evening," he gloated with a broad circular gesture toward the trees.

"And my emerald and ruby bracelet?" she prompted, desperate to keep him talking. Why didn't Sussex return? Whoever was shooting off those rockets—perhaps MacNair's man Forbes—must have accosted him too.

"And a lovely piece of jewelry, that it is," MacNair went on, his voice almost teasing now. She noted he'd let the rougher Scots burr back into his speech. The man was a chameleon in every way. No wonder he had been promoted rapidly for his fluency with languages and other talents, sadly gone wrong.

"So I can call you thief and murderer as well as magician," she said, still trying to gain his confession without vexing him overmuch.

"Your bracelet will soon be en route north to Queen Mary," he explained with another laugh, "as a belated New Year's gift with another set of flagons I bought, but then, those things will pale to the other news I'll be sending her—the ultimate gift. News that the Queen of England has sadly, accidentally drowned in the river with the very whoreson she publicly suggested Mary wed and make King of Scots, so—"

She threw herself sideways and tried to dart away. Thank God she wore man's garb and not heavy skirts and a tight corset. The bank was slick, and she went down, then scrambled on hands and knees as he lunged at her. He hit hard atop her, grinding her face into the snow. He yanked her to her feet, she kicked him, and they rolled down to sprawl onto the hard ice. He seized her again, wrapping hard arms around her and bending one of her arms up behind her back. She almost blacked out from pain as he hauled her to her feet again.

Did he intend to wait until dark to take her and Robin back to the fishing hole in the ice by the palace? To drown them near the Frost Fair among her people, near the site of the boathouse he had burned, even as he or his lackey Forbes must have set the wing at Greenwich afire?

She opened her mouth to scream, but he jammed something in it.

"One of my handkerchiefs to keep coins plucked from the air in," he told her and laughed harshly. "Here I praised you for your impressive intellect and how your head commands your heart, but I have thoroughly outsmarted you, Queen of England. And so you lose the game. You forfeit your place—your throne and crown—to my Scots queen, and so ends the Yuletide entertainment."

MacNair held her in a rough embrace and dragged her out onto the frozen river; at last, to her horror, she saw what he intended. As four rockets went off quite close to them in the forest, four blasts went off on the river ice to blow a hole there nearly as big as the one at the Frost Fair.

She fought desperately as the inky, cold river water surged, then frothed wildly through the hole he shoved her toward. It was her worst nightmare, drowning with Robin in the icy water, for the hulk-shouldered Forbes had appeared and was dragging the yet unconscious Robin. With a splash, Forbes threw him into the hole.

"I told ye, mon," Forbes shouted to MacNair, "I ken how to rig the fuses just right. The wee ones went off the same time in the forest as the long ones out here, so's no one would hear the hole blasted in this bonny ice! And I smashed her other man's skull!"

Sussex! He would not be coming to save her. These demons had shot off the fireworks hoping to lure her men, perhaps her, into the forest. They had lain in wait for them. MacNair had sprung more than one trap, and he had won the game indeed.

"Don't fret, lass," MacNair said, his tone mocking, "for by the next Twelve Days of Christmas, Cecil will be serving Mary Stuart here in London, and everyone will adore her. England will be Catholic again, and your whoreson father's divorce to wed your mother and the Protestant experiment will be mere memory—more stories of the past to tell by the Yule log."

His tirade stoked her strength. Even if he snapped her arm off, she was not going in that black hole, not letting Robin drown or her kingdom go to Mary. Her nightmare flashed at her again, where she and Robin struggled only to sink as the dogs bayed at them. No! She would not allow it!

"I've never enjoyed a bonny Yuletide more," MacNair crowed to Forbes. "Ambassador Melville was wrong, for the English court was anything but wearisome this winter!"

MacNair's voice was triumphant as he slid her across the ice to the gaping maw of frothing white water as the Thames current roared under the ice. She went to her knees and managed to get one of the pitifully small gold forks out of the top of her boot. She wished she did not wear gloves, for it was delicate and she wasn't sure she had a good grip on it. Swinging the fork upward, she jabbed at MacNair's face behind her. Then she twisted her body away, jerked, and, with her back on the ice, kicked up at MacNair's crotch as hard as she could.

He shrieked and, covering his face, doubled over. Forbes came at her, but he slid past. Ripping the gag from her mouth, she began to scream, trying to dart away from him.

Cursing, bleeding, half blind, MacNair too stumbled toward her. She tried to change directions again, but Forbes snagged her hair, spilling it loose and nearly pulling it from her scalp. Robin, she had to save Robin. She had to keep from going in, but Forbes and MacNair together dragged her toward the freezing water where Robin, conscious now, flailed but kept going under.

As in her dream, she heard the dogs coming closer, closer. Was she in the water already, drowning, dying?

When the first dogs leaped at MacNair and Forbes, she knew it was no dream. The entire pack of them, yipping, snapping, twenty at least, attacked the two men, but they knew their mistress and did not harm her. Backing away from the onslaught, MacNair and Forbes tried to kick the hounds away, but MacNair's face was streaming blood, and he couldn't see. Forbes tried to help him at first, then seemed to slip in MacNair's dark blood on the graying ice.

With a shout, Forbes fled toward the Greenwich forest with dogs in hot pursuit. With a massive splash, MacNair fell into the hole. At that very moment, Elizabeth saw the first of her huntsmen among the hounds.

"Oh, pardon, milady," the man cried when he saw her, "but the fireworks drove them to distraction, an' somehow they got loose. That a hole in the ice? Back, my boys, back!" he cried to the dogs, which circled it now, barking into it.

"Fetch a board or some rope!" she screamed, shoving her hair back from her face to see better. "We must get the men out of the water!"

Both huntsmen stood among their yapping charges, staring at her. "Your Majesty?" one said.

"Yes. Quickly, do as I say!"

"We'll fetch him out," the second man cried, " 'cause there's only one."

Still standing amidst the remains of the writhing pack, the queen turned and gasped. Only one man was in the water. She fell to her knees and, trembling, crawled to the edge of the ice.

Robin! Thank God, it was Robin!

"Where did he go?" she shouted, lying down flat amidst the dogs and reaching a hand to him.

"Tried to hold to m-me. I hit him of-f-f," he said, through chattering teeth. "W-w-went under."

She held on to him while the keepers of the pack fished him out with a tree limb. "Despite the darkness," she told the men, "I want you to follow the hounds on the trail of the one who fled."

"Oh, aye, Your Majesty, we'll fetch a coupla lanterns, and he'll not get far, not with a few of the lead dogs on his tail. They musta had the scent of wild animal on their persons for the dogs to act like that."

"Yes, wild animals indeed, unless the pack just came to rescue their queen," she muttered, offering silent thanks to the Lord for her deliverance. The moment Robin was out of the water, she swirled her cape around him and carefully led him toward Greenwich.

"T-that f-f-ire will f-feel good," he told her. "Look, it's almost out. But w-what h-happened?"

"MacNair and his man were behind it all." She tried to stay calm, to help him walk quickly toward the shelter of the palace. But she stopped in her snowy tracks when she saw who walked toward them from Greenwich—and the single man approaching on foot from the forest.

"Ned! Jenks!" she cried. "And my Lord Sussex!"

Her servants looked like two blackened, singed scare-the-crows as they limped toward her, arms around each other's shoulders. But she could not stop here: Robin was slowly turning into an ice man, and Sussex was shouting something about being hit over the head.

In relief and joy, Elizabeth cursed anyone who claimed she lived by intellect and not her feelings, for she burst into tears. She hugged each man in turn, the most precious Yuletide gifts she'd ever seen. And never had she been more proud to be their friend and be their queen.

Afterword

Twelfth Night Cake

In a bowl, combine ½ cup of juice of orange with 1 cup golden and 1 cup dark raisins and let stand. Cream 1 cup butter, 1 cup sugar, 2 cups wheat flour, and 4 fresh hen's eggs. Add the undrained raisin mixture and a pinch of cinnamon. Stir all together and bake until a knife inserted in center comes out clean. Do not overcook, or it can become hard as a rock. Melt 3 tablespoons of honey to glaze the cake, decorating it with ¼ cup of candied cherries. In Scotland and rural shires, they add a pea and a bean, so that the finder of the bean is king for the evening and the finder of the pea is queen. But we do seldom follow such practices in civilized London town.

TWELFTH NIGHT

JANUARY 6, 1565

"OF ALL THE YULETIDE HOLIDAYS I'VE HAD, LOVEY, THIS was the best!" Kat told Elizabeth and reached to take her hand as they sat in armchairs facing the low-burning hearth. "Why, I had to laugh at the look on Master Stout's face when you told him the extra meat pies you ordered were all to be sent to the kennels on the Isle of Dogs. Kind of you to think of your hunt packs there."

The old woman chuckled while the queen fought back tears of relief that these holidays were officially over, and that Kat had not known all her queen had been through to keep Christmas for her. After the Twelfth Night Revels in the Great Hall tonight, led by Ned Topside, since Robin had taken to his bed with a dreadful cold, the two old friends sat late in the queen's privy chamber before the hearth.

"I've asked Ned, Meg, and Jenks to come up when the corridors clear," Elizabeth said, gesturing toward the three other chairs she'd pulled up. "In all the chaos of Christmas, I failed to give them their gifts."

"I thought you were just holding back for Meg's marriage."

"I've intentionally not pressed her on that. No, I mean to give them their gifts tonight."

"I suppose I should not have spoken so fondly of these holidays with the deaths of the two Scots on top of Vicar Bane's and poor Master Hodge's sad demises," Kat went on. "Your royal Catholic cousin will say you've sent her wretched news for the coming year to have her envoy and his man fall through the ice and drown."

Elizabeth said nothing, but that is the story Cecil had written to Mary of Scots. Though MacNair had drowned under the ice and his body had not been recovered, Forbes had been caught but had hanged himself in his cell before he could be questioned. However much the queen would have liked to accuse the Scottish queen of being privy to their plot, Cecil had found nothing in MacNair's or Forbes's effects to prove such, though he had found her stolen bracelet.

"I am sending Queen Mary a gift she will like, though," Elizabeth said, more to herself than to Kat. "Lord Darnley is the messenger Cecil is sending north when the roads clear, and the stage is set for Darnley to entrance her."

"Hmph. You must have known she'd never trust Leicester, your Robin," Kat said, taking another piece of Twelfth Night Cake from the small parquet table between their chairs. Like a child, Kat always ate the candied cherries off the top first.

"Yes, I knew that well—from personal experience," she said, her voice almost a whisper.

The queen also knew the battle lines had been drawn between her and Mary, however cordial and correct they might be to each other in the future. In a single year, more than MacNair had tried to plot against Elizabeth in the Catholic queen's name, and, no doubt, more would. But she, with her friends, her true friends, would be ready for the next onslaught.

Elizabeth herself rose to answer Meg's distinctive knock on the door and let the three of them in. Meg looked as if she'd been crying; Jenks seemed glum, and Ned either exhausted or pathetic. Ned and Jenks still had bandaged hands and singed eyebrows and hair from the fire at Greenwich, which had been successfully put out after some dreadful damage to the east wing. It, like the boathouse, would need to be rebuilt this spring, along with a feigned, polite relationship with Queen Mary.

"Welcome all," Elizabeth told them as she gestured them in. "Take the chairs and warm yourselves."

To her surprise, the two men sat in the seats on the other side of Kat, while Meg took the single one by the queen. "Let me serve, Your Grace," Meg said, popping up when she saw the queen pouring ale for them, but Elizabeth pressed her back into her chair.

"I've asked you here tonight to thank each of you for all you've done for me this holiday season," she said, not mentioning specifics, for their endeavors of detection had been kept from Kat as well as from most of the court. "Also, your friendship and support these first six years of my reign have been invaluable."

"And many more years to come!" Kat chimed in.

The queen gave an ale-filled, heavily embossed silver goblet to Meg, Jenks, and Ned. "To the new year and the future," she said and lifted her drink to them.

"Oh, Your Grace, it's beautiful!" Meg cried, the first to catch on that the vessel from which she drank was her gift. "Look, such shiny silver with entwined roses around the queen's name: *From a grateful monarch, Elizabeth the Queen, to my dear Strewing Herb Mistress Meg Milligrew.*"

"Tudor roses, of course," Ned put in, coming to life at last as he perused his goblet. "Why, on this side it has my name and *Master of Queen's Revels* scripted in. Done by our St. Paul's pewterer, Your Grace?"

"He got out of his sickbed in a minute when I sent him the order for them," she said with a smile. "Meg, you see, yours has herbs as well, and Jenks's has a saddle and bridle."

"That's a good one," Kat put in, "seeing as how he's about to get bridled and saddled himself in holy matrimony with Meg."

Silence fell. Only the hearth crackled away.

"We have decided to delay that," Meg whispered.

"To delay it indirectly," Jenks added.

"Indefinitely," Ned amended. "The three of us—well, for my part, after Jenks saved my life, I just realized all I owed him, that's all."

The queen could see that was not all, but she'd question Meg about it later. Elizabeth sensed that the men, in their new-fledged friendship, had somehow decided for Meg. Not wedding because something better and grander was at stake—yes, the queen grasped that full well.

The five of them sat, staring into the settling fire in companionable silence. In that precious moment of peace, Elizabeth felt that no memories of the past could hurt her, nor did the future frighten her. With friends who were dearer than family, she could not only look forward to Christmases to come but enjoy life each day, beginning here and now. Somehow, that was the greatest gift of all.

AUTHOR'S NOTE

AMAZINGLY, MANY TUDOR RECIPES REMAIN, ALTHOUGH I WOULD NOT recommend following those I've included here, since some of them are shortened or amended, or just plain untrustworthy with unusual or vague directions. Sources for these recipes include some fascinating books such as Thomas Dawson's *The Good Huswifes Jewell,* 1580; Gervase Markham's *The English Housewife,* 1615; and anonymous, The *Good Huswifes Handmaide for the Kitchen,* 1594. Also, a book with excellent drawings about food and banquets is *All the King's Cooks,* by Peter Brears. *Food and Feast in Tudor England,* by Alison Sim, was also a great help. Thanks to Sharon Harper for her recipe for Maids of Honor.

I am also appreciative that Kirrily Robert has an excellent Web site with original old English recipes to be found at http://infotrope.net/sca/cooking.

As in all the books in the Elizabeth I Mystery Series, I take key plot points from history. On December 21, 1564, the Thames froze solid for the first time in years, and it is recorded that "the queen walked upon it." The years of 1608 and 1683 are listed as excellent freezes for Frost Fairs; 1814, the last year for such a fair, saw a catastrophe when the ice cracked and booths and people fell into the river. I have taken literary license with the fact that Lambeth Palace traditionally housed the archbishop of Canterbury rather than the bishop of London.

Under the Protestantism of Edward VI and his sister Elizabeth, some of the early raucous, pagan Yuletide practices and Catholic customs were halted, but "Elizabeth herself paid for holly and ivy to deck the palace each Christmas." As the queen could be tight with her money, this was no small concession to these holidays for her.

The queen's beloved Lady Katherine (Kat) Ashley, early governess, confidant, and the only mother figure Elizabeth Tudor had ever known, died, "greatly lamented," in 1565. It was the same year in which Mary, Queen of Scots, wed Henry Stewart, Lord Darnley, and lived to rue that day. Their child, King James VI of Scotland, later James I of England, followed Elizabeth on the throne in 1603. But in the thirty-eight years between the time of this story and the queen's death, there are many momentous events—and mysteries—to come.

I hope that those of you who have or know of book discussion groups will find the "food for thought" questions that follow useful. Although each of the Elizabeth mysteries can stand alone, this series is also an extended study of a fascinating woman and her times. The queen was a powerful historical figure but also an amazingly modern woman in many ways.

READING GROUP GUIDE

The Queene's Christmas

DISCUSSION IDEAS

1. Many amateur sleuth or detective stories are told only from the main character's first-person point of view. Why do you think the author of *The Queene's Christmas* uses multiple viewpoints?

2. In what way does the Prologue frame or foreshadow the action to come?

3. We are all partly products of our pasts. What family baggage does Elizabeth Tudor always carry with her, despite her position of power and prestige?

4. Although Elizabeth is the heroine of the tale, she is all too human. Cite examples of her honorable acts and her underhanded ones. What strengths and weaknesses does she exhibit? Do these make her sympathetic or not?

5. This book in the series and the previous one (*The Thorne Maze*) emphasize the queen's growing conflict with her cousin the Catholic Mary, Queen of Scots. How is Mary contrasted with Elizabeth, even though the reader never meets Mary? (Elizabeth never met her, either.) How do their contrasting personalities act as strengths or weaknesses in their serving as rulers?

6. How do the recipes that begin each chapter tie in with the

action and intent of the story? How do they throw light on or foreshadow events?

7. Food imagery is used throughout the story to tie in with the holiday recipes theme. Beginning with the Prologue, can you cite examples of this?

8. Comment on customs in the story that have their roots in Old England, such as drinking a toast.

9. Discuss clues laced throughout the story to hint that the villain could be any of several characters. Did you at some point suspect, like the queen, that the culprit could be Ned Topside or the Earl of Leicester? At what point were you certain who was the guilty one? Did you figure it out before the queen, with the queen, or after her?

10. Although the book is set in 1564–65, did you find some characters' thoughts of and reactions to the holidays modern? Perhaps even like your own? In what ways?

11. How is Elizabeth's relationship with her people similar to or different from that of Queen Elizabeth II or an American president? Have we lost or gained from the differences?

12. Elizabeth's longtime relationship with Robert Dudley, Earl of Leicester, was an up-and-down one. Why do you think she never wed him? Did she really wish to? (Earlier books in the series, especially *The Twylight Tower,* expand on this turbulent relationship.)

13. Many of the folk poems commonly called "nursery rhymes" hail from early England. Examples include "Ride a Cock Horse to Banbury Cross," "Sing a Song of Sixpence," and "Humpty Dumpty." If the political and personal origin of Mother Goose rhymes is of interest, you might peruse *The Annotated Mother Goose,* by William S. Baring-Gould and Ceil Baring-Gould. Note that "Mary, Mary, Quite Contrary" is supposedly a comment on Mary, Queen of Scots. Can you find other Elizabethan-era links?

14. There were remnants of pagan superstitions amid the Christian Christmas celebrations of Elizabethan England—for example, the one about holly leaves in Chapter One. Are there others you can find?

15. Last names in Tudor England (in this book, Wainwright, Thatcher, Stout, Green, etc.) obviously come from occupations, physical traits, or even dress. Do you have such an English last name, or can you think of anyone who does?